White Death

Blizzard of 77

BY ERNO ROSSI

PRIME MINISTER • PREMIER MINISTRE

Ottawa, K1A 0A2,
August 25, 1980.

Dear Mr. Rossi,

    It was kind of you to favour me with an autographed copy of your book, White Death, relating to the blizzard of January 1977 which struck southern portions of Ontario and parts of Western and Northern New York State.

    With appreciation and with my best wishes.

Sincerely,

Mr. Erno Rossi, M.A.
  147 Tennessee Avenue,
    Port Colborne, Ontario,
      L3K 2R8.

The Premier
of Ontario

Parliament Buildings
Toronto, Ontario
M7A 1A1

August 12, 1980

Dear Erno:

    Thank you for sending me a copy of your book entitled "White Death - Blizzard of '77".

    It is a fascinating subject and I look forward to reading it soon.

    Kindest regards and best wishes.

Sincerely,

Bill Davis

Mr. Erno Rossi,
147 Tennessee Avenue,
Port Colborne, Ontario.
L3K 2R8

WHITE DEATH - The Blizzard of '77©
Millennium Edition

BOOKS BY ERNO ROSSI
Many Cultures – Many Heritages
Nombreuses Cultures – Héritages Varie
Full Moon
White Death – Blizzard of '77 *(1978)*
WHITE DEATH – The Blizzard of '77 *(Millennium Edition Revised 1999)*
Thank You Mrs. America *(a memoir from the 1930's to 2001 to be published in 2004)*
King Tut Gunner *(his yellow Labrador Retriever twice of Guinness Pet Records fame to be published in 2005)*

WHITE DEATH - The Blizzard of '77
BY ERNO ROSSI M.A.

Seventy Seven (77) Publishing
147 Tennessee Avenue
Port Colborne, Ontario, Canada, L3K 2R8
Tel: 905-835-8051
E-mail: erossi@whitedeath.com
Fax: 905-835-2928
Please visit me at www.whitedeath.com

Mail orders by check or money order payable to
77 Publishing or paper currency to above address.
Gift books shipped around the world and personally
signed to your instructions since 1978.

Total cost $22.00 US. Postage paid and delivery insured.
Total cost $25.00 Can. Postage paid and delivery insured.

COPYRIGHT©1999 BY ERNO ROSSI M.A.

ISBN 0-920926-03-7   Millennium Edition

Printed In Canada

Acknowledgements

Many thanks to the following for their assistance:

Aldo Palma
Joe Rossi
Dave Woelfle
Mike Seredine
Doug Minor
Roscoe Reilly
Lori Campbell
Lori, Lynn and Martha Di Carlantonio
Ilona Karow
Colleen Schickluna
Karen Turner
Teresa Duchesne
Michael Kovacs
Brenda Lee Eagles
Clara Hudak
Jayne Smallbone
Peter Ivankovich
Linda Penrose
Shelly Elliot
Mike Daniels
Deborah DeAngelis
Ann Blackwood
Mary Margaret Wegrich
Doris Siba
Arlene Barnai
Elaine Rossi
Cindy Rossi
Lisa Rossi
Carolyn Zapp
Helen Guhl

Rachel Siba
Cathy Neff
Cathy Marsden
Pam Lochead
Lori McLean
Loralee Legault
Caroline Hogue
Annette McGill
Lisa Sargus
Brenda Puhl
Barb Sanko
Roscoe Reilly
Norm Sheffe
James J. Warde, M.D.
Karen Terfry
Lori Stouth
Lori Trembley
Janet Rossi
Susan VanKralingen
Cindy Webber
Lori Vittie
Kathy Cobb
Tammy Gamm
Edith Perez
Leanne Boulton
Sandra Buccione
Bonnie White
Brenda Daly
Anna Giarrantano
Sheila Dick
Carl Turton

Susan Minor
Joanne Votano
Irene Lens
Ann Ryan
Joanne Barrick
Janet Shanes
Jackie Houde
Carol Tennier
Sandy Reeves
Barb Green
Barbara Wajda
Scott Wolfe
Ester Brown
Bob Dockrill
Dana Rodgers
Carol Siddall
Tom Stamp
Keith Rossi
Reg Bernier
Peter Clancy
Vicky Pivoriunas
Nola Corey
Peg Stroth
Steve Krar
Greg Motolanez
Mayor Allan Pietz - Welland
Mayor George Bukator - Niagara Falls
Mayor Girve Fretz - Fort Erie
Larry Fritz

A special thank you to the following:

My brother, Gerry Rossi
The U.S. Army Corps of Engineers and **Andy Piacente**
Tops Friendly Food Markets
Welland Port Colborne Evening Tribune
Buffalo Evening News and its Research Library
The Port Colborne News and The St. Catharines Standard
The Times Review, Fort Erie and The Watertown Daily Times
The National Guard
The American Red Cross Disaster Centers of Buffalo, Cincinatti and Boston
The Buffalo Red Cross and Lucy Mysiak, Jim Casey Sr. and Ed Brady
The Buffalo Police Academy and Lieutenant William McLean
Hugh Smith, Director of Business Education, Stamford Collegiate
Buffalo Police Department and New York State Police
Ontario Provincial Police and Niagara Regional Police
The Buffalo, Fort Erie, Welland and Port Colborne Fire Departments
CHOW
CJRN, Mike Farrell and Bob O'Brien
WBEN and Gary Gunter
WKBW, WEBR and WGR
John Dyet who designed the cover
Bell Telephone and Jim Price
The Regional Municipality of Niagara and John Kirby
The Greater Port Colborne Chamber of Commerce
Jim Morrison, Librarian, Port Colborne High School
CHCH-TV
The hundreds of people who made this book possible.

White Death — Blizzard of '77.

The Title

News reports concerning this storm flashed around the world and when described in the East African newspapers, the Blizzard of '77 was called "White Death".

Blizzard

A wind of 32 miles per hour or greater, low temperature near 10 degrees Fahrenheit and sufficient snow in the air to reduce the visibility to less than 500 feet.

Whiteout

An optical phenomena of the polar regions in which the observer appears engulfed in a uniformly white glow. Neither shadows, horizons or clouds are discernable. Sense of depth orientation is lost. Only very dark and near objects can be seen.

Ice Storm

An ice storm occurs when rain falls through a freezing layer of air near the surface of the earth. When the rain strikes a surface, it freezes and forms a glaze of up to an inch in thickness, causing many hazards.

Contents

Part One – The Canadian Experience

5.	What Happened?	102.	...squirrel shit.
8.	The window exploded about 10:30.	103.	...ledges for an antenna.
9.	The dogs would urinate on the TV antennas.	108.	We put the ladder up...
12.	Baby Blitz	112.	...tear the ass out...
12.	Buried Alive - 21 Hours	113.	...25 snowmobilers...
14.	God Help Us	113.	...blizzards in Austria
16.	My wife has left me.	114.	...youngsters were whizzing around...
16.	Old nails are off.	115.	...converted into a bathtub...
21.	Remove the ring.	116.	...trying to catch and eat...
21.	I will take the gun...	118.	...my hair became freezing...
22.	Seat Stuffing	120.	I remember back to 1895...
22.	He landed on my front room floor.	120.	...so we had to pull the plug...
25.	The higher the nest...	121.	...the dog had instinct.
25.	Drug Addict	124.	...no weather reporting stations.
30.	...drug overdose dropped...	124.	...I couldn't breathe.
30.	Thank God For A Pile Of Shit	124.	...she had her baby.
32.	...our water pipes froze for ten days.	127.	You're a faggot.
32.	...our cat was frozen to the window.	133.	Barbara Frum couldn't believe it.
36.	...I got to the graveyard.	133.	I lived in the Arctic.
39.	...covered with chicken shit.	135.	When helicopters landed...
39.	...good side effects.	138.	...she saw the snow moving.
40.	...stranded with 13 women.	139.	Her fingernails turned black.
41.	Suspicious Wives.	139.	It was buried under 35 feet of snow.
43.	What? Beer? Where's your car?	140.	...take your snowmobiles and go...
43.	She had firm breasts...	143.	...she was wearing a skirt and jacket.
45.	It was utter chaos.	145.	Hitchcock movie setting...
49.	I dragged him into the snow...	152.	We don't have to leave.
53.	We had 24 people for the weekend.	156.	...five of 57 doves returned.
56.	I was crying.	158.	...many dead birds.
57.	No storm upset her constitutional.	158.	...claws frozen into clumps.
61.	...the loss of blood...	158.	...she cancelled our wedding.
63.	...stealing radios...	159.	...we were getting married.
64.	...about 15 feet over my head...	160.	...they were so thankful.
70.	She broke the phone in 3 pieces...	162.	...the groomer and the ambulance.
71.	...like a swimming pool.	162.	She hugged and kissed him.
76.	...embarrassed at opening themselves.	165.	The Americans had more tracked vehicles...
78.	...two thousand students stranded...	168.	There was a 30 foot drift...
81.	...putting her feet in my face.	170.	...the cracking of timbers in the roof...
82.	...they were homesick.	171.	...we skied throughout the blizzard.
83.	...the girls were trying to sneak the boys over.	173.	...we had a lot of booze.
84.	...the greatest experience of my life.	173.	...two hours to cross the road.
87.	...where you stand in your community.	174.	I couldn't see my hands...
88.	...kids were glad to see us.	174.	...ten below zero in the living room.
88.	...five inches of snow on the bed.	176.	...birdseed and birth control pills.
90.	...rubbing snow on his body.	177.	...work 16 hours then sleep.
95.	...sleep on boards.	179.	...he was screaming.
96.	...more dependent on Him.	181.	...one drift 30 feet high.
96.	...like driving in a pillow.	181.	McDonald's Golden Arches.
97.	...more friendly when frightened.	182.	...hands like small footballs.
97.	...in the snow bank screaming.	191.	...Canada Geese survive.
98.	My husband, my husband!		
101.	...dug into the mattress.		

1

Part Two – The American Experience

- 192. President Carter
- 194. Chip Carter
- 196. ...he was dead.
- 201. ...so every body struck out.
- 202. ...13 calls of people dead in cars.
- 204. Silent Killer
- 204. ...caskets were stored.
- 205. Tops Friendly Markets
- 207. We had a very pregnant camel.
- 215. God hears and answers prayers.
- 216. We had 220 people in here.
- 219. ...blizzard named after a man.
- 219. Births - Nine Months After
- 219. Abortion Clinic
- 221. ...grand mal seizures and death.
- 226. ...drinking, drinking, drinking.
- 226. ...would kill himself or a policeman.
- 229. ...the city would burn to the ground.
- 231. ...push you off the bridge.
- 232. It was a boy – 7lbs, 13ozs.
- 236. If I had a gun...
- 237. My baby was so alert.
- 238. ...the only two survivors.
- 243. Count Your Blessings
- 243. They came on snowshoes...
- 249. ...a city completely paralyzed.
- 249. ...the Brinks truck with a quarter million.
- 250. Buffalo people are nice...
- 251. ...the parrot flew out the window.
- 252. How much for a snowmobile?
- 253. I was scared shitless.
- 257. The YMCA and women...
- 262. ...we fed 7000 people.
- 266. Dumped Milk
- 266. ...the child was brought in alive.
- 270. National Guard threatened with kindness.
- 270. ...the looters would return...
- 271. looters robbing beer trucks.
- 272. Shotgun Justice
- 273. ...accident report – 50 cars and 113 people
- 273. Looters
- 274. We hired 1300 people...
- 278. ...one big party.
- 280. ...film called Naked City.
- 283. Happy Kids.
- 283. ...like having a baby.
- 284. ...about 70% girls and 30% boys.
- 285. ...three freaky looking dudes.
- 285. ...29 people died.
- 289. Buffalo Sabres
- 295. Voice of The Sabres
- 298. ...my leg got pinned and broken.
- 299. Volkswagens are OK.
- 299. ...six ladies who rented rooms.
- 300. ...the baby was safe.
- 301. ...we dug caves into 25 foot drifts.
- 301. Mayor of Buffalo
- 307. ...keep cars out of the city...
- 308. ...what the hell was going on?
- 312. ...he prescribed a cold glass of water.
- 313. ...a heavy duty generator.
- 315. ...about 6 million dollars.
- 320. ...price gouging.
- 320. ...friendly dog in the cafeteria.
- 327. ...over 200 inches at the end of April.
- 329. ...a second disaster.
- 329. Clint Buehlman
- 333. ...freezes your eyelids.
- 334. ...keep their heads out of their bottoms.
- 336. Over 26 Feet
- 338. Salvation Army Looted
- 352. Refuge
- 354. Where's my car?
- 354. Weather Facts.
- 354. Niagara Falls.
- 354. Rest in Peace Stormy

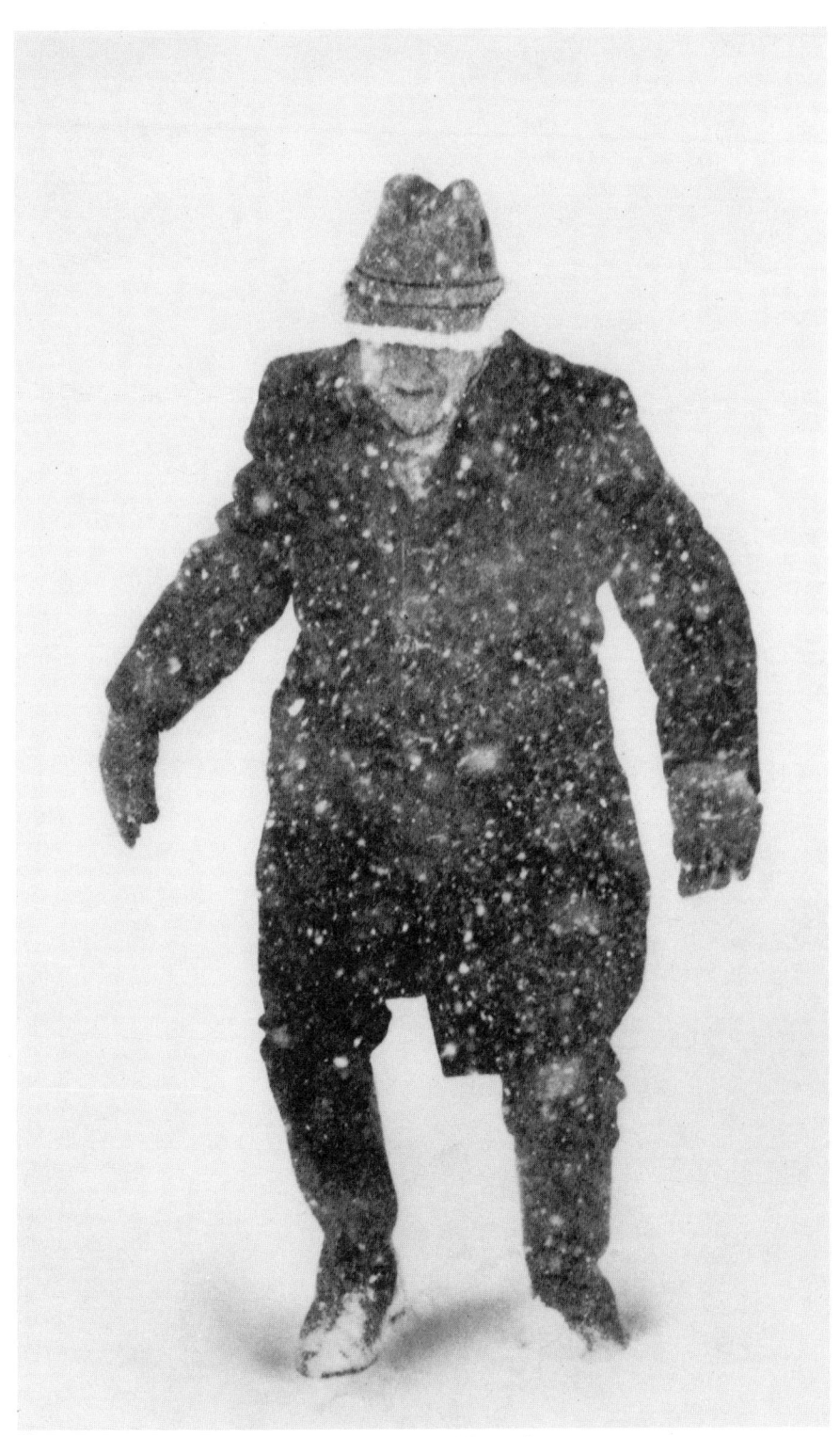

The beginning at Buffalo City Hall by Ron Moscati.

The Beginning. Courtesy, The Tribune

PART ONE

THE CANADIAN EXPERIENCE

WHAT HAPPENED?

On Friday, January 28, 1977 a natural disaster struck Canada and the United States. Southern portions of the province of Ontario and parts of western and northern New York State were besieged by the blizzard of the century and millennium. During this winter hurricane, the temperature plunged to near zero Fahrenheit as hurricane force winds roared across the frozen surface of Lake Erie. Temperature and wind combined to create a wind chill of 60 below zero. Visibility was also zero and remained there from 11:30 a.m. on the 28th until 12:50 a.m. on the 29th of January. The storm did not subside until February. Wind gusts over 50 miles per hour occurred each day with official peaks ranging between 69 and 73 miles per hour.

Lake Erie has a surface area of ten thousand square miles. This water surface had frozen by December 14, 1976 an early freezing record. Here formed a desert of ice that was flatter than any prairie or desert of sand. As hurricane force winds swept across the frozen lake, no natural barriers broke the force of the sweep so that the northeast shore areas felt the full blast of this natural disaster.

The deep snow that had built up on the surface of the lake had not melted during the cold month of January so that ten thousand square miles of snow powder blew inland from the frozen surface of Lake Erie and buried people in their cars and homes.

By the night of Friday, January 28, 1977, thousands of people were stranded in office buildings, schools, police stations, fire halls, bars, factories, cars, buses and in the homes of strangers. Most highways were impassable, train lines were blocked and airports were closed. Snow paralysis had set in during this unique winter hurricane.

On Saturday, January 29, 1977, American President Jimmy Carter issued a "declaration of emergency" for four western New York State counties, permitting government agencies to move in and help with rescue efforts under the authority of the Federal Disaster Assistance Administration. Later five additional counties, including two northern New York State counties were added. These counties by name are: Chautauqua, Cattaraugus, Erie, Niagara, Orleans, Genesee, Wyoming, Jefferson and Lewis.

With international attention focused on this disaster, on Saturday February 5, 1977, President Carter declared the nine counties a "major disaster area", the first and last such declaration ever made for a snow emergency. This allowed more extensive federal relief, including direct reimbursements to local governments for snow removal expenses.

Across the Canadian border, the Canadians were met with the same disaster, aggravated however by the presence of approximately 2000 students who were trapped for several days in urban and rural schools. Many of the young people had never been separated from their parents for a long period of time. The reaction of parents, teachers and children is very interesting.

In response to the blizzard, the whole of the Regional Municipality of Niagara was placed in a state of emergency on January 29 and this remained in effect until February 2, 1977.

We have a lot to learn from weather emergencies. And we should learn as much as possible from the Blizzard of '77. Cities should be especially careful that find themselves near the shore of a lake that has the potential for freezing. Inland areas as well would be wise to beware of the build up of snow powder, so beautiful and yet so dangerous when aroused by a wind.

Friday January 28, 1977. Where were you on that day? What happened? That is the essence of this book. Lives, property and spirits were devastated for some survivors. For others, there was an exhilaration of having met and survived a unique natural disaster. Beginning on Friday January 28, 1977 and often running into the next week, the experience of survivors is captured. If there are lessons to be learned from the survival of others, here is your chance. It could happen again. It could happen to you. Beware of snowflakes!

Price tag on the Blizzard of '77 was about 300 million dollars.

The Feinen living room. Courtesy Inco. By Dino Innandrea.

Kim Feinen—15 years of age

"The window exploded about ten thirty."

I was home with my little brother in the house when the storm hit. The window exploded about ten thirty. My mother was talking to me on the phone when it happened. She was stranded just up the road from here but there was no way anybody could get to us. So she got in touch with a whole bunch of people trying to get somebody down here to help us.

We couldn't get out. I looked outside to see what it was like and then I stepped outside. I fell about ten feet away from the house. Then, when I turned around the house was gone. So I went back in the direction I thought the house was in and I stumbled upon it again. The house kept filling up with snow. It blew through that broken window and we were in there for about seven hours.

The living room was clogged with snow. It was everywhere except in the kitchen because I nailed up the sleeping bags to block off the kitchen. There was no door to shut between the living room and the kitchen. I nailed up the bags and blocked it off like it was a door. This kept the snow from coming in the kitchen. Eric is nine years old. We just sat there next to the heater with a bunch of blankets. It was one of those space heaters. It's an upright that's hooked on to the wall.

Kipper tried to make it home. He's my older brother. He left my mom at the house down the road which was about a half a mile and he came to try to get us but he couldn't. He got as far as Concessi's store. It took him a couple of hours to get there and from there he got lost. He was walking from the store to us and he fell down. He lost his direction. He was just wandering around. Then I think he broke into a cottage, because it was getting dark out and he wrapped himself up in a curtain in the cottage. He stayed there until morning but he said he didn't sleep.

We didn't have any heat in the house. The snow was blowing right through the sleeping bags and around them. It wasn't until about four thirty in the afternoon that the Leslies from way down the road managed to get into us.

We got all bundled up and they took us to our neighbours. It's two doors over, it's not really far. When we were walking there we couldn't see anything and when one of us looked up, the wires were behind us and we were going out towards the field instead of over towards the house. We had to come all the way back to get to the house but we got there finally. We stayed there five days. Finally, my older brother got through with his truck. That's my brother Dennis.

We have a dog too. His name is Digger. He was real good during all that time we stayed in the kitchen. He stayed right with us and kept us warm in the kitchen. He's a big dog and he didn't mind snuggling up with us to help us keep warm. He's a really good dog. He's almost a year old but he's big. I didn't get any frostbite but Kipper did on his face and his feet. In the morning when he got up he could see the power wires, so he followed them to the store.

When he got back to the store he had to dig the snow away from the door to get in. But he finally got in there and his feet were all swollen up and they didn't want him to move.

All through the night he didn't know if we were out or not. Like the people at the store said, if we had stayed in the house we would have frozen to death.

We could talk to our mom on the phone which was in the dining room. But I had nailed the sleeping bag between the dining room and the kitchen and I would have had to go all the way around the house to get to the phone once the area was blocked off. I could hear the phone ringing but I couldn't get to it. I could have but I would have had to go through four feet of snow to get there and there was no sense in doing that.

My little brother was scared. Yes, he said he was. We had lots of food to eat in the kitchen and after they took us over to Duffet's we had lots of food there.

I was thinking about Kipper. Throughout the storm I knew that he was trying to get us. Then I know he got lost or something. I was really worried about him.

Mrs. Feinen

"When the dogs went outside, they would urinate on the T.V. antennas."

Kipper was taking me to work in Buffalo when we got as far as Port Colborne. Then the storm hit us. We had left two children at home, a fifteen year old and an eight year old and so we started to come back. There were lots of accidents. Kipper was bulldozing his way through. He had a Volkswagen bus and he couldn't see where he was going so we went blindly, hoping that nobody would be walking on the road. We got as far as the Station Road just past the garbage dump, opposite that little cemetery there. That's where we got stuck.

Kipper said let's go and he'd push and pull me along in the cold and blinding snow. I didn't even want to move but he kept dragging me and finally we stopped at the the first farm house. He pushed me into their house and we found ourselves at Grabel's.

When we got in there we wanted to call home so we used their phone and we were freezing and all wet. When I called home, my daughter answered the phone and while we were talking she let out a scream and I heard this crash. We had a twelve foot window facing the lake and one section of the window blew in. It was about four and a half feet wide. She screamed and she's not the hysterical type and she said that the snow was up to her knees in no time at all. I told her to get a hammer and nails and block off the kitchen doorway with blankets. I told her to get blankets and candles and get into the kitchen and do the best they could there.

Kipper wanted to go but I told him it was useless. I didn't want to lose everybody and I knew I would because you couldn't see. He got as far as Concessi's store and he called me and said he had made it there and he was getting warm and he thought he could make it to our house.

I knew there was no way to get there. I never heard from him again for seventeen hours. I figured he was finished.

But he was pushed by the wind against a cottage. By then, the snow was up to the tops of the windows and one window was open. Kipper went in. He figured at least he'd be alive. It seemed lik the end of the world but he was thinking it would be only a few hours and he could save the kids.

The owners of the cottage had cleaned it all up. They had taken every blanket. There was a whole bottle of whiskey there which he was afraid to touch for fear he would go to sleep. I was cold and he would have liked to have had a drink. He took the drapes off the window and took his clothes off down to his long johns and wrapped himself up, head and all, in the drapes. Then he lay down and rubbed his legs together for seventeen hours and stayed awake.

I imagine he was going through the same nightmares I was because we thought maybe it would stop and it didn't. If you got a little sleep, you might never open your eyes again.

In the morning, he could see a little bit better by six o'clock and he put his clothes back on. They were all frozen. I don't know if he left the drapes over him but he got as far as Concessi's and by then Concessi's had been covered by snow and he had to go up and slide down to the door. The women saved his life you know. They put him in water. His feet were frozen, his face was frostbitten and they called me and said he was alive. I couldn't believe it. They said he would call me later when he was able to talk, and an hour and a half later he did.

In the meantime, I called everybody we could to see what happened to the kids. The people next door are the Duffets. They went out to try and get the kids who were about a hundred and fifty feet away from their place. They had Newfoundland dogs and they thought that maybe with the Newfoundlanders they could get over to the kids. The dogs just followed them and they went around in circles and they lost sight of their house. He lost his breath and they were afraid he might have a heart attack so they were glad to get back in and they said they wouldn't leave again.

In the meantime, my daughter thought she could get over there and she tried by going out of her house and she lost sight of the house. She fell down and in between gusts she could see something which was the outline of the house and that's how she got back in as soon as she could. She said she would never leave again because you just couldn't see anything.

So the children lay on the floor in the kitchen with the dog in between them and they left a candle going. There was some heat coming from the heater but there was so much wind coming in the house that it was extremely cold.

Finally, they got some young guys who were very heroic. They were Brian and Danny Leslie and they were at Lowbanks. They had snowmobile suits and they were young and strong and they knew Kipper and the kids. When it looked like no one could get them,

Brian and Danny decided they were going to get them. It took them seven and a half hours and they stopped every place where there was a candle or anything. They'd stop and try and get warm. They kept coming and kept coming. They kept calling us as they went along. It was agony. I knew they were still so far away.

If we called my daughter, she had to go around through the snow to the phone and she finally said please don't call me again. Don't call me!

The Leslies finally got them. They couldn't see and they got way out in the field and the kids were crying and freezing. They were carrying Eric and dragging Kim. Finally, they walked right out of the snow into the field and then they had a hard time getting back. They saw the power line when there was a break in the blizzard and they got back that way to Duffet's. They were all there safe.

They came and got Kipper on Sunday as soon as there was a break. Then they came and got me with a snowmobile suit and a toboggan and they got me as far as Concessi's. They dragged me half on the tobaggan to the Duffet's and we were stuck there again until Wednesday night.

The Duffets have an antique shop in their living room so we stayed in the kitchen. They had our dog, Eric, Kimberly, me and John and whoever. They had five giant Newfoundlands in their utility room and two Newfoundlands were trapped in the garage. When the dogs went outside, they would urinate on the T.V. antennas on the top of the roof. The Duffets had lots of wood outside but you couldn't even tell where the wood was because of the snow. We had tree branches getting in our eyes and we fought off these branches to get into the house because we were thirty or forty feet up on the snow. We had to slide into the house.

We didn't get back into our house for quite a while. Kipper and Eric got back in a week. Kim moved in with my sister. I stayed in Buffalo because I work there. I guess I moved in about six weeks later. I came back once in a while but there was no place to park. It was like cutting through a ravine and you had to climb up to get to your place. We have a long lot and that meant we had to drag all our wash out and all our garbage out and all our food in on toboggans. My daughter at one time, fell down on the road because we had snowsteps. She almost gave someone a heart attack because they thought she had gone under the car. I fell down the steps on Sunday trying to get to church and finally we were able to cut in a little path for the cars but they weren't able to cut it in too deeply.

We had an awful lot of damage and that damage wasn't anything compared to the experience of thinking everyone was dead or dying and you couldn't get to them.

You could walk, and there were so many sightseers. They were climbing up and looking around and taking pictures from the backyard. They'd be walking all over and saying such things as, "Oh, are you living here?" It was sort of like Niagara Falls for a few days. People came from all over. They were on snowshoes and they were able to walk around. I guess there were reporters at our house and they took pictures inside and outside. It seems as though there were a lot of news people who were interested in it. However, we never heard much about it after that.

Pregnant Woman

A Port Colborne woman who became pregnant during the blizzard said that she was thinking of naming her baby Blitz.

Mr. Paul

Buried Alive—21 Hours

  I left my home in the morning, with my daughter Linda, to go to the Welland Hospital to have some blood tests done on her. She had to have a knee operation the next Tuesday so the blood tests were necessary. I had a dental appointment in Port Colborne afterwards and so I headed towards it. When that was finished, it started to snow. I decided to get down to the Pioneer gas place where the gas is cheap, and I filled up my truck. We went over to the Dominion Store and bought up a bunch of groceries. When we got out of there it was bad already and I thought we'd better get home before it got worse. The closer we got to home the worse the weather became.
  There were four or five of us in a row and we were able to move ahead a little bit and we'd stop and then we'd go and we'd stop and we carried on like this for a piece. We met a snowplow then and the driver said that he was going to put the plow in the yard because he couldn't see well enough to do anymore plowing. It was he who warned us of the school bus accident up ahead. That scared us so we went ahead a little bit and stopped. There were four or five guys in a line and I was at the head of the line. The guys seemed a little bit disgusted, and they sort of encouraged me to go along since I was in the lead. I tried to go a little further and it got so bad I couldn't see the front end of my truck at times. I stopped. The other guys stopped and they decided to go around me. They did and went ahead and of course I never saw or heard from them any more. We just couldn't see and I thought to myself that I had a tank full of gas. We'll just sit here and wait it out. I figured the snow would stop and in a couple of hours it would be all over.
  Near us on the road was a truck loaded with emergency stuff for the hospitals. I didn't know at that time but he was the last truck that went by and he said he was going to go ahead and try it anyway. We found out later that he didn't get very far. Anyway, we sat in the truck for awhile and there was another car behind us. Eventually a man came up and asked if he could join us in the truck because he was low on gas. He was all by himself and I invited him to join us in the truck.
  I tried once or twice after that to budge the truck but the

drift had me snow bound. We had been stuck since noon hour so at about four o'clock I decided I'd better go to the other guy's car and listen to the radio because I didn't have a radio in the truck. So, I got out and walked to his car behind our truck. It was so cold. I never realized this until I got into his car and the snow that had blown in my hair fell from my head because it had been melting and before it hit the seat it was just like little ice cubes.

Anyway, I listened to the radio and they were forecasting that this weather would let up later on in the evening so we weren't all that worried. We figured things would slow down and we'll just walk out because I knew just about where I was since I lived in this area since 1952. So we tried to make ourselves at home. It was comfortable in the truck. We had the heat going so it wasn't really cold inside. Then we had the wipers going most of the time but they soon gave out because of all the snow.

We sat there and we ate some cookies. We had purchased about fifty dollars worth of groceries so we had a lot to eat. We got a bag full of milk open and we drank the milk. My daughter had a book with her so she read that and after she finished reading it, she gave it to Mr. Korsch, the chap from Burlington and he read it too. Then we just sat there. We didn't really do too much talking. I wasn't really worried. I found out later that the guy from Burlington was quite worried and of course as the night worsened he got more worried because he could see the snow building up.

First of all we couldn't open his door anymore. Then the snow crept up over the windshield. Little by little it crept up over my door. Pretty soon, his door, the windshield and my door was covered.

I had no idea what time it was. I'm guessing that at around ten p.m. my daughter was sick to her stomach. I don't know who woke up who but we were all drowsy and sick. The snow had covered the exhaust and the fumes were starting to back up into the cab so we opened the window to let a little fresh air in. I can remember fighting off the drowsiness and asking the other guy if he was all right. We kept each other awake. It was very cold for a while but we got over that and we never turned the truck on anymore.

I rolled up the window again and since a lot of snow came in when the window was down it was cold for a while. We shivered for a bit but pretty soon the door was covered and there were no more drafts. It started to warm up. It wasn't comfortable because there was snow melted on the floor and there was water dripping off the ceiling from condensation. In the cab of the truck the three of us were pretty well jammed in.

The only thing we saw, after we got snowed under, happened around midnight. A snowmobile went by and we blew the horn. He never heard us. He never saw us. We had a light on in the truck and I guess the windshield wasn't quite covered yet because we saw him go by. We kind of dozed off and on until the morning. During the night the windshield cracked on us and made a terrifying noise. It was really weird.

Must have been around eight o'clock or eight thirty in the morning when we heard somebody walk over the top of the truck.

We blew the horn again and he never heard it. This really amazed us. It still amazes us. That snow must really be a good insulator because he never heard us and we were hollering and screaming and carrying on. I had this long scraper with me and I stuck it out the window and pushed it up as far as I could. Nobody saw it. Mr. Korsch had reminded me through the night that if we ran out of oxygen we'd be in a great fix. So throughout the night I would occasionally push the scraper up and let a little fresh air in and with it came a lot of snow. That snow was just like pepper and salt. It was so fine and so dirty because the wind would pick up the dirt from the bare fields and send it flying through the air. The minute the snow hit the seat, my clothes got soaked. We were all getting uncomfortable. My feet were cold. But the rest of my body was okay. I was wearing a light pair of boots. My daughter had snow boots on. Mr. Korsch had a bit of a suit and a low pair of shoes.

We heard somebody walk over the top of the truck again and we heard this noise from what sounded like a big machine. We heard it coming and we heard somebody walk over the top of the truck again. I shoved the ice scraper through again and somebody tugged at the other end.

After I had pulled the scraper back, all I could see was this hand with a camera on it. The Regional Police were attempting to get the big front end loader through there in order to take Mr. Mulko to the hospital.

Gary Berg saw the ice scraper come through the snow and he had quite a job convincing the authorities that there was somebody under the snow. There was two feet of snow over the top of the truck. Finally, they got some shovels and they dug us out and they took us to the nearest farm house. That was about nine o'clock Saturday morning.

Linda Paul

"It seemed as though God was the only one that could help us."

We started driving home and it was terrible. I had to roll down my window and stick my head out and tell Dad whenever we were getting too close to the ditch. It was the only way we could see and I think I began praying a lot at that point.

We decided to stay in the truck because it was really really cold out and if we had gone out of the truck we wouldn't have been able to see a thing. We would have been lost or frozen to death, and besides, my knees weren't very good. I kept falling all the time. My knees were weak and they would collapse and buckle under me and I wouldn't know when it was going to happen so I was in no condition to do any walking, let alone fight through the blizzard.

At one point, Dad and Mr. Korsch were getting quite dozy. Mr. Korsch noticed it first and poked my Dad and shut off the engine and opened the windows and they were really worried. I

Beware of Snowflakes! Courtesy Betty Leslie, Wainfleet.

had been dozy all afternoon, but I don't know why I noticed it before they did.

It helped that I had a book to read. It was <u>Moon Raker's Bride.</u> I'd read it before but it was the only thing I could find in the house to read on the way. Then Mr. Korsch read it after I was finished.

I was praying all the way through this. It wasn't just for me but for everybody. I knew there must be other people in the same situation as us. There was nothing we could do. It seemed as though God was the only one that could help us.

We were lucky because the snowdrift covered us completely. Without that coverage, we might not have had enough heat and we could have frozen to death. The truck would have been exposed more directly to the wind. We were lucky to notice the fumes because they could have killed us.

They dug down to our window and I don't think I've seen any bigger looking policemen. They were the only people that I'd seen in such a long time except for Dad and our buddy Mr. Korsch. They looked so big and strong and handsome, and one of them half carried me to the farm house. This was the Stouth's place and I couldn't even see until we were just a little ways from it because it was still blowing pretty badly.

Other people were stranded in the Stouth's farm house. Some were from North Carolina. They rushed me in and wrapped me all up in blankets and put me on the couch and tried to get me to relax. Dad couldn't sit down. He kept walking and walking because he said it felt so good.

What really impressed me was how much everybody helped. They had the radio and it was all emergency broadcasting. The neighbors were helping out at the Stouth's. One of the neighbor's furnaces broke and they all came over to the Stouth's. They all pitched in. There was a bunch of little kids that I helped to babysit after supper that night so that I felt that I could do something to help too. It just made me feel good to live around here. Everybody was so helpful.

Male, seventeen: We stayed up most of the night listening to the radio and how strangely some people were reacting to a situation like this. It was a lot of fun. We listened to things like, "My wife has left me and I need a bottle of whiskey, I'd pay anything."

Mr. Mulko

"And now the old nails are off and the new nails are growing in."

First, my name is Alexander Mulko and they call me Alex for short. I used to be a professional wrestler, Kalmikoff brothers

Survivor Alex Mulko with frostbite. By Charles Agro.

by name. We were very famous brothers. We wrestled at Maple Leaf Gardens, Billy Watson, everybody else, and I wrestled all over the world. I have lived in Japan, Australia, Germany. Went to Czechoslovakia eight times. United States I lived and wrestled in every city, Hollywood, Florida, Alabama, Tennessee, North Carolina, Boston, Maine, all over the States. I lived in Newfoundland in Canada, Calgary, Vancouver, Winnipeg, almost every city in the world anyhow. I like Canada the best so I retire in Canada. Especially I'm liking Lowbanks.

I have a friend and Thursday he's calling me up and saying I have a gas well on the farm and the gas well is freezing and I'm afraid to go to the well because the storm and everything and I might have a heart attack or something so two of us will go, no? Maybe something would happen to me and then two of us could help each other. So I said fine. This is about ten o'clock. So we go and we fix up the place on Thursday. Then the storm goes down a little bit and the road is cleaned.

Friday morning he's calling me again about eight o'clock and I got scared and he's calling me up and saying my house is freezing and I need your help. He had no water or anything so I must go and help my friend. So I said okay and I got in the car and it's blowing already and I said to my wife I'm going for helping my friend but I'm afraid I might never come back. I might be getting lost and I told her about two or three times the same thing. So I went there and he's bragging because he bought this small German car and he says how good they are on gas and everything and I have a big oldsmobile and so we got in the small station wagon and we go and get some straw from the neighbours. It's about twenty below zero or something like this and his windshield is freezing and I said what the hell! I would never be having a car like this especially a foreign car in this country and you can't see where you are going, and your windows are freezing, and there's no heater that's working good. And you are saving gas? So we quickly strap on the sleigh, and we fix it up with wire and we start to burn and clean around the well and everything is going good. It is starting to blow so bad and I said to my friend, "Let's go into the house because it's so bad here and we'll get blown over." And he said, "Oh no. We've got to keep working." Then he's afraid of a heart attack and now after it's burned out we don't need it anymore so he's going to the road and bring some more tires. So I followed his dog and I reached the house and it was so bad there I put his dog in his car cause I'm feeling sorry for the dog and the house is closed.

Anyhow, I started to go home and from this farm I had to go on the road and I knew there was deep snow so I knew I must speed up and get on the road. So I speed up and I come close to the road and I stop. I thought maybe I hit some car or have an accident so I just stopped. So I slowed down and I went on to No. 3 highway. I couldn't see which way to go so I opened the windows on both sides and I saw no cars. So I started to come into Lakeshore Road and by Concessi's Store. Then I thought, well I should stay here but there were so many cars on the road that I thought there are too many cars. So I keep on going and I see a car blinking in front of me. I pass the car and I got stuck and I couldn't go back from that place. Naturally, I didn't know where I was then. Then I thought that the snow was not going to blow much longer so I stay a couple of hours. It was eleven o'clock in the morning.

I started the car every half hour. I didn't know where I was. The snow was already so high on the hood that I couldn't even get out of the car. Then I'm thinking my wife will get me somehow. She knows I'm on the road some place because I always call her if I go some place. I call her and tell her I'll be home such and such a time because she has the stomach trouble and all that.

It was already about twelve hours that passed. I started the car again, then the exhaust fumes is coming and stinking and burning my lungs. So I shut the car off and I remember we had some candles in the glove compartment so I thought if I start a candle fire maybe I'll keep warm. I looked for the candles but I couldn't find them. I was surprised not to find but two weeks before we were at a funeral and my wife had put them on the grave so I thought no candles for me.

I don't have any blankets but I am pretty well dressed up. I have on three pairs of underwear and a good winter hunting pants and then I had on three undershirts and I have a vest and hunting shirt and then I have a big hunting jacket, a parka jacket. Then I have a good hat too so then I think I'm going to sleep a little bit. I went to sleep and I passed out.

After I passed out, those boys come because my wife sent them to look for me. So they came and one of them stumbled or fell from the snow down to my trunk. Our car was already covered from the snow so the car wasn't visible. He fell from the top onto the back of the trunk and he said, "Hey here's a car." and that's what they were telling me them boys. So they opened the car and they found me and they shook me and I responded and they said I was still alive. Then they had some wine and so they washed my face with the wine and they shook me up and everything. I responded so they closed the door and they went to look for a house. They found one empty house and they thought maybe there was another house some place and they couldn't find a door or anything, cause the house was buried under the snow. But one window was there so they knocked. Finally the Agro's opened the window and these two boys go into the house through the window and one guy says, "I'm going to get him." The other one says, "I'm not going because he's dead anyways and I'm freezing to death myself." He didn't have enough clothing, my friend the neighbour, so he stayed in the house. So this one man he got me out of the car. Then he gets me out and drags me for eighteen feet and then he gets so exhausted and cold because there were sixty mile-an-hour winds. That's what the paper says and there was twenty-five feet of snowbanks up and down. So he's pulling me and he was so exhausted and I couldn't help him. I don't remember anything and I was alive but I don't remember it. He says I weighed three hundred and fifty pounds or more but in weight I am two hundred and fifty pounds exactly. The first time he went to look for the car, he couldn't find the car and then later he finds it and he pulls me out and drags me about eighteen feet and he gets so exhausted. He was for fear of losing his life and so he digs a big hole in the snow and hides himself a little bit and he counted to himself. I'm laying there belly down. He says to the snow, "It is bad." He's pulling off his face mask and putting it on my face. But while he is pulling me in the snow I loose my glove. Then I get to the house and he's warming up and starting to yell to the other fellow, and he says, "Come on", and the other fellow says, "To hell with him. He is dead already. I'm not going to loose my life." I don't blame the guy you know. I don't blame him. So anyhow both of them went and they tied a rope to the window and then they followed the rope and they come and they get me again in the snowbank where I'm waiting patiently to die. And they start to pull me into the house and I'm very grateful to both of them.

The lady in the house she says they are pushing me in head first through the window and then my head went on the floor and my feet are up. I was frozen stiff. They get me in the house. They get into the house and I'm remembering while they're dragging me that they say, "Push! Push! Push!" And I thought I was hunting someplace with the boys and I couldn't get over the snow. I was dreaming of hunting wolves. While I was close to the house I remember peeling the ice from my eyes while I was lying down on the snow and the snow's melting on my hands and then froze on them.

While I was in the house, I don't remember. They took all my clothes from me. They cut some sleeves and they got some clothes for me. They put me in the bed and that was four o'clock in the morning.

My wife told them, "Go please, look for my husband." They had a couple of drinks and they said I'm calling a friend. So at ten o'clock they start that morning to look for me. It was exactly two miles from my house. It took them maybe five hours to get there and they say the power lines were hitting the snow and they were orienting where they were. Now I am in the house and I can remember the talking of this lady who is knowing about nursing at one time because she was giving me some aspirin. Then at seven o'clock I come to and they give me some tea and coffee and it is good. But I was in shock.

Then I stayed there and Saturday was bad all day. I was hurting. And Sunday is coming one helicopter and they are taking me to the hospital and this Dr. Wilson, he's looking me over in the hospital and saying, "Boy, if you wouldn't be in such good physical shape like a good wrestler you are, you would be dead long time ago." Then my hands were so big and blistered.

The doctor put me on the operating table and the doctor's cutting all the skin and I could see my veins and meat and everything underneath the skin. And he's washing the hands. And he's putting on bandages and then gives me some antibiotic pills and I stay in the hospital.

On the fifth day my wife can come finally and see me, Tuesday. The helicopter comes back and they take some pictures of the house. So they come and she is pleading with them to fly her to the hospital so she can see me. And I'm glad.

Then people come to visit. They bring some gifts and then I said, "Where these gifts from?" I don't remember that either.

Then they clear the roads and Dr. Wilson is releasing me to go to my own doctor. So I go to Dunnville hospital and altogether I stay eighteen days in the hospital.

All the time in the car I was thinking about my wife. You know she went to Jerusalem a couple of times and she's bringing a holy medallion. And I'm taking this medallion, it's a magnetic thing and I stuck it onto the mirror and I touched that medallion and I thought, "Well, the devil calls me to look for a house someplace." And St. Paul says, "Stay in the car because if you are going to go, you are going to die." And one of my friends, Jim Cooke, he says, "Hey, want some good luck?" And he had a jackrabbit foot. So he gives me the jackrabbit foot and I keep in my pockets. Imagine, I'm over sixty years of age and I'm not very religious but I pray to St. Paul. Anyhow, I am safe. I am just so happy I have good friends who take risk of their life to help an old poor wrestler.

And now the old nails are off and the new nails are growing in. I'm thankful for people like these friends who risked their own life by pulling me into the house of the people.

Frostbite Precaution

Remove the ring from your finger if caught in a situation where your hands may be frostbitten. Blood circulation will be less restricted and you will avoid the painful process of having your ring cut from your swollen finger.

Mrs. Mulko

"I will take the gun and kill myself".

I've been twice in Jerusalem, in 1958 and 1964. I pray there. But I never pray more in my life than I pray in those five days. I pictured my husband dead in the car. I say my husband is dead. He is in the snow.

I remember one time in 1956, we were driving to St. Louis in the car and we got stuck in Erie, Pennsylvania - big storm. We stay there for three days. I know that snow can kill because they find people dead in the car.

The neighbour families come and stay with me for five days. I never survive without these good people. Lots of neighbours came and they spend time in helping me. Danny shovel the snow and clean all around and make safe for me because the house is cracking under the snow. We have a dog named Buddy and he could not go out. He cried. They shovel the door for Buddy every two or three hours.

I don't listen to the radio because I was scared they were going to announce that they find my husband dead. The police tell me they were looking for him. After the announcement on the radio for Alex Mulko to call his wife Irene, I tell the police, "He's not alive." "Oh," he says, "maybe he is in some house." I say, "No, no. I know my husband. He phones me any place that he go - always. Something has happened to him."

We got gun in house. I find gun and I am going to kill myself because I am blaming myself for not stopping Alex from going to help his friend. Mrs. Jennings my neighbour, is hiding the gun so I cannot kill myself. But I know my husband is dead. I wait for the police to tell me he is finished and then I am going to be finished. I will take the gun and kill myself. I am scared and in tears and everything is bad.

Larry and David go look for my husband. David not dressed so good like Larry. But they go. I give them some wine to carry with them. If they can find Alex alive, they can save him those boys. They find him alive and they had a hard time to pull him out of the car. They got to go 25 feet over snow and then down to the house because the house is covered with snow. They take him to Agro's house.

They call me from the hospital. The police call me and say he is safe and I don't believe it.

Then the helicopter is landing in our yard and he is taking pictures. Mr. Jennings begs them to take me to see Alex because I don't believe he is alive. This young fellow is the boss in the helicopter and he came here and I beg him to take me to the hospital. He took me. I see Alex's hands and they look like mush. I am afraid he is going to loose his hands.

What I went through, I do not wish on my worst enemy.

Seat Stuffing

One young man was stranded in his car all night and he ran out of gas. He was freezing so he tore all the stuffing out of the car seats and all this material helped to keep him warm. His hands were frostbitten pretty badly.

Mrs. Agro

"They had to turn him on his side and shove him head first and he landed on my front room floor."

We were awakened by a pounding on the back window about three in the morning. Of course we had no way of knowing that Mulko was fifty feet in front of us on the road and he didn't know

Queen Elizabeth Highway between Niagara Falls and Fort Erie. Courtesy St Catharines Standard.

that we were here. Concessi's store had phoned earlier and said that someone was missing and as is our custom we put the lights on along the Lakeshore. I had forgotten about the light and the pounding on the windows aroused us. There was no way to get in. Whoever it was had to go around to the front window. Eventually we broke it open. It's called a bay window and it has three sections. The two boys broke in the window first and they said there was someone missing and we'll never find him because you couldn't see a foot in front of you. Away they went out again and as luck would have it they found him in front of the house right near us. Apparently he was in the car and Charlie went and got a rope and tied it to the window so that the boys could follow the rope back as a guide.

When they did get him out, he looked like a snowman. I'm not laughing but he did look weird. His eyebrows were full of snow and his hair was frozen. They heaved him into the house. They tried to get him in through by the shoulders but there was no way. The man was so huge. They had to turn him on his side and shove him head first and he landed on my front room floor. It's a wonder he didn't crack in half. He was subconscious. I think he knew he was safe but he didn't care anymore. He was with us about two days. I think it was Sunday afternoon when we were shouting at him to try and get him to move his arms.

Finally, he got flown into Port Colborne Hospital by the helicopter. That's when they broke the back window and took him out the other window because the snow by this time had covered the front window over again. So they were forced to break another window to get out the back way. The army and the police were all here. The helicopter landed on the lake right here beside us, then, they took him to the Port Hospital.

The boys who found him were born around here, lived here and they know their way around like their own backyard. It was so bad that they even lost their way. Everything was covered. There was no way of identifying anything. We have a large tree in the front and it's the only one around here that size and one of the boys said he remembered that tree was from Agro's so he knew where he was.

We were without power for about twenty eight hours. We had a fireplace. It felt like we were camping out in the middle of winter. The generosity of the people, and this love for your fellow man, I'll always remember surely. People you speak to and nod at because it's respectful are standing at your door saying take this because you might need it. It was great. That's something that stuck in my mind. People were beautiful. Later on we would sit at the table and laugh at what happened—the stupid things we were saying because nobody knew what to do.

I have two large dogs, and they were very frightened because they're so used to running the house and here they were faced with all these people coming in a steady stream like Grand Central Station. The dogs stayed mostly under the table or in the cellar and then to do their constitutional we had to push them through a hole in the snow. They'd come right back into the house and go under the table. Seems strange thinking back now with the flowers all up and the warm weather. It gives you goose bumps just thinking of what it was like during the storm. I didn't get cabin fever even though I didn't get out for about eighteen days. I said at that point to Charlie, "Please take me down town so I can see people moving around."

Wild Bees

Naturalists noticed in the fall of 1976 that the wild bees had formed their nests very high in the branches of trees, the highest in living memory. Indian folklore states that you can predict how much snow will fall that winter by the height of the bee nests. The higher the nest, the deeper the snow.

Drug Addict

"I was like a guy with rabies, thinking of people I was going to bite."

On Friday morning I was spaced. I had been to a party the night before with some friends from Buffalo. Ozone—Disneyland that night. I was really loaded and couldn't cope with what was out there. This disaster was the farthest thing from my mind. For me, the biggest disaster was waking up.

It was really strange. The old lady left me in December and I was kicking around. I was out of work. I had been with a band in Toronto for about two years. I had a lot of things in my head—like I was going to straighten up. I was going to put the super band on wheels and everything was going to work out.

I met some friends from Buffalo and we were partying and into some dynamite coke. I got a pretty good buzz-on with that stuff.

It was a strange story—me messing with heroin and the whole thing. I was talking to this friend of yours at a party and he said you were doing a book about the blizzard. He told me to give you a call. We got into a rap about it and I . . . it's freaky cause he comes on to me like I'm some kind of junkie and he wants the whole tune. No junkie ever thinks he is a junkie unless he has been into it for a million years. Nobody wants to be hooked on anything—even cigarettes or coffee.

I got mixed up with junk and I had been at it for a couple of years. It's not like that bull shit on television when you do it once and then you go screaming around after that. You do it—it's a big buzz—nothing matters for a while and that's what I was into. Before I knew it, I was into it every day.

So it came down to this Friday morning and I'm hung over in a big way. I needed a fix but I was dry. The storm was starting to blow and I couldn't reach anyone. I had a lot of good smoke so I did a couple of good numbers first thing in the morning. I was supposed to be in Buffalo that night. There was going to be a party with some

Good Insulation, Wainfleet.

people in town and I hoped I could get hooked up with them. That was out of the question as the Friday went on.

What happened was that I started to come down except that I didn't know what I was coming down from because I never thought that I was anywhere to begin with. It was weird when I started down. It was somewhere between the flu and madness. I got sick.

A junkie never says he's a junkie, never admits that he needs anything. I found myself scooting around the house looking for any shit that I had on hand-whisky, aspirin, a couple of downs. They were immediately devoured. I lost Friday because I was spaced out. Downs are mean things anyway. Just like junk, you just get settled down until disaster. I wasn't worried about a disaster outside. There was one in my house.

When the downs started to go away on me I started running into some real trouble. From then on it's what happened in my mind. I got sort of super tired you know—when you can't go to sleep and you get paranoid and crazy. It's a strange state where you don't know whether you are sleeping or dreaming. You lie there sweating. I couldn't live with it at all. It was Friday night I guess. That storm was so strange.

I never knew night from day. It blew and blew and I would look out and it was always the same. I had a place by the lake in Fort Erie. It got so bad after I started to come around that I would lie there and start to fall apart. Nothing was working.

Suicide popped up. There was no doubt about it. If I had more guts there was a time when I probably would have blown myself away on the spot.

I got afraid of myself. I had no place to run. Friday night was the killer. I didn't sleep because I was animated. I couldn't deal with the fact that I wanted to start banging with that needle.

Then I started calling people on the phone. It was weird. I called that buddy of yours. I didn't make much sense and that alienated me further because you rap to somebody and they don't want anything to do with you and you pick it up. Never occurs to you that you are so weird that you just can't communicate at all. You blame it on them. You slam the phone down. By the time it was over, everybody was responsible. You keep picking one scapegoat after another.

Saturday was a real trip. Nothing was right. You're not comfortable no matter where you sit. It wouldn't quit storming outside. That snow came into my mind. That blizzard came into my head. Everything that had gone wrong in my life became the blizzard. It became the whole problem. I went through so many changes. Then I went outside and attacked the storm. There was this huge drift in front of the house and it was as hard as cement. I started shovelling. The street was black and there was no place to go. But that drift got hell I'll tell you. It came apart. I went crazy with it. I exhausted myself and I had the shakes really bad. Yet I drove myself on. I was wearing every piece of clothing that I owned.

I shovelled towards the people next door. They're real innocent you know. I couldn't relate to them at all. Loud music late at night was never their cup of tea and there was always a bit of a hassle. I started to shovel their sidewalk. I wanted to do a favour but I didn't want them to know it was me. I shovelled within three feet of their door and then sneaked back to my house.

I was sick but I refused to admit that the dope had anything to do with it. When I wanted to kill myself I'd call for help and then I was afraid to ask for help. I called the open line radio station and then hung up on them. I was in tears. I was going to talk to them. I wanted to talk to somebody but I hung up on them. I was afraid of them too. I called the finance company to say that I owed them money. I wanted to shout at them but there was nobody there. They were responsible. I was like a guy with rabies thinking of people I was going to bite. I called up my ex-wife. She was on my mind. But I wasn't together. I screamed at her and hung up.

I called the man in Buffalo. I wanted him to come over and bring me some good shit. Nice try. He's going through things I can never imagine. In Buffalo he has a place on the West side. He's down around Elmwood and he is going through crazy things there. He called all over and there is no way he can get to any shit. I hung up on this dude because he cannot get shit together at all. They were all down and they were going crazy. They were trying to rig a game. They were trying to deliver drugs to people—all through that emergency service. They thought they could get some downs but they would take anything. Barbs - anything. They were making up these outrageous stories to tell people so they could get the emergency vehicles to deliver them some shit. They called the police. They tried everything. A three year old knows that they couldn't do what they wanted. I'm sure they are going to call the hospital and ask for dope and they are going to send it right over. It was that stupid the way they were coming down. The man isn't cool at all. He thinks he is Mr. Conman and he couldn't con a full twenty dollars. I hung up on him.

With each call I made, I thought that this would be the answer. This would straighten the whole thing out for me. Yet every call was another disaster.

I never dreamed that drugs could con a person. All of a sudden you realize that there was no place to go. You are running from yourself and there was no place to go.

I was in that house for three days. But I had a fire place. I got a fire going and I kept staring into the fire. I'd shovel snow and come into the house and fire would be there. It was the only friend I had. I was praying by the time it was over. I prayed that I could get my head together.

Sunday came and the storm was still blowing. At least by Sunday I was rational. I started thinking about things. I hadn't eaten and there was food around. I remember eating an orange. While I was eating I saw daylight.

The lifestyle had me and so did the junk. Junk is a riot, a bounce. There are no hassles. Nothing bothers you. You are untouchable. You are sitting on your cloud and you are in charge of everything. They never show you that part of life and maybe that's OK because that is what catches kids. That was experience. I guess I was lucky to get a taste of the other side. Then you realize how you wanted to blow yourself away and how sick you really were.

I was in debt like you wouldn't believe. I had taken a loan before that. I had sold the guitar. Without an instrument, how does a musician work? I sold twelve hundred dollars in equipment and I blew that in no time. When it starts to go, the dude at the loan company gave me another loan. Unemployment insurance, that's what he called it. First he said he wanted to see my records from the bank. I told him that if I had any kind of record from the bank that I wouldn't be seeing him for money. He got a piece of me and I hated it. After all that time being so cool on the street, you realize how cool you really were. Some dude in a checkered jacket with striped flood-pants has got you for such a bundle and he's laughing. I'm not out from under him yet but I have a job. It's in construction. And I've never got back into heroin. I still get high now and then. I smoke a bit and I do the odd toot of coke but never junk. Never again.

I ran with some well connected people for a while. They were loaded with bread. They were mostly in music and they had all kinds of turkeys to take care of them. Some were dealing on the side, some were doing a little shit. They would come to town and have a good time with some turkey like me. You realize that you are not much more than a groupie when you are doing a number. That cat is cool. He plays a guitar. Come in here. You sit down. You get high. Right? Sure a good time. They hit the road and you hit the dirt.

I want to get back to music but I don't know if 1 can. I've thought about putting the storm to music . . . It's in my head but I've got nothing to play it on. I'm not going to have anything for a while.

For me, it was like three days in the insane asylum. I was everybody. I was in charge, I was the patient, I was the cure, I was the problem and I wouldn't want to go through it again for anything.

In a way that storm was a blessing. I got so self-centered. There were people dying out there and I was far more important than they were. I was flipping-out when I called the radio station and I thought: Who is going to listen to my problem when there are people out there freezing, starving and dying?

I love music. I turn on the radio and this man is telling me there is a storm. That's my problem! Get off it man!

I've been to a doctor since the storm and of course he was going to straighten out my life. He told me to take the old lady back. I called her during the storm. I was on my hands and knees crying that I thought I was going to die and she says: "You bastard, you ain't got a job!"

We are finished. She was another thing. I knew it was just a matter of time until she met somebody else. Romance is just another phase. That came with a storm too. No doubt about it.

It's a fragile world you know. No matter what kind of band you are playing, there are always people who think you are hot shit. As long as those people are around you, you never have to look at yourself. You never have to count up the points because you can see it in their faces. Then when everything starts to go to shit on you, you stop and look at things. I was hanging onto the band while the old lady and the fans were hanging onto me. Clumps of people all hanging onto something else. If something falls near the top, the whole thing comes apart.

I bet there are lots of people who got to thinking about themselves during that storm. I'm kind of jealous of those people who were able to think of others. They went out of themselves. Then there are other people who went out there and helped those folks who had all that trouble. If I had to do it over again, I would shovel right up to my neighbour's door.

Thomas A. Rejent, Chief County Toxicologist

We service approximately 38 area hospitals in Western New York. Because of the blizzard, our volume of work concerning drug abuse and drug overdose dropped by probably eight to nine hundred percent.

"Thank God For A Pile Of Shit"

I was in the marsh around eleven o'clock in the morning and the hunting was good. I had already bagged two cottontails. I had heard that there was supposed to be more snow that day but I never paid much attention.

Then the snow started to fall and it was different than I had ever seen. Such huge flakes and they were falling straight down and it was so silent and so thick that it gave me a weird feeling. It kind of made me feel like something was going to happen and I got the shivers just standing there watching all this snow fall.

With so much snow falling, all the rabbit tracks were covered. It wasn't worth hunting any more, so I called my dog to heel and I started out of the marsh. Then this wind hit and the snow started to blow and the tops of the trees started to bend at quite an angle and whoosh I couldn't see a thing. I had a lot of protection from the brush at the time but I thought—Good God!—What is this coming on?

I waited and thought that when this gust of wind passed, maybe I could see again, but the wind never stopped. I figured that I'd better ride this one out. So, I sat down on a log and tried to light a cigarette. Impossible!

From what I could see of the dog, it acted kind of strange. It's a black Labrador Retriever but it was pretty white by now. He kept his ears flat and it had a strange look on its face and it kept watching me as if he was asking me what the heck was going on here.

I decided to move so I unloaded my gun and pointed the dog into the wind. I've done this before when I've come out of the marsh at night. I figured that the dog knew where it was going. I pointed the dog ahead of me and I said, "Car! Car!" This meant that we were going for a car ride. So the dog started out ahead of me.

We were going very slowly because I was holding the dogs tail Yep, I strapped the shotgun over my shoulder and held onto that long pointed tail with both hands. I had confidence in my dog because it had led me out of places at night.

Well, we walked and we walked and we walked. I couldn't see the head of my dog when I was holding onto its tail. But it kept going and going and going. Finally it stopped.

I looked around and I couldn't see anything. It was a complete whiteout. I figured we were at the car. I felt my way over the top of the dog and reached around in front of him. I felt something that was higher than me so I knew I wasn't at the car. I started to dig my hands into this thing in front of me and I felt heat. Believe me it felt good because even though I was in hunting clothes and long johns I was freezing. That wind went right through everything and my face was on fire. So I kept digging and I noticed a smell as I dug downwards. It was a manure pile. There had to be a barn nearby. There was no way I was going to look for the barn because I was really tired by this time. I was freezing and I was a bit up-tight because the dog was supposed to bring me to the car and it brought me to a manure pile.

He followed me around to the other side of the pile where the wind wasn't so strong and I tried to see a barn. I couldn't see the dog when it was standing on my foot.

I slung the gun off my back and with the butt of the gun I dug a hole into the side of the manure pile. It was a little mushy. When I got inside the hole I saw steam coming off the manure. The dog was out in the wind and that was no good because the wind was so strong that it blew the snow into your lungs and made you feel like you were suffocating. So I got out and dug enough room for me and the dog so we could both fit inside. The snow covered us over except for a little hole that I kept open by poking with my gun barrel. Believe me it was really warm in there. I won't say anything about the smell.

After about four hours, the wind let up for a minute and I could see the outline of a house. "Let's go," I said. So we ran towards the house. But it disappeared because the wind was blowing again. But I banged into the side of the house and then I found a door half covered with snow. I banged and banged at that door and finally a man came and opened the door inward.

I must have been quite a sight with all the snow and the manure on me. Here was a farmer who couldn't believe his eyes or his nose.

He made me take off my clothes—down to my long johns—right there in the back room and I piled them on the floor. The dog curled up on them. I was stranded there for three days before a snowmobiler got me out. I picked up the dog about a week later and my car was buried for two weeks.

As I think back about the storm I think that my dog knew more than I did at the time. There was no way I could have got that car out of there and we could have frozen to death. Now I've got a CB unit in my car.

You know what? I never did get the two rabbits in my backpack out of that manure pile. Anyway, as I think back about it, I thank God for a pile of shit.

Hunters

Hunters commented on the very early migration of ducks and geese in the autumn of 1976. Predictions were for a cold fall and an early and severe winter in 1977.

Mushroom Pickers

Collectors of wild mushrooms complained in the autumn of 1976 that it was the worst mushroom season on record because the weather was too cool for mushroom growth. The prediction was for an early and cold winter.

Female, sixteen: During the storm we had our water pipes freeze for ten days. We connected a hose to our next door neighbour's and we had to let water run through it. We filled up the bathtub, but the hose kept freezing and breaking.

Ilona Karow, 15, Pine Motel, Port Colborne

"Our cat was frozen to the window!"

The first night my father was stranded at Maple Leaf Mills. People in our motel couldn't go out for supper so we decided to serve supper to all our guests in our breakfast room at $3.00 a head. My mother had ten pounds of stewing beef so I went to the neighbours and borrowed vegetables and my mother made a hearty German goulash with salad, buns and potatoes. We had complimentary coffee all day for anybody who wanted it.

We had people stopping at all hours, people who were trying to get home along the lake or people on snowmobiles. The police brought in a few people who were stranded and the motel filled up quickly. Our cable T.V. didn't work and we couldn't make any outgoing calls on our telephone although we could receive them.

The next morning (Friday) my father decided to walk home

from the mill, a distance of one and a half miles. The snow was drifting very badly but he was able to stay on the road by following the telephone wires. When he got home we discussed the food situation and my father decided to take his hunting pack and hike downtown to buy food. A regular at our motel and also a good friend, Mr. Mohino offered to join him with another knapsack. We bundled them up in scarves, ski masks, hats and 3 pairs of gloves and mitts and sent them off. They filled the whole hunting pack full of meat and the knapsack full of bread and vegetables. In the Bank of Nova Scotia they discovered five girls who had been called in from Toronto to install the computer service. They hadn't been able to get back so they had slept on the floor. My father and Mr. Mohino also found Mr. Borgman, the owner of Doughnut 68 and his son who had also slept in their shop. Their volkswagen was running so five girls piled into it and the four men led them home (pushing on several occasions) with plenty of fresh doughnuts for energy.

At the motel we provided sandwiches for lunch and the people entertained themselves playing cards or shuffleboard. There were about five radios turned on to CHOW.

My sister and I were kept quite busy all the time. We had to clean the rooms in the morning and do the laundry and mangling because our help wasn't able to come in. In the afternoon we had to peel all the potatoes for supper. It took us about an hour and I hated every minute of it.

The motel was so full that we had people who had never seen each other before, sleeping together in the same room. We used up all our cots and some slept on air mattresses. Nobody seemed to mind. Everybody was very co-operative. My parents had given out their bedroom. They slept in my bedroom and I went to sleep in the linen closet.

Shell had brought in two people who brought fuel oil for furnaces and serviced homes in the area by snowmobile. I remember that we rarely saw them. They would go out all day and come back for a few hours sleep and leave again.

Many people who were stranded didn't have a change of clothes so at night we went to each room and collected clothes for the wash and returned them in the morning. We also had to lend out our own night gowns, night shirts, combs, toothpaste, shampoo and all kinds of things because nobody had expected the storm to last.

Everybody took the storm exceptionally well. One sailor brought in a lot of alcohol and opened up his room for free drinks. Everybody was happy then. There was one elderly couple who were quite frightened by the experience. They couldn't get home to St. Catharines nor could they phone. Their car couldn't start and they were extremely upset. The man was glued to the radio and reported every bad thing that happened. He kept predicting the electricity would go off and we'd all freeze. The only things that happened to us though were that we lost a lot of pine trees and our new aluminum siding.

Then we heard over the radio that the city was having water problems and that there was a water shortage so my mother had to go to each room and ask the people not to shower or bathe. We decided not to use the dishwasher but to wash our dishes by hand. We had about 32 people staying in our 16 unit motel. Have you any idea how many dishes there are after supper? It took my sister and I over an hour to do them. My father and Mr. Mohino made the trip downtown a second time to get more food.

My sister let the cat out to go to the bathroom and she forgot about him. My father found him frantically meowing at one of our windows. He tried to open the back door but there was about four feet of snow jamming it shut. My father went out the front door and all the way around the back and called the cat but the cat wouldn't move from the window sill. My father went up to him and discovered that our cat was frozen to the window. My dad tried to open the next window beside it so that he could lower a Super Max hair dryer. But that window was frozen shut so he ended up taking a knife and literally scraping the cat off the window. There was an outline of torn fur left on the window and the cat was nearly frozen to death.

One of the more tragic incidents that we had at the Pine Motel during the Blizzard of '77 occurred with a man and his child. The man arrived a week before the storm and paid for his room in advance saying he wanted to stay for at least a month. He wanted the smallest, cheapest room we had, a room with one double bed, saying the child, a little girl of about two years, could sleep with him. My parents didn't like the looks of him, he was dirty, uncombed and he smelled but my parents had sympathy for the little girl so they agreed he could stay for one week on a trial basis. The man was loud and vulgar, he didn't look after his child properly and was quite often drunk. So, we told him well before the week was over he would have to leave on Friday. The man raised quite a fuss saying he had no place to go but he finally agreed.

The blizzard started, so we could not make them leave. My father was out collecting food when this man argued with my mother. Since she was afraid of him, she accepted another week's rent. In the meantime, the motel was filled with stranded people and we were all living in very close conditions. The man smelled terribly but always insisted on socializing with the other guests who tried to stay away from him. This got him angry. From the day he moved in we had not taken out a single used towel or changed any soap. We had to change his sheets every second day because they turned brown. The room smelled worse than he did. Before the storm, our help refused to enter his room and he left his door open when he walked out of the room. Before the storm, there was no food in the room except for potato chips, jelly beans and pop from our pop machine. I asked him once if he thought it was bad for her to be drinking only pop and he said, "Well, I give her C-plus for the vitamin C." He also gave her some of his toast in the morning and took her out to McDonald's for supper occasionally.

During the storm we hoped the child would finally get decent meals but they were still not good enough as far as I was concerned. She got her father's dinner rolls, some corn or potatoes and some of his dessert. "She won't eat meat, fruit or vegetables", he said. To me the child looked really unhealthy. She was very pale and thin with rashes on her bottom and her nose and face were constantly inflamed with a cold. Her nose was always running and I was always wiping it because her father refused. Her bottom was red because she sat in her dirty diapers for days. "They were so expensive," he said. I am sure she only had two dresses and one sock (not a pair just one sock) none of which were ever washed. Many times she ran around naked and unattended. When my parents said something, he'd start swearing and told us to stop telling him how to raise his child.

Our motel is set up like a lodge with one main entrance so that everybody sees everybody if they're not in their room with the door closed. This man would go into the lounge and sit beside someone and start bragging. The mother of his child was British and came to Canada to get away from her husband. They were going to get a divorce. She met him, this man, and they fell in love. Her visa ran out after three months but she was pregnant so they got a statement from a doctor saying she was unfit to travel. She had the child and after of couple of weeks was deported from Canada, thus legally she would never be allowed to return to Canada. She stayed as long as she could before she was forced to return and when in England she went through the divorce procedures with her husband. She left the child with her boyfriend in Canada in hopes of using the baby as an excuse to return. She wanted to return, marry him, and remain in Canada.

In the meantime, he had to go to work and apparently he took his child along leaving her in his van all day in the parking lot while he worked. The company found out about it and fired him. He also had a home somewhere. Why he couldn't occupy it I don't know, but he returned several times to get things from his home. One time he came back with a huge hunting rifle which he kept propped up beside his bed.

When the father left his room and wandered around talking to other guests, most often he went to the room where the sailor was serving free liquor. The girl would come to my sister and me or the other women in the motel. We played with her, washed her face, combed her hair and found some clothes for her to wear. We'd try to give her apples and milk but she'd only eat candies. She squealed with delight when we played with her. Then her father would come stomping in and try to take her away and she'd scream with fear and grab our legs until he wrenched her away. I really hated that man and was ready to adopt her myself.

The five girls from the Bank of Nova Scotia often took the little girl into their room to get her away from her father. One girl said that she'd like to take the girl home with her and never let her see her father again. The men in the motel also felt sorry for her but when they tried to approach her she'd cry and run away in terror. We all felt so guilty.

Finally, the blizzard died down and most of the guests departed but the man still had a few days with us. He was able to go to the liquor store and stock up on whiskey again so for the last few days he was drunk. On his last day he started to beat the child and screamed obscenities at her. My father was out and wouldn't be home until later that night. My mother and I were really terrified. When my father finally got home, it was too late to do anything. But we agreed to phone the police after he checked out in the morning.

They came to see us and to make a report. They said that they had found the man and the girl was O.K. If we had called when he was actually drunk and beating her they could have taken her away on the spot. They would keep a close check on him. That was the last we ever heard of them. But we still feel very guilty that we did not act sooner and we'll know better if the situation ever arises again.

Other than that, I enjoyed the blizzard and I think everyone involved would agree that it was a learning experience that we will always remember. The people that stayed at the motel really appreciated what we did for them. My mother got all kinds of flowers, and my sister and I shared thirty dollars in tips.

Attila Nagy—Teacher

"I got to the graveyard and thought to myself, what a place to go!"

I was at school that morning and we saw the snow coming. We were apprehensive. We kept saying, "Let's close it down." The superintendents finally made a decision. Close it down.

Bill Marshall and I took some kids in the car and we shot down to Sugarloaf to deliver the kids to their homes. We had our heads out of the windows while we were driving. Ice caked all over our faces. We got the children safely home but there was no way we could go back to the school for another load.

It dawned on me while sitting at Marshall's that my laundry room was going to be a complete shambles because my door to it was closed. This meant that all our water pipes and heating ducts were closed off. This began to worry me. I knew my children were all right and that my wife was going to remain in Welland and I took it upon myself to head home. I was told by Marshall that I was crazy to go out. However, they did give me some clothes. I had three pair of pants on, a face mask and two jackets. I figured it was worth it because I could probably handle that walk along the shore road. I was familiar with it. From Marshall's it was about three miles.

So I left Bill's place and started walking. It was very nice to start with. A walk down Walnut Street and up the Lakeshore. The snow was up to my knees in spots already so that every step I took, I had to lift foot upon foot. I could barely see anything when I got to Sugarloaf Hill. I just put my hands in front of my face. Even with that mask my cheeks were starting to burn. I could feel the frostbite starting. I turned around with my back to the wind and walked backwards for a while. Without exaggeration, the drifts were up to my waist. I'd hit the bottom with one foot, I'd crawl up and then go down in another one. This is the way I crawled past Sugarloaf. Then it dawned on me, "Am I going to make it?" That started to get to me.

Suddenly I saw footsteps in the snow. I thought, "There is

Attila Nagy's home. Courtesy, Welland Port colborne Evening Tribune.

somebody else who is crazy in front of me." I started following these footprints. I hit a car and walked up on the roof. I scraped away at the window but it was empty. I kept walking and suddenly these footsteps began to go back and forth across the road in circles. I could tell the guy was in trouble. I yelled and there he stood. I walked up to him and the guy was almost finished. He didn't know where he was going anymore. He said, "I'm really glad you came along. I have to talk to somebody. As long as I can talk to somebody, I'll be all right." This guy had been walking for five miles already. He still had another two miles to go. We walked that stretch going through Sand Hill and suddenly we started laughing. We got so darn tired; we got the giggles. The snow was blowing. We were laughing. Couldn't see a damned thing! We were up again, down again, falling up to our waists in the drifts, tumbling over drifts, sliding down the other sides into these ten foot holes. The power and telephone wires were buried. We wanted to follow this fence, but we lost the fence. He said that he lived close by, so I said good-bye. I found out later that he got lost. He found his way back eventually. About fifteen minutes later I realized I was lost. I had no idea where I was at that time. That's when I began to panic. I remembered all those stories that I had read to the children in school about what you are supposed to do. I was tired and frightened. Now what was I going to do? I could always stay here and dig a hole in one of those snow drifts and spend the night. I thought I'd give it another try. So I just kept staring in all directions hoping that in between gusts I would be able to see something. I didn't. So I kept walking and I ended up exactly where I had started. I had walked in a circle. I tried again. This time I followed the fence. I walked on top of the fence and I was able to follow it for a while. Then the fence was gone into snow. I spotted the power lines so I followed those. Then between gusts, I spotted a light. It was Clark's. I headed in that direction. I finally made it to their place and I was exhausted.

Her husband was stuck at his school, so I used his clothes. I changed completely. There was still some light outside and I decided to try again. Again, I was told that I would never make it. As I walked, I saw a few lights in the houses on the right. It was all right up until Reebs Bay, then there are no more houses and no more lights and that was the worst stretch ahead of me. I started walking and again I had no idea where I was.

It hurt my eyes to stare at things. I felt crunching under my feet and I thought my God this is a little different. I bent over and felt with my hands. I realized I wasn't on the road. I was on Lake Erie. Ice under my feet! I started running. I was terrified. I stopped running and sat down for a while. I kept saying to myself that it couldn't happen to me. I spotted a dark shadow and I ran for it. It happened to be a tree, thank God! I knew a tree has to be on land. I found the road again. I found the power lines. I followed them. I was getting really tired because the drifts were high. I was on my hands and knees half of the time crawling up and down, up and down. I got to the graveyard and thought to myself. What a place to go! That got me up. I raced through the graveyard as fast as I could. I started talking to myself. I got confused again. I kept going and again followed the power lines. Finally, I spotted my place. Oh God, O God I was so excited! I crawled up to my house over the drifts. I got there and there was no place to go into my home. The entire bottom was snowed in. I climbed up to my upstairs deck but the sliding doors wouldn't open. I crawled downstairs to my back porch. It was covered. I couldn't even see it.

I started digging with my hands and I don't know how long I dug. In the meantime I guess people were going crazy, worrying about me. My parents were phoning everybody. My mother was crying. I finally got underneath the porch and I was up against it with my back just lying there for a long time. I almost fell asleep. It was so nice. Then, I dug again and I made it to my back door. Accidentally I broke some glass. The phone was ringing when I smashed into the kitchen. Everybody phoned. I told them I was okay. Then I just lay there.

Dr. Pond—Psychiatrist

I know of four people who ended up in the psychiatric hospital because of the storm. There was a man, a woman and two young people. If it had not been for the blizzard, those four people would never had been admitted.

A number of people told me that they wanted to do a lot of things while stranded in their houses. They didn't do anything. I can relate to their feelings because the same thing happened to me. I intended to do a lot of reading and studying, but I didn't feel guilty about sitting there drinking tea or coffee while I stared out the window for several days, watching nature at work.

Female, Seventeen

"I couldn't get the board off and it was covered with chicken shit."

I was at home climbing the walls - in Wainfleet - out in the sticks. I was going nuts because there was no place to go. There are seven kids in our family and the two youngest ones were always getting on my back. My mother, well you'd laugh at what somebody says on the radio and she'd go nuts. All I had to do was take care of my horses and I stayed in the house most of the time.

When I first got home during the storm I had to go and get the horses because they were out in the field. My mother wouldn't do it because she is afraid of them. When I brought them in I had to scrape them all off because there was ice and everything all over them. And after I got done I shut them in and my father told me to put this board across the stable so the snow wouldn't get inside. The wind was really strong and it was hard to hold onto it because the board was very thin. The wind pushed it and almost pulled me along with it. I was trying to put the board up, when I opened the door. The board was lying on the ground on a slope. The wind picked up the board and it pinned me against the stable. I couldn't get the board off, and it was covered with chicken shit. It was all over my face and my cheeks and everything. My father was laughing at me. I didn't think it was so funny. It was stuck all over my face, caked hard. My father came out and pulled the board away and I took some snow and wiped it off my face. It was really getting on my nerves. Then my father came over and put the wheelbarrow in front of the board so it wouldn't fall down. I had to go in and check the horses every half hour, see how they were and see how much snow was getting in. I had to go through the same thing, putting the board down, this time I stepped on it. I wasn't going to have it fall on me again.

My sister is married so she wasn't at home, but there were six of us and then the neighbour boy who couldn't get home so he came to our house. They were making me go nuts because they were squealing all the time. For three days I was at that house banging at the walls. I was really pissed off because you couldn't do anything.

I couldn't do anything the whole time I was there. Once me and Vicky went out. It was at night, we went out behind the snow banks and threw snowballs at cars. I threw a snowball and I hit this truck. The driver came over to our snow bank. My little brother was out there too so we all took off and we were hiding. The man caught my little brother. My little brother was running through the snow, he was going squish, squish, squish. His legs were going so fast. The guy got a hold of him and he goes, "Did you throw that snowball?" He was so mad he almost blew off. He was a bit spastic. My mother said he came to the door at our house. My mother thought that maybe he was a bit retarded—you know how people are all jumpy and everything? She said that if he would have touched my little brother she would have given it to him good because he was kind of loony. It scared me though. I never ran so hard in all my life. It was all Vicky's idea too. That kid is unbelievable. Everytime she's got something new like spying in the next door window and throwing eggs at their house. The kid next door, he throws eggs at her house all the time so she says, "Let's go do it back." So we pick up this frozen horse manure and we whip it at their window. The manure was frozen so when they hit the wall they sounded like a baseball bat hitting there. It was really weird. Then the people came out the door and they'd look around.

It was boring. If we have a blizzard next year, I want to get stranded somewhere else.

Mr. Sutton Smith - Social Worker

"There are good side effects to an emergency."

Some people who have mental illness have to be able to get

outside. Being shut in is very bad for them. I remember one case that worried me. He was beginning to climb the walls and we had to get him out.

People, especially in the rural areas, really began to feel shut in. But this was not a lasting feeling.

Some of our regular returnees would come back for two or three days a month. Because of the blizzard, they returned to us sooner and stayed a few days extra. Again, there was no permanent effect. The storm seemed to aggravate problems which were already there.

As a marriage counsellor, I noticed that many couples found so much to do from the point of view of clearing snow, getting food and surviving that there was little time to argue with each other. Many people forgot about their personal problems and pulled together in the face of this emergency. This is a very common reaction.The opposition will co-operate with the government in wartime. People share their cars during transportation strikes. There are good side effects to an emergency.

Male, Seventeen

"Can you imagine being stranded with thirteen women. He came home in a good mood."

We were pretty isolated because most of our neighbours were stranded elsewhere. The cleaning lady was stuck at our place for several days so she just kept working. When she wasn't working she sat in front of the door with her coat on, thinking her brother was going to pick her up. She kept bugging me to take her home so I tried and I ran into a snowbank. My car was half buried there for four days when a tow truck finally pulled it out.

My father was stranded in the Port Colborne Club along with 13 women and some other men. They slept all over the place. They had lots of food and booze and the men didn't have their wives on their backs. Can you imagine being stranded with thirteen women? He came home in a good mood.

After a while some of the men were getting pretty restless and they started to play jokes on one another. One man phoned up a tow truck to come pick him up and the men started joking with him. They said, "Oh, there's a school bus outside waiting for you," and "Somebody's coming with a bicycle to get you."

SUSPICIOUS WIVES

A number of husbands who were stranded complained that their wives were suspicious and refused to believe conditions were as bad as they said.

"It's here somewhere!" Note the car aerial in the foreground. Tribune photo.

Joe Apolcer

"What? Beer? Where's your car?"

We were stranded in Port Colborne Quarries. There must have been thirty three people there. We were all feeling rather depressed around seven p.m. when it became evident that we were going to be stuck there for the night. Around nine o'clock, one woman suddenly came out of her daze and said, "Oh my goodness, the case of beer in the trunk is going to freeze." She had been shopping and she had picked up a case of beer. Two guys jumped up and said, "What? Beer? Where's your car? She had encouraged them by saying, "Well if you can get it, you can have it." The boys came back in fifteen minutes and said, "The car's locked." "Oh my gosh she exclaimed, the keys are in the car." "No sweat!," they said. "We'll get them." About half an hour later they returned. They were white, their eyebrows frozen, but they had that case of beer. They brought it back and we devoured it. They brought the keys back with them. They had to break into the car to get the keys.

I got home late the next day to a big surprise. My son was visiting with his new bride. Unknown to me, they had eloped and had made it home just before the blizzard stopped all the traffic. So I met my new daugther-in-law.

"She Had Firm Breasts And Her Nipples Protruded Slightly"

If you ever tell anybody my name, I'll kick your ass across town.

I was stuck at home alone for three days and had no choice about leaving the house. I was snow bound. Since I'm a bachelor, I didn't mind being alone.

There I sat on the sofa and drank coffee and watched this white freak of nature blow past my patio windows—for three days.

It was about the end of the first day that my mind flipped into a fantasy-scene and that scene repeated itself for at least a hundred times for the remaining two days of isolation. I stared at the snow and began to see it melting. The water from the run-off gathered in a natural swimming hole somewhere in the country side. The sun was warm and it shone on me as I sat on the grass at the edge of the pool—a bottle of beer in my hand.

There was this 18 or 19 year old chick with me and she never said a word. She would undress, grab this long rope that was suspended from nowhere and swing out over the water. She'd let go of the rope and fall into the water, her long hair trailing behind her. She'd enter the water with a splash, swim to shore, get out of the water, smile at me and then go for another swing on the rope. All this is in slow motion. She had firm breasts and her nipples protruded slightly from the fresh cool water.

Never once did I feel horny with all this. I was captivated with

Calling car 77, where are you? Tribune photo.

the scene. I can't recall ever taking a sip of beer during these fantasies.

Yet I knew that this was a fantasy, the likes of which I've never had before or since. I was starting to wonder what the hell they were putting in the coffee these days. Whatever it was, I liked it and I'm kind of hoping for another storm next winter so I can try to recapture my rope-swinging friend.

Bob Smart - Niagara Regional Police Officer

"Initially it was just utter chaos."

I was scheduled to work the 4 to 12 shift on the 28th of January. But I was called in at 12:00 o'clock noon because the storm had moved into the area. Originally everything was tied up with accidents. They called several additional officers in as well. They wanted to put us out in the extra cars because of this rash of collisions. By 1:00 p.m. the visibility was so bad our cars couldn't get tow trucks to pull them out. I advised at this time that members of the CIB should contact CHOW radio station and request that snowmobiles be sent to this location because our vehicles were totally useless. I was then instructed to set up a communication system in central office. I waited there and one by one the snowmobiles reported for duty and eventually we ended up working 60 snowmobilers and 15 four-wheel drive units.

We started out with a portable radio answering police calls with snowmobiles. We had one or two break and enters reported and since we couldn't transport by car, we used the snowmobiles. Then we had medication and food calls. It is hard for me to imagine how people live from day to day with that small amount of food but apparently quite a few do. They appear to be living out of the corner store.

Initially it was just utter chaos. We couldn't use the cars at all. So I would dispatch a snowmobile to a certain drug store to pick up medication and then have it delivered to a certain destination. As the weather grew worse, we started sending the officers in two's and four's in case one machine broke down. This way they could return to the office through that unbelievable storm.

As we began to get caught up we had more snowmobile operators coming in than we had calls to answer. Then we had a chance to attend the desk in the other room. Then when we started dispatching within the city limits, two units could answer the calls for medication and food. If it was in an outlying area we would send 4 units out together, with their names recorded along with time of their departure. They would complete the call and report back to the detachment for their own safety. We then knew that they were okay. It worked very well.

Later in the evening a C. B. outfit came in. They were positioned on the desk to the left of me. They were working on a citizens band frequency with the four-wheel drive units. Quite a few of them had citizens bands, and that was a real asset. It was really good.

Eventually the EMO called in the army. We had contact with them as well. They were working in convoys but they were working under police directions. As a result we had two forms of communications with them. They had their own radios which had a very short range so we had a constable with them carrying portables. Our range is better with this unit. In this way we were able to keep communications with the larger convoys. If we had a very serious call, we would send an officer on a snowmobile with a portable radio to make sure that the call was answered. We had no trouble talking with Toronto, or even London with these portable radios so there was a good 100 mile range.

We had no trouble with communications through the storm at all with the possible exception of the telephones. We received so many calls and before we would dispatch help it was our responsibility to check that they weren't crank calls. In order to do this we would phone and the phone lines would just be flooded. The switchboard was just jammed solid. However, the Bell Telephone system was absolutely magnificent. We would just wait and try to get hold of the operator. As soon as we contacted the operator she would cut in on the line we requested when she was informed it was the police. No problem. They were really good at that.

We sent several convoys to Wellandport and three or four out to Winger. Now that doesn't seem too far but in that type of weather that is a very long distance. There were medication calls and later on there were children to be evacuated by helicopters. We used three helicopters during the storm. One OPP helicopter was used and two out at the Niagara Falls airport were at our disposal. We had communications throughout. Police were up in the helicopters with their portable radios. We worked in conjunction with them and the Militia convoys on the ground.

We had problems with the snowmobiles breaking down. The runners seemed to give them the most problem. Fortunately we had a man come from Canadian Tire who managed to open the store to get the parts for the snowmobiles and he would bring them back here. He brought oil and spark plugs and runners. Consequently, whenever a machine broke down, we had the parts here. For the major repairs it was necessary to have two mechanics here at all times. We repaired the larger four-wheel vehicles as well. These units were brought into the security section here, where they were heated up. If they needed repairs the two licensed mechanics were right on the spot with access to the parts that were needed.

In our office here, our communication set-up was something like this. We had the citizens band people to the left of the table and our communications link-up was in the centre and the other side had a man in charge of supplies such as equipment for the snowmobiles. The people would call for food supplies and medication and these calls would be transferred to that man to my side. He would take all important information that was directed to me and pass it over to me and I would find the men to make the delivery. Thorold region had been covering their own area but they didn't have access to the machines as we did. So on occasion we had to send units up there. That was always a four machine operation. We had several calls to transport doctors into the hospital and nurses to duty and they were moved by snowmobiles. Six children from the school in Winger were brought in here to this detachment by helicopter. They attempted to get as far as Forkes Road where they bogged down with the four-wheel drive vehicles. So the kids had quite an exciting day.

As the storm progressed things got better here. The Militia came in and set up a mobile kitchen. We had all kinds of people in the office. Stranded people initially. When I was first called in they couldn't get anybody home. The cruisers were as stranded as the motorists. The people were put in a large hall and we thought it would blow over but as you know we needed to bring in food. Some of the constables managed to get home and they brought in boxes of food that lasted throughout the period.

Everybody seemed to be on the telephone. Consequently when people needed to call the police or to seek assistance they couldn't make a connection, if they needed food or medication. Mostly diabetics were calling in. Then the Bell Telephone would cut in on the phone line and get through to the residents and verify it and we would also verify the directions to the house. Nobody was sent out without specific directions and a description of the home.

All the CB calls were verified. They were working beside me and they worked in conjunction with a base station set up over on Kolbec Drive. We even received a call from stranded people going to Port Colborne from Vineland. Through the CB, the call was related right to our station and their location was pinned down. Information was related back to CB and units were sent out from that division to pick them up because the weather wasn't bad up there. Consequently these people were picked up, taken to One Division and then they were relayed to Welland and through to Port Colborne. This type of work was done all through the CB. Their ranges are very short maybe 20 miles. It may not be 20 miles but the base station was contacting Poncho who had a larger receiver and he in turn contacted the Vineland outlet and made the connections for us.

There was no trouble with communications at all. Even the units up in the helicopters were able to make communications in spite of the noise. It boomed in well. Our mobile units were totally useless. They couldn't move in the snow. They were just abandoned. Also, one of our men set up with the emergency measures organization station. I don't know where the EMO received the calls from or how their communications was set up but they did receive requests for assistance. I must have been in contact with the EMO 300 times in those three days.

I was working alone here and they seemed to forget about me and my little nitch. But eventually another officer was able to come in and help me and constable Bowle and I alternated. He was working the late night shift 8 at night to 8 the next morning. But we found that we were the busiest during the day. Fortunately we only received three crank calls. They were all from the same area and they came in by CB. It just indicates that there was one person abusing it.

If we ever have another thing like this again, the best that I can recommend would be a portable radio. But I don't know if we could go out and buy a hundred radios. As a matter of fact more forces are changing over to the portable. I believe that our system is being changed so that every officer will carry his own radio instead of using the one in the cars so you will be in direct contact with the officer. It is a terrific idea. I believe Hamilton has this system right now and I know a few departments in the U.S. that have this communication directly with the officers. When you leave your cruiser you're not going to be cut off from the communications desk. We are supposedly coming out with this next year. If our communications move along that line then that brings us to the only other problem I see and that is transportation. Our vehicles were useless.

I think the main thing to remember is that response from the public in that storm was terrific. The thing is to keep track of what is going on, who is working where, who is going where, is someone overdue? That's the main thing. Know who you have working, know where they are going, know what time they left and what time they came back. In the city it's not bad because if a machine breaks down they surely can get into a home for some heat. When you're moving in the outlying regions and the machine breaks down you're not going to last too long in weather like that. Of course this was why we sent them in groups of four and we had communications with them. I don't believe we sent anyone anywhere without communications. This was a must.

One occasion, we did have a unit of two machines sent up to Forkes Road. We thought they were overdue according to the check list. They should have been to the residence and should have called us and confirmed that they made the rendevous. The phones were jammed so we gave them adequate time and when they didn't get back we sent four more units with communications to look for them. As it turned out, a snowmobile had broken down and the other units decided to stay at the location and attempt to fix it and they were both transported back here. It was important to remember that without the check list, it's possible we might have missed them in the activities going on here.

The thing that stands out in my mind the most was the people I met during the blizzard here and whom I have met on prior occasions when the feelings wasn't so good. During the storm we sat down and had coffee together and worked together as if we were a big family. The attitude of the people coming in here really surprised me when I saw how some of them were such good heads. They were really great. Another thing that stands out in my mind was the Welland Snowmobile Club. I can say nothing but good about that unit. It's just unbelievable what they did with their snowmobiles and four-wheel vehicles. They were sleeping and eating here as well.

We didn't become informal at all. We had a good feeling among the snowmobilers and the dispatchers. The snowmobilers took on the attitude that this was their job. There was no carefree or laxidasical attitude. Those guys responded immediately to a call. There might be fifteen of them sitting here. As soon as the call came in, they would jump up and be gone. What can I say about them?

They were just magnificent. There was no laxity in radio procedures at all. That's why officers were sent with the men. We had to maintain control over it and all broadcasts were monitored by headquarters. So we had to follow proper procedures. We couldn't pass our radios out to members of the Militia or people coming in. They always had to be controlled by a police officer.

As far as the CBers are concerned I am not familiar with their system at all. I do recall that they were very busy. There must be an awful lot of CBers out there. They surprised me the most with their super attitude toward this disaster. It was just magnificent.

Male, sixteen: I didn't think there was really that much of a crisis. People were phoning in to the radio, they were running out of food and that. I ran out of cigarettes. Things got pretty hectic. I couldn't get down to the store so I started picking at ash trays, smoking butts. I had a neighbour who finally got out. She got me some. Christ! I would have sold my soul for a pack of cigarettes.

Bob Eden - Niagara Regional Police Officer

"He sure revived when I dragged him out into the snow."

To tell someone what happened on January 28th, 29th, and the 30th they would say that you were a bit off-side. There's no way that anything like that could actually happen in this day and age. Mother Nature sure taught us a lesson.

My lesson began right across from my residence. People got out of their cars. They had been sitting in their car, a man, his wife and two boys and they made it into my place. My family had gone shopping earlier and they were unable to get back home. It was just marvelous to see her in action. At first she was quite shy, not wanting to go into another person's cupboards and not wanting to use this bowl or that. She fit right in and after a while she looked like she belonged in my home. She would be cooking for her own family plus my one child that was at home. My main objective was to get to Port Colborne because that was where three of my kids and my wife were stranded.

I know of one lady who was stranded at the Old Fashion Food Parlour on Main Street. She was with quite a few people there for three days and when she finally did reach her residence in Sherkston she found all the hot water radiators had burst. The water was flooding through her house. She had damages totalling thousands of dollars just from the radiators cracking.*

---

* Antifreeze in the hot water heating system can prevent this.
   Regular water lines can be drained.

I got out on my snowmobile checking the highways here. I found a bus and there were four or five women on that one. They gave me their names and had me phone their husbands and children.

I continued to check the area and I almost ran into the back of this truck that had been stalled. I didn't see it until I was actually there—my snowmobile actually touched it. I came to a stop against the truck. I checked that area around there and found two women in one car. There was a man in another car and a third man had his car running and he was lying down in the car with all the windows wound up. He revived when I dragged him out into the snow. I got them all into the bus. I managed to get three men out of another truck and into that bus. At this point I found a rope. It was maybe twenty-five or thirty feet long. I instructed everybody to hang on to that rope and cover themselves up as best they could because we were going to leave the bus and walk to a house. You couldn't see where the other person was in front of you.

The lead man on the rope line was now along side my snowmobile and he began to laugh and make a big joke out of the whole ordeal. He thought it was a big joke that we were doing this and it wasn't really needed. After one or two steps out of that bus and into the wind and snow he wasn't laughing anymore. He was the first to rush for the house when he saw it.

One of the ladies on the rope didn't cover her face. She got into the house and down into the basement. Her nose was white up to her face. She couldn't do anything; her hands were so cold. It was fortunate that the gloves I had on kept my hands quite warm so I kept my hands over her nose for about five minutes. You gradually began to see the colour coming back into her nose and fortunately she had no after effects from it.

When we got those people settled, I answered calls to the various parts of that region. There was another instance, where we had a lady who was going to have a child up in the Wainfleet area between Chambers' Corners and the old Two By Four Restaurant. There were several of us who tried to get up there by using four wheel drive vehicles and snowmobiles. We worked from the Port Colborne end to try to reach her and we also worked from the Welland end. A doctor came into our office and we had to get him a snowmobile suit. At that moment another chap came walking into the office and overheard our conversation. The gentleman said that if you want a snowmobile suit you've got one. He zipped his off right there, removed his boots and handed everything over to the doctor. The doctor put it on, got on the back of the snowmobile and we managed to get to the lady. By using tracks and snowmobiles we moved her into the Welland Hospital where she gave birth to a healthy baby. It made everybody feel quite good that we were able to help in a situation like that. Under normal conditions the trip would have taken no more than fifteen minutes. During the blizzard it took us four hours. As it happened, I broke my snowmobile. The track broke and I had to lay it up.

Different snowmobile dealers came forth in the area and volunteered snowmobiles, gas and oil. One chap came up to me and offered me a new seventy seven Yamaha. It had never been used before. And this is the way people actually helped out during the storm. If you needed anything at all there was no hesitation. It was there at your disposal.

I got a bit of frostbite on my neck from the blowing snow. I saw people, however, with ears, nose and cheeks which were badly burnt. We had police officers, the likes of which I'd never seen before. They were dead on their feet. If somebody had said stand in the corner they would have been asleep. Yet, when calls came in these guys were right on those snowmobiles again and gone into the wind. There was nothing said. No arguments, they just moved out.

I don't know what day it was that we received the call to go to an area around Oakwood Street here in the City of Port Colborne. So the fellows shot out there and went in. When we got to the residence to help this lady, it turned out to be the opposite way around. She had packed buckets full of food. There were roasts of beef, potatoes that were mashed, different vegetables and even a bottle of Vermouth. She had packed boxes and it was her gift for the army and the police department here in the City of Port Colborne. She was one of those ladies that didn't want anything. She wanted to give something and it was marvelous to see people giving whatever they could spare to help out. It was something that I'll never forget.

I would suggest that if a person is going to use a snowmobile they should by all means get some type of instruction. In this way you know what you need. We had persons that just got on the snowmobile for the first time. There was one fellow who had a brand new machine. He started it up and started running it and in fifteen minutes he came back and there was no windshield on it, the skis were all bent, and it was a mess. He had never been on one before. He tried to do something because of what was taking place and he wrecked the machine. The snowmobiles were breaking down. They were freezing up. You had to have your de-icer and you had to have it mixed properly. If you had too much, it wouldn't run. If you had too little, it would freeze up. Your oil had to be just right so your plugs would not foul. In that storm, if you ever got stopped three or four miles out of town in a bush area there was just no way that you were going to get back. If you are going to run a snowmobile, by all means join a club. It's just what you need to learn about the equipment. By covering my skin with vaseline, I cut down the severity of the wind. Even then I got some frostbite.

I never saw so many people that could band together like they did with no instructions. They came in voluntarily here in Port Colborne and gave the use of their machines.

Some police officers had their own machines. Someone was put in charge and everybody listened. It looked like an army. I never saw anything work so smoothly in my life. The snowmobilers and the CB radio people got along so well that it took only seconds from the moment someone needed help until the snowmobiler was dispatched to the scene.

I had never flown in a helicopter before and when we arrived in Welland they said we were each going to go in a separate helicopter. I got in with the pilot and we took off. I was frightened looking out the front of that machine and finding nothing in front of me. Just a piece of glass between you and five hundred feet of air.

We were flying over the Robin Hood Mill at about two thousand feet and I asked my pilot if he had ever had any close calls while flying helicopters. He mentioned that he had and this didn't make me feel much better. Since I had taken off there wasn't much I could do about it. Then I asked him how long he had been flying. He said that he received his pilot's license yesterday. Of course he was kidding. Sort of shakes you up at two thousand feet.

We flew at about four hundred feet over the Lakeshore area. It was our responsibility to check the houses by hovering over them for as long as it took to see if there was any movement. Anyone who wanted anything would motion to us to come down. The majority of the people simply acknowledged our presence and continued about their survival work. We were primarily concerned with collapsed homes and injuries that people may have received.

We flew the Lakeshore down as far as the Sherkston area and also into the farm districts. Some farms were four or five miles away from neighbors. We saw most of them out with their tractors or plows. The Humberstone area was not as badly in need as the Wainfleet area. In Wainfleet, particularly the Long Beach area they really got hit hard. We couldn't see the lake. The snow was so bad that it was virtually impossible to see anything. It looked just like a white cloud that was always there. At four hundred feet you couldn't actually tell the depth of the snow until you saw a chimney sticking out of the snowbanks from the homes buried beneath. At this point you could surmise how high the drifts were.

A part of our responsibility in these flights was to try to locate a train which had left Fort Erie and had become stuck in a snowbank somewhere. At one point we were flying to the east of Welland over the new railroad tracks and it was beautiful. We were in sunlight and you could look across and see the snow about three quarters of a mile away from us. The snow was coming down so heavily that you couldn't see through it and yet around us it was a beautiful winter's day with the glorious sun. In a matter of seconds we were completely gobbled up by the snow and we couldn't see again.

We could not see the front of the helicopter. Seconds later it would clear up again. The train was finally located on the railroad tracks just near the Port Colborne Country Club. The crewmen had managed to get to a nearby farm house where they waited out the storm. Can you imagine losing a complete train?

While flying the helicopter and landing in the Wainfleet area we could see the drifts were so high that the telephone wires were presenting a problem to people walking over the snowbanks. People either had to roll under them or in some cases step over them. The power lines were presenting the same sort of problem along the Lakeshore. I saw large homes that were actually buried in the snow so that you couldn't see any part of the house with the possible exception of a chimney sticking up.

While we were flying, the only animal that I was able to pick out was a red fox which we followed. It was scared by the sounds of the helicopter because we weren't flying too high at that time.

Other members of the helicopter team did report seeing quite a few herds of deer over in the marsh area. Interesting enough, they weren't in the bush. They were in the open fields. Anywhere where there was a bush or any type of wind break, the snow built up and it would be virtually impossible for an animal to go through a woods. The last snow that I saw was the end of the first week of June when the banks finally disappeared from the Cedar Bay area.

Sam Yallowica

"My wife had just said that we hadn't had any company for a while. There was a knock on the door and we had 24 people in the house for the weekend."

It was about noon hour on Friday, January 28 when Bob Eden, the policeman knocked on the door and asked if we could take in some stranded people. He returned in a while on his snowmobile. He had a rope extended behind his machine and about 20 people were walking through the blizzard holding on that rope. Some people had frost bitten noses and others complained about pains in their hands. We got them thawed out in the basement.

About three o'clock that afternoon we had a power failure and the power stayed off for 30 hours. That meant that there was no water because we need the electricity to operate the water pump. I stayed up all Friday night melting snow on the gas stove so we could have water for the toilet. While I was melting snow on one stove, my wife cooked ten pounds of potatoes on the other stove. With guests and four in our family we had a total of 24 people.

With all those people in the living room and dining room we stayed pretty comfortable. They came on Friday and most got home by snowmobile on Sunday. Some didn't get away until Tuesday.

We played cards, cooked, melted snow, cleaned the house and slept wherever there was room on the floors or beds. Three fellows went out in that blizzard and walked about a half mile to their cars in order to get cigarettes.

It was like a big family. Hardship really brought us together. It was a lot like the old days when we had much more hardship. There were closer ties between people then because we needed each other more. Maybe we are too independent today. I'm 53 years old.

Mr. Seko

"My mom's on fire, my mom's on fire."

I got a call to come in as a volunteer mechanic to give the police a hand in keeping some of their units mobile. A bunch of us were

53

Will it ever run again? Courtesy, Welland Port Colborne Evening Tribune

rounded up and we went down to the Welland Police Station. The police don't have a garage but they've got a little place where they keep a couple of cars. It's not even heated but we were pulling the cars into the bay there and trying to get them going. There was a problem because we didn't have any air pumps. We managed to get hold of one of those trucks with an air compressor on them and we backed it up and that way we got the compressed air and we used it to blow the snow out from the engines.

One of the problems that we also had from a mechanic's point of view was the snowmobiles that were freezing up. Even with the de-icer in the gas, the lines would freeze. That's the problem with blowing snow. It covers the engine. The only thing to do is periodically open the hood and make sure that all the snow isn't building up around the engine.

One of the local citizens had lent the police a four wheel jeep and while the police were using it, the fan stopped turning. The snow got under the rad and it would melt. This melting water would freeze and eventually a chunk of ice would build up behind the radiator and this ice interfered with the fan. Since the fan couldn't turn, the engine overheated. A lot of cars had this problem.

You should have de-icer in your gas tank and always carry a full tank of gas because you go through a lot of it just sitting around. You also can use the weight of that gas over the wheels for traction. You might also carry some of the spray that you put into the carburetor.

From a mechanic's point of view you should in the winter have light oil in the engine, number ten oil for example. Although most people get by with a Ten W Thirty all year. By all means, snow tires would be in order. I would recommend that you carry a couple of sand bags in your trunk. Not only does the sand give you the additional weight but you can use it for traction by sprinkling it around if you ever need it.

I remember the incident about the death of the lady in Welland. It appears the woman's husband was stranded at work and couldn't get home all night. She was pretty upset and I guess didn't sleep much during the night. A neighbor had called her about nine o'clock in the morning and asked her if she needed anything at the store because the neighbor was going to walk up there but she said that she didn't need anything. Another neighbor had stepped out of his home about ten o'clock in the morning to do some shovelling of snow and he saw one young child running around in his pyjamas over the top of the snowdrifts. The neighbor yelled to the kid and asked what was going on. Over the noise of the blizzard, the little child screamed back, "My mom's on fire, my mom's on fire." The neighbor dashed over to the house and found the older child inside the door. The neighbor shoved the kid outside and told him to stay there with his little brother. Then the neighbor got on his hands and knees and crawled in through the kitchen under the smoke filled air to see what he could find and as he crawled slowly into the living room he saw what the young boy was screaming about. Sitting in the couch was the mother with flames shooting out from her. She was on fire; burning in the chair. The smoke had probably knocked her out and we presumed it was from the cigarette. By the time the fire started she was probably dead. The children were probably down stairs watching television. Can you imagine what memories they will have of this blizzard?

Reg Bernier, President, Welland Snowmobile Club

*"The father and the two kids were crying.
I was crying and so were the three police officers."*

As soon as I got home on Friday, I checked my snowmobile and then the phone rang. It was Sergeant Brant of the Ontario Provincial Police and he wanted 15 snowmobiles to go to highway No. 140 for an accident. We met in my driveway and left even though we couldn't see ten feet in front of us. It was a prank call, there was nothing there. But two of us almost lost our heads. We were standing beside our machines on the highway and the wind picked us up and blew us to the other side of the road. We had trouble finding our snowmobiles again.

One of our fellows had a machine that broke down. He kept trying to start it and when he stood up, the wind and snow hit him and he couldn't see or breathe. He panicked. He ripped off his mask and helmet and started to tear off his snowmobile suit. Several of his friends grabbed him and settled him down and took him home. Next day he came back and started helping people again.

Constable Smart of the Regional Police called and he needed two snowmobilers to get to a pregnant woman out in the country. Two snowmobilers drove ahead of my four wheel drive and when I couldn't go any further they went on their own and we brought the woman out at 4 a.m.

I got a couple of hours sleep and a call came in to go to Bridgeview School because it was full of kids. I contacted our club members who were working out of the various stations in Welland and we headed for the school. When we got there, the people were too frightened to leave. The policeman who was with us had to convince the people that we could make it out of there. We delivered them to the police station which at that time was full of refugees. With snowmobiles and four wheel drives we took about four hours to clear the school, except for the principal and several others who refused to come. They said they were safe in the school.

There were about 600 people stuck at Niagara College with nothing to eat since Friday afternoon. We delivered food there and then started using my four wheel drive as an ambulance to get people to the hospital.

Then there was a family out by the airport and they had no fuel or food. Constable Smart sent five snowmobiles to follow my four wheel drive. When I got bogged down, we loaded the food and fuel onto the snowmobiles and they finished the delivery.

We got a call to go to Moyer Road, on the way to Niagara Falls, where there were 60 people stranded in one house. Two four wheel drives and four snowmobiles went out and we hauled people to their homes in Welland. We worked until daylight Sunday morning.

I returned home, went to bed and the phone rang. There was a woman having a baby in Wainfleet. The doctor rode in my truck and the snowmobiles followed. He finished the trip by snowmobile and we got the woman to the hospital where she delivered. It was Sunday evening and the Army was starting to move in. Since they couldn't handle it, we were still needed.

One old man in the countryside needed medicine or he would die. I got the drugs and drove to Port Colborne Block where I turned them over to an Ontario Provincial Police Officer who gave them to a snowmobiler who completed the trip.

McDonald's were great. They fed snowmobilers, the police and everybody who was helping — free of charge.

There was a bad fire here in Welland where a woman lost her life. They couldn't get to it except in my four wheel drive so I took five policeman there. The City of Welland sent a front end loader to clear the way for the removal wagon. I was asked to take the deceased woman's husband and two children to relatives. Three police officers, myself, the husband and two children rode in my vehicle. All the way from the west side of Welland to the east side, the father and the two kids were crying, I was crying and so were the three police officers. That was the saddest experience of my life. That's when I went home to check on my wife and kids.

No sooner did I get home than a call came through about a woman who was having a heart attack. Paul Dion and I rushed her to the hospital and we thought several times that it was too late. We have seen her since and she couldn't thank us enough.

I reported to the police and told them I had to get some sleep. They checked my chart and I had logged 57 hours on the road. Then I went to bed.

Fred Butler—Snowmobiler

"No storm was going to upset her constitutional."

From a snowmobiler's point of view, there were many hazards. There was the frostbite factor. Then you could get lost going across a field. Some of us were still going to work and then coming home at night and performing these emergency runs till two or three in the morning. A lot of people were extremely grateful for that. I know it gave us a great deal of satisfaction; the fact that we were able to help people.

Funny things happened. We were down in Sherkston off one of the side roads. There was a family of four stranded, no electricity, no water. We had to get them out. We brought the mother and father and the two children into Port Colborne where there was light and heat. Getting the mother and the father on the snowmobile was no problem, but when the kids heard the loud machines they cried and they gave us an awful time. They didn't want to get on the machines. We got them into Port Colborne. The funny thing was that they wouldn't get off the machines. They wanted to go and ride some more, and some more, and some more. The kids loved it.

Another incident that happened involved a small child about 6 or 7 months old. I was worried about that baby coming in from Wyldewood to Port Colborne so I put the little girl inside my snowsuit, and about three quarters of the way to Port Colborne, she decided she had to go to the bathroom and I got the benefit of that. Can you picture her little nose sticking out of my snowsuit and relieving herself all over my stomach? No storm was going to upset her constitutional.

Another incident occurred out in the Wainfleet region. I was zipping along and came to the top of a high snowbank. I stopped the machine and got off. I walked three quarters of the way down to the other side of the snowbank and there was a car parked in the driveway with about a ten foot drop down to it. I didn't even realize that I was on top of a house.

Another time we had to stop on the top of a snowdrift just to check ahead to see what was going on and one of my buddies accidently stubbed his foot in the snow. He said there was something underneath and as he looked down he saw a windshield. The car was completely covered over. All sorts of things like this happened.

Other things happened that weren't so funny. There were some stories how some people took advantage of others during the storm. We had people who were two or three blocks from the grocery store saying that they couldn't get down to the store. They were complaining about having no light or heat or food. We of course, answered every emergency, it didn't matter what. You couldn't separate the real ones from those who were taking advantage. On this occasion, I pulled up to the front door with my machine and caboose loaded with groceries. I knocked on the door. It opened and there were four people drinking beer in the living room. They had the kitchen full of groceries and they just kept accepting more. Somehow, that doesn't grab me as being the proper thing to do when there were other people out there who really needed the food.

One of the best examples of people who really needed us was the family in Gasline who had taken in eighteen or nineteen people. They were Italian Canadians and they had a well stocked larder when the storm first hit. They had exhausted their supplies after a couple of days and they were now in need of more food to help these people who were stranded at their place. We got out there as quickly as possible only to find that the head of the household and his young son had actually gone across several large open fields to get some food from a neighbour who had a bit extra, just to help these stranded people. They got side tracked somewhere in the middle of those big fields and this created another emergency. We had to go and find the man and his son and bring them back because they were walking on foot. These people got burned out previous to the storm and they said they were so appreciative of how people helped them during the fire that they couldn't do enough to repay. They cleaned their home out of everything during the blizzard.

Snowmobilers saved a lot of lives by pulling a lot of people out of those cars. The army, the police and the snowmobilers all seemed to be going in the same direction. Lack of co-ordination in the beginning solidified into concrete action as things progressed. I think that people can pull together when they want to and when they have to. The fact that there were no storm related deaths is a real tribute to the people who helped in this region.

There were a lot of people who never thought that they had the courage to get involved in something like this. Suddenly they found themselves with courage far beyond their dreams. A lot of people got a tremendous personal lift from their accomplishment. I guess it's quite a thing to take on mother nature and come out the winner. I guess we learned a lot about ourselves under those conditions.

We received a call that these people needed help. It took us about two hours to get to the destination and that's only three miles at the very most. We had to break trail, exhausting ourselves. Finally, upon arriving, we found out that the guy wanted a loaf of bread. He had everything else that he might need and we had taken twenty or thirty dollars worth of supplies out. It's enough to make you want to break down and cry at times like that. We turned around and headed home. One of our machines broke down and I was pulling that machine out with mine and I'll be a son of a gun if mine didn't break down too. It was too much for the machines. Here we were, half way between Lorraine and Port Colborne in a very serious situation because it was eleven o'clock at night, in the middle of a blizzard in the country. This chap's telephone had been working so we walked back to his place and called in to the police office. They sent a squadron of six snowmobilers out to pick us up. The point was, over a silly loaf of bread we created an emergency. However, these sad little stories come out with good ones and certainly in the blizzard the good ones far out numbered the bad.

No particular type of machine seemed to be more reliable than another one. The lower power machines proved to be better because they were more of a work-horse. The hot machines, the big 440's and so on with all their special gadgets were not able to work very long because they weren't accustomed to this slugging.

The snowmobile clubs, in the early part of the storm were the only people who were available to deliver medicines to heart attack victims and insulin to the diabetics. We made only direct deliveries from the pharmacy to needy people. We even delivered a pregnant mother to the hospital in time for her delivery. We brought her in from Wainfleet area to Port Colborne. I was worried at the time that she might deliver in the middle of a blizzard. I chuckled to myself and said, "Well, I had one pee all over me so what the heck." I could take anything after that.

My expenses for running my unit were more than one hundred dollars. A fund was set up that was administered by the Chamber of Commerce to help defray costs. People donated voluntarily to the fund and we in turn submitted our bills to the fund. Mostly parts and things like that involving breakdowns were covered. There wasn't a payment for gas. I received a check for sixty-three dollars in the mail a week or so ago to cover the cost of my parts. And I know for a fact that most of the people who were involved in the storm did receive coverage for their breakdowns and repairs. A fund like that is very worth-while and I'm sure that you're going to see it in existence on a continual basis. With a possible exception of one or two units, most of us paid for our gas. This was quite fair.

I think we're going to be in much better shape should another emergency like that arise in the future. I suppose being prepared now, it may never happen again. This lack of preparation was quite evident in the early part of the storm. For instance, I got phone calls form people who knew that I had a machine. Ron Lampman, our President, had numerous phone calls, and he would direct the calls to members of the club who he knew would or could respond. When things progressed and got a little worse, we began to respond from the Niagara Regional Police Station who were then handling the calls. The Niagara Regional Police were located in downtown Port Colborne. They had rented several snowmobiles and their original idea was to take care of the emergencies themselves. Great idea until they realized the magnitude of the storm and they couldn't handle it by themselves. We answered their appeal and happily responded to their directions out of the Port Colborne office. These are the communications that I mentioned earlier that now began to come together. We became a cohesive compact unit and we were able to direct our actions in a particular way instead of going helter skelter around the country. It really became easier for us from that point on.

I don't know whether most communities have what you could call an emergency measures organization but I think that any community that could face possible hazards would be well advised to set one of these up. For instance, we have the lake here and every once in a while we get a bad storm. I think our community should have some sort of emergency organization set up to deal with a situation like this. When an area such as Port Colborne is finished with an emergency like this, people tend to forget about it. We tend to relax and I think this is what is happening here. If a situation were to develop tomorrow we'd have exactly the same thing, whether it was rain, hail, wind, lightning, flooding or a tornado.

One of the things we noticed was the distinct lack of trained people in emergency measures. The lack of first aiders was a real shocker to me. With possible heart-attacks and everything else imaginable, there were very few of us who knew what to do. I think it's important that any organization should have the trained personnel available to them in a situation like that.

I see that there's supposed to be an emergency measures organization working out of St. Catharines that was to provide expertise in cases of disaster. The part they played was very minimal. They didn't have the people and they didn't have the set-up. About a decade ago, they had been so stripped by local, provincial, and federal authorities that they were almost helpless. When they were first set up there were a certain number of people who were alotted to each area and they received a broom, a shovel, and a pail and that was the extent of their equipment, with a little bit of training thrown in. I was very disappointed in seeing that it fell flat on its proverbial in this storm. I don't know what the answer to this problem is. Thinking back a few years ago, we had that tremendous scare about the atomic bomb. Build your shelter and that kind of crap and they were at their height at that point. Since then, everybody's got the bomb so why worry about it. The organization virtually disappeared. Now let's face it, we'll have people who'll say that we have such an organization, and who's going to deny it? The organization will say, "Ya we got it," and they probably have. Did you hear anything about the EMO? No, I never met an EMO guy or representative or anything throughout that blizzard. I don't know where they were or what they were doing. Where were they?

I think anyone who's interested to the point that he bought a snowmobile should join a club because in a club they receive special training. They not only learn how to ride a machine, but to ride it properly. There's a vast difference between the two. You receive advice on what type of clothing to wear to counteract this frostbite which is the greatest hazard we have. The ability to be able to handle your machine and to be covered up properly while so doing is critical. Most snowmobile clubs teach these things and certainly ours is going to be better prepared to do a more effective teaching job after our experiences. We now have a first aid ambulance sled. We made up our own. We're ready for our next storm. With this sled we can transfer people on a stretcher.

It's important that if we are going to have snowmobilers, we're going to have people who should be trained properly, not only for greater satisfaction personally, but to be able to respond more effectively when we are called to duty. Who knows when we will be called next?

Every square inch of your body must be covered. If you have even a half of one square inch exposed when you have a chill factor of about fifty below zero, you will have frostbite in that small patch.

Larry Butters - Ambulance Attendant

"He was going into shock because of the accident and the loss of blood."

There was a car accident about 2 miles out of town on No. 3 highway and it took us about 20 minutes to get there. We arrived about 11 a.m. Friday morning and picked up a man who had a pretty good gash on his head and he had lost quite a bit of blood already. The storm by then was upon us and everything came to a stop because a tractor trailer was stopped in front of us and four cars had piled up in front of him. One of the cars had pushed the truck's bumpers against his wheels so he could not move.

So you thought you had an ambulance in an emergency? Courtesy, St. Catharines Standard

We called for the big city road grader to come out and free the tire from the bumper and pull the transport trailer out of the way. Then we followed the grader into town.

Our ambulance kept stalling on us and we had to clean the wires and clean out the distributor several times. We used towels to clean and dry everything.

Finally we got our man to the hospital over 5 hours later. He was going into shock because of the accident and the loss of blood but because we kept the ambulance warm he was all right.

Randy Butler - Teenage Snowmobiler

"Others were opening the car doors and stealing radios."

I was taken totally by surprise by this blizzard. I was getting ready to go snowmobiling up north and then I didn't have to. I got stopped on No. 3 highway where a tractor trailer had jack-knifed and a car had smacked into a pole. I climbed into the back of my friend's van and dressed in my snowmobile suit and helmet. I sat on top of the van and directed my friend with my hands and that was the only way we could get home. It took us 3 hours to go 2 miles.

We were at home until my father called up and said that there was an emergency in Port Colborne and my snowmobile should be put into service to help. We stayed up that night until 2 a.m. helping people.

It was very dangerous because you barely could see from the blizzard. We were going down the road on which cars were stranded. We would go over a snowbank not knowing what was on the other side. We headed straight for the Legion Hall. Three of us met there and we began transporting people from the legion. Following that we went over to the Inco and we took people out of there. Later on we went to Port Colborne High School where there were a group of teachers stranded and we transported them all back home. That was quite the experience because one of the ladies was new at snowmobiling and she clinched me very tightly around the waist. Going over the hill we rolled the machine because she was so scared.

There were a lot of people involved on their snowmobiles. It turned out to be a very valuable experience for everybody. I think we learned a lot from it. I think a lot of bad things happened as well. For example, there was a lot of looting along No. 58 highway which was closed. We drove up there as part of our routine, looking into the cars for people who were stranded. I remember seeing a cola truck there and a lot of people who were on snowmobiles were helping themselves to the pop. Others were opening the car doors and stealing the radios.

The fact that snow had piled everything up forced us to drive over cars that we didn't know were there. Unfortunately, we would come down on the roof of them and occasionally we had to drive away knowing that we caused damage. We were digging underneath one snowbank and we broke a back window of a car. We couldn't tell that the window was in that position. Several times we dug under the snow to see if there were people trapped. Most of the time while we were riding the machine, the snow was packed like a rock and the machine would not break through.

I think calling the Militia could be called a waste of time. When they were called they went to the police station. There must have been ten snowmobiles out there just sitting. All they did was sit. We were dispatched from the police station. The army would be in the back there drinking coffee. After a couple of days of going up and down hills, I was exhausted and I loaned my machine. The army got stopped because of those 25 foot drifts that went straight up and down. When they couldn't get through they called upon us to help.

Sometimes the CB'ers did a good job. They helped us a lot by telling us where to go. Sometimes they were not much help because they would say the highways were open and they were not. People heard these reports and jumped in their cars and raced down there trying to get through and ended up stuck. It was a worse mess than before and we had to go in there and take them out by machine. Some people had CBs set up on their snowmobiles but that was pretty poor. I remember one lady called CHOW radio and said that her baby was starving. There was a store just around the corner with milk. My father and I along with five other snowmobilers went to her aid. There were a bunch of people at her home already just to get a quart of milk when it was really not necessary. One person could have gone.

CHOW helped a lot, but they hurt a lot too. They would give reports that 58 highway was open and I went down with my machine. It was hard to get through because the cars were piled up. There were at least 2 police cars in the ditch, a tractor trailer had jack-knifed and there was a Trans Am right in the middle of the jack-knife. Two cars were head on right in front and there was no way anybody could get through. However the radio said it was fine.

The snowmobilers did what they were expected to do. It seems as though they got a good name from it anyway. I think their help in the storm was probably the best of all the people who were involved. Taking milk out to people, food, bread, drugs, certainly helped their reputation. But the reaction of the people in some cases was very disappointing. My brother went out to Lowbanks answering an emergency call for bread and milk and he delivered it to these people and they just said, "OK give us the food" and they shut the door in his face. He had come 7 or 8 miles and they wouldn't even offer him a cup of coffee or invite him in to get warm before his return trip. Most people however were very generous. They would offer money for gas which we had to refuse. It makes us feel good that we were doing a good deed.

At one point when we were making our rounds I ran out of gas. Luckily my friend was with me and we had to syphon it out of one of his tanks and into mine. We used a little piece of rubber tubing, got a mouth full of gas and began to syphon.

We would carry the bread and milk and those things in a bag held between our legs. If somebody needed medical help we would rig up a stretcher and get them out. Randy Zapp and I found a man who was hurt about 2 o'clock Saturday morning. He was mostly shaken up and scared but he was walking the streets and he collapsed. The way the wind was blowing that night he shouldn't have been out at all. He recieved frostbite and passed out. We got him on the stretcher and dragged him into the hospital.

I was extremely disappointed in the army. Everytime we went in there and asked if we could help they said, "Now we will tell you when we need you for something." Then the army would be sitting back keeping warm and having a cup of coffee. I didn't see one thing that the army did. I saw a picture in the newspaper of them transporting goods but other than that they were all bunched up in the police station in Port Colborne with all kinds of food stacked up in there. There were canned goods, crackers, bread, powdered milk, everything that you would ever want was stacked up in there.

I think the milk for babies was a necessity but the older people could have drank water. If their water wasn't running they could have melted snow. I think a lot of these people were screaming emergency when I'm sure they had some kind of canned goods at home or something in the fridge that would have got them through.

I think at times our services were really being taken advantage of. One lady on Lake Shore East put in a call for help. We responded. Her house was reasonably comfortable, she had coffee, she had milk, she had bread, she had everything except someone to talk to. We walked in and we walked out twice as fast.

The winds from the blizzard caused a lot of damage. Trees had fallen down on homes. We were out at Lowbanks and I was following this one guy on his snowmobile and suddenly he smashed into the chimney of a house. He totalled his machine completely. Houses were buried that badly. Power lines were crashed down and this was pretty risky business driving your snowmobile around in it. One of the high schools in Welland was opened up so that the snowmobilers could get their units into the school shops, where they could fix their machines. It would have been a good idea if they would have done the same thing in Port Colborne. My machine broke down at the high school when one of the spark plug wires got split. I was loosing all of my power that way. When I was out there by myself, I had to hold it with my hand and I was getting quite a nice jolt. So I got it back to the school and one of the janitors brought it around back and we fixed it there. So it would have been a good idea I think if the school had been open for these emergency type repairs.

One thing which stood out in my mind was the number of cars that were wrecked on Highway 58. There were at least 57 cars that I counted myself. The hoods were up, the batteries were missing and everything was in shambles. Snow was packed into these cars. They were a mess.

While we were riding around in the storm we were going against 50 to 60 mph winds. This was packing the snow in around my helmet. I sat at home close to an hour before I could get my helmet off. My goggles were frozen solidly to the mask and my moustache was stuck against it. I had to sit there and thaw out.

If they had put a driving ban on I think it would have been a

The St Catharines Standard

good idea. It certainly would have made the job of the snowmobilers a lot easier. If we are supposed to be getting very bad winters for the next 8 years, I think we had better prepare now. The police and even the army should change some rules as to what to do on a snowmobile. They should be taught how to make repairs that are most likely to be needed on a snowmobile.

One of the gas stations refused to give gasoline except to emergency vehicles. That way curiosity drivers would come in with an empty tank and not be able to get served and it would force them off the roads where they shouldn't have been in the first place.

Many people were worried about their animals. They wanted to take hay out to their horses or dog food out to their dogs that were stranded in their homes or cars and so on. All this worrying about animals was logical, I suppose, but I think the snowmobilers should have worried about the people first. One chap stayed at our house over night and we gave him a bottle of whisky and he was happy for the whole night. His life is all tied up in his horses. So we drove him way out No. 3 highway and he fed his horses the next day.

Jim Wright, Teenage Snowmobiler

On Friday night we had our snowmobiles down on No. 58 highway and we were taking people from the stranded cars to the Port Colborne Block Factory.

On Saturday this guy came in to the garage and said his wife was trapped in her house in the country with no power and there was no way he could get to her. We loaded the snowmobile onto the truck, went as far as we could that way and then unloaded and drove 5 miles by snowmobile to get the woman and bring her back to the truck and then to town.

That night we snowmobiled to Zudel's parents on Forkes Road. The snow had covered their house and if there was an emergency they couldn't have got out. So we kept an exit shovelled out for them.

Lloyd Goss - Snowmobiler

"He was about fifteen feet over my head when he passed over top of me with his big snowmobile."

We were taking insulin out to Sherkston and taking stranded people home. For delivering groceries we towed a sleigh. I went out to the dump and picked up a fellow that had been stranded there all night, the fellow who looks after the incinerators. He'd been stranded out there all day Friday and Friday night. I went Saturday morning and picked him up. He was stuck in this little shack all that time

Buried house with owner at window. Wainfleet. By Norman Rockwell

by himself. For heat he had this little cone with a wire wrapped around it.

Sunday morning, Fred, Randy Butler and I went out into the marsh and brought a whole family out. There was a man, his wife, two children and a seventy-three year old woman in a farm house there. They had no power and no heat except for a fireplace in one room. We used a skiboose to get them out. Bud Noyes went over top of me on his big John Deere when we were coming back from the Mill. I went up over a hill, up over the big snow drift and down. He was behind me and he gave it too much gas and he went up over the top and just took right off with a girl on the back. He came down on the other side and he was about fifteen feet over my head when he passed over top of me with his big snowmobile.

We should have a central location on the east and west side because it is rough crossing the bridges on snowmobiles, especially with the machines that have the slide suspension. Once you hit the grates where there's no snow you lose all your lubrication, and then if your're not careful you tear lumps off your belt.

I always ride on one knee if I'm riding alone. I hunch down over the handlebars and get my face in behind the windshield. Then, I don't have much trouble seeing except in the whiteouts. Always carry spare spark plugs, a spare drive belt, wrenches, a flashlight, and always use gasoline with de-icer. Then you will never have any trouble. I put in about four or five ounces to every five gallons. I never have any trouble with my machine now. I helped a lot of fellows whose machines were iced - their carburetors were iced and they just wouldn't run. One fellow was stalled on the bridge and I stopped and we put gasoline with de-icer into the carburetor and tank and once it thawed the ice, it worked well.

If you haven't got a proper snowmobile suit, then you might as well forget it. You have to be dressed properly or you will suffer frostbite. A short coat will creep up and you'll get frostbite across your stomach or on your back. I got frostbite under my chin and on my neck when my scarf opened up. It looked like a rope burn around my neck. I noticed my frostbite about four o'clock at night when I went up to Emergency at the hospital. They advised lukewarm wash cloths and then rub it with vaseline and do that about every twenty minutes. It was about two weeks later when it started to peel. It blistered and peeled just like a burn. It was painful for two weeks. Exposed parts of your body should be covered with vaseline or grease in cold weather. It keeps the heat in the skin.

When I drove people home in the country, I would stop and check cars and school buses. Then when we delivered the person, I would call the police to see if there was another job in that area or if someone needed to be brought into the city. This saved a lot of time.

I found that the face shield didn't work for me because it always had fog on it. So I switched to a helmet and goggles with a green lense for day driving and yellow lense for night work; no fog problem then and no ice on the eye lids.

My snowmobile used about 30 gallons of gas and I bought it myself. I've put in a claim for a few drive belts and a set of spark plugs. There will be a meeting to settle the claims.

Female, seventeen: I was at home during the storm and my father was stranded at work for 24 hours. When he came back, he took our snowmobile out and took a bunch of guys home. One guy had a wife out in the country without any formula for their baby. We had to take a bunch of things out to them and on the way dad ran over a bus and a volkswagen and smashed up the snowmobile so he couldn't do much for the rest of the storm.

Farmer Twerdohlib

"There is a strong need for a snowmobile driver program for all police departments in communities which can be hit by blizzards."

People should know their snowmobile clubs because they can help you first in a snow storm. If such clubs do not exist in a community that can be hit by a bizzzard then at least one such club should be formed and there should be liason between it and the other organizations in that area.

There is a great need for a snowmobile driver program for all police departments in communities which can be hit by blizzards. Some police took off on snowmobiles and they had never been on one before. They had to go out just the same.

We were lucky and it was more luck than good management. I hope we are as lucky next time.

People used to bitch about snowmobiles, thinking they were a nuisance. Now they are a pretty good thing.

Winston Siddall - Four Wheel Drive Owner

"She broke the phone in three pieces on his head"

I was down at the shop when it all started. And then I got round to get the kids. I went up to Steele Street school and offered to take anybody home that was interested in a ride and I took a couple of kids home. I delivered one boy and his father was there and I asked "Is your wife around?" and he said, "No, she just walked over to the school to pick up my son." I thought, well good luck. I hope she makes it. I said that I would go back there and look for her. I found her on the corner and she didn't know which direction she was going. She was almost finished.

Then we went down to the canal. Guy was injured down in

the hold of a ship. Fellow had a boom come down on top of him; broke his shoulder. The hoist wouldn't work and the rest of us all had to carry him up about three flights of stairs to get him up on the deck and of course he was in the back end of the boat and the ladder was at the front so I had to walk all the way along the side. Then we carried him over the snow drifts and finally made it to my Blazer.

Then we got a Saturday night special call from the lower east side. The guy was bleeding pretty badly. He had a big split in his forehead. His partner said to me, "Get the hell out of here. He's not going to any hospital." The injured guy had been pestering the lady next door and when he got his nose in the door, she cracked him with the telephone. She broke the phone in three pieces on his head! So finally I said, "Well good luck buddy."

Nobody was on the road at that point. We ran into really crazy people at that point. A guy asked me for a ride, going down Elm St. I said, "Where are you going?" He says, "Welland." I says, "I'm sorry, I can't take you."

We needed to follow a big snowplow into the country in order to get out an eighty year old man. We had to carry him down from the second story. The snowplow went down a little further, turned around and came back and stood by while we loaded the old fellow. By the time we got ready to head for town the road was closed in again. The snowplow had to plow us all the way out again.

I went up to St. Catharines. The roads were still blocked off as far as the army was concerned. You weren't supposed to go on them. They would check us all the way down. We got hell a couple of times because the police would stop us and say, "What the hell are you doing on the road?" We explained that we needed the parts for a diesel tow truck that had dropped its clutch.

In St. Catharines it was just like a different world. Everyone was driving around like any normal day. The busses were working. People couldn't leave just because everybody else was snowbound.

I had to go into the neighbour's garage and when I opened the door there was every kind of bird in there that you could think of. At least four or five species came flying out. Later a lot of them were found frozen to death.

Don Reilly - Superintendent, Niagara South Board of Education

"The school had about four inches of water in it. It was like a swimming pool."

Well, for my part, I came to school early that morning of Friday Jan. 28. I came early because I had a meeting out at the Child Development Centre. I went out there and was there at 9:00 when I got a call from my secretary that I'd better hustle back. They had warnings to close the schools.

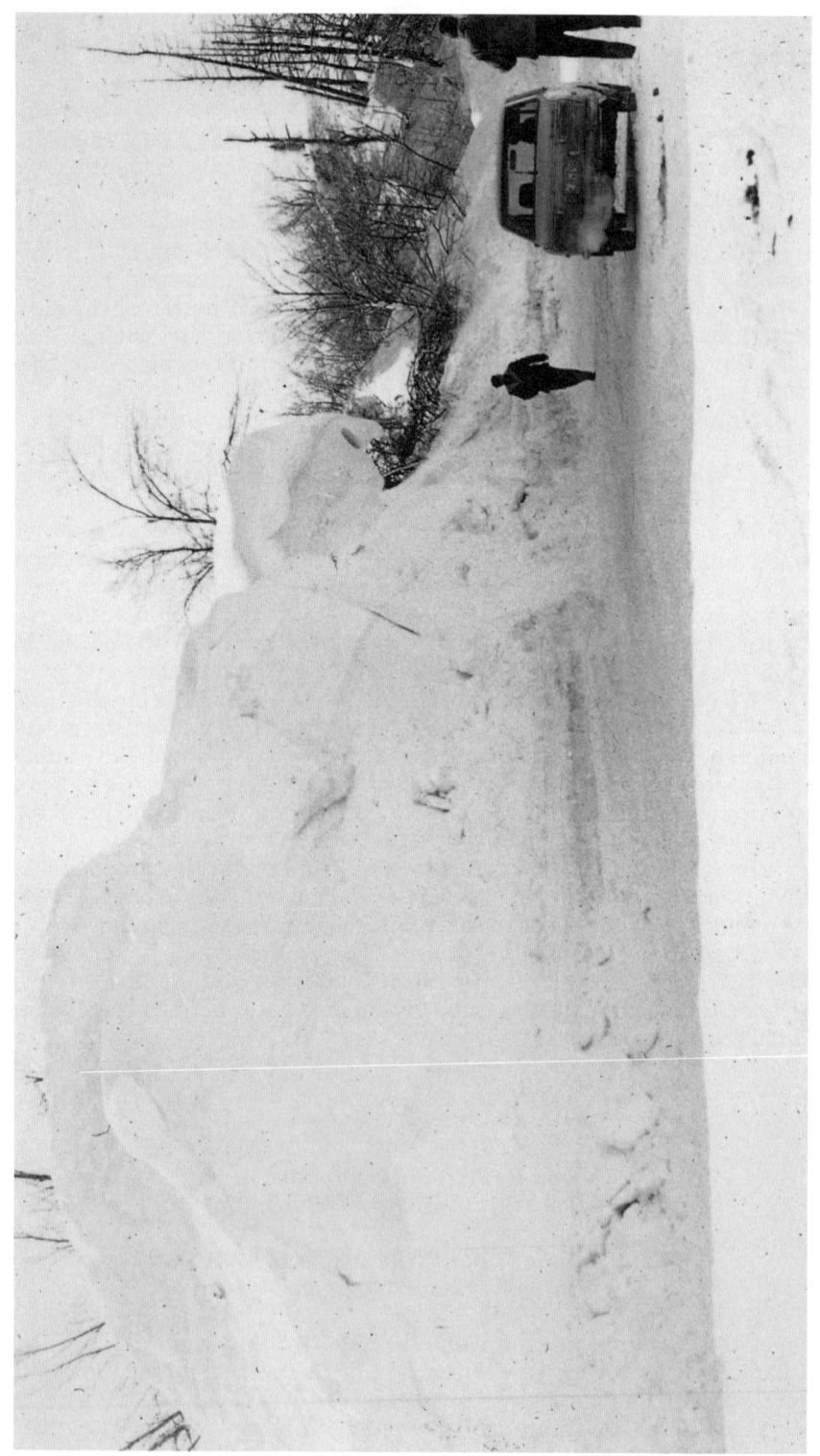

Canadian Snowdrift - Wainfleet. by Richard Hughes

In the TMR program (trainable mentally retarded) we have children who are mostly handicapped and there was a delay in the buses. If the buses had begun their runs at 9:00, we wouldn't have had any trouble. As it happened, the buses dropped off the children and started back to their depot and we had to contact them to get them to go back to the school. By this time it was almost 10:00 and they just couldn't go because there was so much snow. Some got back to the schools all right but by the time they got the children loaded, some of them in wheel chairs, the buses couldn't budge. So they called in here and I was on the phones along with Doug Silcox. The girls here in the office had gone home because we were afraid they would get stranded. I was on the switchboard directing an army helicopter as to what school and kids we wanted to move. We had a big chalk board here that we brought up from the basement. On Friday night, we had about 1,500 kids and 250 teachers stranded in schools. My daughter is in grade 12 and she dropped in here because she didn't want to walk home in the blizzard. So I put her to work on the switchboard. Then I got on the telephone with the CB people and we got food into the schools. In one case, a lady was stranded at Lorraine Central School. She just happened to have done her weekly shopping. So the kids ate all her groceries, Friday and Saturday.

At Gasline School, two law officers had a prisoner in hand cuffs. They were stranded and they had this prisoner with them and they commandeered one classroom. The kids were feeding the prisoner hot dogs. Apparently they stayed there over night.

We had a couple of emergencies with children in these TMR schools. They are children with I.Q. scores below 60 and a lot of them are subject to grand mal seizures from epilepsy. A lot of the kids are on a drug called dylantin and one of the children, without the drugs had a seizure about every hour. In the school we always insist that at least an extra day of drugs are available for every child that has to take them and this has been the practice for a number of years. Well for a long stay like we had, he ran out of drugs on Saturday and we had to get a police snowmobile and four wheel vehicles to go to the hospital and get the drug that he required and then take it over to Pauline McGibbon School so we could control the boy's seizures. Everytime a child has a seizure, a certain number of brain cells are burned up and so you have to diminish the seizures of the children.

We had one child develop—we thought it was pneumonia. We had to get the child wrapped up in blankets and a four wheel vehicle came in and picked the child up and took him to the hospital. I just had to take the responsibility for it because I couldn't reach the parents.... the phones were out and the parents weren't all that appreciative of what I had done until they heard what the problem was.

We stayed here all night, kept in contact with the school by phone and by CB radio. On Sunday afternoon there was a spell where it cleared up a bit and that was when I had the army helicopter evacuate the kids from W. E. Brown School. The chopper picked up 8 kids and landed in their own back yards.

We had one little lady, on the telephone, about midnight one night. She called and said her children were stranded with the bus driver in Niagara Falls and her husband was stranded at McKinnons and she was all by herself. The nearest neighbour was a mile away and she had to talk to somebody or she was going to go crazy ... so I talked to her for half an hour then I turned her over to Doug and Doug talked to her for a while ... just to keep her from climbing the walls. She called back at about 2:00 in the morning then again at about 4:00 in the morning ... she just needed someone to talk to ... two ladies like that as a matter of fact. They were all alone on farms ... Finally, by late Sunday afternoon, we got all the children into billets some place.

One guy who really impressed me was Lloyd Emerson. He ended up in the hospital from exhaustion after it was finished. He and another guy ... each of them had white diesel tractors ... 3 big brutes ... and they started from their home right at Chambers Corners and they headed toward Wainfleet South School. We were in touch with them by CB radio and it took them 8 hours to go across the fields on their big tractors ... they stand about 12 feet off the ground ... he and the other guy took 12 hours to get from there to Wainfleet South School. It was an emergency because the power kept going off and if the school would get cold we would have been in trouble with the 60 kids and 5 teachers that were there. Finally they got the school bus and with the help of a chap down there, who had a big bull dozer., they hooked up one of Lloyd Emerson's tractors in front of the bus, then the bus, then the other tractor behind. They put the bull dozer in front and it just pulled the bus between the tractors. We got the kids in the bus and billeted in 2 houses that were close to the highway so that in the event that the highways opened they could get to their homes. One lady had 26 kids at her house up there.

One thing that was a saving grace for all of our schools for the retarded children was that each of them has a home economics room and some of them have freezers. They had enough food stock piled. The kids had roast beef, chicken and they made out very well. I'm interested in the vocational programs with the secondary schools and at Fort Erie secondary the wind loosened one of the glass tiles in the greenhouse and blew it off. The greenhouse is in the southwest corner of the building and the wind of course was coming from that direction. It froze all the pipes and here these poor kids had been working at horticulture to propigate plants. It froze all the pipes and wiped out about two thousand dollars worth of plants that the kids had been working on. It was a fantastic loss for the kids. I called the Minister of Agriculture and I called Mr. Allen who was in charge of the Parks Commission and explained the problem to them and 2 weeks later, a truck pulled up in front of the school with a donation of plants, the likes of which the kids had never seen. Exotic types of plants that only grow in green houses were donated from the experimental station at Vineland and from the Niagara Parks Commission. That didn't cost us anything really ... they were glad to do that.

Jack Dobney who teaches at Westbrook had an interesting

experience. A kindergarten bus had broken down and it couldn't go any further than Westbrook. So Jack Dobney who owns this 4-wheel drive jeep pulled his jeep into the auto servicing shop at the school and got it all warmed up and protected with rubber and plastic covering where ever he could. He took the kids home 1 and 2 at a time. Then he'd come back into the shop and wipe the snow off the machine and let it get warmed and the battery charged and away he'd go again. It took him 9 hours to get those kids home.

Interesting story about Bob Blake. He's a teacher at Westbrook. He decided on Saturday he was going to get home so he borrowed one of the trucks one of the guys had from Westbrook and he borrowed a snowmobile and he put the snowmobile on the back of the truck. He lives in Dunnville, so we monitored his progress by the helicopter in the armed forces and he started out from here and got as far as Wellandport with the truck. The truck broke down and he got the snowmobile off the back of the truck and he covered the rest of the distance by snowmobile. When he got home his wife called here and said that he made it. It took him 5 hours to get from here to Dunnville - that was 15 miles.

The police and the army were terrific in their help. We were in constant communication with them all the way. I have a short wave radio and I brought it in here so we could monitor what the CB people were saying to us instead of using the phone because the phones weren't working very well.

Bill Wales who works for us has a son who lives in the Chippawa apartments just near here. It's a high apartment building and the son put the antenna on the roof. By telephoning him we would relay a message and he would relay a message and he would pipe it out to Wainfleet South School. At the school, John Mastroianni has a CB radio in his truck. If we couldn't get him by telephone, we'd raise him on the air with his CB. Now Mastroianni would get in touch with Bill Wales' son and he would call back in here on the telephone. So we used that link 3 or 4 times because the power was a 3 phase electrical system and the one phase kept going out and then some pipes froze and water flooded into the library. There were a lot of problems over there at Wainfleet South School.

Elsie English Memorial School in Fort Erie was really hard hit. We got the kids out of there and they had to tunnel through a 20 foot drift to get out in front of the school. They billeted the children in nearby homes and then they locked the door. It was starting to get cold because the furnace was on the wrong side of the school and the draft intake was on the windward side and the flame went out. The pipes froze. Bill Wales went to walk into the school 2 days later and the total school had about 4 inches of water in it. It was just like a swimming pool.

McDonald's were fantastic. They sent in free food for us. CB people would bring us free breakfasts and free lunches and suppers all on McDonald's. An old lady across the road brought us a bottle of wine.

Precautions to take that we are concerned about include such things as making sure when a child is on medication and that the parents are informed that we need 3 days supply of medication in the school with the directions for administering the medicine. We put these in an envelope and we mark the child's name on it and put it away in the vault. Then we'll renew it every fall to make sure that the medication is fresh because some of it loses strength. Another thing for certain is that we will put cases of high nutrition canned goods and a couple of boxes of powdered milk in all the schools. We thought about CB radios but it's just too expensive. We are going to set up an emergency system where we can get to more than one phone, like 2 neighbours that are willing to co-operate. We'll get the names ahead of time of possible billets. We've asked Bell Telephone to check and see why the phones go out everytime it rains. They just don't bother. It's kind of handy if there are CB'ers in the neighbourhood of the school, just to alert them in case of an emergency. We could use the CB instead of the telephone. Other than that, a lot of the suggestions are contained in a written document which would be easy for anyone to receive if they so wished.

Kathy Hiseler

"Once the danger was over, people seemed to go back into isolation, feeling embarrassed at opening themselves to each other."

"Is it le printemps or la printemps", I muttered to myself as I struggled through my French exam.

"Excuse me people. Please put your pens down for a minute. I'd like to speak to you."

I looked up at the sound of our Vice Principal's voice. It must be something important to interrupt an exam.

"We've just heard on the radio that a severe snowstorm is on its way here. The rest of the day's exams are cancelled, and the buses will be here at eleven o'clock to take the bus students home. Okay, go back to your exam."

I looked down at the paper, and it came to me — le printemps, the spring. I wrote it down and hurried on to the next question.

When I finished the exam, I handed it in and went down to my locker. I put on my coat and walked out of the school to meet my mother. Softly falling snow was just beginning to coat the sidewalk.

"How did it go?" she asked as I sat down in the car. I told her, and added the news about the approaching snowstorm. We looked doubtfully at the gentle white snowflakes, and decided to get the groceries at the plaza.

As we stood in the check-out line with our groceries, a woman came in from outside. She was extremely agitated and began telling a woman nearby that it was absolutely awful out, snowing like crazy.

"You can't see a thing, I'm not kidding. I hope the kids are still at school. They'll never make it home in this. Oh it's unbelievably thick," she raced on excitedly. I looked over at mom and surpressed a shiver.

We carried our groceries out to our Mazda. The snow swirled all around us, making it nearly impossible to see a foot ahead. I put out my hand to the car door and struggled to open it against the force of the wind.

Once we were in the car and got it going, we headed down Highway 3, towards home. The car began to make strange popping noises — ominous sounds to our ears. My mother didn't say much and neither did I. We were both intent on watching the road and finding our turn. "This is it." I said to my mother. She turned, but as we were half way into the turn the car popped, banged and stalled. Mother tried to start it again and again, but the engine refused to co-operate. She told me that we would have to get out and push the car back to the roadside.

I forced open my door against the wind. We ran to the front of the car. We heeved until it rolled back to the side of the road. We got in. As I sat back, my eyes watering from the pain of the blowing snow I thought about how we could easily have been hit by a car if one had come while we were pushing. I thank God for protecting us, and thanked Him again as mom successfully started the engine.

We turned onto the Golf Course Road and slowly crept along, going more quickly between the gusts of wind. The car kept up the series of bangs and pops as we went along. Then we saw the tail lights of a car directly ahead. A man walked up to us and said to follow him. We could make it together. We followed his flickering lights for a short piece until he disappeared as quickly as he had appeared. My heart sank a bit — we were on our own again, alone!

When we were about three quarters of a mile from home, the car quit again. We tried over and over again to start it, but knew it was useless this time.

A truck stopped. The young man asked if they could help. We piled the groceries into the back of their truck and they drove us home, with one of them riding in the back of the open truck. Then they were stuck and could not get out.

With a hot coffee in front of us, we sat and exchanged names and stories, while we watched the raging storm. I figured it would be a couple of hours before the storm calmed, so three of us played cards while mom called on the phone, trying to locate the rest of the family.

That was Friday. On Sunday, my father, younger brother, younger sister, and her friend were brought home by snowmobile.

Tuesday I said good-bye, a little sadly when the two young men left us. I knew we'd probably never see them again, and they had been terrific to help us in a time of need. That storm had brought us closer together as it had done to many people. Once the danger was over, people seemed to go back into isolation, feeling embarrassed at opening themselves to each other.

After they left, I looked at the towering snowdrifts surrounding the house. I realized how lucky we had been with heat, food and power through the whole thing, snug in our own home. I hoped that everyone had been lucky enough to escape the death that had loomed so near.

My mind began to wander to thoughts of exams still to be written. I knew the blizzard of '77 was over, except for the snow it left behind and the memories in the hearts of all those who lived through it.

Doug Silcox—Superintendent—Niagara South Board of Education

"There is nothing as loud as the sound of a snowflake falling on the roof."

"We had approximately two thousand students stranded in schools across the county."

It was on the twenty-eighth of January, about nine o'clock in the morning when we had the first storm warning from the weather bureau. It was unusual because we normally don't get such information direct from the weather bureau. At that point we had an emergency meeting with all superintendents who were here and the ones by phone who were in other jurisdictions.

We moved as fast as we could to hurry the buses to make alternate arrangements in picking up the children. We went on the radio two or three times to announce what was happening.

By eleven o'clock it was bad and I was getting reports almost every ten minutes from the schools regarding conditions. Many of the buses that did arrive at the schools were unable to get away or got only a few hundred yards away. The hardest hit places in terms of student population being stranded was in Wainfleet where almost one hundred per cent were stranded. Port Colborne's eastern section was hit badly. From that point, panic began to set in many people's minds.

We tried to get as many people out of here as we could. We kept one girl as long as we could to operate the switch board and then we made sure that three or four of us could manage. I made the decision that I was going to stay. There was no way that I was going to leave for the night and by that time you couldn't get anywhere anyway.

In Welland we couldn't move. Some people donned heavy parkas and tried to walk. We started at that point to set up a kind of long term operation here. We set up blackboards. We kept a running count exactly of how many kids were in the schools, the conditions of the school, how many teachers, how many principals, how many people from the community were stranded. We continued with that kind of monitoring. We contacted every home. In many cases we started at that point to have communication problems. The phone would go out. Winger and Wainfleet South Schools gave us the first communication problem and it went out quickly. At that point, we used the Bell Telephone operators who devised a method of communication into a school.

Parents pushed the panic button because they could not reach the school. What we attempted to do was to go on the radio and ask

Checking a school bus for survivors. Courtesy, The St. Catharines Standard.

the parents not to worry. We kept them informed that the kids in Wainfleet were safe and warm and they had food coming. That helped quite a bit. I think the first night we had approximately two thousand students stranded in schools across the county. One thousand of them were in Port Colborne and Wainfleet.

By the second day, there were some people able to get out by snowmobile and four wheel drive trucks. When students were evacuated we had their names and their phone numbers and where they were going. Some were taken to neighbours, some were being taken to homes in the immediate area. Remember that many parents were stranded away from home. The Gasline-Sherkston area lost all power and had no heat and we had a breakdown of communication. At one point the principal of one school got across the road to a house and got a phone call through to me and arranged to get the children to a nearby home. They had to tie the kids to a rope and in that way they got them to safety. There were fifty or sixty kids. We got in touch with the parents of those children and pacified them.

Going into the second day, it cleared up in the morning a bit. The roads were still impassable in most of these rural areas and then it hit again that afternoon shortly after dinner time. According to the weather bureau, it was the same storm that turned around and was coming back again. By six o'clock that second night we had about eight hundred still trapped in the schools. Six hundred were in Wainfleet and Port Colborne.

The most difficult problem at this point was the human emotional reaction to what was happening. Naturally the parents were worried sick. The principals were carrying an extremely heavy responsibility at this time and my job was to monitor as much as I could what was happening and to make sure that I arranged to get necessary things for survival into the buildings.

In Wainfleet South School we again lost power but we were able to get snowmobilers in sufficient numbers to get the children out of the school and into nearby homes where there was heat. The principal returned to that school and remained there throughout the next day. By late afternoon Saturday, it became obvious that the emergency was beyond our coping. The militia started out with a convoy of sixteen and they made it with four vehicles on Sunday. They took out the balance of the kids that Mr. Emerson had not been able to move and got them into nearby places.

At the same time, the militia moved another group of vehicles into William E. Brown School and started transporting those children out. Wainfleet South kids stayed where they were in the homes.

The last kid in our family of schools to get rescued was from William E. Brown. They were stranded in these army vehicles on Forkes Road at about Highway No. 58. A plow was trying to get them from the other side and they were both stranded. The storm was due to hit again and at that time they took a helicopter and flew these kids across Forkes Road and across the highway into two or three homes there. That was the end of that particular thing!

From that point on it was a matter of picking up the pieces. There were the odd ones stranded but they were in no particular discomfort. It was an emotionally exhausting experience for everybody that was directly responsible for these children, principals in particular. From our point of view, it was exhausting for me because there was no sleep from Friday until Sunday night when the worst of the problem had been conquered. Then it was a matter of trying to determine what happened, what could we have done to make it function a little better and it was at that point that the planning stages began for the document which we have now worked out.

This document is our Board of Education paper for the whole system. It will include an emergency procedures manual which will go to every home in the Port Colborne, Wainfleet areas identifying exactly what happens in an emergency.

One of the initial problems we had of course was the fact that in most of these schools you have only one telephone line and every parent was trying to get into it. This ties up the principal because he can't use the phone for emergency calls such as we were expecting. We were highly criticized for not shutting the schools down earlier. One hour would have made a great difference and we would have avoided most of what happened. A storm of this proportion has never been experienced before and we didn't really have sufficient warning. We didn't lose anybody which was a blessing and a miracle and no one was seriously injured. We had a lot of isolated cases where a child needed special medical attention. There were all kinds of close calls but nothing disastrous. We can joke now about the fact that I should never travel around as Superintendent of Wainfleet and Port Colborne without a snowmobile in my trunk or at least a ski-doo suit and a full supply of food.

The people were nervous after that one. The favorite saying around Wainfleet was that there is nothing as loud as the sound of a snowflake falling on the roof. If it got cloudy after that, the people were on the phone to me and asking when I was going to shut down the schools. It was those same people who criticized me in the past if I had to close a school. Now I get calls that go something like this. "What the hell are you doing? You should be closing them down now!" We hope we never go through it again!

Lisa Jacques

"Tina kept kicking me in the back and putting her feet in my face."

Grade 4
Wainfleet South School

The blizzard of 1977 was on January the 28th. When we left for school we waited for half an hour and the bus still did not come. My mom came instead and drove us to school. We got to school, and all the kids were inside. My sister and I came into the school and entered our room and began to play Clue with David and Jamie.

Then we put Clue away and sat down in our seats. Mrs. Rigg came into our room and said it was getting bad out so we had to go home. We got our coats on and waited for Bill's bus to come. Bill called and said he was stuck in his driveway and refused to come because it was too bad out. He could not see out his own windows.

We went into the library and watched TV while the power was still on. After that we went and ate our lunch. After lunch we went in the gymnasium and played floor hockey for an hour and came back to our room.

By then it was dark and it was time for supper. We had soup, peanut butter sandwiches and a drink. After that, some men came and brought us some blankets and somethings for breakfast for the next morning. We got the blankets and lay them on the floor. We watched Donny and Marie for an hour. Then we saw Roots. Then it was time for sleep. I slept beside Carol. She kept pushing me off my mat. So then I went and slept by Tina. Tina kept kicking me in the back and putting her feet in my face. So I went and slept by Carol. In the morning, we had hot chocolate and tarts. Then Mr. Murphy came in and said we will be going home. Was I every happy!

Male, sixteen: We missed about seven days of school but we didn't really miss that much because the teachers gave extra assignments.

Angel Interisano

Grade 5
Wainfleet South Elementary School

In January 1977, we had the worst storm in the history of our times. It all started with small winds. The snow thrashed against the windows causing them to rattle. No one could see anything. Many were stranded in their cars and many almost froze to death.

The buses weren't able to come and pick up children so we were stranded at school. Eventually, some people made it through to us and brought us food and blankets. We had a warm supper. Some children were too upset to eat. After our supper we played floor hockey. During our game, the lights went out, so we lit candles and sang songs. When night came we all nestled down to sleep. Many children were lying in the dark crying because they were homesick. Many of us were afraid. Just the sound of the wind chilled us to the bone, making us feel hollow and lonely. Even though we were nestled up, the emptiness was still there. Morning came but the storm hadn't stopped.

We were transported to different homes, where we were treated very kindly. The next morning, we were able to go home. Boy was I relieved!

I would like to speak for all of us children and parents and say thank you to parents and staff members for taking care of us throughout that awful storm.

Those Girls!!

My little sister was stranded overnight in Humberstone Senior School and all they had to eat were some chips left over from their lunch hour. Next day they were taken home on the back of snowmobiles in large garbage bags.

My sister didn't mind staying overnight because the girls slept on one side and the boys on the other and all night the girls were trying to sneak the boys over.

Bert Murphy, Principal of Wainfleet South School

"So we had to build a little dam across the door out of bricks and beanbags and that held the water back."

We had forty-one students and eleven adults stranded in the school. To keep the children amused, we used filmstrips and we watched television and played games of floor hockey. We lost one third of our electricity about two hours into the storm which shut down our heating system. We did not have heat in the school proper from Friday afternoon to Saturday night but we did have an electric heater that we ran in one classroom and that's where we kept all the students.

The first day we used what food we had on hand for supper. We had potato chips, concentrated soup and some bread. When that was used up there was a little store at the corner and I was in contact with the owner. I told him that we needed things and he and another man gathered all the stuff that they had in the store and they walked down here with it. We also had some parents and neighbours who brought things in and that got us through the day.

When we lost our electricity we found it necessary to override the circuit breakers on the pump and cause the furnace to come on manually. At our school we cannot get to the furnace room from the inside of the building. We have to go outside. So when necessary, another teacher Mr. Mastroianni and myself would make regular trips every hour to the furnace room to keep the pipes from freezing. On Saturday we were in contact with a neighbour by telephone who said they had another electric heater which we could use. So Mr. Mastroianni and I walked about one quarter of a mile to the electric heater and food and brought them back. During the really bad weather of Friday and Saturday, the children were all kept inside.

We had one door on the southeast corner of the school that was completely drifted over right to the top. Two other doors that had drifted up to about chest height were kept open by using the shovel. These were emergency doors.

The lines out here became very quickly overloaded. During the day, it was almost impossible to phone out. We did have quite a few parents phone on Friday for children who were stranded but once they knew that the children were safe, they didn't call back. We got the children out of the building on Saturday and to some houses down the road. Mr. Rod Campbell got to us with a bulldozer and opened the road down to the corner, took the children out to some houses and spent Saturday night there. So on Sunday morning when we could get them out, we got in contact with the parents and we told them the children were on their way home.

I think this will be a milestone. I know that in my own case I remember my father talking about a very great storm in the forties which was kind of a milestone for him and I think this will be a similar situation for our generation.

We had one funny thing happen on Saturday night after the children had been taken out to homes where it was warmer. They had full electricity. The power came back on in the school about eleven-thirty that night and Mr. Mastroianni and I had just literally closed our eyes to go to sleep in the staffroom. As we were just dozing off, the fire alarm blasted. So we scurried around and we found that a pipe in the air conditioner had burst in the library and in bursting, it had shorted out the air conditioner and set off the fire alarm. We spent about an hour and a half Saturday night rushing around trying to find the valve to shut off the water which was pouring into the work room of the library. While Mr. Mastroianni was busy running up and down to the boiler room, I was getting directions over the telephone from the head of our maintenance as to which valve to try to shut off. This water was building up in the store room and was starting to pour on to the library carpet. So we had to build a little dam across the door out of bricks and beanbags and that held the water back until I could get the big vacuum cleaner and suck up the water and keep it out of the library. That was probably the most humorous thing that happened through the storm.

On the whole, it was a pretty serious situation but I think that the children and the teachers here took it quite well.

Carol Leppert - Rural Teacher

"I would have missed one of the greatest experiences of my life"

We had a hundred and seventy-six students stranded in the school. The neighbours were very good in sending in things. I remember one chap in particular who lives probably a mile from the school. He walked that distance during the blizzard on Saturday, carrying with him heads of lettuce and several loads of bread. The neighbours around the school developed a phoning system and they sent in homemade cookies, cakes, and extra bread. One farmer brought in a big milk can filled with milk. The store down the road was very good at sending up whatever we wanted. For instance, we took all the cans of soup that they had in the store. We got most of our bread from them too. We got twenty dozen eggs which we cooked for Saturday morning breakfast—hard cooked mind you— in the big canner that we use here on Hotdog Days. The bus drivers were here also all Friday night and some of them went home on Saturday before dark.

The telephone company arranged to have an operator just standing by for the school. We had no dial tone. You just had to pick it up and wait until the operator answered. Calls came through directly.

Actually, the children were really terrific. On Friday night we put all of the kindergarten classes, the grade ones, twos and threes on the carpeting in the library. We had very few blankets on Friday night but the kids used their coats and their snowmobile suits for covers. The older children in grade four, five, and six were divided into four rooms; two rooms for the girls and two rooms for the boys. The first night the girls had the use of all the gym mats and the boys were left on their own with the few blankets we could scrape up. We moved all the desks in the classroom over to the side and we slept on the floor.

Saturday we ran games in each of the classrooms. There were two teachers who were responsible for one classroom of children. As it happened there was not nearly the full enrolment here so that two teachers would look after twenty-five children.

On Saturday in the gym, we rotated so that one group exercised for three quarters of an hour. We continued with this rotation all day. At meal times, staff members who were not looking after children assumed the responsibility of cooking. The teachers were relieved every hour. They could look after any special problems. The children were never left alone at any moment. Any of them who were concerned about their mother or going home could always seek some comfort from a nearby teacher with whom they could talk. We had a minimum number of problems because the majority of the kids were super.

The first night some of the youngsters in kindergarten were quite upset. Other than that, there were few problems with getting some of the older ones to sleep.

We just put cushions on the floor as teachers. The teachers from the primary end were with their little ones in the library. There again, we took shifts, rotating around to make sure the little ones were covered up and just making sure that nobody was having any problems.

There was one little boy in kindergarten who was upset and he started to cry because he wanted his mommy. He had gone to different teachers to see if he could phone home and talk to her. All the teachers, in some way or another, told him he could not because his mommy couldn't come anyway. When he came to me, I sat him up on my knee and was rocking him back and forth. He asked what we were going to have for supper. I answered by saying that it will really be something nice. "We're going to have hotdogs, ice-cream, chocolate chip cookies,—it's really going to be a fun supper." "Oh yah," he said, "I want a steak!"

We had soup on Friday night for supper along with the hotdogs, and we had soup on Saturday at lunch with sandwiches and we had soup on Saturday night. Sunday morning, the children lined up, the small ones coming first, the older ones following. A little boy from grade one came along with his cup and as he was going down the line he took a look at me dipping out the hot chocolate and he very sweetly put his hand over his cup and said, "No thank you, I don't care for anymore soup."

The teachers of the older children didn't seem to have any problems on Friday but by Saturday afternoon some of the older children were getting quite concerned about not being able to get home. A couple of the grade six teachers had to sit down and talk to them eye to eye and reassure them that everything was going to be all right.

One thing we were lacking were flashlights and we figured we should have a good supply in the school from this point on. We never really ran out of water at all or heat so it was really quite good that way.

By Saturday afternoon the neighbourhood people had sent in garbage bags full of blankets and sleeping bags to take care of the sleeping situation. The snowmobilers around here were really terrific. They visited the neighbours and brought the stuff in.

We had several television sets and we used them for entertainment. We didn't encourage the students to listen to the radio with all the blizzard phone calls on it. Perhaps a stock pile of dried soups would be an advantage in the future.

Most of the teachers were here until Sunday at noon hour. The secretary of the school was tremendous. She did much of the organization as far as the cooking and phoning and making parental contacts and taking messages. Some of those who weren't supervising the children on Saturday were asked to make out a card for each family showing the name of each child who was here, the addresses, their phone numbers and what road or highway they lived on. This would help the snowmobilers to evacuate the children on Saturday afternoon and Sunday. Then came the job of phoning each parent to make sure that they were going to be home on Sunday when the children were delivered. Some parents were stranded themselves and were stuck at other places. We had to have alternate drop off points such as the neighbour or a relative that was living close by. We started evacuating as early as six thirty on Sunday morning. We got the children bundled up and loaded on the snowmobiles. Usually there were two or three snowmobiles that went together with a couple of kids so that they could deliver them in the same area that had been mapped out before hand. Later on in the morning, the army showed up and they took the remaining kids in these heavy trucks to the different sections of the townships.

We had two medication difficulties throughout the stay here.

In both cases, snowmobilers were sent to the homes of the children to pick-up prescribed medication. They brought it back to the school with instructions as far as dosage and so on was concerned.

The thing that stands out in my mind about the storm was how great everyone got along. Our staff all pitched in together. Getting meals ready, supervising the children, checking on the kids at night, was a super smooth operation.

Friday night, many of the children had trouble trying to get to sleep but Saturday night, they were zonked and they collapsed on the spot. We had all the children in the library. By eight thirty it was lights out and they all settled down. Second night however, we had things a little better organized. We learned from the first night's experience. Rather than having bodies all over in a haphazard arrangement, we had the children sleep in rows on Saturday night to prevent us from stepping on the little innocent fingers as we patrolled through the rows during the night.

Some of the teachers went home by army truck and some went by snowmobiles. One of the board members had this big cab tractor up here at the school and he did a lot of things like clearing the roads and helping the vans get in and out.

I remember phoning Mr. Emerson, the Board of Education member out here. It was Friday morning in preparation for school when it became evident I couldn't make it because of the drifting on my road. I said if you can get me to school I'll be there. He took me up on it. He got his tractor and with the blade on the front he busted through the drifts. He picked me up at home and proceeded to take me in the direction of the school. Then I was dropped off in a station wagon driven by a chap that took me to the school. So if it hadn't been for all that trouble that they went through, I would not have been at school and I would have missed one of the greatest experiences of my life.

John Gilmore - Principal of the Rural Winger School

"You should know where you stand in your community . . . ."

Friday night the power went off for about 45 minutes. We were rather concerned because of course we had no heat or water or anything. When it returned, that put an end to those troubles. During the black out we went to the store and we bought anything that would create light such as candles and flashlights. By the time they got the power back on, we were all set up. I think the one thing we need in this school for future emergencies is a stand by power unit run by gasoline. This would keep the furnace going and the lights on in the hall, at least emergency lighting.

I think the main thing as far as advice to come out of this is that you should know where you stand in your community. All the police and emergency measures people could do was call and to tell you, "Look I know you are there." It was the local people around the school that kept us going and kept us out of trouble. They brought in food and blankets by the truck load. This is the sort of thing that I meant by the support of the community around the school. They brought in sandwiches and bread and milk. The Emergency Measures Organization and the Regional Police would call and talk to me. The point is that any help we got was from our own people right around the building. The Emergency Measures Organization couldn't do a thing.

Lloyd Emerson

"But the kids were sure glad to see us."

Two other fellows and myself worked all Friday night and got a pathway opened up to Winger School. We used a bulldozer, a blower and a tractor. A local machine dealer said that he would help and he gave us a snow blower. It took us about six hours to make a clearing just wide enough to get a car or a truck through. It must have been a distance of about three miles.

It was cold out mind you but we were inside the cab of the tractor and it was heated. The guys on the bulldozer and the blower would come up in the cab of the tractor and get warmed up for a while, so no one suffered from the cold. Everyone was tired to start with and on top of this we worked all night long. The kids were sure glad to see us when we got there and it certainly made the hard work worth while. I think it was about seventy-five kids that we took home before the convoy arrived. No one wants to see another storm like that again.

Mrs. Cuff - School Teacher

"Five inches of snow were on the bed."

The Catholic teachers were attending a workshop at the Refractory in Niagara Falls and we were stuck there over the weekend. I had started on my way home and got caught. I got as far as Uncle Sam's motel and spent the night there and there were about thirty of us.

That was Friday night and it was cold in the motel and they had run out of food. One of the teachers from a couple motels down had walked up and got us and then we all took our cars and managed to get down to another motel for Saturday night and then we came home Sunday. Apparently, many of the teachers stayed at the Refractory the whole time and they had a dance there on Sat-

There will be a slight delay in traffic. Courtesy, Niagara Regional Police.

urday night. They had all the equipment there for a dance. I guess they had a good time so they didn't mind it at all.

In the motel where I was staying, the snow had come in under the door. Five inches of snow were on the bed from a crack in the window and we had to clean the snow off the bed before we could go to bed. It was so cold that we had to get out of there Saturday night. We slept with our clothes on and all the blankets that we could find there in the room. They charged us twenty-eight dollars for that snowy room. Twenty-eight dollars for that room, and the next night at the other motel the fellow charged us ten dollars and the room was warmer and a lot nicer. The people who stayed at the Refractory weren't charged for anything. They got their meals for the whole weekend. That's at the Victoria Park Restaurant. They were wonderful to them. It's that big restaurant that faces the falls.

Gerry Rossi - School Teacher

"Can you imagine in that raging blizzard, this hairy chested truck driver rubbing snow all over the top part of his body while singing an aria from an opera?"

Everything was calm and white as we looked out from the breakfast table about seven thirty that Friday morning. Across Lake Erie was a reddish sky. My wife said that she didn't think she would send Rhonda, our seven year old to school that day. "I've got a premonition," she explained. I learned a long time ago not to fool around with my wife's premonitions. The old saying went through my mind at the time, "Red sky at night—a sailor's delight. Red sky in the morning—a sailor's warning." I wasn't going to be doing any sailing on a frozen lake so I dismissed it and got ready for school.

As is my custom, I put on my spring top coat, kicked aside my overshoes, forgot my gloves and pointed the station wagon southward. As I pulled away, several large snowflakes floated past my windshield.

Around eleven o'clock, an announcement said that all bus students would be released. I was released with that group of students who had to go out into the country.

I moved into the traffic coming south on Highway 58. The road at that time was still passable. However, I started to get the feeling that I was driving in a jug of buttermilk. As I approached that overpass at the Forkes Road, I remember thinking that as I get higher on this overpass, I'm going to get better visibility. Stupid thought. The higher I got, the thicker the buttermilk. The speedometer read ten miles per hour.

Out of nowhere—in front of my bumper—there was a shadow. Instinctively, I pulled my wheel to the left which brought me into the on coming lane. Stupid thing number two. The right front corner of my car plowed into the back of Gary Gilbert's car and his vehicle bumped ahead into Margarie Davies'. Both of them were sitting there innocently and I came along and botched up things. My car carried into the on coming lane because I glanced off Gilbert's car. I drove as far over on the left shoulder as possible and turned the car off.

Now I had to get over to Gary's car. I didn't know if anybody had been hurt and this was foremost on my mind. I stepped out into the blizzard and I suddenly realized just how bad it was. I screamed across the highway at Gary who had by this time rolled his window down and was making motions that everything was okay. I inched my way across the icy pavement and jumped into the back seat of his car. Margarie, the girl ahead, had already got in the front seat of Gary's car and as I climbed into the back she asked me how Roots was coming. Margarie had been to parents' night at our school a week earlier as a concerned parent and during the discussion someone had directed a question at me. I responded by saying that I was sorry because I didn't hear the question. I was too busy reading Roots. It was all the rage at that time. Television was carrying the series and I was trying to keep ahead of it in the book.

We exchanged driver's licenses and insurance numbers and then settled down to think about what we could do. Margarie was from that area. She lived up Forkes Road. She knew it quite well. It was her suggestion that we try to make a dash for the Pakrul home which was about a hundred yards distance. We decided that she and Gary would hold each other and I would follow behind with a blanket and try to break the wind for all of us. As a group of three, we might be able to make it.

We jumped out of the car into the blizzard. Margarie, our beacon of hope, led the way with Gary holding her arm. I held onto their coat tails with this blanket draped over me, trying to break the wind from behind. I must have looked like Lawrence of Arabia but I'm sure his blanket was in much better condition than mine. Next thing I knew, my feet blew out from under me. The wind hit the blanket and much like a sail pushed my feet forward. I was tangled up in their snowboots and legs. They grabbed me, untangled me from the blanket and helped me lift myself. We followed Margarie. Women's Lib jumped about a hundred points in my estimation. She shouted back with words of encouragement as we moved under the underpass where she thought the wind would be broken. She was right. If someone had said to me here's a hundred dollars Gerry if you can tell me where you are going, I couldn't have taken the money.

It seemed like a long time before we got there with the slipping and the sliding and the wind pounding down my flimsy spring top coat. My legs were numb and my bald head screeched from the snow pringing off it. Sure enough, out of a drift appeared the Pakrul mailbox and for all practical purposes we were safe.

Mrs. Pakrul had finished her shopping that morning and had arrived home thirty minutes before we got there. Little did she know that her weekly shopping was going to be demolished by about six o'clock that night. By the time we got there, Mrs. Pakrul had a feeling that there were going to be a lot more of us. And I'll be a son of a gun if she wasn't already preparing things. With Margarie's help they jumped into making these dishes that she felt she could get together quickly. She hadn't encountered anything like this before. It was a good logical conclusion that she made. There was going to be trouble on that overpass. She was the closest home to it. Therefore she'd better get ready for what eventually turned out to be twenty-eight people. By about twelve thirty, we had been fed hot coffee, scrambled eggs and cakes. Mrs. Pakrul already had in the oven two or three big trays of cake. The storm carried on all afternoon and it kept rising in intensity. More stranded people were coming in all the time.

Some of the guys who were equipped for our winter weather, decided to band together and go out and check the cars. We were getting the reports from the radio that the snowmobilers were working their way out of Welland down to the West Side Road and by that time of night they were just at the Provincial Police Station. Well, there was another mile and a half or two miles to go before they got to this interchange and it's quite possible that there were people in the cars. Some of them may have been in their cars for close to nine hours by that point. There was a group of four of them who got dressed in their snowmobile outfits and insulated jackets and face visors and they tied themselves together with rope and out the door they went with a couple of hand-held spotlights. Within forty-five minutes, they brought back another six people. Some of them had virtually given up. Their gas tanks had run out, they had nothing to eat since morning and at this time of the evening after sitting in the extreme cold they figured that they were finished. Now when these people came into the house, they made me appreciate how lucky I had been to have arrived there when I did. Some of that group were actually in physical shock. One of the guys from St. Catharines refused to have anything to eat or drink. I'm sure he wasn't acting rationally. I don't think he knew that he was turning down coffee, cake and those high sugar things that we were trying to encourage him to take. He sat in the corner of the family room all night long, about four feet away from the heater, and never said a word. He never had anything to eat or drink until eight o'clock the next morning.

The evening proved to be very interesting. We watched an episode of Roots in the family room. We sat around in groups and told stories and compared notes and just had a great time. We played euchre, talked a lot, drank coffee and generally tried to get our minds off of what was going on outside. It was interesting to watch the nervous reaction of the smokers while the cigarettes were being depleted. I'm a smoker and I had no hesitation of going back to the butts when the big ones were finished and we smoked them down as fine as we could until there was no more tobacco to smoke. A chap who had been sleeping at the far end of the family room woke up about one o'clock in the morning and came over to join the group. He turned out to be a smoker. And when he pulled from his pocket a package of tobacco and cigarette papers, it was like a breath of fresh air had blown into the room. All the smokers were a bit nervous and uptight and were going through their withdrawal symptoms. At the sight of the tobacco our eyes began to twinkle and it seemed once again that life was worth living. It didn't take us long to go through that package of tobacco and we were left with some cigarette papers. Then we broke up the cigarette butts and rolled new cigarettes from these. You would take one puff and pass it to the smoker next to you and it would go around the circle of smokers. It was consumed before it got back to the starting point.

You could see the effect of the nicotine on our system. But from that point on the smokers were happy again, until we ran out. However by that time, some of the brave souls dressed up again early in the morning and decided to walk to the Dain City store. That's a couple of miles and it took them several hours to get back. But when they tumbled back into the house with their four cartons of cigarettes, a big cheer went up as if we hit the jackpot in Vegas. Everything was fine with the world again.

It was probably one of the most interesting nights I'd ever spent anywhere. I was fascinated by the stories that the truck drivers were telling. They're a great group of guys. We compared notes, told fish and hunting stories and soon we covered every continent in the world that night except Australia. We had nobody in the group who had ever been to Australia. I remember a story of a Livingstone Truck Company driver and his experiences in Algeria and in Ethiopia. Then this brought us to my experiences in East Africa and South Africa. Then that led to excursions into the Alps in Switzerland. From there we jumped to Afghanistan and then to the west coast of Canada; then into the North West Territories. Virtually every state south of the border was covered and it was like going on a convoy with these truck drivers through the night. Trying to get some sleep was the last thing on my mind. I was really charged up and enjoyed it immensely.

From the moment I left school that morning, the one thought that bothered me the most was that I knew that my wife had taken the two children and the dog shopping in Port Colborne. If I had known that the family was safe, I would have never tried to come through the storm. The thought that they were stranded on No. 3 Highway, no better prepared than I, had been gnawing at my guts and I think that's what kept the old Ford moving through the blizzard, trying to make it home. There was no way those little peanuts of mine could have survived without help if they had been stuck on No. 3 Highway.

I was finally able on that Friday afternoon, to get through to my father-in-law in Port Colborne. Then, I found out that my wife had smashed her car within the same half hour that I did. Fortunately no personal injuries were suffered by anybody in either of the accidents. I learned that she and the children and the dog were safe at my mother-in-laws. It was as if someone had lifted a ten ton concrete block from my shoulders. From that point on, I can honestly say I enjoyed the experience of the blizzard. Up until that point however, I kept fighting back the lump in my throat. It seems that the storm made me aware of my priorities in life.

Anybody who sits back and says "Well, what the hell, it was just a snowstorm", speaks from a position of total ignorance. Unless they've come to a situation in life where they've had a challenge thrown at them like this, they just don't appreciate how awesome and powerful nature can be. I was impressed with the responses of citizens throughout the course of that first night. The people in the Pakrul home came from all over the peninsula and from as far away as Goderich, North Bay and Windsor. So it wasn't a local clanish thing. It was a people thing, and people made it work.

My wife and I have over forty years combined driving and we've never had an accident. Never had a claim. We've driven throughout Europe, throughout Africa, throughout Canada and the States. We have driven through all kinds of conditions and suddenly within an hour our numbers came up. That's kind of a freaky thing in itself. The insurance company didn't raise the premium. The clients, at least of my insurance company, were not penalized for accidents during the blizzard.

On Saturday afternoon, a group went out ahead of us and made it. I went in the second group, and with borrowed apparel from Dan Pakrul, we slugged our way through the storm. We walked over the tractor trailers that must have been fourteen feet high, danced on the roof and went down the other side. It was the same tractor trailer that belonged to one of the truck drivers in the Pakrul home. He had returned after checking his vehicle that Saturday morning. He was clean shaven and really looked super. I asked him what hotel suite he had rented. He said he had stripped in the lee of the truck and had taken a snow bath. Can you imagine, in that raging blizzard, this hairy chested truck driver rubbing snow all over the top part of his body while singing an aria from an opera? I asked him what he used for underarm deodorant and he quickly snapped back that he slapped on a couple of handfuls of anti-freeze.

The walk to the pick-up point was something else again. I had a ski mask over my face but nothing to protect my eyes. I was forced to put my hand over my eyes and peek out between by gloved fingers. Even at that, some of those particles of snow managed to sand blast through and ping off my eye ball. The sensation was quite similar to having a wart burned off your hand with that electrical device in the doctor's office. A matter of fact, I couldn't help thinking this would be a good way to rid your nose of a big wart if you had one. Cover up your face and just let the wart stick out and have the snow sand blast it right off. At least it would be frozen. In any event the CBer's from the Port Colborne Club were waiting at the end of the glacier on No. 58 Highway and they ran us up to the Mall. We had a bowl of soup and arranged for a ride in a convoy that was being driven by another volunteer group in Port Colborne. He dropped me off at my mother-in-laws and for the following week we stayed with them.

We were lucky at our house in the country. The power had only gone off for a short time and we received no damage. My neighbour down the road, Joe Torkas, had borrowed a front end loader and he single handedly opened up our road by working on it for three days. The big equipment of course was designated for the major arteries and so it should be.

As far as preparations for another snowstorm are concerned, there are a few things that I am going to do. If I get at least a couple of hours notice, I'm staying home. If the wind is over two miles an hour, I'm staying right in my bed. I'm not going to fool around with mother nature. But seriously, I think a basic survival kit should contain candles and an empty tin can to insert the candle in. I think I'd stay away from alcohol because you might be tempted to go overboard. Have something to eat like chocolate bars and peanuts. I think blankets might be critical, or even better a two piece snowmobile suit. I will in fact make sure I do have one this year in my trunk. Butane lighters are a must. You know very well that when you're out hunting and your hands are cold, that matches are useless. Batteries that run a flashlight are certainly in order. With the candles I think you have a psychological advantage in that one light from it gives you a good feeling. The darkness can be frightening. I remember being in the bongo caves in South Africa and everything was darkened as part of the effect of the show and one tiny beam of light was generated and the audience was just aghast at the effect as it opened up the total expanse of the cave. I think a shovel and a broom should be top priorities. So very basically, if a person can remain warm and relatively calm and have a little bit of light, they're going to make out all right through a blizzard of this magnitude.

I was extremely interested in the reaction of our children, Rhonda, seven and Frankie, five. They thought the blizzard was fun. They loved it. They had no fear of it because of course they were safe and they're looking forward to the next one. Frankie is associating going to school in the winter time in Canada with having lots of holidays. So he wants to go to school so that he can stay home. That's his reasoning. Winters are fun according to them and that's the way we want them to think of it. It's like counting the lightning flashes over the lake during a severe thunder storm; something sent by God to be taken not in fear but as a show of nature. I think it's a healthy reaction.

So the next time one happens, I'd like about twelve hours notice so that I can get on United and fly south. I think the older generation has finally had it's come uppance. No more can they put us down by quoting the storm of such and such or the blizzard of such and such. This was the storm of all storms.

When you look back to the ice storm in March of 1976, then the blizzard this year, you can see some relationship. Without that ice storm, we would have been in a hell of a position during the blizzard. Mother nature did a tremendous pruning job of tree branches during the ice storm that would most surely have cut off power supplies throughout this region during the blizzard. Nature did us a favour with the ice storm. Then the blizzard forced us to sit up and really pay attention to nature. This is something we should be doing all the time.

Male, sixteen: I was at home most of the storm but my parents were trapped for two days where they worked. They had to sleep on boards.

Mrs. Pakrul

*"I think that God's message in this was that
we should realize that He has a say in our lives and
that we need to be more dependent on Him."*

A lot of the people who stayed here were very grateful afterwards. We had a lot of gifts given to us. In fact, I think we were really thanked more than we needed to be. Our experience taught us more than anything that we really aren't our own masters. I think that God's message in this was that we should realize that He has a say in our lives and that we need to be more dependent on Him.

I guess there's a message in everything that happens to us in our lives. I'm a Christian and I believe God directs my life and I believe everything that happens to me could be a message in some way but I don't think that it was a great omen. I think we should look at things like this and realize that we are not as self sufficient as we like to think we are.

The intensity of the wind and snow stand out in my mind. My husband works in Port Colborne and headed home that noon hour and he had to abandon his car on the highway. He has lived here all his life and because of the intensity of the wind and snow he became completely disoriented and turned around and was actually walking back towards Port Colborne. He came upon another car. There was someone in it who knew him and knew where he lived. Once they were turned around in the right direction, my husband and his friend just kept walking and I think they picked up someone else along the way whose car was also stranded. The three of them finally got into our house. They held on to one another as they walked. My youngest son was stranded in Welland.

I suppose a lot of people are going to be a little bit more resourceful around their homes and have alternate fuel supplies. I hear that many people are buying old wood burning stoves and gas stoves as an alternative to the electric furnace.

Mrs. G. Rossi

"It was weird — like driving in a pillow."

It was weird, like driving in a pillow and suddenly I saw this swirl in front of me and I realized it was a person standing like a ghost in the middle of the road. I smashed into the back of her car. I yelled out to the lady, "My God, you're in the middle of the road, someone could kill you." The lady had stopped because she couldn't see where she was going and she got out to have a look at what was ahead of her. In the meantime somebody stopped behind me. I don't think I could have made it out further into the country with my two children because my sense of direction was completely gone and I think many people felt that way during that blizzard.

I don't think any of us really knew what a blizzard was until we were caught in one.

After being excited about the lady getting out of her car, I proceeded to get out of mine, and I went to the chap behind me to see where we were and where we could get shelter. We didn't get home for five days.

When I get to be an old timer, I'm going to tell all about that blizzard of '77. How can a perfectly beautiful day turn into such a disaster — a total living hell in so short a time.

Mrs. Brown

*"I think that anytime people are frightened
they are much more friendly."*

I was up town at the bank thinking that I'd go and buy groceries, but I didn't. I came home. I'm very glad that I did.

I think we had a lot of fun. We had neighbours in and we watched TV and the kids played cards. We took a sleigh and we went to the store the next day. It was just like when I was a kid you know. I had fun!

I think that anytime people are frightened they are much more friendly. They kind of rely on each other. I think everybody was frightened. We are not accustomed to winters like that. We are not accustomed to the severe cold so we don't dress properly. We don't have the equipment to clean up the area in the fashion that we should.

Cameron Romaine

"We came upon two girls in the snowbank screaming."

We were in our car travelling from Port Colborne to Welland. We got involved in the pile up on the Forkes Road overpass. It was like a parking lot. I started in my car and when it stalled we entered another car. This person would drive about 2 miles per hour and we would proceed in his car and go about 25 feet. Then his car would stall and we all got out of that one and moved into another. I think we were in five cars and then finally we came to the empty bus and we piled into it.

We lost about two or three hours on the bus and people began to realize that they didn't want to stay there. There were college kids on the bus from Niagara College. They were wearing those little jean jackets. They had no hats, gloves or boots. I really felt sorry for them. They looked like they were ready to go to Florida. There was one youngster, a teenager whose skin was purple and his shaking was out of control. It was quite sickening just looking at him.

At first, people were moving around, talking and trying to keep warm. Gradually, they stopped moving. There was no activity. Then there was silence. It was serious.

We finally got out of the bus and started working our way down Forkes Road. One lady kept falling and we had to stop and pick her up. She fell again and again until we were dragging her. We started to panic. When you can't breathe and you can't see, it's a scary scary feeling. It was on that walk that we came upon two girls who were in a snowbank screaming. They had been stranded in the car for a couple of hours and they got out of their car and couldn't see anything. They fell into the snowbank and remained their screaming and screaming. We dragged them out and pulled them with us. After walking for a while, I started to have a feeling that soon it was going to be every man for himself. Some people had lots of clothes and some had very few clothes and things were getting pretty serious. I'm glad we bumped into the trucks before it was survival of the fittest.

They were Bell Telephone and Cable T. V. vans. It was amazing that they were still running. It took us an hour to go one mile, from that point to the Dain City school.

There were lots of little kids there who had been stranded. The teachers kept them in one classroom.

Saturday morning was unpleasant because everyone was rather tense. It was still storming very badly. It seemed like we were going to be there for the rest of our lives.

The snowmobiles started to dribble in with suits and equipment and they began to take out the children one at a time.

It's really difficult for people who didn't live through it to understand how dreadful it really was. How you could be out in it and walk for five hundred yards and feel that you could not take another step. It felt as though you were going to turn frozen solid.

After I got home, I felt guilty as hell listening to all those disasters over the radio. Everything was fine with me. But what could I do? I wasn't supposed to use the phone. The neighbours were all fine. But I felt guilty about not being able to do something and I was left with this feeling for a long time afterwards. Other people confessed to this same feeling. That made me feel better about this guilty conscience.

Mr. Ginns, Bell Telephone Construction Foreman

"She kept screaming, "My husband, my husband!"

I guess we were a victim of the blizzard because we were working down on No. 3 Highway when the storm hit. It moved in pretty fast and I made a run for it to see if I could get my boys off the road because I had four large trucks and I was hopeful that we could make it through with them. We made it to McDonald's corner and were having a bit to eat when they announced that the restaurant would be closing in an hour. We decided to make a convoy thinking that if one us went into the ditch the other could help pull us back and so on. That way if we stayed together we'd be okay.

We got the convoy together which included at this point a TV truck and headed down No. 58 Highway going north to Welland. We were able to get as far as the Block Factory on the West Side and we got jammed in. There was a fender bender of an accident that started it all and the works just clogged up.

As I was parked there, the blowing wind came under the hood of my little truck. The motor stopped. I asked the big truck to push me into the ditch. This he did. Then we moved the big trucks back and forth, punching into the snowbanks — retracting then punching again. We were able to get as far as the entrance to Forkes Road.

This was about two o'clock in the afternoon. We proceeded down Forkes Road toward the old canal and we came upon these eighteen people walking on the road. They had left a bus that had been stranded. They couldn't see where they were going. But seeing the eighteen of them walking along in the blizzard with little suit jackets or windbreakers really flabergasted me. I took half of them and put them into the back of the TV truck and piled the other half into the big telephone truck. I had jumped out of the truck, opened up the door and said, "Push in, push in." I pushed them in as far as I could. I knew their own body heat would keep them warm when they were so close together. At least in the vans we had heaters, so it represented some kind of safety. I remember as we were pushing these people, there was this one little Italian guy. I'm sure he has a boot mark on his back where I had to put my foot and push him in order to get him over the mob. I gave him this tremendous shove with my boot and slammed the door shut. At least we were able to get them all over to the school and God only knows what would have happened to them because they were heading down the highway into the marsh. I'm sure they would have fallen asleep or frozen along the side of the road.

Another episode along the road was finding this woman who was hysterical. She was really concerned because she kept screaming, "My husband, my husband!" Apparently the husband had gone off looking for someone. And she wasn't about to get into the safety of the trucks. I said if you don't come now, you'll be in the same place as your husband. "Forget him! Get in!"

I remember a car blocking the road with four guys sitting in it. We told them to get over to the side and we would blast open the snowbank with the big trucks. So we got them out and pushed them over and started to blast through. I'll be a son of a gun if he doesn't move his car back onto the road. I had my eight fellows there and we jumped out and moved them off again to the side and sure enough he moved right back in front of us. Finally we ditched him. We left him there with the three other fellows sitting in that car. Not one of them was willing to get out and help. All they were doing was obstructing the road. The funny thing is that time plays such an important part in this. Each time we piddled around trying to get his guy off the road, we wasted of couple of precious minutes and that was a critical factor. I don't understand their thinking. Maybe they were in no condition to understand what was really happening.

I remember stepping out of the truck at one point and the blizzard winds grabbed my hard hat and took it flying. It was white. I couldn't see where it landed. When the snow started to melt, I kept looking for that hat. It's still out there somewhere.

We started the convoys up again and got going down Forkes Road. A couple hundred yards down Forkes Road my van truck stopped. It broke down. We took the people out of there and stuck them in the back of one of our big line trucks. I remember one woman. She must have been sixty years of age and well over two hundred pounds. We couldn't get her in the back of the truck. So we hoisted her up in the front of the truck and from there on we were able to travel down Forkes Road and get into Bridgeview School. That's where we spent Friday night and Saturday until the afternoon, when I was able to walk out. We were down to one truck by the time we got to the school. One truck that was working that is. The TV truck gave out just at the bridge. We hooked onto him and pulled him the rest of the distance right up to the school yard. Then the big truck gave out too. Then there were no vehicles operating, but we got everybody safe into the school.

I can remember that we passed a couple with a small infant. They had been in a van. We offered them the comfort of our truck because it was still running. They turned down the invitation because they said the road would open up a bit. We couldn't force them of course. Half an hour later, while we were still jockeying the vehicles around, I recognized this man, woman and baby of a couple months. They were walking back up the West Side Road towards Welland. There's not a damn thing there for the next few miles. We talked them into turning around and if they were going to walk anywhere, we suggested the Forkes Road. We knew there were a couple of houses there. Apparently they made out all right because we didn't hear of any deaths along there.

I can't say enough about the people at Bridgeview School. When we walked in there, they had coffee, soup and hotdogs from their kitchen. They had the place running ship-shape. They really had everything under control. They had a telephone for calling in, a telephone for calling out, and they kept it organized that way.

The thing that really amazed me was the children in that school. I don't know how many there were but those kids made no noise at all. You wouldn't know they were even around. They went to bed a certain time. When they had to walk down to the toilet, the teacher was with them mind you. The kids were kept in their own classrooms and we never heard a peep out of them. I was amazed at that.

Our gang was sitting around and we asked, "Where are the kids?" They said that the kids were to bed. Funny part of it was that you'd hear the teacher say "Get into that sleeping bag. Get underneath those blankets." All of a sudden you'd hear somebody say, "Miss Smith, Miss Smith" and then you'd see a little kid hanging on to the teacher's hand going down to the washroom. It was cute to see.

When I got up in the morning, I walked around and felt like a sore thumb. I looked into this one room and there was a whole bunch of little kids sitting around small tables having their breakfast with not a peep out of them. God they were well behaved. That is the first thing that I mentioned to my wife when I got home.

I remember on the convoy trip, walking over a snowbank and stepping right into a guy's open window of his car. You couldn't stop for a minute because the drift would pile up underneath your car and then kill the engine. You had to keep going. One person I was concerned about was this chap who was driving the bus. He must have been between sixty and sixty-five years of age. When we got him to the school he was white and his face, ears and hands were frozen. We wrapped him in blankets and set him beside the radiator with a sixty-five year old woman. Her two hundred pounds presented quite a problem when we were packing her into the truck. They thawed out in a few hours and then seemed to be okay.

Mrs. Krueger

"Then he dug his way down through the blankets and sheets and into the mattress."

My husband called our neighbour on the Sunday and asked him to go over and let George out. George is our dog. When the neighbour arrived, he found George had no problem of getting in and out because the front door had blown open and it had been open all the time during the storm.

When we got home on Sunday, the snow had melted and there was water everywhere. The pipes in the upstairs of the home had frozen and when we got the water running again we proceeded to have hot showers coming out of the ceiling fixtures. Upstairs, we had cold water running out of the fixtures. We had water running everywhere because it was seeping out of the breaks in the pipes.

George managed to do a very interesting thing. As the winds whipped through the house and created huge snow drifts, George jumped up on the bed. This is something he had never done before. Then he dug his way down through the blankets and sheets and into the mattress. He dug into the mattress stuffing until he had a huge pile of fluff and into this he snuggled himself. In this way he protected himself from the freezing temperatures in the upper part of the house.

I guess animals know how to take care of themselves in a natural disaster. At least it makes you wonder, doesn't it?

Female, sixteen: I stayed home and played cards, and shovelled the driveway. I didn't listen to the radio very much but when I did, there were a lot of people asking stupid things. Like this one old lady phoned in and asked if they should set the clock back half an hour. In the middle of a blizzard she wanted to know if she should set her clock back.

Arnold Leslie

"It was a real mess, squirrel shit from one end of the house to the other."

We got socked in at work and I was stuck in the plant until noon Saturday. I stayed with a friend in Port Colborne for three days after that. My kids were out in Wainfleet and my wife was in Welland. Finally the wife got to Port Colborne on Sunday and we got her out to the kids by snowmobile on Tuesday. I bought a snowmobile on Tuesday morning and rode it home. I had to break an upstairs window to get into the house. I have a two and a half story house and the snow was right off the peak of the roof. Twenty-three feet off the peak of my house when I finally got home. Our road was closed for eight days.

This dog of mine is a beagle and it had been without food or water for five days. He was pretty well dehydrated when I got to him and we kept an eye on him for a couple of days but apparently he's as healthy as hell now.

He reacted a little funny when I came in from the inside. He was in an outside porch and it was buried. So I broke this window upstairs and I came down through the house to the dog. I think he felt that I had left him out on purpose and had just ignored him for five days. He seemed a little afraid of me at first whenever I'd come near him. But after we got him fattened up and got the water back into him, he was all right. He's two years old.

I got one of those one and half car garages here and it was completely demolished under the weight of the snow. It had a flat roof and there must have been six feet of snow on top of it and it just caved in.

I had a couple of squirrels running around inside the house when I got home. I've got one bad spot up in the eaves of my roof and they got in there somehow and I guess with nobody being in the house for four or five days they figured this was home for the winter. They made themselves right at home. It was a real mess, squirrel shit from one end of the house to the other. One of the guys that I had met had heard about my dog being locked up and he came down here trying to get him out but he didn't want to break any windows so he couldn't help the dog. While he was here though, he looked in the window and he said he saw these squirrels running around on a big spinning wheel that's in my living room. They were having a ball. I had to chase these squirrels around the house with a hammer. Me and the other guy finally got them. We had to kill two of them and we found another one outside in the eavestrough. It apparently died from rat poisoning that I had used to get rid of a rat. We killed the squirrels right in the living room. We were chasing them around the house and we couldn't get them out. We smashed them with a hammer. My wife wasn't too happy about that.

My neighbour called into the radio station. He described the conditions of the homes near him when it suddenly dawned on me that it was my home that he was talking about. I thought maybe the story was a little far fetched. When I got home, all I could see was my chimney.

Any old timer who tells me he can remember a worse storm is going to have to look at my pictures.

Male, seventeen: After the storm, we finally got the car started and we were able to drive around the corner and we ran out of gas. Oh well.

Dave Brown - CB'er

"Look for such things as ledges where you can set an antenna, a post that might do as an anchor, or a chain link fence."

I was at work and in the early afternoon my boss said that I should go home. At the corner of Quaker Road and South Pelham I had to stop and help several cars out of the way. I had to contend with a truck that was stuck and blocking the better part of the road too.

I was lucky to get my car off the road. It stayed there for several days. I listened to certain broadcasts - the police and one or two other stations that I could get. It was on a special short wave receiver, a public service monitor. We also have a CB so that we were monitoring that as well.

Everybody and his brother was on the air giving information on what was happening so that you had a good idea that it was getting pretty rough outside. I normally stay off as much as possible and because of the heavy traffic relating to the road conditions, I made it a point to stay off the air.

I went to bed and it wasn't until morning when it was still blowing pretty bad that I realized it was a little worse than anyone ever expected. I made sure they knew that I was standing by ready to help. My equipment was available. We were talking to a local Ontario Provincial Police officer who was licensed on GRS and he asked if I would mind going into Regional Niagara. I told him I might have trouble getting there but they arranged a pick-up for me. So I grabbed what I figured I'd probably need which was the radio-a marine type antenna, some cable or lead in and a tool box. I might need this for an emergency repair. I took my sleeping bag as well and I got a

CB people lend a hand. Welland. Tribune photo.

ride out to the Regional Base Station.

I was taken into a general information area where I met a stock room clerk from Canadian Tire. He seemed to know what was going on. He was in charge of the maintenance, servicing the snowmobiles that were working out of the Niagara Regional Base.

We tried to organize the antenna to be fairly high up so that we could get a half way decent range. I went upstairs in the Criminal Investigation Branch and the antenna was put out through a window between the screen and the edge of the frame. The antenna was about nine feet long. It's a marine type antenna designed for use on a boat. That's one reason why I took that particular antenna. I figured an ordinary antenna would be awkward. I could have easily made up an antenna but there are certain characteristics with different antennas which will make a difference between the station getting you or not. That's kind of technical. In any event, Officer Smart would take the information which I was receiving and act on it accordingly. I remember hearing about the big earth remover which dug into a snow drift and came out and up with a small sports car dangling from the bucket.

I was on CB channel nine which is generally considered the emergency channel. The party that I worked with mostly had a handle of "Poncho". My antenna was stuck in a snowbank outside on a lower platform. It was too close to the building which meant that the matching on the antenna to the set was very poor. The result was that I wasn't getting any fantastic range. That is why I worked through another station which is a good procedure anyway.

There were groups on other channels also. There was a group on eighteen, there was a group on six, the hospital base is on channel one. I understand that there was a base station at the OPP and there was also one at the Fonthill Fire Department that had the snowmobilers working out of there.

The requests were mainly for food or general information on road conditions. Some of the vehicles that were sent out from Regional Niagara had CB equipment on board and were monitored by us. If they got out of range we had to arrange with Poncho who slipped down to another channel and stayed in touch with his extra power. We were following a convoy and we found out when they arrived safely and then we'd advise them on their way back. Many roads were closed of course and those vehicles that were permitted to travel were only allowed to do so in pairs. This made it kind of awkward to control and this is where the CB helped.

We did have a number of requests for information pertaining to the roads and we would just say they were closed or bad. Stay at home. I know there was one party out on Forkes Road who was equipped with CB's and the guy was in Welland and his wife and kids were out at the house along with the dogs. They have a dog kennel out there. Information was relayed to us that they were running low on food and needed help. By that time, we were getting coordinated enough that we were getting phone numbers and names so that police could call back and confirm just what was needed and what the situation was. There were a lot of calls that were coming in via CHOW radio that were received by some of the CB'ers and relayed to us by a CB. Some of the information was not always accurate and the result was that it was causing problems.

The army of course, came in. There wasn't too much by way of food or cooking facilities at the police station—just a hotplate. Doesn't mean we weren't getting half decent meals—we did. We had a concoction of beans, ham and wieners and just a matter of what they could get together. One of the office girls was looking after that end of it.

I was operating a CB unit that actually is referred to as a GRS in Canada, General Radio Service to be exact. It was a six channel transceiver, an old tube set that I first started out with. I chose the tube type set rather than the transistor for the simple reason that it's more rugged—it would take any abuse that I could feed to the transmitter and I was throwing a fairly severe miss match into it which means that I was losing a good part of my power in the miss match. The fact that my antenna wasn't overly high, restricted my range. It was this reason mainly, that I was working through Poncho. He had the base station. He had a good strong set-up. So this helped a lot.

That was about seven thirty Saturday morning when I set up. I spent the night at the police station rather than come home. There was a base station in Welland and a lady there came over and relieved me between eleven and two in the afternoon. She was called Cornflower and most of us go by a nick name or skip or handle.

Sleeping quarters consisted of one of the little interrogation rooms off the main offices. The first night I had a sleeping bag spread out on the floor. I was used to this from my camping experiences. Sunday, things weren't too busy until around nine o'clock when they began to pick up. The army moved in that morning and it was suggested that it might be better to move down closer to the army officer.

The main reason I had gone upstairs in the first place was to get the antenna to a different location—a good location up fairly high where I could feed it, rather than down off the snowbank at the side of the building. I went down and re-arranged the location so I was downstairs where the main co-ordinating occurred. Downstairs I had a better idea of what was going on. I was able to communicate directly with the officer involved and it worked out a lot better.

The Armed Forces were also there and they were co-ordinating right from that general area. They moved in some gas stoves and started cooking fairly heavily for their personnel. It was at that time that I got a little better scope into what was going on with regards to snowmobiles, four wheel drive operators and so on. I knew that when they needed parts they called that young fellow from Canadian Tire and snowmobiles would deliver the goods and repairs were made right on the spot.

I remember one emergency call. It was an accident and someone was hurt badly. The information was sketchy. Two snowmobiles and a four wheel drive operator thoroughly checked the region. They could find no accident. It was a false alarm. It was a frustrating experience.

Later on, arrangements were made for a chap by the name of Jack Sibbit, an amateur radio operator, to get out to CHOW radio. We had him transported by snowmobile to the radio station and we transferred another fellow by the name of Dennis Dubois to the central firehall. They did a good job. We passed a lot of information down to the amateurs in St. Catharines who made local phone calls concerning stranded people. This relieved a lot of the anxiety.

The amateur radio is different from the GRS in many respects. One, by the number of different frequencies that are available to amateurs. Some of them like the two meter amateur, which is up in the police frequency at one forty seven megacycles. Therefore, you could have a small one and a half watt walkie talkie sitting in the police station and because of the repeaters that we have, which the GRS cannot use, we can have the equivalent in this case of an eighty watt transmitter with an extremely high antenna. Consequently you can get almost anywhere in the Niagara Peninsula. I have heard stations from as far away as Orangeville, London and Toronto getting into the repeater.

Out of this could come some advice from amateur radio operators or CBs or GRS—whatever you want to call them for future emergencies. First of all, I think the amateurs will put down GRS operators but they're the first to admit that they do serve the purpose by their sheer number. And the numbers of mobile units and portables have to be a factor that we should consider. I think what would have been an ideal situation would be for the amateurs in the Welland area to have a base station at the police station or the fire station or the mayor's office or at CHOW. We could do the same with Port Colborne, Dunnville, Fort Erie or wherever there is a need to handle inter city traffic. We could get the police chief, for example in touch with CHOW, so he could make a direct broadcast by the amateur radio to the amateur circuits. The GRS boys can handle a lot of routine traffic and this is good because of their sheer numbers. I'm not saying that the amateurs can't handle some of the other stuff, some of the routine traffic, because I think there is a place for that too. The channels are clear and that is why I suggest the main centers of communication be connected by amateur. You don't have the masses and you've got a lot clearer communication and more power. You have the ability to get out better.

When I got down to the police station, I should have taken a walk around the outside of the building and checked the situation. I think that's the first thing for anybody to do, if you're setting up in an emergency situation. Set your equipment down and take a walk. Look for such things as ledges where you can set an antenna, a post that might do as an anchor, or a chain link fence. When I collected my equipment at the end of the storm I found such a fence. We normally like to use a steel post as an anchor. Now if you can put up a good high antenna on a steel pipe and you've got something to which you can anchor this pipe, it's a simple matter of a couple of turns of wire and you get the thing up in a hurry. The important thing is you have to have something to anchor—a good solid support for the pipe. Apart from that, the height is important too. The greater the height, the greater the range of your transmitter.

If I had walked around, I would have discovered there was an aluminum ladder in the utility storage area at the back of the police station. I didn't know about it at the time. So I suggest that a person move slowly and think. The aluminum ladder for example could have served two purposes: it could have gotten me up on the roof where I could have put the antenna and got it much higher or it could also serve as a tower for an antenna system by itself. By fastening it to the chain link fence, or using a rope and fastening it between two police cruisers, or cars or whatever as an anchor point for guide ropes for the tower. Then I could have come down from there with another type of antenna and anchored it say to the building. I could have used it as a form of tower.

A little more co-ordination could have been had in the use of the different channels. There were a number of people who were up extremely late—a lot later than necessary and there was a lot of traffic handled that I don't think needed to be handled. Messages and requests were handled on a number of different channels and the result was duplication. When you get duplication you get confusion. So I think a little more co-ordination could have helped.

At the time of the emergency, the GRS operators could have been more co-ordinated and could have produced a greater effort then they did. If they had a better idea on proper communications procedures, that would have helped. I think there should be two or three base stations, but only one of them should be active at any given time. The advantage of having two or three stations is that should someone have to leave the one channel, another could pick up and the fellow posted there could keep the communications moving. It would lead to a much more co-ordinated effort and in an emergency that's what we want and that's what we want fast.

CB'ers

People used to complain about the CB'ers before the blizzard. Then they helped so many people during the storm that I haven't heard any complaints about them since.

John Marsh

"We put the ladder up and that's how we got out of our house."

Saturday noon the storm hadn't dropped and you really couldn't see at all. I decided to try and go out as far as the car. My wife had some groceries in the car and we thought that we should try to get them inside. I was really looking to see if I could find the car at the end of the property and of course the car was buried. We sunk a

What summer cottages? Courtesy Betty Leslie, Wainfleet.

couple of exploratory tunnels and finally hit the car.

Just trying to get out of the house was an interesting problem because we had a tremendous amount of snow. All Dad's windows were sealed for the air conditioning and all his doors opened out and you couldn't open any of the doors and you couldn't open the windows. The only door we could open was the one in his basement. It was solid right up as far as you could see. So we got a step ladder and a shovel and started the tunnel up. We had the tunnel up a good six feet from the top of the door sill when we broke through and we put the ladder up and that's how we got out of the house. That's how we brought the groceries back into the house.

We got through to our dog on Sunday. She was in the kennel outside and the kennel is six feet high. The snow was over the top of the wire and there was no dog in sight. We shouted for her and could see just a little hole in the snow. We hollered down the little hole and Christ — one little paw came up and then the other paw came up and the paws started to go like hell and the dog popped out. So she'd been okay.

We got into our house with very little difficulty. Lost our electricity on Monday and we were without power for twenty four hours and again no real problem because we were well insulated.

One of our business associates tried to reach our place. He also lives along the Lakeshore. He got as far as Cedar Crest and got stuck and thought since he wasn't that far from my place he would try to walk in. He got down into the gully and got totally disoriented and he tells of stumbling off into the woods. He had no idea where he was and he actually stumbled across the road and didn't realize that he was on the road until he tripped on the top of the green mailbox. If it hadn't been for that, the poor guy would have wandered into the woods and right into the swamp. He found his car, got warm for a while then came back and followed the fence line into the subdivision there. He was frostbitten. When we finally got out on Tuesday we could literally walk on the snow at the front of our house right over the roof of our house.

In the farm itself, where our tennis court is, you could walk right over the top of the fencing there and that's fifteen feet high. We had to replace the fencing around the court because the weight of the snow eventually collapsed the whole thing. Half of the barn collapsed. At Dad's place he had a drift that was estimated at forty feet and I don't feel that's any exaggeration because I know the white birch trees there are a good thirty feet high and it was well above those trees. You looked down on top of the house from the snow. That was the snow drift that remained here until the first of June.

The horses in the barn didn't have any great difficulty because they had an automatic watering system. They were shut in until Sunday noon. When the storm abated for that hour or two it was like being in the eye of a hurricane. We got down within the hour and checked the horses over and saw that they were all right and left.

The children thought it was the greatest thing! We had a hell of a time keeping them off the roof of the house. The kids thought it was just great to be able to walk up on the roof and scream and holler. The only way the Ontario Power could get in here was to fly their crew in by helicopter. That's how they finally repaired the lines. That was Tuesday and remember the storm started the Friday before.

Trying to open up the roads was another story in itself. First they tried with one of those big front end loaders. It couldn't touch it. They tried it with a large bulldozer. It couldn't do anything. Then they got a small bulldozer with a bucket on it and the driver spent two and a half days trying to punch through from the Lakeshore Road to our place and that's only about three hundred yards. There were eleven houses on the strip and we all split the cost of that two and half day operation.

The power was off for twenty four hours but that was good fun. We brought in all kinds of wood although the first night we couldn't get out of the damn house to get wood and that was a bit of a problem. When the power went off on Monday, the storm was still blowing so badly that you really couldn't get out to get any wood. But come Tuesday morning it had abated and we got out and we brought a lot more wood in and ended up with the fireplace going. We cooked in the fireplace and made tea and coffee in the fireplace and there was really no hardship at all there. We managed to keep the house at about fifty degrees, so while not warm, it was certainly comfortable. The pipes didn't freeze or anything. But boy, the wind whipping off the lake was something to behold. If you came inland two hundred yards it seemed like it wasn't even the same storm.

I think to better prepare ourselves for another storm like that, I think we're going to keep a four or five day supply of canned food in the house. That's really the big thing I suppose. For Christ's sake, never go out wandering for any reason. There's just no way that you can walk around in a thing like that. You couldn't see twenty feet from the house. I know, for example, that at Dad's place there was a bird feeder that is exactly ten feet from his window and you could not see that bird feeder during the height of the storm.

In digging for the car we sunk these exploratory tunnels. I still got the shovel marks on the roof of the car to show where we hit it.

Our dog surprised me the most. She had been outside for that length of time - about two days and she was able to cocoon herself right inside a snowbank. There's no wind in there and there must have been a temperature of thirty two degrees. But she survived through this instinct. She knew what to do. As a matter of fact, this may be a strange comment but there appears to be a tremendous number of young rabbits and chipmunks and squirrels around this year. There is no less wildlife because of the blizzard. Maybe the animals realized they couldn't do anything else but stay inside and multiply. As a human, I knew I had a very cosy feeling. Actually, it was a pretty exciting thing. Even during the height of it, the feeling was one of disbelief that this could actually happen in our area.

CJRN - Niagara Falls
Bob O'Brien - Operation Anti-Freeze

"Awaiting him were the very sharp teeth of a large German Shepherd dog which proceeded to tear the ass out of his snowmobile suit."

Operation Anti-Freeze was set up years ago and it is a system which allows fifteen minutes of news followed by fifteen minutes of phone calls. By screening the calls we can eliminate a lot of repetition and consequently be more effective with our radio audience. We put the system into effect during the blizzard and soon we had 25 people processing the calls about missing children, parents and buses as well as school and plant closings and all those worrisome questions which arise in an emergency. The operation lasted 90 hours.

We had snowmobiles and four wheel drive vehicles lined up on the street in front of CJRN. These people were able to respond to emergency calls which we received on our twenty phone lines. What made the system most effective was that listeners would phone in and offer food, shelter and clothing to those in need. We then could pick up and deliver food and people and by everyone working together we created a very effective tool for assisting those who were in trouble.

Rick Generet happened to mention on the air that the drivers were spending their own money on gasoline. Rick was paying these people a tribute which was well deserved. Within a half hour of that tribute, we had received one thousand dollars in donations towards the expenses of the rescue workers and that soon climbed to over ten thousand dollars. Most interesting is that ninety percent of the contributors did not want their names mentioned on the air. One fellow made a large contribution because he had been struggling against the wind and driving snow and one of the snowmobilers gave him a ride to and from the store—the liquor store. "He saved me!" the man kept repeating as he turned over his contribution to the fund.

One young man was compensated out of the fund for his slashed snowmobile suit. The weather was so bad that the only way that he could tell where he was going was to read the numbers of the electrical tower coordinates. Eventually he struggled through to the residence of an 87 year old woman whose house was almost buried in snow. The young rescuer dug down through the snow drifts and he had to force open the door to the old lady's home. Awaiting him were the very sharp teeth of a large German Shepherd dog which proceeded to tear the ass out of his snowmobile suit. Eventually the dog was brought under control and the lady was moved to safety.

Another man phoned us from Stevensville where he had sought shelter at the first house that had a light shining on the porch. The man asked his mother not to worry about him because he was safe in the company of five women and a neutered dog.

I felt sorry for another snowmobiler who answered an emergency call for bread. He risked his life to make the delivery and when he turned the food over to the lady at her door she exclaimed, "What the hell, I don't like Italian bread."

I was impressed with the CB'ers and how quickly they co-ordinated and fed information to us and the police. They did a great job.

Denise Harris, President, Niagara REACT

"There would often be 25 snowmobilers responding to one request for assistance."

My base was the cordinating headquarters for the whole area. We had four wheel drives and snowmobiles and we worked with the different authorities from Beamsville through to Fort Erie and across the border into the United States. We worked with the American Niagara Frontier REACT and Central Niagara County REACT. When there were Canadians stranded on the American side and Americans stranded in Canada we exchanged people at the border and took them home when possible. When an ambulance couldn't get through to sick people we brought these people to the ambulance. We evacuated people from their homes when there was no electricity or heat. Many people had their water pipes frozen and we got those people into shelters.

We discovered at 3 a.m. that there was a bus load of children from Buffalo stranded on the Niagara River Parkway and with the help of the police and a very large snow plow from Queenston, we got through to the kids. We kept CJRN Radio posted so that they could report to their listeners because they were concerned about stranded people and especially kids.

All REACT members have standard first aid training and we are associate members of St. Johns Ambulance and they are associate members of REACT. This makes sense because we are all concerned with helping people.

We learned that when an emergency call went out over the radio, there would often be 25 snowmobilers responding to one request for assistance. This was a wasted effort. The radio stations did not intend to get into this type of situation, it just happened. To avoid duplication in future emergencies, the various organizations which can help people, must draw up a master plan in advance and work from it.

Klaus Peter Weyers

"I've seen blizzards in Austria and Switzerland where I go skiing. But they never hit that fast."

I'm an exchange student from Germany. I've seen blizzards in Austria and Switzerland where I go skiing but they never hit that fast. I never experienced such extreme wind chill, down to -68° F and the wind was incredible too.

After the blizzard I went through Port Colborne, especially to the lake and it was amazing, up to 30 foot drifts. Incredible!

The storm was on T.V. and radio all over Europe and a couple of weeks later I received some newspapers which my parents sent to me and on the front page there were big headlines: "Blizzard hits North America, houses under snow, people in emergencies, no water, no food."

We had the radio on day and night. They warned of food and water shortages so we put water in the bathtub and in pots in case we would have really run out of water. We were lucky. No pipelines in our area broke or froze. We didn't have any shortages of food or power at all

After the blizzard was over, you could buy T-shirts and drinking glasses in the U..S.A. which had written on them, "I survived the blizzard of '77." That was quite interesting, because I wouldn't expect that would happen in Europe after a catastrophe, making money from things like that is typically American. I didn't see it in Canada.

Lake Erie surprised me to be frozen over. It's a real lake compared to the European Lakes - much, much greater. I have never seen a European lake totally frozen.

Female, sixteen: The night before the storm broke out we went to New York City and we were stuck there for a couple of days. We left on Tuesday and we were stuck until Wednesday of the next week. When we got to the Airport in New York we saw that the flight to Buffalo was cancelled. We thought we were going to have to sleep in the airport, but we didn't. We didn't have much money, but the airport paid for our hotel and food. It was nice in New York, about 40°. We then flew into Toronto and it was nice there too.

Rick Dolphin

"Some youngsters were whizzing around in shopping carts."

I was stranded in the Seaway Mall but things weren't all that bad, in fact, things were pretty good. I was dropped off at the mall by a friend on Friday. All I wanted to do was to get to the bank and then take a bus home. Ha! Some wish!

"Welland transit wishes to announce that the bus service has been discontinued until visibility is better." Great! Who could blame them? Looking through the front doors of the mall was like trying to see through a glass of milk. Vicious rumor had it that the storm would keep up for four days.

Then came the one p.m. announcement. "The stores in the mall will be closing at two p.m." Slowly, brave people with cars ventured into the wasteland outside. Then they returned, ruddy faced, shivering and swearing, to stand inside, gazing aimlessly through the glass doors.

The lights in the store started to blink off and the people began to thin out. Those of us who were left, either through lack of transportation, motivation or guts, talked to each other about the pile-ups we heard about, and of course, the weather.

Luckily the billiard hall, a couple of coffee shops and a restaurant were open to serve the captive consumers. But boredom reigned supreme that long afternoon.

Little groups of humanity were clustered here and there; some playing cards, some chatting, some youngsters were whizzing around in shopping carts, and others sat in the Fountainbleau Family Restaurant. As the evening drew on, and it seemed that a hundred or so of us had been abandoned by the civilized world, more and more thirsty souls found comfort in the beverages offered by the Fountainbleau.

The general mood of the inmates had gradually changed from one of frustration and annoyance to cheerful resignation, partly because most people had contacted their families, established their safety and then discovered liquid enlightenment. The manager of the restaurant kept his establishment open until one a.m. and opened again Saturday morning to serve breakfast. He also provided, free of charge, coffee, tea and sandwiches of brown toast.

"We gotta be nuts to be out here", the manager said. We all appreciated his brand of insanity. Dave Walton, the manager of Miracle Food Mart, should be commended for opening his store to provide the food for toast, sandwiches, and bar-b-cued chicken. It was delicious.

There was a cross section of Welland society at the mall; young, old, businessmen, housewives, managers and floor-sweepers. And they all got along well, these different people in the same predicament.

D'Arcy McHayle, stranded Niagara College Theatre Arts teacher said that he had met a whole lot of people who really were having a great time. "People are at their best . . . you enjoy the people and the situation." D'Arcy was seen dashing around the mall in a fetching afro wig, lent to him by a hair dresser.

It soon became apparent that we would be there for the night.

Mike Hogan - Canadian Theatre Group - Welland

"So we converted it into a bathtub and lots of people used it."

On the Friday night, with the help of a couple of other people in the mall we were able to set up lodging here and we brought in food and cooked it for a couple days. We had people sleeping in the theatre for four days. We made do with the carpet mats on Friday night. We were able to get a hold of some foam rubber from Woolco. It wasn't the classiest hotel in town, but it was the best one going at the time. We had snowmobilers bring in blankets and sleeping bags for Saturday night.

On the Friday night, there was a captive audience in the Seaway Mall. I made the announcement that there would be a free showing of each movie. You had a choice; Clint Eastwood "The Enforcer" or Led Zepplin "The Song Remains The Same". I forget exactly the time that we put it on but it was later on in the evening, before everyone decided it was time to get to sleep. At that time we knew we weren't going anywhere. People started to make plans to sleep in the theatre, after the movies.

On the Saturday and Sunday we set up a bathtub for the women who wanted to take a bath. We had a big plastic container like they use in the hospital for linen. It was delivered here when we opened the theatre but it had never been used. So we converted it into a bathtub and lots of people used it.

Hiroshi Kinju - Japanese Exchange Student

"The first time when I saw snow falling down I was trying to catch and eat. I wondered if anybody scattered the cotton."

I come from a very small island in Japan. I never saw the snow before. I saw the picture of snow and the ice, when the snow become ice but I never saw the snow. The first time when I saw snow falling down I was trying to catch and eat. I wondered if anybody scattered the cotton. I didn't think that was snow. I just wondered, "What's this?" I heard of the snow in many books. I can imagine the rain falling down so fast, but snow is slowly and I couldn't imagine!

We had bad storm. Many people say so, but I like that. During the storm I wanted more like that. My house mother was home. My house father was not home at the time and my house mother was worried about him. I don't care like that. I like snow and I just wanted more snow.

I didn't know that sometimes people died by the snow. The snow covered my house. House has two floors but our house was completely covered in snow. Except the top of the roof. That was not covered. We had to dig to get out of house. And we used the saw to cut down the snow in little blicks. That's hard work, I didn't like that! I like the snow but I didn't like the snow shovel. It took a few weeks or more to saw all those blicks of snow out. The first door is completely covered with snow, the downstairs door. We have the kitchen on the second floor and the kitchen door was not covered with snow so we used that door. We have to shovel the snow downstairs because if the snow melts, the water come into the house. We have electricity all the time and we have lots of food. But some neighbours didn't have enough food and we have to take to them some food. Some neighbours came over our house and sleep over for nights. During storm we were watching TV. Oh yes, people helping each other, I think this is very nice. I did not want to ride on snowmobile in the snow. This is the biggest thing for my family in Japan because they never see snow. I took about 200 pictures, all of snow.

My family in Japan saw the storm on the TV and they talked of Buffalo. They wonder and they worry about me and they called on the phone.

During the storm I took some groceries to my neighbours and that's all. I went out into the house of my neighbours and when I came to the house of mine I missed the house. I passed my driveway. It was covered with snow and I couldn't find my house. I was never afraid at any time.

I enjoyed the snow but I didn't like the cold too well. It was good experience. But I don't want to live where you have snow like this every year. I don't want to live. But I like to visit. I want to come back after graduating from university.

My island is sub-tropical, always summer. It was quite different for me but I heard before about the snow. Before I came here I met two girls who were the exchange students. They were here last year. You know Chimi and Mikie? I met them and they say they have ice storm when they were here. They say it was very cold. You know, I live on the island and it is sub-tropical and I worry because Canada is so cold. I find it cold a little but not too much. I like cold too but I like hot better.

After I go to Japan I will miss my friends over here. I miss my family back home in Japan too. I have one brother who is older and one brother who is younger. I have no sisters. I always fight with them, especially my older, he always hit me. I hit my younger brother and he tell to my older brother and it comes back.

I couldn't speak English when I came here. I studied English in Japan, grammar and reading but they didn't teach the total speaking. When I came here I couldn't hear what the people saying, I couldn't recognize the words, I just hear ya, ya, ya, ya, ya. I couldn't understand. I didn't speak too much you know. I think I speak more my English when I get back to Japan. But I will lose it again I think. I have to keep my English. I am very glad to have met this winter. Most people say this was the worst winter and I am very glad to catch this winter.

I am very glad to catch this visit to Canada too. People over here are completely different than people in Japan. Here everybody speaks to each other but in Japan there are two people and they always meet in the bus all the time through the year but they don't speak. They just sit in the bus and never speak. They speak to their friends but they don't speak to everybody. Only people they know. Over here the people are very friendly. I like these people and I wish Japan's people were like here. If they like that I can make more friends. I don't speak too much.

I very scared this first year I came here but I am glad that I came. You know in Japan the students have to take the English, they have to take it in school. In the high school they taught six years English. They studied but they can't speak English. Just like the French here. If I didn't come here, I never speak English.

Tatsuya Matsura

"So my hair became freezing."

My name is Tatsuya Matsura. I come from Japan. I am an exchange student on International Fellowship. At first I surprised of snow storm in Canada. Because in my city is too hot. We seldom see snow in Japan. During the storm I was too boring, because just stay home and listen to records and play the billiards and play cards. So we couldn't take training, jogging or somethings like that. So just gained weight and that's not good. And one day during the storm I went to a party, it's like a crazy party, 20 or 25 guys and girls get on the back of the truck and sing madly and go to the church or some house and say Merry Christmas. Some lady and man drank wine. But we couldn't drink the wine. So I became too cold, freezing. I have a problem of the hair and skin because it's too cold so my hair became freezing so I needed a hair conditioner and medicine for the skin too.

I did the push up and sit up and something like that. Only in winter time I jog 2 miles in the day. In the summer I do not jog because of the swimming. I went out and not friendly outside; too cold. Everyone stay home. I shovel snow. It's hard work but was good training you know.

The water is frozen in the house during the storm. We went to the neighbours and take the water to our house in the bucket.

I brought some clothes from Japan for winter. But it doesn't work. The winter jackets, it doesn't work. Too cold. In Japan the winter is not cold. I do not like the cold. I get sick two times in nine months. In Japan I never had a cold in 10 years. I healthy you know.

People in Japan are quieter. They don't talk as much. In the morning they go to the railroad and sit in the crowd. They never talk to each other. They never say anything about the weather or anything like that.

What I am wonder is every winter you have snow, on the ground. So, what the farmer do in the winter time? Is he free of the farm?

Male, nineteen: There were a lot of crazy things that happened. My friend was driving down Lakeshore, he wanted to see how bad it was. He was really crazy. He got stuck and a guy came out with one of the big bulldozers. My friend asked if he could pull him out and the guy said, "Yes." He pushed him into a snowbank and then he took off. Later when the garbage trucks were collecting garbage, they pulled my friend out.

The force of the wind finished this barn in Wainfleet. Courtesy of Inco. By Dino Iannandrea.

Rach Knoll

"I remember back to 1895 and there was never anything like this."

I remember back to 1895 and there was never anything like this. My personal experience was with my big barn. The wind broke the windows on the south side of the barn and since there were no openings on the north side, the wind blew the complete east side of the barn right out. Right to the ground. It took part of the roof with it.

I had a big copper kettle in there, a very large one, that was used in making apple sauce and it was flattened—I had a table saw and it broke the frame of that completely.

I had about ten feet of snow in the driveway and on my own home I had a bank of snow about twenty feet high. I shovelled through by hand in the driveway so that I could get through. In this storm, it's not only the snow but it's what happened afterwards. I lost about twenty big trees that just broke off. I was impressed with the co-operation. Everyone seemed to be so willing to help without looking for money.

On the other hand, I think it has created a lot of fear about calamities. It wasn't just the snow falling. There was the heavy wind that was bringing the snow off the frozen surface of the lake. That's why it came in clouds. You couldn't see anything. Because there was such a big area of the lake that the wind could sweep across, the snow came for miles and miles. It just dumped it here on this area. Soon as it hit the beach, the trees and the homes, the snow would pile up. Just a mile or two inland from the beach there was no snow in comparison to the lake shore.

I know the mice deep down under the snow survived all right. They chewed around the trunks of the trees, knawing all the bark off for their food. They had tunnels underneath the snow where they'd go from tree to tree and eat their little hearts out. It's fine for the little animals, but now the trees are dying so there's going to be a lot of work ahead to get things cleared up. For some reason or another there seems to be a lot more groundhogs around than I've seen for some time.

Mrs. Augustine

"So we had to pull the plug in the bottom of the tank and let the milk go down the drain."

I was at home on our farm here and everything went along pretty well. The power was off for thirty six hours but we have a generator that attaches behind the tractor so we made our own power for that time. We have to have something like this because of the milking that must be done. The cows have to be milked twice a day. If you miss a milking, you're in serious trouble with cattle.

The cattle also drink a lot of water which is pumped by electricity so my husband has this generator to hook up and switch on. It makes all the power that we need.

We have a milk storage tank in the barn. It holds two days milk and it was completely filled. It was time for the truck to come and pick it up. The truck couldn't get through so we had to pull the plug in the bottom of the tank and let the milk go down the drain. This was a financial loss of about two hundred and fifty dollars.

This may sound kind of silly but I just more or less sat and watched the storm and listened to the radio. My husband and I both have our amateur radio licenses. We were listening to that also and helping out whenever we could by getting emergency calls through from one place to another if a telephone wasn't working.

A ham radio is a little different from a citizen band. The set-up's quite a bit different too in that what we have here we can pretty well get through all over the place. Our range is greater while the citizen band radio is kind of limited as to distance. We found that the ham radio was very beneficial.

It's kind of amazing, when you look back, and wonder why there weren't more serious problems than there were. I know of one of our neighbours, just down the road from us, whose husband and her were both away and their children were home alone. The parents were brought home by helicopter because they were worried about their children.

I can't recall seeing my neighbours during the storm. Our phone only worked occasionaly so I really didn't call anybody because I had no reason to call out. I thought the best thing for us to do was to stay off the phone and leave it for anybody who needed it . . . . so I really felt as if we were rather isolated. I didn't feel any closer to my neighbours at all during the storm. I knew they were there and realized they might be having problems I didn't know about. But I couldn't do anything about it anyways. Maybe pray for them, which I certainly did, but I didn't feel close to them because I had no direct contact. I didn't feel scared at all during the storm; I had no fear.

When it was all over and they went out to have a walk, they came back to the house simply amazed. Cottages were covered completely and if you didn't know they were there before, you would never have seen them or found them. I had to be content to look out the window from the beginning of the storm till the end because I'm in a wheelchair.

Mrs. Schaefer

"The dog had some kind of instinct that told her she wasn't going to make it through the drifts."

We have a cabin which is close to the house and that almost disappeared. We could see the chimney and after we could get out you could walk on the roof of it. We were actually snowed in for 19 days. We were ploughed out on the 14th of February, 1977. One neighbour came with the ski-doo and brought us milk and eggs when we needed them. We had snow 40 consecutive days before the blizzard hit.

Be sure you have flashlight batteries and candles. We had a battery radio that was working and that was our only contact with the outside world. The telephone wasn't working very well. We intend to get more heaters which run on gasoline or kerosene.

We were wearing our outdoor clothes and we had to run down and run the furnace a couple times an hour. We kept the fireplace going as well. We also had to keep wood piled up next to the fireplace. The power was off for a long time.

We were fortunate because we never even got a cold. I think you don't have time to get sick. We ate sparingly also. We survived and that's the main thing. My husband is 68 and I'm 65. It's not as though we are kids. We have 6 grandchildren. Our cat and dog also survived.

We have a guest cabin. It's right next door to the house, 25 feet from our back door. It's a complete house. It has a gas heater so it was warm the whole time. It happened that my husband was in that cabin with the cat and the dog when the blizzard started. I was in the house and he came in about 4:00 in the afternoon. He could hardly reach our door. There was an awfully big drift between the houses because the area is exposed to the lake. On the way over to the house, the dog had some kind of instinct that told her she wasn't going to make it through the drifts, so she turned around and wouldn't come. So my husband turned around also and took the dog back to the cabin and put her inside and told her to stay there. He came back to the house and I couldn't open the door so I had to take off the storm panel. The drift was getting more than half way up the door. This was Friday. Well, he got in all right but he said he wouldn't dare go back out there because he couldn't see a thing. He was actually exhausted just coming that distance. We left the cat and dog over there. It got much worse at night and the next morning. We felt really bad about leaving them over there but what could we do? At least they'd be warm. Our dog is really attached to us and we knew she'd be having a fit. She's house broken. It really distressed us. We never went out the next morning either, it was still so bad. Finally that Saturday afternoon two neighbour boys in their 20's came over to see if we were all right. We managed to hand them a shovel out the back window and we explained about the dog. I gave them a leash. They managed to get over to the cottage by walking on the packed drifts. They dug out the dog and they brought her back to us. She was very happy to be with us. The cat stayed there for 2 weeks with her pan and her food.

In order to even walk outside we had to make steps in these mountainous snow banks. It was weeks before we were really shovelled out in any sense at all.

My husband had written in his diary that we had 53 consecutive days of snow in this area. We still had unmelted snow on the ground in May.

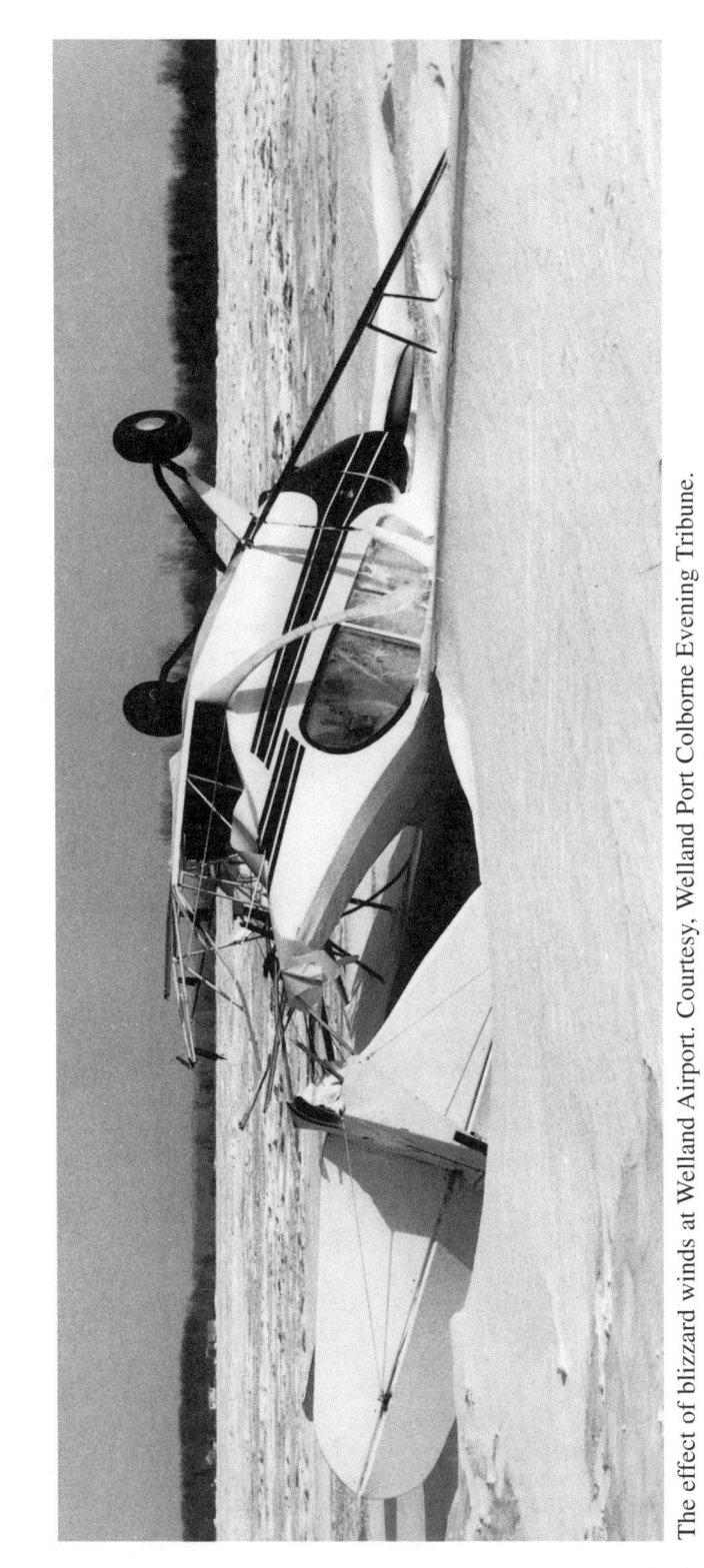

The effect of blizzard winds at Welland Airport. Courtesy, Welland Port Colborne Evening Tribune.

Mike Daniels - Welland Airport

"There is no weather reporting station on this side of the escarpment."

On Friday, they landed the helicopter in my back yard in Fort Erie and flew me back to the Welland Airport. When I got here, two of the aircraft had already blown over and were completely demolished. We kept the helicopter refueled for emergency situations and gave hourly weather reports and pressure tendencies. There is no weather reporting station on this side of the escarpment. We were getting a storm while on the other side of the escarpment there was nothing. St. Catharines was actually clear and it wasn't too bad in Niagara Falls. This is why we were giving hourly reports to the police.

We were spotting the pressure tendencies so we could tell when the wind would intensify. In this way we were able to keep the helicopters flying between the squalls and we'd also fly a Cessna 172 with two Army Majors in the back. We would find different routes by which they could get their equipment through to buried areas. Several times we got caught with a 100 foot ceiling and 50 feet visibility for landing. A few more grey hairs!

I was at the airport for seven days before I received my first warm meal. I was taken with the military to Sunset Haven, the place where all the senior citizens stay. I got the shock of my life when I looked in the mirror. I had lost ten pounds and my eyes were sagging and I couldn't see much difference between the appearance of the senior citizens and myself.

Mrs. Buchannan

"I could not see at all and I couldn't breathe."

The school phoned up at 11:00 a.m. and said they were going to send the kids home on the bus so I proceeded to drive out the driveway and I got stuck. I left the car there and I walked to the corner and waited for the kids. I couldn't see and I was cold. I met a lady and she told me they weren't going to send the kids home from school. I had to get back home because my mom was sick. She was 74 years old and she died a month later. My husband was stranded in Welland. We got to that lady's house and that was all because the blizzard was so bad. I waited there for about 2 hours. Then a neighbour phoned and was worried about me. She sent a neighbour boy who was 16 and he helped me walk home. If it wasn't for him I don't think I would have made it. I could not see at all, and I couldn't breathe. The wind was 60 mph. I followed him and we stopped by another neighbour's house by the trees. It took about 3 hours to get home, and it was only a short distance away. Then our electricity went off for 24 hours and thank goodness we have a fireplace. I blocked off the family room and cooked over the fireplace. The children got home Sunday by snowmobile. They had problems at school because the power was off. The neighbours behind the school had a space heater so they kept all the stranded kids at their house. Actually the teachers were excellent because when the children arrived home, it seemed like they had a good time. They were not frightened. Our daughter is at the stage where she had never been away from home. When she came home, she didn't cry. She liked the ride on the ski-doo. So I thought that was great. Just knowing they were OK made me feel better. I kept in touch over the phone.

Things worked out for the best. We had enough food here but it was just a problem preparing it and cooking it on the fireplace. I would now purchase a gas stove. I would recommend a fireplace to people in this situation, or a gas stove or propane. Have a plentiful wood supply and lots of candles.

My husband finally got home on Tuesday by snowmobile and it took a week before we were plowed out. We lost some food in the freezer when the power was off.

Gordon Burnett - CHOW Radio

"She phoned back later and said that she had her baby and that everything was, OK."

At 5:00 p.m. we decided to cancel all our programs because we were getting frantic phone calls from various people, organizations and particularly the police departments. By 6:00 there was no music at all because the messages were coming in so quickly. So we cancelled scheduled programs and all commercials and went to emergency broadcasting only. By this time it was dark.

Calls were becoming more frantic and more urgent. People were stalled and stranded. The snowmobiles got into action and emergency sections were set up at various communities. About 7:00 we started getting emergency numbers that had been set aside for them. Fire halls and city halls were on this emergency list. The city halls were the first emergency numbers and then they transferred them eventually in all the various communities into the fire halls and that sort of thing.

We announced over the air the following morning that we were short of food and the snowmobiles came through. They dug out a door-way for us, a tunnel out to the top of the snowbank. By this time the snow had completely covered our cars to a depth of approximately 8 feet. Snowmobiles were coming in on a cloud of snow, arriving with blankets, sleeping bags and food. These things came from different sources.

We carried on the following day with basically 3 or 4 hour shifts. We were so geared up on Saturday with the realization that this was our first emergency, that we couldn't sleep. This nervous tension took us over and we were walking around like mechanical people or robots. We knew when we were on the air and we knew what we had to do and we did it.

By Sunday we got some of the girls out and Joan Blanchard froze one of her hands when she was moved out by snowmobile. We tried to wrap her up as best we could and apparently we didn't do a good job. The girls didn't have any snowmobile jackets and the cold got through the blankets that were wrapped around them. We got a few of them out and other volunteers came in and joined us. Brian Green and a few of the boys from Niagara College came in on Monday and let a couple of our fellows go. But Frank Sernak, Tom Murphy and myself stayed right through until Tuesday. We resumed normal operations Tuesday morning around 9 or 10. And the three of us got home Tuesday afternoon around 3 o'clock.

We really got hit with the severity of the situation around Long Beach area and the Lowbanks area around 2 o'clock Sunday morning. We received a phone call from a man up there who very calmly explained the situation. I can remember him saying that he wasn't complaining, that he didn't feel that they needed any help at this point but he thought that we'd like to know what the situation was like in Lowbanks and he proceeded to give us the story. His windows had been smashed in. They had boards against the doors because they had collapsed and he couldn't get out. They were burning their furniture and were huddled around the fireplace. He went on for almost 20 minutes in telling of the trials of his family. They had taken another family in with them and they were all huddled in this room and the only thing that was working was the telephone. Power and furnace was off. He said they had plenty of food for which they were thankful but many other people didn't have any food. He said he thought we would like to know that they were buried alive. From that point on, the phone calls picked up again. They had sort of tapered off and they picked up and my God we went until 5 a.m. and most of them were referring to Lowbanks. Lowbanks sort of came alive and we were made totally aware of the situation because of this gentleman's initial phone call.

The people in Lowbanks were in serious trouble. So we phoned Ray Haggerty, the member of parliament of the province and got him out of bed. We explained the situation to him and said that he had to use his influence to bring any help that he could to these people without electricity or heat who were burning their furniture in their fireplace to stay alive. We heard from the Emergency Measures Organization saying that they heard about the situation on the air but they weren't aware of it. The EMO then notified the army and the army was then alerted and they came in with their trucks on Sunday afternoon. The helicopters then arrived of course, but it all started from this one phone call.

Financially this emergency cost us a lot of money. We had our salaries to pay during that time for Friday, Saturday, Sunday, and Monday. There was the overtime as well. Then there were the people who came in to help us. I paid them. Then we have to consider the business we lost. It's gone! If there is a sale on Saturday, it's on Saturday. It's no good on Monday. In total, I would say our losses totalled around 10 thousand dollars.

It's very difficult to pass on any advice to someone who might be in a similar situation some day because these things happen so quickly and they're gone before you can set the wheels into motion. We should have an auxilary power plant available for an emergency. As it happened we had a power failure. We were off for one point for something like a half an hour but fortunately we came back on again. And we had about 4 or 5 blackouts, the longest one was about two hours. I can recall that we were off that long because we had electric heat here and by the time the lights finally did come back on we had our blankets and coats wrapped around us because of the cold in the building. The wind was blowing through the cracks around windows and under doors. Had we gone off completely for eight to ten hours, I'm sure that we would not have been able to be of service to anyone.

At one point I was talking to my wife. She phoned me a couple of times. One time I was on the air. She said something to the effect that, "Honey I think you better have some sleep. You've been on now for 4 hours." I said, "Thank you very much for your call St. Catharines." She answered by saying that this is your wife, Suzanne, talking and I answered by saying thank you very much St. Catharines. I had been concentrating on things and was not really aware that it was my wife calling.

Another episode occurred when a lady phoned and said that her husband was in Welland and that she was in Port Colborne, apparently out on a farm just outside of the city. He couldn't get home and she was waiting for him because he was supposed to pick her up and take her to the hospital for a baby that she was expecting. She didn't know where he was but she was okay. A little while later she phoned and said, "My God, I'm having the baby!" This was on the air. I asked her if she was all right and if she was capable of looking after the situation and she answered yes that there was no problem. She said she'd keep in touch by phone. She phoned back later and said that she had her baby and everything was okay.

One woman was delivered by snowmobile from her place in Sherkston to the Fort Erie hospital. They got her through and into the hospital within minutes of the delivery. Now that was quite an exciting thing and they phoned us back and let us know that she had a bouncing baby. After that snowmobile ride, it must have been a bouncing baby.

Tom Murphy - CHOW Radio

"The weirdo at the other end said something like, "You're a faggot!"

It hit quickly and we didn't realize that we were going to be in here for the next five days. I saw something that we had talked about for thirty years — a whiteout. Standing by the window we were limited to seeing two inches away. It was like looking into a sheet, a completely white sheet and that's a cut-off experience.

Then we started getting calls from school bus drivers. They were stranded but their children were okay at such and such a house. This was the really frightening part because we were so afraid that some of these youngsters were going to be stranded and lost. There were people who were going to sleep with the radio on. They wouldn't leave that radio. They developed an amazing attachment to our station during that period. They depended on it for everything, even the ones without power that were fortunate enough to have a battery operated radio. It's really an amazing tale.

The food supply was interesting. There was the man who owns the Fish and Chips Place in Welland. He got a hold of a snowmobiler and sent these fish and chips out - free. He stopped selling and gave everything away. He ran out of food. Anyone that was coming through like road workers or snowmobilers were fed for free. Then McDonald's did a great job. However it was the lady on the farm across the road from our station who came over with a big pot of stew. We will remember her best. We saw this figure crossing the snowdrifts. All you could see were eyes. She had a snowmobile suit on, a hood, and God knows what else. She got into our place here and said, "Oh my God I forgot the salad! Imagine!!" She went all the way back home. It must have taken her another half hour to return with the salad. These were the kinds of people who surfaced in the storm.

Snowmobilers would drive in here to see if there was anything we needed. Then they'd sit and try to warm up. Our basic worry was that we would run out of water. We could advise other people what to do such as filling their pans or bathtubs. But we didn't have any of these facilities and water was running low. We truck our water here and there was no way that the water truck could get here. We didn't have the slightest idea of how much water remained or how to go and check it.

One of the big problems that we faced was the phone lines. It wasn't troubling us as much as it was the telephone company. Their circuits were literally burning out. Our lines were so tied up that if some of the officials had something to say, they couldn't get through to us either. In fact, my wife was angry at me because I didn't call her. I couldn't get through for three hours. We couldn't get out. I think there are six lines altogether. Then we started to get bug calls. These would be basically kids and we would appeal and appeal to keep unnecessary calls off the line. It was an impossible task and this is the thing that worries me very much. I think if we ever got into another disaster, this could break our communications. These kids were home. They were out of the supervision of their parents and obviously the parents didn't seem to take this thing seriously enough to keep their kids off the lines. Most of them were youngsters that were tying up these essential lines. They could have blown the whole communications system. If that had blown we would have been in an awful mess.

We got a few obscene calls that bothered the girls in our office. I don't know what the answer to these calls is, but it seems very strange that every time we would broadcast an appeal for emergency calls only, these nonsense calls would pick up. I'm afraid parents were lax, very lax in curtailing their kids.

We were getting some calls too that were rather frightening. These kids were sent home from school and some were out tobogganing on snowbanks where cars or trucks couldn't see them.

We were fascinated to find the range of our station during the blizzard. We discovered that we have listeners in areas such as Barrie, Ontario. We didn't have the slightest idea we could get into that area. They called afterwards and said we've never heard of your station. We found it on the car radio and we have been listening constantly. We've had people from New York State drop into the office since the blizzard. They were tuned into us during the storm and they would come in and thank us for our storm effort. That made us feel a closeness with them.

As far as we can determine none of the American stations went to full time emergency broadcasting. I assumed it's because they are more commercially competitive than we are or maybe they didn't have the desire or the same community feeling that we seemed to have here. We just automatically figured this was something that had to be done. This is what we are here for. This is why we are licensed. We rolled up our sleeves and had a go at it.

People took it upon themselves to monitor our station. They would leave their phone numbers so that the CB'ers could make contact at these various numbers and they relieved the pressure from us because a lot of people couldn't get through to us. For example, let's say somebody in an area needed insulin. They would call us and somebody would take it upon themselves to jot down all this information. Just an ordinary listener. They would leave numbers and we'd keep putting their numbers on the air so a snowmobiler would check in with them or they would call the firehall. They could then say that they heard on the radio that somebody at such and such an address needed insulin and the snowmobilers would be out there in no time.

There was another thing that occurred on Sunday night. We had a Ham radio outfit move in and set-up in the office and they started to do some direct air stuff. They did some very fine things. This one guy was working here constantly. We weren't doing this for dramatic purposes and these things didn't get on the air. It was just a case of expediency. To the best of my knowledge, he got insulin to a couple of people that needed it desperately and I think he even got a pregnant woman by way of ambulance to the hospital where she delivered. We thought we would be working hand in hand with them but it wasn't necessary. These Ham guys were in many cases faster than we were. They just utilized our physical facilities and they really let it go. They did a super job.

Do you realize that we had a snowplow that actually got lost? One of the plants sent a snowplow and it disappeared. We were putting out reports for it and looking all over the place. We knew it was to go down Forkes Road. Finally a plow did get in and we got on the air with it. We said we found your plow. They were getting pretty worried about it.

That snowplow from Owen Sound was supposed to be coming

down and we didn't have the slightest idea what the width of that machine was. This was going to be ironic if we here were doing everything to get all cars off the road and our own staff cars were going to be blocking Forkes Road. We knew for sure it was to come down Forkes Road. It arrived about eight or twelve hours late. We got on the air and made a plea and a farmer came in here out of nowhere. He had a plow and he was able to plow out this big drift that was blocking our parking lot. We were then able to get our cars off Forkes Road, otherwise they would have been side swiped into the ditch on both sides. That farmer didn't even drop into the station. He did his job, in a matter of fact way, brought his plow down in a truck, unloaded the thing, did his work, and disappeared again. He didn't even wait for a thank you. Sounds like the Lone Ranger, Hi Ho Silver. I think this is the kind of positive thing that you are always going to remember.

We were taking hundreds of calls you realize. At one point I was sitting across from Frank and we were punching the phones in as fast as we could possibly do it. I received an obscene call. The weirdo at the other end said something like, "You're a faggot!" I handed the phone to Frank and said, "This one's for you."

We didn't use a delaying system on these calls. Ordinarily, we could delay the discussion for eight seconds or so, but when you get weird calls like that it throws you into a panic anyway and before you know it, the situation is probably made worse with you pushing the bleep buttons and so on.

Our accommodations were quite nice here. I slept on the curtains for the first couple of nights and after five days of doing that, I couldn't get used to a bed. It's kind of strange how you could dig into the curtains on the floor and feel really comfortable. I was peeved at my wife for saying that here we are with a bunch of single attractive gals floating around and I didn't worry about her one bit.

One of the big jobs we were doing on the last day of the storm was to handle the bread shortage. We were giving on the spot appeals to these bread trucks. We'd report for example that a truck driver would be at a certain store, or he was on his way along the Lakeshore. I think that these store keepers did a great job. They would call up and say that they were going to stay open twenty-four hours and that they had bread and milk or whatever. Don't forget that this happened to be before payday. This created a major problem because there was a lack of ready cash in most people's pockets. The pension checks didn't get through. We have never heard of one case where anybody got turned down for the lack of cash. All reports said that the shopkeepers were extremely kind in this regard and I feel these small merchants that worked it out actually found that it cost them money to stay open. Some of them were a one man operation and they just kept on going. One chap in particular went through seventy-two hours without sleep, keeping his store open.

We did everything in our power to appeal to the region around us. We tried everything to reason with people and we sometimes bordered on rudeness. For example, part of the thing that tied up our lines was that these kids started calling and saying that they had a snow shovel and that they could go out and shovel someone's porch. On the one hand this was very good. But the reaction didn't come across this way. These kids wanted some kind of recognition. They all had to call up and say things like, "Me and my brother have a shovel." Now this tied up our lines and it's a very tricky situation. You can't be rude to the kids and hang up because they really want to do something and yet at the same time we couldn't discourage them from doing what in their estimation was the right way of going about it.

To my knowledge I can't recall any radio station or town that has ever got tied up like this. We had a couple of little trial runs there in Port Colborne along the lakeshore with a couple of floods. It helped us out in that regard as if it were a trial run for something greater to come. I was peeved that the town had no contingency plans. The same thing happened in the ice storm. People just left it up to us to try and put it all together.

The storm was a very positive people thing. There is a sociological factor that I'd like to mention. Near the end, we had done about all we could and it was virtually over and we felt like a winner in a friendly poker game. Everyone at the station was hesitant to be the first to leave, no one wanted the other guy stuck and stranded there. We also had this feeling that this was the end of it. Tomorrow was an ordinary working day and back we go again.

Throughout the storm we had anywhere from 5 to 25 people at any given time in the station. These people were at nerves end. A lot of them were under constant pressure and yet they all got along beautifully. It was amazing. You would think that there would be some kind of snapping at each other or behaviour like that. It didn't happen. Not one incident occurred. I've always heard that in submarines that you never have two people together—you have three—or the two will kill each other. So it was that we had more than two people at various times rushing about. Everybody seemed to be worried about everybody else. It took us about two weeks physically trying to get over it. We were literally bushed. I think the best plan was exactly what we did — we kept on going at a normal every day pace. It made our group much closer I think.

The Port Colborne Chamber of Commerce awarded the station a beautiful plaque. The Welland Chamber of Commerce gave everyone at the station a scroll. This was nice and we appreciated it.

There was more too. A lot of letters and thank you cards came in. Cakes and flowers were sent to us. You'd think they were setting us six feet under for a day or two. Actually, we ended up with quite an exuberant feeling. We felt that we had actually accomplished something. When we were working on a one to one basis and you felt responsible for getting an ambulance, it made you feel that you had contributed something. You figured you had done your part. Something had to be done and we tried to do it. If anybody ever asks what the highlight of our careers would be, there's no question in my mind that it would be the blizzard and the part we played at the radio station.

I had a thought that really touched me a bit. I saw a guy come in, a snowmobiler who'd been out about eight hours, and he had ice hanging down from his moustache, he hadn't been able to shave, he was freezing to death and the guy came in to the station because he happened to be passing by and he says to us, "Thank you". There we are in this air conditioned building, snug, well fed, well looked after and he's thanking us for what we were doing. A great mutual admiration society started to take place but the one thing that you realized right from the beginning was that you were only one part of it. You saw other guys and you knew how well off you were! It's a little unfortunate in a way. It seems unfair that we were foremost in the public eye and we might have been getting a hog's share of the credit when the guys who were getting blisters on their hands, frostbite on their cheeks and blocked nassal passages were really doing a tremendous job.

There was a fantastic number of calls that came in from maintenance people who were wondering about going back to work. They were Gung Ho to get back and get it done and get everything in operation again. The plants were the very same way. With the way our lines were tied up, it must have been extremely frustrating trying to get through with a message that a shift was on or a shift was off or the maintenance people should report here or not report there.

Bell did a tremendous job with the telephone lines. This was the basic fear that we had constantly. If we had lost the telephone, where would we have been? Do you realize that we lost power for less than one minute throughout that entire time? If we had lost our power, that would have been the end of the transmission because there is no auxilary system. No major power loss, no phone breaks, and even the water held out till the last few hours.

Possibly the greatest invention in the world as far as communications is concerned would be the transistor. During the storm, everyone had access to either a portable radio or at least a car radio. The Japanese did a heck of a job on our behalf.

I'm a heart attack victim. My coronary left me depressed, worried and with a very negative attitude towards life. Then the blizzard hit and I worked as hard as people who were much younger than myself. I survived in far better shape than those who were supposedly far healthier. Consequently, my whole attitude towards life has changed. I'm now very happy, positive and enjoy life. That's what the blizzard of '77 did for me.

Male, seventeen: I stayed at home during the storm. I live in Wainfleet, out on the lake. I listened to the radio, but what bugged me was that people were calling in for stupid things, like this lady had to pay her rent. She was two months overdue and all of a sudden she had to pay it, so she needed a ride. Another lady needed Pampers, all kinds of stuff.

Frank Sernak - CHOW Radio

We had calls from all the stations in Hamilton and Toronto and from the National News. They couldn't believe what we were going through. People from British Columbia were calling their relatives in Port Colborne, attempting to find out what was happening. They couldn't imagine Port Colborne being isolated as it was. Barbara Frum from Toronto said that no matter what we said, she could not believe it. Hamilton was in fair shape and Niagara Falls was all right. In St. Catharines, the sun was shining.

Paul Davoud - CHOW Radio

"I used to live in the Arctic."

A little hassle started in a form of a debate during the lull in the storm. People phoned in criticizing the skidoers whom they claimed were taking all the credit. Then we had the other groups phoning and saying the CB'ers should get more praise because they were doing so much. The radio station shouldn't be taking any praise. While all that crap was going out over the open line radio show, I was just waking up from the floor of an office here and I wandered out into the lounge of the radio station. There is a speaker in the ceiling so that one can hear what's being broadcasted anytime. There was a man named Jack Sibbet in the office. I don't think that he had any sleep and he was operating the CB radio base, sitting in the lobby with two kids. A boy and a girl about 16 years of age were both dressed up in their ski-doo outfits. The boy's face was badly scarred and blue from frostbite. His girl friend was frozen. They'd just come in to get their first meal in twenty-four hours and they're sitting there trying to get thawed out, getting more stuff ready to go on the next mercy mission and working together with the radio station and Sibbet. I looked at these two kids sitting there, both of them freezing and I listened to this crap on the air above us about who is going to get all the glory for this thing. And I thought that while all that nonsense is going on, these young kids are on their way out again. There's Sibbet struggling away on his CB, keeping going day and night, monitoring the radio so he can help co-ordinate with the radio announcers. And the men from the radio station here are continuing to stagger on through the day and the night.

It was a really great experience. All the rules break down and it becomes kind of humorous. When I was dealing with people in need of food or with people who had fuel oil running out, or with people who needed medical help, I started thinking of how just a few days before, things were so normal. For example, around here we would lock up the office and the station at night. Time cards had to be filled properly, proper date lines had to be on the top of each news story and initials to identify who wrote it, so that you make sure you're going to read professionally and with authority; all those little day to day things. Then you walk in here and there's teletype paper all over the place. The whole teletype system has been ignored. Everyone is into handwritten notes because you don't have time to type them. Everyone is into huge lists of industries that aren't going to be opened the next day and you're not even sure if they're up to date. Here you've got a bunch of house wives and neighbours who are in there manning telephones, writing news that they've never done in their lives, taking emergency phone calls, transferring information between control rooms, guys working until they fell over. No one even has a clue if they're getting paid or even cares about getting paid. It was really good.

I used to live in the Arctic and started as a radio announcer at Frobisher Bay and I have worked when we had storms up there. Sometimes the temperature was 58 below zero. But in an environment like the Canadian Arctic people expected weather like this and they dressed for it; you prepared for it. The police, the authorities and the citizens expect it. If you go outside you don't breathe deeply because you will freeze your lungs. Down here no one is prepared for a storm like that. Everyone is dependant on normal transportation, on open roads, and normal telephone lines and power. No one has emergency equipment. Up there everyone is ready for it. Here, it becomes a disaster. And that's the only difference between areas. They are ready. We are not.

Frobisher Bay is 1500 miles north of Montreal. It's the capital of Baffin Island, and CBC has 6 radio stations across the North. Frobisher is the smallest manned radio station in the world. It has a population of about 1800, most of whom are Eskimos and it's the biggest Eskimo settlement in the world.

The whiteout situation is quite common up north but this is the first time I've ever seen a whiteout down south. Up north everyone knows that you don't go out in a whiteout. You don't make a move. The one night in my life that I stayed in an igloo, I stayed with a couple of Eskimos who had built the igloo for fun about 50 feet from a house. When we woke up in the morning you couldn't see the house and no one had to say anything, you just didn't attempt to go to the house unless of course, there's a rope tied to the house that you can follow. If you can't see your hand in front of you, you're in trouble. You'll be into frostbite, you'll be lost and there are all sorts of accounts of men simply going in circles, four foot circles, eight foot circles within twenty feet of a house and freezing to death. Your perspective goes to hell.

If you're caught in a whiteout like this you should stay where you are. Try to cover yourself up. Build an igloo if you know how to. Don't go wandering around. You'll just wear yourself out and wear down your resistance. Try to protect your body, especially from the wind, and if you were out on your own you would dig a hole in the snow and get into it and keep down to the lee side with an air hole.

Frostbite is a very common problem up there. You get guys who are out on skidoos hunting and a storm comes up when they didn't expect it and it lasts longer than they thought it would. Sometimes you're not aware you're getting frostbitten and suddenly your nose or your cheeks have been frozen too long and the blood is restricted from flowing and you get really bad scarring or you end up with gangrene. I think they've changed the medical approach to treating frostbite now. They used to rub snow on it but that is incorrect.

I got the impression that people are generally really decent. After two or three days you know when you're generally running around bitching about the government, bitching about taxes, bitching about car service or what ever the hell your complaint is that day, you generally realized people are decent. We had an odd case of a car being vandalized or someone over charging on a loaf of bread or one hotel which was inhospitable. Generally, people were really busting their asses for each other with no thought of reward and the whole question of payment and money and books being written about it was not in their minds at all when they were doing it. I know that nobody in the radio station or the skidooers or the CB'ers were looking for money. I really felt good after it all. I was pleased. It created a whole new positive feeling in my mind towards people.

Female, seventeen: I was at home during the storm listening to the radio. My mother made me do some work.

The storm was a bad and good experience. It made people think about how to get along without. We ran out of food so dad had to go out into the blizzard and get some. We were all right with heat. We have a gas stove. The power was off but we have a gasoline generator.

Rita Leslie—Concessi's Store

"When the helicopters landed, we all ran outside and you'd think we hadn't seen anyone for months."

Around noon hour the Feinan boy came in and he was walking as if he was half frozen to death and he stayed with us for an hour. We got some soup into him and got him warmed up. He was heading home because he had word that his front window had blown in and his younger sister was home alone with the younger brother. He started out. He didn't come back. When he left he said he would call us when he got home because we wanted to know if he made it. He didn't call and it was getting very late in the afternoon. It became obvious that nobody was going to leave the store so we got supper ready and we sat around and played cards. Nobody slept. Everybody was too anxious to know what was happening.

We put the store lights on and sat up all night with the radio on. The two fellows next door would come over once in a while to check to see how everything was and in the morning they shovelled the snow from the door so that we could get it opened. Each morning they did it. Now Saturday morning the Feinen boy returned to the store. We thought we heard a noise in the front of the store so we all ran that way. And we could see him staggering up against the door. He could hardly navigate. He was so cold. We got him inside and got his socks off and he said that his legs from his knee down were numb. We worked on him for about three hours until we got him warmed up. We kept rubbing his legs and feet and we got blankets around him. Now this was Saturday morning. Four men came with toboggans and sleighs and they were taking milk and supplies to all the immediate neighbours. Fortunately for us, the power in the store didn't go off for long so we were never cold or without heat. And I think that's what saved our lives. The radio was such a help. We listened to it constantly.

Then after Saturday night we felt sleepy and we got some air mattresses out of the warehouse and we just blew them up. We cat napped. And so it was this Saturday afternoon that the big snow-machines tried to open up the road in front of us. They were trying to get up to get Mr. Mulko to the hospital. They got just beyond the store and they couldn't go any further. They turned back. That's when the driver thought he had a heart attack. This was a pay loader type of machine and there was a rescue team behind him trying to keep up. They couldn't get beyond the store.

On Sunday the Campbell boy came up with the bulldozer and they didn't get quite to the store. They just got in front of the warehouse and they couldn't go any further. They turned back. And I remember him saying, "Oh man are we ever in trouble up here." We got flags from the store and we went out and pulled the car aerials up that we were able to reach and tied the flags on them so that we could tell where the cars were. A couple of snowmobiles came in on Sunday. I'll never know how they got here or how they could see.

Young Peter Reker with his snow experience walked right over the telephone poles. He came up to the store everyday and he brought us fresh water because our water system, the Long Beach Water Works went off. It froze up and we didn't have any fresh water then. We had to melt snow to use for the bathroom.

On Monday afternoon the younger boys got outside for half an hour. The wind just sort of let up a little bit that we could see a few feet in front of the store. Then it started all over again and we were back inside. On Monday night we had the radio on at one o'clock in the morning when we heard our neighbour, Al Duffet, calling CHOW radio. He really told the station what it was like. We had phoned CHOW on Sunday and they just kind of laughed at us when we told them the snowmobiles were running over the tops of cars that were buried. At least that's the impression we got. They thought it was rather humorous. This changed however when Al Duffet phoned. He told them they weren't just going to plow any road out up here. They were going to have to get some big machines.

On Tuesday afternoon when it cleared up, the helicopters came out. From the time Al Duffet got on the radio, the police called the store every once in a while to find out how we were making out.

Note the flags marking buried vehicles. Concessi's Store. Wainfleet. Tribune photo.

When the helicopters landed, we all ran outside and you'd think we hadn't seen anybody for months. They landed out behind the store and they were taking pictures. It was quite late Tuesday night when the snow machine got up to the store. Snowmobilers brought milk and bread up from the highway. Wednesday night we finally got home.

Norma McIntee - Concessi's Store

"Suddenly she saw the snow moving"

Our telephone went out in the store and Ron Murray took his CB out of his truck and installed it for us in the store. And Chris who was stranded here with us knew how to operate the CB. He kept in touch with different people. That went on all night long and was a wonderful experience. I think without the CB we would have felt really isolated.

Then in the morning, the front door had been drifted in so completely that it took two men to dig us out. This went on each morning, trying to keep that door opened.

We ran out of bread and milk but some of us were good old farm cooks and we make our own bread. We managed to get along quite well. Even though the storm was bad on the Monday morning, when we were finally able to see outside, it was just like a fairy land. It was beautiful.

We could have gone out by helicopters but the store was the only place between Dunnville and Port Colborne for the local people to buy their needs.

The power lines were drifted right over and the police wanted to keep people away until they found the dangerous areas. Then the snowmobilers made their regular trips over routes that they knew were safe. Some of the drivers had to travel on the frozen ice of the lake because of the snow covered power lines.

Mrs. Rivers was coming from her home and she walked by a person's house and she saw that the snow was right up to the roof of the house. Suddenly she saw the snow moving. She started to dig too because she thought it was an animal that was trapped. Coming out of the snow was the owner of the house. He was taking the snow from the tunnel and placing it in his bathtub where it would melt for water and he would return for another bucket full. In this fashion he managed to dig himself out of his trapped home.

—Male, sixteen: I was at home, RR2 Port Colborne near the lake up on Sandhill. We didn't do much, we were just listening to the radio. We were snowed in for about a week. It cost us $500.00 to plow our driveway. It's about 100 yards long.

Mrs. Rodgers

"Her fingernails turned black."

I drove to my mother's house with my head out the window. My son got out and was guiding me because I couldn't see if there were any cars ahead of me. We were stuck at my mother's place for a week.

The power was off for two days. When we got home, we found all our pipes had broken, our toilet was cracked and everything was frozen that was sitting in jars. Then we had to stay at my brother-in-law's place for two weeks until everything was repaired.

The bathroom taps had to be replaced along with all the copper pipes in the house. The shingles blew off the roof so we had to buy new shingles. The ceiling tiles were ruined in three different rooms and they had to be replaced. The attic was full of snow and that added to the damage.

But, I really felt sorry for this woman that my mother took in. The poor soul got frostbite really bad. She had blisters on her legs and hands. They had to get her to the hospital. About three weeks later, her fingernails turned black.

Male, sixteen: I found that a lot of people were being really dumb. Like, you can do without bread and milk for a few days if you have enough of the other stuff. You don't really need it. Then people were calling in saying their cable T.V. was out. So other people were calling in and telling them to put coat hangers outside of their door. That's stupid.

Mary Minecci

"I didn't have to worry about my car. It was under 35 feet of snow."

I've lived up here for thirty years and we're always prepared for bad weather. We are quite a ways from town. But I wasn't prepared for thirty-five foot snow drifts over my car. I live alone. And during the storm the ceiling collapsed in the living room. I don't have any close neighbours and I was a little uptight. I didn't have to worry about my car, it was under thirty-five feet of snow and it wasn't going anywhere.

How can anybody be prepared for anything like that? The TV was of no help. It was doing the coverage about the Buffalo area and it wasn't hit half as bad as we were. So we tuned to the local radio station.

I remember one man with a CB radio was stopped at the corner there by Mrs. Dawdy's. He wanted to drive on but of course you couldn't drive the road the way it was. The snow was up to the power lines by this time and when the police stopped him he got out of his car, put the CB under one arm and the antenna under the other arm and away he went. My dog barked. Who could it be? I peeked out. There, coming over the drifts was this little man, looking for all the world like Admiral Perry heading for the pole. He came over that thirty-five foot drift with the radio under one arm and the antenna under the other and he spoke with quite a French accent saying something like, "Now we'll know how you are Mama." I'll never forget him because during the storm, every morning, he'd call on that CB at six o'clock saying, "How are you today Mama?" Those things you don't forget.

I did have to do the living room all over. It was painted and now the ceiling is two different colours but, other than that it's just part of living. When you live along the lake for a long time, you see so many versions of nature that nothing more amazes you. I hope that's the last big amazement I'm going to see.

My neighbour put my ceiling back up for me and it's really nice to have neighbours like that. As a matter of fact you couldn't live here without that kind of neighbourliness. You couldn't do it. The young boys, God love them, they were around here shovelling and shouting and cheering me up throughout the ordeal.

Mr. Yohn - Ontario Hydro

"So you just take your little snowmobiles and go."

It was the worst storm that we've ever had in our memory and that's about thirty years. Some of the guys here at the hydro go back longer than that. The thing that was so frustrating was not being able to mobilize because the roads were plugged. We have guys on call twenty-four hours a day all the time. Whether it be lightning, thunder, sleet, we're prepared. What good is all this preparation when your frustrated because you can't move. That was the problem with the blizzard.

In order to get around this, we phoned Toronto and we got them to send us over two bombardiers. They are a heavy tracked vehicle that can carry a lot of equipment. They shipped them to Cayuga and we picked them up at Chambers' Corners the following day. Even those limited us. We couldn't use them everywhere because we couldn't get through everywhere even with them. So we had to rely very heavily on the snowmobiles and drivers that were contracted to us. We had a helicopter standing by at Mount Hope but he couldn't get into the air because the weather wouldn't permit it initially. So for three days we could only go by snowmobile.

Damage wasn't all that great. It was just that we couldn't get to the place where all the damage was done to repair it. We had a lot more physical damage during the ice storm. We had to pay the snowmobilers fifteen dollars an hour. That's what they were charging us and I guess they earned their money. They took the linemen out with their tools to the trouble spots and they were able to make on the spot repairs.

We set up the headquarters here at the sub station and we had power. We ran the snowmobilers from this point. We were comfortable in our sleeping bags here. We took about twelve hundred calls for help over that three day period.

When a person is in trouble, sometimes it's real and sometimes it's imagined. The thing that makes it very difficult is having people phone up and expect individual service. They are one of twelve thousand customers in the area and they feel angry when we don't get to them right away as an individual. There was one family complaining all by themselves for example and the whole village of Stevensville is out. These people call and want immediate service. They can't get out so I don't know how they expect us to get in. So you have to be very patient with them.

There is an elderly lady who lives on Erie Peat Road and we thought she should be evacuated because she was there all by herself. When the two guys came down with the snowmobiles she said, "I lived in this house before we ever had power. I can get along quite nicely, thank you. So take your little snowmobiles and go. Go away and worry about someone else." We checked with her every hour and sure enough she was okay.

Some people had lost their power for as long as seventy-two hours. The average would be twenty-four hours before the plows could break through to get us to some of our larger customers. We got to them within the day. The snowplows were awfully good to us especially out in Wainfleet. Stan Pettit, the mayor out there really went out of his way as did Port Colborne's Saracino. They were fantastic. They sometimes would send two or three plows to break through ahead for us and even at that it was difficult sometimes to open that snowbank.

It's odd how some people panic when adverse situations hit them. They don't seem to be able to cope with it. These seem to be the exception rather than the rule. Most people, when they know something is wrong, realize there's not much you can do about it. We assured them that we would get there as soon as possible. Then they become resourceful. They start looking around for alternatives - ways of getting out or someplace to go or breaking out their camping equipment and getting camp cook stoves, tent heaters, all sorts of things like this. It's a pretty small percentage of people who actually hit the panic button in such a situation like that. At least this has been my experience. As a matter of fact, it seems we like to remember happy times and forget the hard times. I suppose people will try to put this storm out of their mind as quickly as possible.

Those people that had fireplaces could keep warm and could keep the house from freezing. They took the storm more philosophically than those that fully depended on electricity. Now that's the way with almost any heating system anymore. Your oil furnace

Queen Elizabeth Highway, Fort Erie. Photo by Ron Roels

can't function without any electricity. Your gas burner will come on but you can't circulate it. It's usually a failsafe system too. When the electricity goes off, your whole boiling system shuts down and your safety valve shuts the gas off too.

Gus Baker

"So the wire service from here to Singapore was certainly better than what we could come up with during the blizzard."

We left Fort Erie about eleven o'clock in the morning just as the storm started. "Let's get out of here" my wife said so we started back to Port Colborne on No. 3 Highway. Down the highway we got stuck in the snow a bit but I thought we would be all right. It would blow for a couple of hours and then stop. The radio was predicting that this would occur.

The snow blew across the highway. We had one drift behind us and one drift going out from the left front fender of the car about the height of the car hood. We had a shovel in the trunk and periodically I would get out and shovel around the car to keep it clean. We had a full tank of gas so we figured we were in no great danger. By about six thirty that night I said to my wife, "I think we're here for the night." Nothing was moving either east nor west. There hadn't been any movement for a couple of hours.

We had CHOW radio on which was giving us excellent coverage, and I think it was really a great assistance to us and certainly comforting. We knew what was going on in the area and we knew that the power was off in Ward Four in Port Colborne. We were in part of Ward Four at that time. People asked why we didn't go to the nearest farm house. Well we knew there were houses somewhere out there but since the radio warned us that power was off we figured there'd be no lights to guide us. We could have been easily lost and then what do you do?

About seven o'clock that night my wife said, "I think I'll see what I've got in my purse." She came up with some Dynamints and I think we had three each. She dug up some cough candies and that was it. That's all we had in the car as far as food was concerned.

As time went by we got pretty drowsy. We did not actually sleep. We dozed a bit, taking turns. We alternated during the night and at times it got so darn cold. You'd shut off your motor for a bit and then turn it on after a while. By midnight the gas was getting down and I thought we couldn't leave our motor running much longer. We shut off the motor and I got out and shovelled a couple more times. I got back in the car and I was chattering. I had a blanket in the trunk and I got that out.

During the final stages of the night we huddled together and had the blanket over us. We shut the motor off for a maximum of fifteen minutes and we put it back on occasionally and the motor would hesitate each time.

My wife wasn't dressed for cold weather. She was wearing a skirt and jacket. I had my scarf over my hat and I had a big heavy coat on and I had a good substantial pair of gloves on. I would shovel the snow away from the exhaust so that the fumes wouldn't get tied up and come up through the body of the car and kill us.

When the snowplow came it was a happy sign. We felt warmer already just to see it. They went by us, slowed down, but did not stop. They saw our signal lights, knew we were all right and they went about their business. We learned later that they had picked a lady out of a car further down the highway and they were taking her through to their truck center to get her into some shelter. They returned to us about an hour later at eight o'clock in the morning and dug our car out. The car wouldn't go forward because the transmission apparently was frozen but I could manage it in reverse.

People in the Gateway Motel in Fort Erie were really good to us while we were stranded there. They didn't have a dining room or a kitchen or a breakfast nook but they gave us extras that were not required. The Fort Erie Hotel on Garrison Road opened their doors to stranded people. They took people in who were brought in by bus from the Land Mark Hotel that burned down during the blizzard. There were two bus loads of adults and children. The Fort Erie Hotel wasn't equipped to handle this type of emergency. It's an old hotel. They didn't have that type of accommodation, but it didn't stop them from piling mattresses in the beer rooms and all over the place and they put people up. They brought in staff and fed people and they wouldn't take a dime from anybody. As much as you wanted to pay, they refused to accept any money. They were just remarkable as many people were.

There were people in the mall with four wheel drives and snowmobiles and they organized the mall in Fort Erie as a clearing station. They were moving people in from the various schools. There was one school in Fort Erie in which they were keeping a lot of students. Their boilers went out, and they brought all those kids from the school into the mall in Fort Erie and put them up there for the night and fed them. Just unbelievable.

I come from an area near Owen Sound. I was born and raised in Allanford, twelve miles west of Owen Sound and as a kid I remember storms but never a storm of this ferocity.

I know my wife was very concerned. I have a high blood pressure problem but we didn't have any medication so she was concerned. The fact that we were together and we could talk to one another really helped us. We decided to keep cool since there's no use to get excited. I was a police officer for thirty-five years before retirement and you get to know that there is no point in losing control of yourself; so you calm yourself under pretty adverse conditions. Between the combination of past experiences and a good wife for a little guidance here and there we were really fortunate.

There were times when we had some pretty deep thoughts about whether or not we were going to survive. Had the car not kept us warm, I wouldn't want to guess whether we would have made it because within fifteen minutes you got so terribly cold. As a result of that experience I'm going to see that there are going to be certain things in my car that weren't there before. You go further north and they've got snowmobile suits and this type of thing. This is what they actually carry. It's their first aid. We've never had to do this and I think after a storm like this we've got to look seriously at it.

We have a daughter in Indonesia and she didn't know that we were involved in this storm. She was in Singapore at the time. They were out on a rest and recreation leave. They work with Inco over there in Indonesia. She sent us pictures of the Buffalo and Fort Erie storm that were in the papers Sunday and Monday in Singapore. We didn't have any papers delivered here until Wednesday. The pictures she sent us showed the buses and comments of the people taken from the Land Mark Hotel into the Fort Erie Hotel. She had pictures of this stuff in the Singapore paper and little did she know that we were right there in the middle of it. So the wire service from here to Singapore was certainly better than what we could come up with locally in that blizzard.

Mayor Saracino - Port Colborne

"I was in office for only one month when that great storm struck."

The blizzard of 1977! What a nightmare that was! I recall the day started out with a very light snowfall. January 28 looked like an average winter morning. I got right into my daily work. As the morning went on, I could see the snow was heavier and weather conditions became a little more severe. By noon the snow was rapidly increasing and the wind velocity had picked up a great deal. I figured we were probably in for a very severe night.

The office staff became very nervous about how to get out of the building. The City Hall parking lot was full. I became very concerned . . . we were getting phone calls asking when would the roads be plowed out . . . I called the city superintendent asking him the same questions. His answer was that we were virtually bottled up . . . some of the equipment was stuck in snow banks . . . it was very serious with evening coming on . . . I alerted the works department personel. Be prepared for a long night perhaps two nights. Conditions were getting worse. I walked home around 7:00 p.m. winds violent . . . snow drifts monumental . . . at home phone calls . . . constantly . . . concerned people . . . couldn't get into the streets, their driveways . . . what was happening? What are we doing? I had never experienced a storm of that magnitude. I contacted our city engineer and asked how our work force was mobilized? What was happening to our equipment? I got an up to date status an hour later and each hour thereafter I got a report. I didn't sleep all night. I was on the phone until 1:30 in the morning seeing if we could get the works crew going. How were we proceeding? What was happening in the rural areas . . . downtown areas . . . medication bogging down . . . nerves starting to enter the picture . . . a very

Breaking through. Courtesy, Niagara Regional Police.

unpleasant experience . . . was it the end of the world? In the mean time we are listening to our local radio station CHOW . . . they had of course gone to emergency broadcasting and they were keeping us up to date on weather conditions on a minute to minute basis . . . all services in various departments in the city were notified . . . Red Cross . . . snowmobile club . . . health units . . . the cities of Welland, Port Colborne, Fort Erie, the Wainfleet area . . . all calling in for information and all trying to react . . . the evening passed very uncomfortably.

In the morning I walked to work early — a fifteen minute walk took me an hour and a half . . . walking along I saw stranded vehicles all over the road . . . stores closed . . . seemed like we were on another planet . . . Alfred Hitchcock movie type setting.

Two members of the staff had arrived at work . . . switchboards were starting to light up. What was happening? Roads are not being plowed — people stranded overnight . . . abandoned vehicles . . .

Again I contacted personel in charge of the works committee . . . I thought we should sit down and have a meeting . . . what's our present condition . . . what inroads have we made . . . what do we expect in the future?

The storm increased in ferocity. No question—we had an emergency situation. Up to date information on the city's position was made available to us . . . We made a decision to man City Hall here as head quarters to receive in coming calls. Those personel who were at work were asked to volunteer for that duty. They jumped into handling the complaints. I went to the police station and asked if we could have the co-operation of the local detachment of the Niagara Regional Police Force. We set up emergency headquarters working together. We had a tremendous relationship with the police. At that point I instructed our engineer to contact the Ministry of Transportation and Communication in Toronto and ask them to declare Port Colborne in a state of emergency and request all available equipment that the Ministry had at its disposal. We were crippled and I wanted to go on record immediately as having asked them for help.

I knew that once this situation was over, the cost of snow removal alone would be horrendous and I wanted to make them aware of my position. I asked them to send whatever snow blowers, snow removal equipment that they could spare. I felt good in one way knowing that we were the first municipality to ask for this assistance. We were told that what was available would be dispatched to Port Colborne immediately.

Messages to people in distress---emergency rations were needed . . . women calling in . . . couldn't get to the store---no milk---running out of food---kids hungry---they just couldn't get out of their homes. No sign of relief at that point . . . police headquarters worked together with the Niagara Regional Office---were authorized to make all kinds of food packages, canned goods and whatever was needed to dispatch to persons in need as quickly as possible . . . At that point, the police enlisted the aid of the snowmobilers. I went on the air asking their help in this emergency situation. They were to report to the police station where they would receive orders to dispatch food. In less than 2 hours, snowmobilers started pouring into the police office volunteering help. At that point I went on the air declaring Port Colborne in the state of emergency and I asked the residents to remain indoors, to stay off the roads and to give our snow removal equipment the best possible chance.

People were calling in reporting their loss of electricity. Some homes were literally being covered with snow. They couldn't see out their windows. Numerous complaints came from the rural areas of Port Colborne. What was happening the people wanted to know because there was no heat, no power and they were starting to virtually freeze to death in their homes. Naturally they were concerned for their families and children. A lot of their families hadn't even reached home from the previous day. They were stranded at other places when the storm hit.

From that point on, it became a real nightmare. People were disappearing with no trace of them. Some never got home from work or from visiting friends. Right away, our prime concern was people missing. What had happened to them? We received calls from frightened mothers and fathers whose children were stranded in schools. What was happening in the schools? So we started a program here to call all the schools in order to get the situation. How many children did get home? How many were still in the schools? The school board told us exactly the position. They tried to contact all the parents of the children, advising them of the situation. There was a very good feeling to know that at least the children were safe.

The power was still out in some rural areas and remained off for 3 or 4 days in some cases. I know of people who were stranded in their homes and had a very deathly feeling. They couldn't look out their windows because they couldn't see anything. They had no idea how high the snow had gone over the roof. They were freezing ... in their homes. The temperature had gone below zero in one home out there. Small children in that home—mother just petrified ... feeling so alone so helpless ... many families felt the same way. They thought it would be a matter of minutes before it was all over for them. Ordinary measures were not enough. Our past experiences were not good enough---they couldn't help us.

Were other cities in the same situation as Port Colborne? We only knew Welland was being hit, Fort Erie was being hit very severely, and Wainfleet was being hit. However, outside this area it didn't seem too bad. St. Catharines, Toronto, Hamilton weren't bad. What was happening to our area? Was it because of our geography, our location ... adjacent to the lake? Were we being sucked up into some vacuum and everything being dropped down on us? Gives you an ... eery feeling. Were we being penalized? Many things went through my mind.

The day I declared Port Colborne in the state of emergency, I was in touch with the Emergency Measures Organization in St. Catharines asking them for help ... relief ... what could they send? We were here ... crippled ... down and out. At that moment they dispatched an army convoy and this was something, because when you have an army reserve battalion moving into your municipality in peace time ... you begin to wonder ... They brought in food supplies. They brought in numbers of the militia. These members assisted the police in going out and looking for stranded motorists . . . people located in farm houses, in schools . . . they had big heavy trucks . . . jeeps that were mobile in this type of weather. . . a tremendous amount of assistance. I believe that this was the first time that militia ever had the task of coming into Port Colborne under actual combat conditions. The enemy was the weather and we had to fight it . . . and we had to keep in touch . . . and it was virtually every half hour . . . detail . . . more detail . . . keep the public informed . . . keep the situation clear . . . bad as it might be, it had to be clear . . .

The water pumping situation was critical now . . . Water problems were appearing throughout the city . . . and here we are too busy combating other problems when the water department did not know what to do. Hit the air waves . . . ask for conservation measures of water to be imposed . . . We were pumping a fantastic amount of water and we were experiencing water breaks . . . water mains freezing . . . we were having problems beyond control.

What should happen if a major fire of any significance should erupt? No water to combat it. So we asked the people to conserve where possible. Reserve tanks were slowly declining and were becoming very critical with regards to water. Any situation needing water would be hopeless. To the people . . . get the word out . . . get the water breaks in the lines . . . freezing lines . . . bursting lines . . . loosing literally hundred of thousands of gallons of water. This kind of problem we didn't need in addition to the blizzard.

Back to city hall, second day headquarters set up at city hall. I asked for volunteers who would be willing to stay the course of the night to man the phones and to listen to people's problems and offer help if they could. I was very happy to see the city staff volunteer for two to three nights.

Calls coming in . . . literally hundreds . . . asking for help . . . we're running out of this . . . we need that . . . what's happened to my family . . . a lot of information going out through the local radio station. Keeping the public informed as to the conditions in and around the Niagara region. Weather conditions, food supplies, medical help, advice, up to date reports. Twenty-four hours a day throughout the storm, the radio pumped out that vital information.

The scene in Port Colborne began to change a little. The storm was still very intense. The equipment was making headway. We were starting to become mobile! Roads started to open up. Ask the public to refrain from driving and adhere to that request. Tow away any cars that were innocently blocking traffic. Take them to the depot. A lot of people became upset because they couldn't find their cars, they didn't know where they were. So they contacted the police. Then we were hampered with messages running back and forth with people wondering about their cars.

Ugly stories began to appear. Reports of people phoning in for food parcels and they were saying nothing was being done and they weren't getting any relief. Their babies were suffering because they had no milk for baby food. They called the city hall . . . all the radio stations . . . all the police . . . they're not doing anything about it. Well these were all checked out and a couple of the people that were phoning in these distress calls had to give their addresses if they wanted things to be delivered. The reports came back from the police—very very sad reports . . . they had gone to a couple of these homes and literally saw dozens of food parcels and huge amounts of alcohol being consumed.

People used the storm for their personal benefit. They didn't need any emergency help. No children to be seen anywhere. Using the plea of starving children to profit and have a good time. Sadest experience of the blizzard.

The Ministry of Transportation and Communications informed us that a giant snow blower was proceeding toward Port Colborne. It left Owen Sound area well over 24 hours ago and still no sign of it on the Queen Elizabeth Highway. If it hadn't reached the QE in 24 hours, when would it hit Port Colborne?

We needed some relief because we had to get in food supplies and open up those main arteries to the outside world. Children in schools were very worried about getting home. In most cases this was a nightmare for the teachers as well as the children. Children were wondering what happened to their parents which was just as frightening a thought as parents worrying about children. We had to open up some roads . . . but we couldn't do it, we didn't have the equipment available for that. The arrival of the snow blower gave cause for hope. We counted on it to open up the road between Dunnville and Fort Erie. Then the Wainfleet area reported extremely high banks of snow.

Port Colborne people started to move out of their homes in utter dismay and disbelief of what had happened to the city. It looked like a white sheet had blanketed the homes, streets and poles. For a photographic fan the scene was something special, but for the ordinary person it was a terrrible experience to look around and not see homes where homes are normally found. What's underneath those white things? Were there people underneath them? Reports started coming into the police station saying that they found bodies literally frozen in the snow, frozen in cars that were off the road. How many people are missing?

I know personallly that the police were very worried at this time because they had reported many cars that had been abandoned. They didn't know the position of the cars that were abandoned, or the location of the owners who had left the vehicles. People were virtually lost at large . . . all over. They didn't know if they were walking on homes, cars, telephone wires, or what?

I recall that one of our office staff, who lived in Welland, had tried to make it to Welland, and half way there he became panic stricken as his car ran out of gas. He and his friend were alone and they didn't know what to do. They left the car and began to walk. At one point they felt a change underneath their feet and wondering they checked and found it was a telephone line. They were that high up, 25 feet in the air on a bank of snow. He became very tired and wanted to sit there but fortunately his companion moved him on. He did say later that if it had not been for his friend literally dragging him in some instances and talking to him that he would have sat down there and given up because he didn't know where he was and he couldn't see anything. He was very indebted to his mate for keeping him going. They walked half the night. They walked around in circles and returned to where they started. That's one memory he would like to forget. Our staff was still on the phone 24 hours a day. We slept at city hall for 2 evenings. I hadn't seen much of my wife for three days. She stayed at home and listened to the radio and she kept in touch that way.

Traffic began to move in the downtown area. A few stores started to open. The walkers began to emerge and we were concerned about . . . what they were going to find on the street. We contacted the hospital and they were functioning rather well. Cases of frost bite were showing up. The helicopters brought in people who were stranded out in the country. Wainfleet township was still in very bad shape. Some areas were still without power. Snowmobilers were trying to get into the badly hit area of Ward 4, and bringing food and supplies. So after 3 days of intense storm, signs were starting to show . . . that we still lived in civilization. I guess God was good to us. We figured we were going to make it now.

The Militia was still in town, and stationed at City Hall. They set up a radio dispatch unit here as well as a mobile crew and they were assisting very well in the delivery of food, parcels, medical supplies and answering pleas for help.

We were still having water problems because our pumping was in the area of 5 million gallons per day. This is a tremendous amount of water, equal to a very very hot day in the summer months. Well we didn't think there was going to be a summer at that point. So where was this water going? The frozen water lines had burst and some areas of town were literally under sheets of ice because of all the water freezing on the surface. It was treacherous for any vehicle using the road. Fortunately we didn't have any fires at that time. We discovered later that 460 water mains had frozen into individual homes. This is abnormally high because during an average winter you would be looking in the area of 20 to 30 water lines freezing. This was a tremendous cost to the municipality in the area of 70 thousand dollars. That is the cost of any 3 winters all rolled into one.

We had very little help from the provincial authority. They eventually gave the city of Port Colborne 150 thousand dollars. I had an audience with Premier Davis as well as the mayors from the other municipalities, asking for more relief in regards to the severe storm that we encountered this winter and hopefully there will be additional funds coming from the provincial authority on this matter. We had a meeting with the federal authority asking for a similar type of help.

About a week after the storm had subsided, I organized an emergency task force. We have our fire chief appointed to head this force for Port Colborne. Who's to say that we won't have another blizzard? Weather forecasters predict the next 5 years may see similar types of weather again. Maybe there is some movement in the atmosphere that's creating this. I don't know. But we can't afford to take a chance that it won't happen again. We've experienced a situation that I hope we'll never see again. I think once in anyone's life is enough. It certainly was enough for the citizens of Port Colborne.

We all learned an awful lot from the experience. However, I might say that it takes a disasterous situation sometimes to pull a community together. I feel in my own mind that this storm has brought a lot of people closer in our city. It brought the community together... that's the lesson I think we learned and it was a good lesson.

Communications are vital. Co-operation of the people was tremendous. This shows that when we need help, all you have to do is ask. The whole city came to its own rescue. For that I am thankful.

I was in office for only one month when that great storm struck. What a way to be baptized by fire or perhaps snow. The worst winter in history! In all, there were 20,500 citizens in our community who worked together in a team effort and completed the job.

You never know when you open the door what you will find out there. On January 28, 1977 we opened our doors in Port Colborne and saw a hell on earth. I will always remember 1977 as a year of drama and nightmare and I'll never forget the gigantic feeling of relief when it was over.

Stan Pettit - Mayor of Wainfleet

"What the hell, we don't have to leave."

One of the things that came out of the storm from the township was that basically we are an agricultural and rural area and a number of individuals in this region are in the dairy farming industry. We started getting calls from these individuals who weren't able to have their milk tanks emptied after 2½ - 3 days. Most of them have the capacity to hold milk for at least 2 days. However if the milk isn't collected in a certain length of time, the collectors do not have to accept it. The farmers who were holding milk were extremely concerned because there was no way this milk supply could be picked up. So the farmers put out the call over CHOW Radio that there was milk available to anybody who could bring their containers to pick it up. In other words, they would be forced to dispose of it.

Another major hardship was in keeping alive the livestock that were not able to get food. The farmers were out with whatever equipment was available. But tractors couldn't get very far unless they were lucky to be between drifts. Some had snowmobiles that they could use to transport a bail or two of hay. Some of them had sleds that they were able to use to get some feed to their animals. But the big concern was when could they get a road open to their source of supply so they could get it back to their animals. So people extended themselves to care for their animals even at the risk of exposing themselves to serious danger.

Drifts up to the power lines, Wainfleet. By Norman Rockwell.

We tried to open the roads as soon as possible in order to get back to some semblance of agricultural activity. In the main, calls for assistance in terms of food were very minimal. People here are very self-reliant. This was an important factor in helping them get through this storm.

There were a few people who screamed in our ears because we weren't able to get to them and they had to dump their milk. I didn't really hear of anybody who lost any animals because they couldn't get to feed them.

Another aspect of the storm was how much individuals put aside their own hardships in the concern that they had for other people that were a little worse off than themselves. It was this sort of spirit which prevailed throughout the storm. I never really had a flat refusal to do something when a request came in. I guess this is one of the characteristics of a rural area. You rely on your own water supply and when it isn't sufficient you resort to melting snow for a bath or trapping the water from the roof into your cistern. If you are without electricity and gas in certain areas, you rely on wood stoves and coal oil lamps.

I remember organizing all the water haulers in the region to go together and supply these people once the roads were opened. There were about 120 customers waiting for their water to be delivered and these haulers all banded together and took a certain percentage to themselves and met the needs of these people who were waiting for water services. It worked very well and we got through that back log in record time once the roads were reasonably opened between Port Colborne, Welland and the Township of Wainfleet. The volunteer firemen assisted in that program. They would ride with the haulers to the locations where the water was to be delivered. So the spirit of co-operation again shone through and it pleased us all.

I remember leaving the office finally on Thursday night and coming down No. 3 highway. The roads were open and I had a feeling of such great relief. I hadn't been home since the Friday morning previous. The war was over. I suppose it was that kind of feeling.

It was quite a while before I got the full feeling back into my hands. This was from leaning on the table with the telephone in my hand all that time. I could try to pick up something and I would drop it because I couldn't hold it. Even when cutting with a knife and fork I couldn't use any pressure. Coming home that night was such a relief. I kept thinking, "My God I'm finally going home." It was nice seeing Shirley again. It had been a pretty hectic time for her as well since she couldn't get out of the house for that period of time.

The area hit the hardest was along the lake with drifts as high as 45 feet. When we finally got crews up into that region, a suggestion was made that perhaps these people should be evacuated. It was in response to that suggestion that people said, "What the hell, we don't have to leave." That's the spirit that got our region through that disaster with as little loss as we suffered.

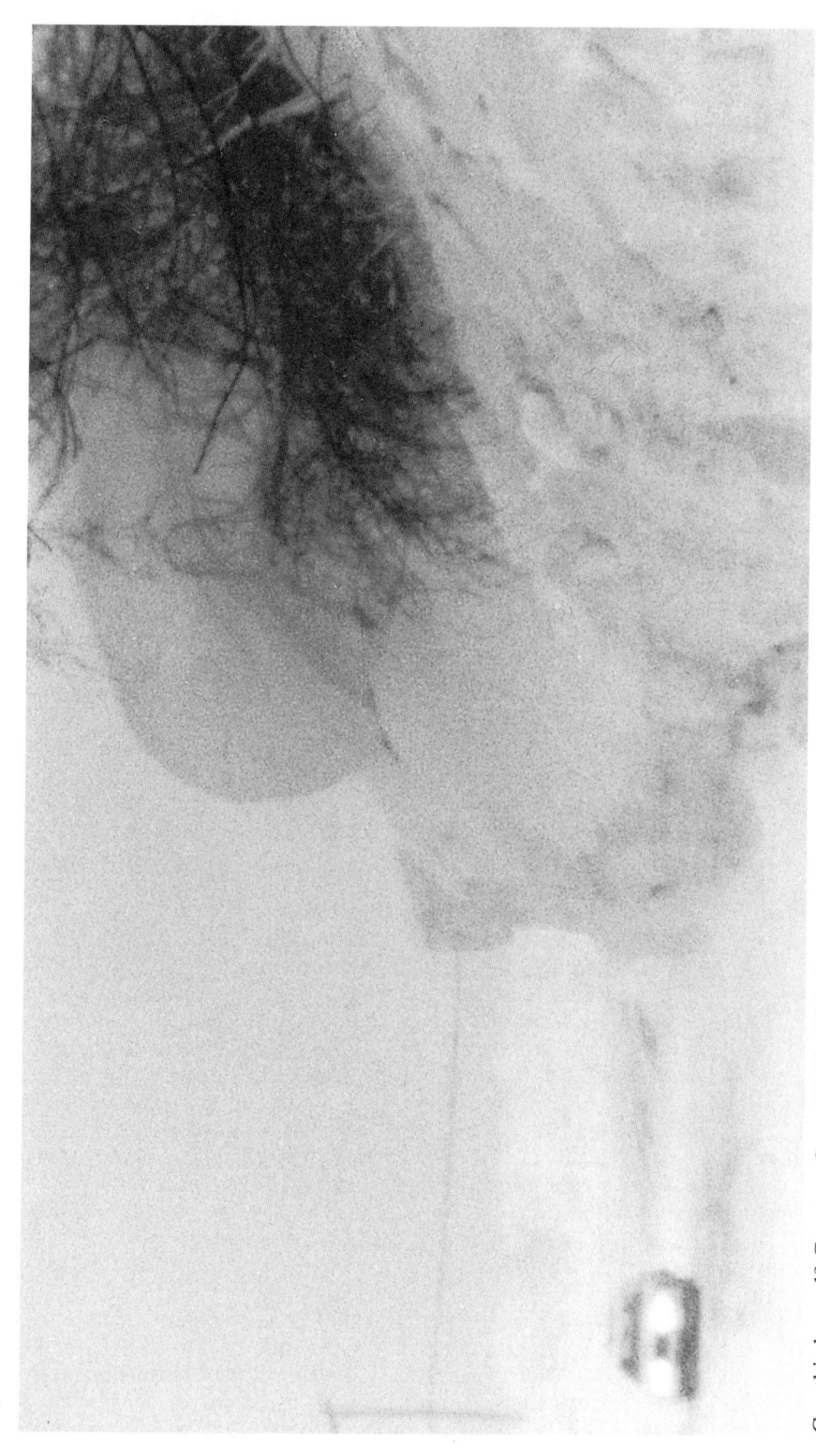

Can this be real? Courtesy Scott Wolfe, Wainfleet

Shirley Pettit

". . . only five out of fifty-seven mourning doves returned after the blizzard subsided."

I am a nut about birds. We did keep track of how many mourning doves we were regularly getting here. We had as many as 57 coming everyday. I feed them about 1,000 lbs. of bird feed during the winter. It's down in the back yard under the bird feeder. I cleared a spot about 30' by 15'. I just went out there and shovelled every time it snowed or if it was a light snow I would sweep it off. Even when the storm was going on, when it was at its strongest, you could watch the birds go up and attempt to get some bird seed from the feeding station, and they could get some off the ground as well. The wind was so strong that if you stepped out the door it would cut off your breath. In this kind of wind the birds were able to get off the ground only a couple of feet and the wind being as strong as it was forced the birds to be suspended in mid air. They just couldn't fly. They couldn't get to the feeder and they couldn't even drop to the ground because that wind was so strong.

My bird feeder was an invention to solve some of the problems we had here. I took an old window screen that must have been 4' by 2' and suspended it from the clothes line. This allows any moisture that might settle on the seed to work right through the screen and not get trapped in the feed for the bird. Another advantage to this rig is that it discourages the squirrels from getting on to this screen because they have to attempt to walk the clothes line to get out to it. They are not prepared to walk that kind of tight rope, so the seeds remain there for the birds. The squirrels are quite happy to get what is thrown to the ground and they certainly get their stomachs full that way too.

The mourning doves came to this feeding station all winter. Along with them we have chickadees, titmice, cardinals, blue jays and just about every kind of sparrow you can think of. For example, we have the little red headed kind and there's the black and white striped headed one that just floats around here in the winter time too. Woodpeckers arrive and we put up the bag of suet out for them and the titmice. It seems to work out quite well. The squirrels stay on the ground, they don't bother anybody and certainly the birds don't bother them from their perch above on the window screen. At one point during the storm the snow had built up higher and higher from the ground and the snow was also piling on top of the bird feeding station so the two were coming closer and closer together. You could almost see the glint in the squirrels' eyes hoping that the two would meet. They never did get close enough for the squirrels to jump from the top of the snow to the bird feeding platform.

When I got trapped in the house and I couldn't get out to the birds and squirrels, I panicked. All I could think of was that I feed these birds and four legged creatures everyday and sometimes a couple of times a day. This is fine, I didn't mind doing that. What panicked me was remembering a point I had read in a magazine about the problem of feeding the birds and the squirrels. Apparently they come to depend upon you so much that if you ever miss feeding them for a day or two in the cold winter, they may very well die. They become so dependant upon us that they need that food to keep the fat built up in their systems. Without it, they could die. All I could think was that I had encouraged them to come and had been feeding them and now I couldn't get out there and they would probably be wiped out because of what I was doing.

In desperation, I remembered that some of the upstairs windows had not had the storm windows put on them. There were summer screens still in place. These windows with the screens on them overlooked the yard where the bird feeder station was located. So, I took my pail of bird seed and up I went. I removed the screen from one of the windows and I must have been at least twenty feet from the feeder. From that bedroom window I began to throw the seed into the wind. The birds sat down below and looked at me as if I were insane. Finally they found a few of the kernels. The snow was so solid that it was like concrete and the seed did not fall through. The birds are able to salvage quite a bit of seed this way and this made me feel a little more relieved that they were getting some food after all. I was really thankful that the snow was as hard on the surface as it was. In spite of this, only five out of fifty-seven mourning doves returned after the blizzard had subsided.

I believe the dove is more vulnerable than some of the other winter birds around here. They are rather slow moving. They are pretty much ground feeders. I don't know for sure why we lost so many. Before we began to feed the birds years ago, I had no idea that the doves actually stayed here during the winter. I thought they all migrated as well. Before I started feeding the birds, I had never seen them here. One year I decided to start feeding a little earlier than normal. It was actually before the weather changed for the worst and before it had got too cold. I wanted to see if I could attract as many as possible before they left. That's when the doves began to come to our place and as long as we kept feeding them, they stayed. That's how I know that they stayed this winter.

I don't think it affected the squirrels. I took pictures of them as they were visiting our feeding station during the winter. They came out of their holes because they had come to be accustomed to feed.

I have noticed that during the fall you can get an indication of what kind of winter we are going to have by watching the acorns in our yards. Other bird feeders and animal lovers have made the same comment about the walnuts. It was a tremendous year for the acorn crop. We had more acorns on the tree this year than I have ever seen in all the years we've been living in this region. This is true for the other trees around here as well. And this was our worst winter.

My birdseed consists of a mixture of sunflower seeds and other varieties with equal proportions of each. I throw in one pail of sun flower seed, and one pail of the other mixture because not every one of the birds will eat the sunflower seeds and not every one of the birds will eat the mixture. They will choose the varieties that appeal to their little diet.

Martin Greg

When the snow disappeared in the spring, I went for a walk in the pine woods and I noticed many dead birds that had died during the blizzard.

Liz Madsen

"The claws of the bird were frozen into clumps of ice."

My mother and I were alone and we were bored and when we looked out the living room window we saw something moving on the front porch. It was blowing so hard that it was difficult to tell what it was. It was a bird flopping its wings. Mom told me to go outside and get it. The snow was too deep at the front door so I got all bundled up and went out the back door with a box and I put the female Cardinal in the box and brought it into the house. The claws of the bird were frozen into clumps of ice and snow so we got a hair dryer and put it on low and started to blow the hot air on the feet and this melted the ice and snow in about a half hour.

Then I put it back in the box and took it out to our garage and let it fly around in the garage - with a lot of bread and bird seed for it. It was warm in there.

On the first clear day I opened the garage door and she flew out and away. She was fine.

Robert Baldwin

"I was really hostile and tense because she had cancelled our wedding."

The storm struck Welland on the Friday morning and Jane and I were to be married the next day. I waited an hour before I left the school to go home. That would give everyone a chance to get out of the parking lot. When I left, I didn't think the weather was that bad because I could see 50 to 100 yards down the road. It was really blowing and it was cold as I drove to my mother's house. It took me about five or ten minutes. I was extra careful when I drove around a few stalled cars.

Then I started worrying about whether Jane was going to get home from Port Colborne. She called me later in the afternoon saying that she couldn't get home because the roads were blocked. I told her that I was going to come down and get her and she said that she wanted me to stay where I was because some people from school had tried to get through to Port Colborne that afternoon and couldn't get there.

I was very apprehensive that evening. I drank 5 or 6 bottles of beer and we talked several times on the phone. It often took us an hour between phone calls before we made a connection. I took a tranquilizer and went to bed.

I got up the next morning about six o'clock, the day of our wedding. Jane called me and I was really hostile and tense because she had cancelled our wedding and had started phoning everyone. We had to call our out of town relatives early in the morning before they left for our wedding. We called the priest and he scheduled us for the following Saturday. The photographers were in a car accident on the Friday and they couldn't have got there on Saturday either. We were lucky that the hall still had an opening the following week. They cooked the food that day and then froze it for the following week.

The cancellation was broadcast over the radio. The thing was that there were two Bob Baldwins and both were getting married that day, believe it or not. We both rented our tuxedos from the same store.

The girl that was going to do my hair went to work and waited all day for me to show up. I forgot to cancel my hair appointment. It was just something that slipped my mind. I said that if it snowed the following weekend we would have never gotten married at all.

I had all my gifts made up for the ushers and the best man and all the dates were stamped on them and it was of course the wrong date on them. That gives me leeway now as to which Saturday I want to celebrate it.

We didn't have any problems with the flowers. They had not cut them yet and we had them delivered the next Saturday right from the greenhouse.

Mrs. Jane Baldwin

"Bob was determined we were getting married even if there was nobody there."

During that Friday morning recess we were sitting looking out the window. The whole staff was there and finally the principal said, "I think we better start for home." I started out about a quarter to eleven and when I got to the high school I was lost. I didn't know where I was. Finally I came upon a car. It was about three feet in front of me before I saw it and it had its flashers on and its bright lights. I decided I'd better try to get back to the school. I made a U-turn and came back.

I was taken over to my friend's home by a four wheel drive truck. He took me there because he knew that I would really be a nervous wreck knowing the wedding was coming. I phoned Bob and told him that I was going to call the hall, the priest, and everybody and tell them that if it keeps up we'll cancel. He got very upset and told me there was no way I was going to do that. I asked him what I

159

was going to do if my parents wouldn't be able to come, none of my family would be able to make it and my sister was my maid-of-honour. My father wouldn't be able to give me away because he lives far away.

Bob was determined that we were getting married even if there was nobody there. I phoned Bob again at six o'clock on Saturday morning and told him that I was going to cancel the wedding. The blizzard was still raging and there was no hope of getting married that day. He said, "Well, if that's the way it's going to be, then that is just fine." Then he hung up on me.

We had booked our room for that night at the Park Motor Inn in Niagara Falls. There is this beautiful Chinese bedroom and we were looking forward to spending our first night there. Believe it or not, this other Robert Baldwin had booked the same room for the same night and if it wasn't for the blizzard, they may not have discovered the double booking of the same room. We could have arrived at Niagara Falls and discovered that we did not have a room. Or even more interesting, we may have moved in with another honeymoon couple, also named Mr. & Mrs. Robert Baldwin.

Our big joke is that I spent what would have been my honeymoon night with Tony Marinelli. I was at his house for the Friday and Saturday night of the blizzard. Tony and I were there together because his wife is a nurse and she was stranded at the hospital where she works. I slept in the spare room. Bob and Tony kid each other about where I spent my wedding night. I finally got to my own home on the Sunday.

Because the blizzard closed the school for a week, we took the time to reorganize. I was amazed that we didn't end up killing each other because of the tension that week. What would have happened if there was another storm the next weekend?

When the wedding finally took place, I decided to forget about formalities and enjoy myself. I was never so glad that it was finally over. I'm glad I went through with it.

Corporal Woodward - Ontario Provincial Police

*"We found the hardest thing to do was to
convince people that this was a bad storm."*

We found the hardest thing to do was to convince people that this was a bad storm and that they should come with us. We were very angry at one fellow who had a number of children in the car and he refused to come with us. He figured that it would blow over very quickly. Finally, we talked the father and children into coming with us. All they could say throughout the remainder of the night, each time they woke up, was that they were so thankful that they had come with us to the restaurant with 50 other people.

We no sooner arrived at the restaurant than the lights went out. Just seemed to be one tragedy after another. So we kept the

The Regional Police and the Military discover a car.

Anybody in there? Courtesy, Regional Police.

161

police cruisers running all night. We ran out of gas with one pretty early in the morning. Our idea was to help people warm themselves by taking turns getting into the cruisers. After this, they would go into the back kitchen of the restaurant and keep warm from the natural gas. This wasn't a safe thing to do but they had to keep warm. It's better than freezing to death. Fortunately there were no leaks in the gas system or someone could have been seriously injured.

On Saturday we attempted to get home. There was no possible way. We were directed to go to a motel and lodge in Fort Erie for the night.

The reverse situation will most likely happen the next time there are a few snow flakes. There will be panic all over. It was quite evident that the first little sign of snow after that storm got everybody frightened. Parents were taking kids home from school. They were reasoning that if it hit once, it can hit again. It seems as if people were waiting for it to happen again.

Don Morrison - Ontario Provincial Policeman

"Both the groomer and the ambulance sled should be kept at the fire hall."

Every municipality that might be hit by a blizzard should have a snowmobile groomer. It removes the high spots on the trails and smooths the way for rescue workers.

It would be wise to purchase an ambulance sled as well. That would cost between four and six hundred dollars. In it you can lay a person down and strap him in. The sled is covered with canvas and has a clear plexiglass window which would be good for people who suffer from claustrophobia. Both the groomer and the ambulance sled should be kept at a fire hall where they would be available at all times.

I'm sorry to say that there were inexperienced people on snowmobiles during the blizzard. That was both foolish and dangerous.

Larry Strange - Ontario Provincial Police Officer

"She hugged and kissed him she was so happy."

I was on traffic patrol in Fort Erie on the Queen Elizabeth when the storm hit. I was dispatched to an accident at Bridge St. I arrived 20 minutes later to find a tractor trailer unit jack-knifed and three cars in the ditch. I approached the scene at 10 miles per hour and then it took me another hour to write up the report.

I was sitting in the car when I noticed that the driver's window had turned white with frost, despite all the heating equipment. I felt that anyone coming onto the highway should be assisted back, because this wasn't like any other storm and it wasn't going to quit.

When I got out of my car and walked 20 ft. away I couldn't see my car. I headed back to Fort Erie, stopping on the way to help people who were stranded in their cars and in the ditches. I met an elderly couple in their 70's around Gilmore Road. I persuaded them to leave their car. They were reluctant to do so because they had all their valuables and were heading for Florida. I dropped them off in the bus station where they spent the night. I arranged a hotel room for them next day but they didn't have any clothes with them. I retrieved two bags from their car for them. Later that night I talked to the lady and she said that I had brought back their bathing suits and towels. She thought that it was kind of funny.

In reference to the mall, I was really amazed that the manager of the A & P in Fort Erie had arranged for food to be taken to the Skillet restaurant in Zellers. The staff in the Skillet had been kept on to cook for free for anyone who had been stranded and brought in.

Some people I thought kind of special through the storm were the people with the four wheel drives and also the CB'ers who were going out and bringing people back in their own cars. I remember about four in the morning, when a convoy of CB four wheel drives came down the highway on the wrong side. Transport trucks and vans which were snowed in on Friday night weren't cleared out until sometime Tuesday.

There were houses along the highway and Officer Bagley could tell you that some people gave refuge to twenty-five or thirty people during the storm in their houses. Some people found it heart breaking that other people were singled out and were told that they did a good job. There were a lot of people I know who did a good job. I had a lot of people at the time who asked me my name and they would write it down and say that they were going to write me a letter of appreciation and they didn't. It is a natural thing. Some people are like that. People mean well but they don't get around to it.

OPP Officer John Bagley was south bound and a guy pulled out and hit him. It was only a minor accident so John continued on to the accident about a half a mile because it was supposed to be a very serious accident. A truck was supposed to be on top of a car and a person was supposed to be trapped inside of the car. We then got another call that a car hit a telephone pole and the guy was cut up. We got another call then that a car rear-ended and a guy walked off into the storm and we didn't know where he was and his head was cut open. We got another call that a guy had been seen carrying a body on Gilmore Road. You couldn't even see Gilmore Road. These were the kinds of calls we were getting and we couldn't move, it was physically impossible. We felt helpless and we couldn't even stand out in it since the wind was so severe. Amazingly there were no deaths.

There was a tractor trailer unit bogged down under Baker Road with a drift as high as the unit on one side. Sunday morning we pulled nine cars out of the drift beneath. John Bagley had pulled a

Snow Canyons

hysterical woman out of a car earlier and she hugged and kissed him. She was so happy she thought she would not survive.

I am from St. John's Newfoundland so I have done a lot of heavy snow driving. When I moved to Toronto I noticed that a quarter of an inch of snow and the city was snowbound. This storm was different because of the intensity and the length of it. It was a three day thing. The drifting was what really made it bad. I have never seen the winds that severe. I felt sorry for the people who were in the mall from Friday to Sunday. But I suppose they were lucky when you think of what could have happened to them. I left my home seven o'clock Sunday night. My kids didn't recognize me when I got home because I had a beard.

From these experiences I now incorporate a CB in the cruiser. I wouldn't go without it. That is something that in a storm situation is a must. A person could use the CB to say where they are and how to get to them. Ordinary citizens would benefit from it. There are a lot of bad things about them such as the foul language but in an emergency situation, I don't think anything could help you more.

John Kirby - Emergency Measures Organization

"The Americans had more tracked vehicles in Buffalo than the Canadian Army has in total."

Breaking through in Wainfleet. Courtesy, Niagara Regional Police.

Staying in shape northern style.

Sun and snow creates a glow but strains the heart and back. A common scene after the Big One. W. D. T.

Welland snow drift by Greg Motolanez

Mrs. Gardner

My husband came home on Monday on a snowmobile. That was a terrible experience for him. He had only been on a skidoo once in his life. He didn't like jumping the snow drifts and the machine tipping over so he decided to walk for two hours down Lorraine Road in this terrible snow. There was a 30 foot drift right next door at our neighbours. You couldn't recognize the road. My husband walked past his own house. Until you were outside, you didn't understand the dangers.

We moved our groceries and garbage on toboggans for 3 weeks. It was the children's best winter with lots of snow to play in. But the birds weren't as plentiful as other years.

Digging out Port Colborne. Photo by Erno Rossi.

From The Tuck Tape to Indonesia

"He was trying to get some sleep when he heard the cracking of the timbers in the roof and sure enough there were vertical cracks appearing in the walls of his living room and in the walls down his hallway."

When we got down to where I had abandoned my car, we couldn't find it. It had been buried. Imagine this full-sized Ford Station Wagon, entirely buried, roof-rack and all. We discovered there was about 18" of snow above the roof-rack. The only thing that we could see was the tip of the radio aerial. We proceeded with the help of the neighbours to dig the driver's door open on the station wagon because all the groceries that Donna had bought on the Friday morning were still in the car. There were four bags of groceries in the car and when we got the driver's side open, the groceries were absolutely frozen solid. The thing that amazed me was the bottle of cooking oil, one of those plastic bottles of Mazola Oil was rock hard. You could have driven a spike into a two by four with it. There was one drift that was so high that an average size man such as myself could have stood on that packed crest and changed the electric street light with no ladder.

The phone rang a short time after 7:30 and my neighbour who lives at the end of Orchard Drive called and asked if I could spare him a couple hours to come over and help him shovel off his roof. His house is designed with a flat roof and the snow had been accumulating there during the course of the storm. I guess he really hadn't noticed it until Sunday night after the sun had gone down. He was trying to get some sleep when he heard the cracking of the timbers in the roof and sure enough there were vertical cracks appearing in the walls of his living room and in the walls down his hallway. He was very frightened. The weight of the snow by that time was tremendous. So, in the peak of the storm and through these massive drifts, I put on all the winter clothes I had, wrapped a scarf around my face and went over to give Pete a hand.

The drifting of the snow had overhung the sides of his roof by two or three feet in some cases, and it was necessary to take our shovels and chop it off, literally like you were chopping wood. The snow was so hard packed that it fell in chunks to the sides of his house and down on his cedar deck which he has at the back. We figured that if we had piled so much tonnage of snow on his deck that it too might crack. We decided to haul the snow to the two sides of the house where it wouldn't do any harm. We did a rough calculation. I understand that his roof area is roughly 1200 square feet. We know that the snow was at least 6 feet deep and possibly a little more in the maximum areas and just doing a rough calculation on the weight of the snow and the weight of each shovelful and knowing what a cubic foot of water weighs we figured that we shovelled in the hours that we worked, in excess of 100 tons of snow. It certainly felt like it.

There have been some rather funny situations too. Sue Benenson got stranded with her Simpson Sears repair man. Her own husband was down at the Port Colborne Mall. She tells a rather funny story and she says she really doesn't know who was more anxious, she or the repair man, who ended up staying for 2 nights while her own husband, Peter, was about ¼ of a mile away at the mall.

The Bridgers had quite a mix-up. Elliston was out of town and was stranded in St. Catharines that night. In the meantime Norm Penrose who is the minister at Morgan's Point had to take refuge at the Bridgers. So Norm was there living with Marcia Bridgers. The hospital was on the phone to Marcia all the time. She's a nurse and because she lived close to the hospital they were trying to persuade her to come into work to relieve some of those who weren't able to get home. So Norm Penrose ended up taking care of the Bridger children.

Des Cunnington went out to pick up Lynn at her school where she teaches in Sherkston when the storm started to break. But once he got out there, there was no way they could get home and they ended up living at a farm house with Lynn's grade 2 class. How would you like to be with 30 little Grade 2 children for 3 days? Their menu was something else. They had oatmeal for lunch and jam sandwiches for breakfast. There was a little store nearby and they just barely got along.

We heard of lots of cancellations. Actually, everything was cancelled, funerals, weddings and so on. The strangest of all, was that the winter survival course was also scrubbed. There was too much snow! A winter carnival that had been planned was also cancelled. Too much snow for it too.

Jamie Dewar - Teenager

"We skied throughout the blizzard."

I just finished the exams at the school. Then I wanted to go skiing. We heard that a storm was on its way but I was willing to take the chance because I needed to get away. So four of us got out of here the Friday morning and headed over to KISSING BRIDGE. We skied throughout the blizzard. It was fantastic. Friday night we stayed in the Chalet at the bottom of the ski hill. The next night we moved to the Seneca Mall in Buffalo. When we got to the Seneca Mall Saturday night, we slept on cots that they had set up there. There was food available such as bacon, toast and eggs that the Red Cross was supplying.

That day I met a lady from Derby, N. Y. who was staying at her daughter's because of the storm. I had this Audi, my father's car and it's a pretty good car and it will go through anything. I said that I would take her out to that place and we could stay overnight because they wouldn't let us stay at the Seneca Mall. So I took her there and we stayed over there the next night.

We were out of Port Colborne for 7 days. It was blowing in the Buffalo area but the drifts did not compare to the size of the

Blowing it away, Port Colborne. Courtesy of Inco.

ones we had around Port Colborne. Two nights were spent at the Regency Hotel. When we arrived at the Regency we had missed all the benefits that the people from Buffalo received. They were nice to us mind you. The free room and board was handed out to those who got stranded there the first and second night. We had to pay for everything with the one charge card that we had. Total costs at the end of it all were four hundred dollars.

Mr. Hoover

"Mind you, we had a lot of booze."

I thought the storm was excellent. I was stranded for two days in Bismark and I had to hitch hike home when the storm let up there on the Sunday for a couple of hours. We survived all right. We went around the neighbourhood and delivered the milk from the farm next door for all the little kids. We delivered by foot and with a little sleigh that we had. Mind you, we had a lot of booze because people kept dropping it off on us and we didn't turn them down. The rest of the time I played my guitar and just sat around.

Mrs. Dawdy

"It took two hours to cross the road."

We were out on the road heading back from Vineland and we couldn't get past Chambers' Corners. We stayed at the restaurant until we could get across the road. It took two hours to get across the road. There were twelve of us that slept on the floor in the restaurant the first night. The power kept going off.

There was very little water. These two guys who were there had a van full of horses and they had to get water and food for these horses but we didn't get any water until Saturday night. In the meantime these horses were given the water. This was fine because they certainly needed it and they drank a lot more than any of us.

The storm was the worst that I had ever seen even when compared with out West. I came from out there and we have lots of storms but I've never seen anything like this one. It felt like hail hitting your face. It was so cold when we were walking back that we had to walk backwards into the service station or we would have frozen our faces. I had a blanket wrapped around me as well because I couldn't stand the wind hitting my mouth and face.

When we got back into our home we were pretty well set. I have three freezers and I always have bread frozen. I have powdered milk for the animals and I used that when we ran out of milk.

I don't know exactly how many people we had staying with

us but it involved seven different families. This included three small children and one little girl who had quite an ear ache but there was no way we could get them out.

Ron Lampman

"I couldn't see my hands on the handlebars."

She hit about 10:30. I was contacted by a Welland Ontario Provincial Police Sergeant. He asked me if I'd go out the highway here and help get some people off the road. On Miller Road near Highway 3, there was a stranded school bus full of children and a couple of cars. I went out to get my snowmobile off the back of my truck. In doing so, the wind caused the rear door of my truck to drop. My snowmobile windshield got smashed. I got the machine going and I drove around my yard for about a half an hour because I couldn't find my way out to the road. I almost ran into my own house. I couldn't see my hands on the handlebars. In a lull in the wind, I saw my own house and I hadn't moved, I was just running around my own yard. There was no use going anywhere. That night, late, I went around the field a few times and out on the road. I didn't see anybody out there. A few cars but no one was in them.

On Saturday morning we went over to Bethel School and helped clean that out. There were 30 children there and we took them home.

We were running heart pills and blood pressure medicine. You name it, we were running it. At 3 o'clock, Sunday morning, we were going down to some of these farms and feeding their cattle and breaking ice so we could get water to them. One fellow had a chicken farm. It was about two in the morning when we took him over there to his chickens. The power had been off. He had frozen pipes so we left him there for a couple of hours while we went up to Brookfield Road and fed some cattle and horses and then we went back and picked him up and took him home. He had built a fire under the boiler, and got the heat on a bit. It was enough to keep his five thousand chickens from freezing. The next day we were supposed to take him back, but we had some emergencies to look after. So he bought a snowmobile of his own. On Tuesday afternoon, when everything was settling down, I took the wife for a snowmobile ride down the road and we went over the top of a school bus. It was buried. You couldn't see the roof. Later, three of us with machines and sleighs each delivered two hundred pounds of chicken feed for our neighbour. This left him free to bring in his own fuel by snowmobile.

My advice is to be certain that you put a little bit of de-icer in your gas, a good tablespoon full for each five gallons of gas. That way, you won't stall the machine. If the snow is packy, be certain to tip the machine on its side and accelerate the engine so that you get the snow free from your track. This saves you from burning out your belt.

Be sure you carry extra plugs with you and extra belts and dry gloves. When transporting the children from the school, I took an extra snowmobile suit. You should have seen a three foot kid in that. But they were warm and that's the main thing. If it's possible, it's wise to pull a small sleigh with you, just in case there's not room on the machine. You can always carry provisions in it too. Sometimes it can bog you down.

Have you ever pulled up to a stop light and a car beside you moves a little bit and you think you're moving and you jump on the brakes? It's that same silly feeling I had during the blizzard when I was on my machine. The engine was idling and I wasn't moving. With that snow blowing past me, I felt like I was really moving. I would even slam on the brakes. That made me feel silly because the machine was not in motion.

Gino Rossi

"It was ten below zero in the living room."

I tried to get my car out of the driveway that morning and it was snowy and icy. I couldn't move the car so I didn't go to work. Around noon hour it started to snow quite heavily. By Saturday morning there was a thirty-five foot drift in my driveway. You could stand on top of it and touch the power lines with no problem. The drift completely encircled the house.

We had no power. Our electricity went out about twelve noon on Friday and we were without it for five days. The only heat we had was in the kitchen and it came from a gas stove. Naturally, the pipes of our heating system broke and I think we had something like twelve or thirteen joints that had opened up. We have a hot water heating system and the water gushed out. I carried out eleven of these five gallon pails of water. Into the second day we were running out of milk and bread because Ethel hadn't had a chance to go shopping.

I think some of our confidence was gained from having a radio. It was portable luckily and with the batteries we were able to keep in touch with these outside reports. We would hear people say that we weren't to panic and that snowmobilers would be out with food. We got help on Sunday.

Our phone was always in operation and that was a tremendous help. We were able to talk to our loved ones. I was able to call the store and check on proceedings there. We actually had a ball in the sense that we were all in the kitchen - one big happy family.

I was thankful that I was stranded at home rather than out on the highway. When we began to hear stories of people in distress I began to realize how lucky I was.

The children reacted quite well. Shawna read her book and we had the mattresses out on the floor so that they could do their tumbling and Shawna was old enough that she was able to understand what was going on and showed no fear of anything. I think we just accepted it as a normal condition and the kids accepted it the same way.

Living out here on the lake you are conditioned to a number of things that can happen very easily. The thing that crossed my mind most often was the possibility of a sick child. Fortunately, that didn't happen.

In the future I know I'm going to stock up with more food in the house and I'm also going to drain those water pipes. If the power is off for at least two or three hours, they recommend that you should do that.

Many people got snow in their attics. When it melted people received all kinds of water damage below. I think another main thing is to make certain that every home has some form of gas. These electric homes may be fine but they were quite a problem. If we hadn't had gas out here we would have frozen.

We have a fireplace, but we may as well have had a fire burning out in the middle of a snowbank. The winds were so fierce that it just drew everything right up the flue. The living room is on the exposed side towards the lake and without a word of exaggeration, it was ten below zero in the living room. Everything was frozen. Ethel's flowers had ice all over them and the thermometer dropped below the registration point on the outside porch.

So we had the phone working, we had the radio working because of the batteries and we had a gas oven that provided some heat. I think those three things got us through.

I know one thing I'll never forget. When the government finally got a snowplow out here to dig out the road, they couldn't find the road. It was not there.

Howie Climenhage - Fireman - Crystal Beach

"We had calls for bird seed and birth control pills."

We had a lot of kids coming around the firehall who wanted to help. When it got to the point where they were getting in the way, we decided to put them to good use. We sent them out in our equipment truck with shovels. We had a couple of firemen in there with them with a map. The firemen dropped these kids off at certain points and they dug out fire hydrants. The truck would return and pick up the kids and take them to another point. We had all our hydrants dug out in that way. If a fire would have erupted we had an instant water supply.

We were running the snowmobilers out of our station here. In fact they were being run out of all six fire halls in Fort Erie. The Ontario Provincial Police were working with us out of a fire station because they couldn't get to their office. We had a ten foot drift down the south end of town close to the lake. The cars were completely buried and everything down on Erie Road and in front of the Palmwood Hotel was completely bogged in. You could only see the second story of the Palmwood Hotel.

We were transporting food to different residents who couldn't get out. They were unable to get their checks cashed and some of these people who were on welfare were having a difficult time. So we ran food to them. You know we have about three thousand five hundred people in the winter time in this area and that's enough to cause a major problem. We were lucky that we had no fire problem because people were using their fireplaces twenty-four hours a day to keep warm. Those folks who needed prescriptions from drug stores got them filled and we ran them back to their home on snowmobiles.

The snowmobiles started to set up at noon on Friday. I never got to the fire hall myself until Saturday night because I was stranded at John Deere in Welland. We had nothing to do in the plant but sit around and play cards. There wasn't any place to lie down and have a comfortable sleep. I remember the canteen truck that was loaded with goods destined to go to Hayes-Dana, couldn't get out of our parking area and we managed to clean out his complete truck over the period of that storm.

Back here in Fort Erie I remember calls coming in from people who were anxious to get bird seed for their birds. They thought they had an emergency with that. We also had calls for birth control pills.

I don't know how the animals were affected by the storm but I imagine that the cat population will be decreased this year.

I think we were a little bit more ready for that blizzard than some areas because of that damn ice storm we had the year before. We organized after that ordeal. The organization carried us pretty well. The majority of people co-operated with us really well. They offered anything they had and the snowmobilers just worked their hearts out for three or four days and never asked for a damn thing in return. That storm was like a war.

Charles Ott - The International Nickel Co.

"They'd work sixteen hours, then sleep, then work another sixteen."

We are prepared in a number of ways at INCO. We have a hundred beds we can make available in an emergency, seventy cots and mattresses stored away in a store room in the separate change house and then we can sleep another twenty people in the club house. We have rooms in the club house with a bath and a number of suites in that area. We have some other rooms with a common bathroom.

We had food in the freezer for overtime lunches, so that perhaps we had a hundred frozen dinners similar to a T.V. dinner but larger. We call it the working man's T.V. dinner. We have an electric oven which will heat fifty T.V. dinners at a time, and we have coffee making facilities, all kinds of linen and silver and so on. We also have facilities and a recreation club, where we can set up various beds. The separate change houses have lots of facilities. We are ready and we have gone through this before so we have some organization. We can easily jump into it and get going.

We've prepared a number of times for snow storms but then things cleared up and people went home. This was the worst, of course. Things started Friday morning and by Friday at four o'clock, nobody could get out of the plant except those who lived in the immediate area. We fed and slept two-hundred and fifty people in the plant Friday night, including the ladies. I put them up in our club house. I pulled the mattresses off the box springs so that each room that was equipped with twin beds slept four girls. Two slept on the box and two slept on the mattresses. Food was a big problem because you couldn't get anywhere to pick up more. We had twenty-one cars jammed in the front of the office. Each one had tried to get out and got stuck, while the next one tried to go around him and he got stuck. Transportation was impossible; so we had to walk.

We took all the bread we could get from the Quality Baking Company on Mitchel Street. We went to DeFelica's and got one hundred pounds of cold cuts. We got other things at the other little stores, at least dry soup, coffee, soda biscuits, butter. We were all right for food. The boys came over in shifts to eat. Those who had to stay on the job and work sixteen hours were given dinners. We managed to get over town and get some more food.

One of the superintendents here has a four-wheel drive vehicle and that Sunday morning they opened Loblaws and we really got a supply of stuff. We had bacon and eggs and everything under the sun.

As far as the plant was concerned, we kept going. Friday morning we had gotten two big front end loaders and then three trucks similar to the ones we have permanently. These three loaders worked steadily from Friday through to Monday hauling snow. We kept our main yard completely clear. We kept up with the storm and the men who stayed and couldn't get home were quite happy to work sixteens so we did have enough labour. Some of them made a bundle over the period. They'd work sixteen hours, then sleep, then work another sixteen. The plant operated.

Saturday morning was a little bleak. I had coffee and soda biscuits for breakfast. But the thing is, we left all the staples for the men who were working. All we did was walk around and worry and keep things going.

We had a lot of people come from out lying areas, some from Fort Erie, Gasline, Welland and so on. And of course the roads were closed so they had to stay. As things got a little better, the snow plows got streets opened.

Those who lived in town gradually got home. We got all our girls out Saturday. We had the fifteen of them in the bunkhouse. Some walked, some went out by Ski-doo. So by Saturday night we had it down to one hundred and fifty people. By Sunday there were only fifty of us left. It was an experience, not the kind you want every winter.

There was a lot of time and a half paid which amounts to money when you're running your whole plant on overtime. But I suppose the food cost us a little. The snow removal was expensive. We had big machines in here at thirty dollars an hour, trucks at twenty dollars an hour moving around the clock. There was a certain amount of loss of production but we managed to keep things pretty well moving. We couldn't ship of course, nothing was moving on the roads. That wasn't awfully important because we were able to catch up the next weekend when the highways started opening. I think probably it was expensive for us in the same ways it's expensive to the city. The tax payers and so on have to pay for the snow removal equipment.

One roof collapsed in a storage shed because of the heavy snow. It was an older building and there was nobody in there.

That happened all over the place. Some of my neighbours lost their garage roofs at home because the snow got piled up. The serious area, of course is in that belt along the lake. People further inland didn't know what snow was. I live on Lake Erie, just west of Port Colborne, just past Sugarloaf Hill, and I had a fourteen foot drift in my backyard. You could walk right over my garage on the snow. People in Welland thought they had snow and they had a foot and a half.

We got some very nice letters from people regarding the care they received. For those who weren't working, we dug up some radios and a couple of television sets from the club house. Some of them played billiards and bowled in the recreation club. When you have a group of people held inside like that you've got to do something or it gets pretty difficult and people get arguing. So you've got to keep up morale as well as keep them fit.

Mrs. George Furry

"He had frostbite on his hands and he was screaming and screaming."

The people in Port Colborne and Welland had nothing to compare with what we had out here. In fact we had quite an emergency at my brother-in-law's. We had a guy stop breathing on us. He had been out trying to help people all day long knocking on doors and so on. Finally, he just broke down with exhaustion. We called the Wainfleet emergency number and they said, "We can't do anything, it's up to you." Fortunately he came to by himself and snapped out of it. He could have died very easily, he was in such bad shape. He had frostbite on his hands and he was screaming and screaming. What really got me was the way the emergency number told us that it was up to us and there you were right back to zero again. I suppose that's what it all boils down to. It's up to yourself in a disaster like this.

Far above maximum. Courtesy, Betty Leslie, Wainfleet.

Mrs. King

I have two small children who were at home. But my husband never got home until Sunday morning at 2:00 a.m. Our power was off for 17 hours. We blocked the door way with blankets to keep one room warmer. We stayed in the kitchen. We'd turn on the oven for cooking and of course it would keep the room a little warmer. We don't have a fireplace. I brought a mattress into the kitchen and we slept there all together at night, wearing a lot of clothes.

Ray Prophet

There was one drift thirty feet high. Underneath it we knew there was a snowmobile. We tried to dig and find it but we couldn't locate it. When that giant snowblowing machine came along it touched the buried snowmobile and crumpled it.

McDonald's Golden Arches

"One move and that whole window would have blown in on us"

When the storm hit we locked the doors first off, but it turned out that certain people were stuck. They had to leave their cars on the highway out in front, because they couldn't drive any further. So we unlocked the doors and let the people come in. We were not prepared to have anyone stay here. The full-time ladies wanted to go home to their families, and I wanted to go home too. But if people are stuck, what are you going to do? You got to let them in. As the storm got worse, we had to let more in. So we wound up with about forty people in here, along with five of the full-time ladies and myself. The storm didn't let up at all. Come night time, everyone was getting pretty hungry, so we lit the grills and we served them supper which consisted of quarter pounders and french fries. We didn't charge them for it because we knew that some of them didn't have any money anyway.

The storm was getting worse and everyone was getting nervous. We had some older people here, they were getting kind of upset. So we decided we had to get some help to get them out of here. So I called one of my friends on the telephone who had a CB radio and I knew that the CB'ers were out with their skidoos. He called on the CB and he got us a couple of snowmobiles. So, two snowmobiles showed up and they started carting the people off to motel rooms. And we also had a Bell Canada truck here and he took some of them down to a motel room.

That pretty well took care of all the customers except one older fellow. He was afraid of a snowmobile. He said, "Well I don't really want to go down there but I've got my wife's medicine here for her heart condition. She needed her medicine four hours ago." So I said, "Look! You get on the skidoo and get home to her right now!" So one of the guys took him down on the skidoo. The one skidoo couldn't go by himself, he had to have a backup just in case something happened to him. So he went seven miles by snowmobile.

So, it came to getting all the ladies out of here and they didn't want to go because I wouldn't go. You see, I couldn't go. The front window, the big bay window with the golden arches on it, with the wind blowing as strong as it was, curved the window right in. One move and that whole window would have blown in on us. So, we stayed here overnight. It cleared up a little bit in the morning. Finally, we couldn't take it any more, so we called for help and they finally got us home on Saturday morning.

On the Sunday, the snowmobile rescue squad was set up here by the CB'ers. This was their base station.

Major W. A. Smy - Operations Officer
Lincoln & Welland Regiment.

". . . his hands were like those small footballs that kids play with."

The storm blew up on the twenty-eighth and about four p.m. the Lincoln and Welland Regiment was placed in a stand-by position, mainly because the military are not allowed to respond to a civilian emergency until they have the authority from their command headquarters, which in our case is in St. Hubert. They don't authorize the employment of the reserves until a request is formally received from the civil authorities. This is to protect the individual militiamen who may injure himself or injure someone else in the performance of his duties. If he hasn't been formally placed on duty, he is civilly liable for his actions; so the reserves are not allowed to respond until they have been formally placed on duty.

The regional authorities asked for a military commitment in the afternoon on the twenty-ninth of January and F.M.C. headquarters called out the unit at fifteen-thirty hours, that's three thirty. F.M.C. means Force Mobile Command, it translates back and forth into French and English.

We sent a liaison officer to the Emergency Measures Organization headquarters at Church Street in St. Catharines and established an operation centre at Lake St. Armory and militiamen were ordered to report to both Lake Street and Niagara Falls Armories. In some cases, militiamen like myself who live in Fort Erie or Port Colborne, couldn't respond because we were snowed in. We were forced to wait until the military came and got us in the wee hours of Saturday morning, when the first vehicle convoy started reaching Port Colborne and Fort Erie.

At five o'clock or seventeen hundred, the Twenty-Third Service Battalion in Hamilton was also called out and phased under com-

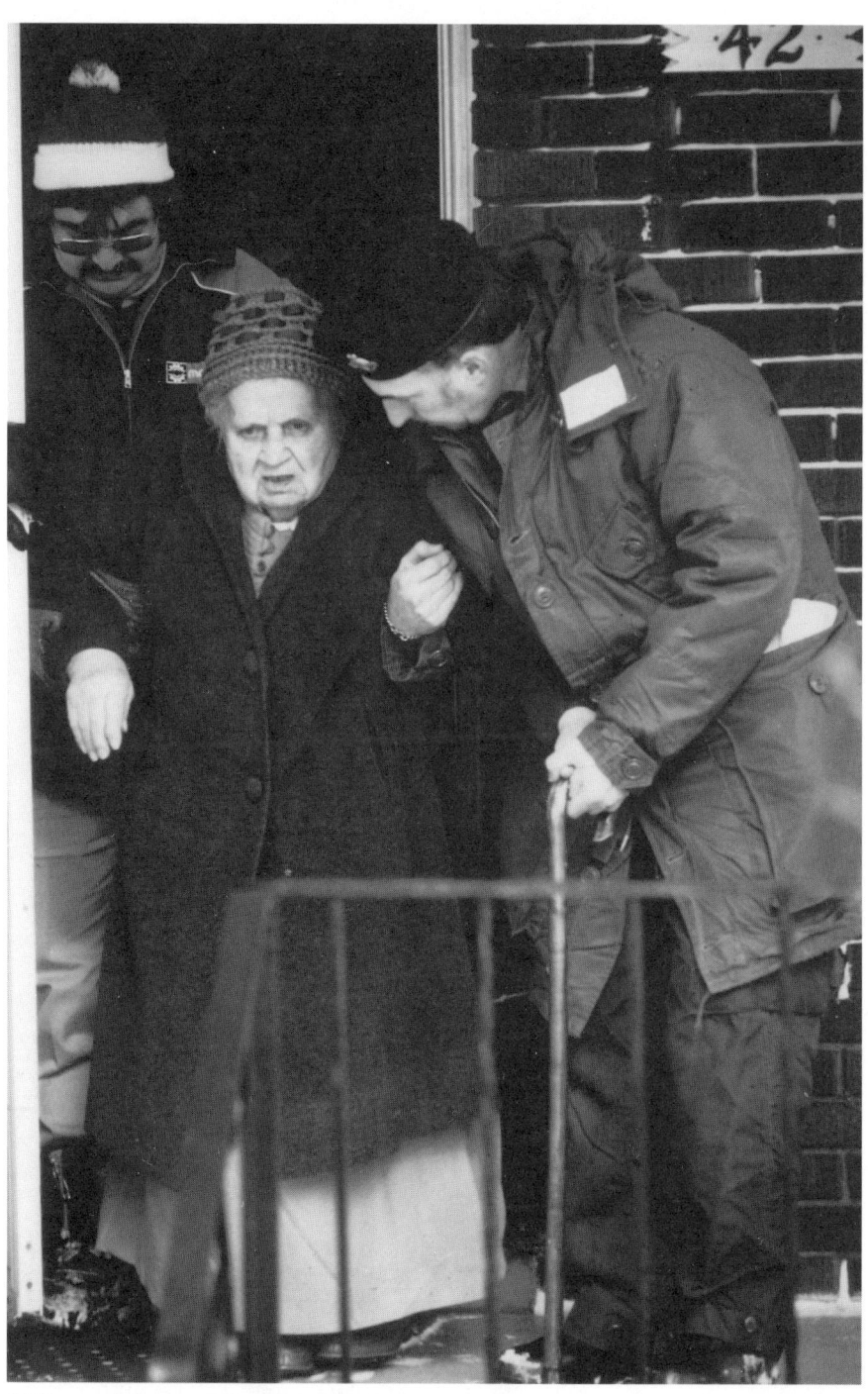

Military assistance. Courtesy, Regional Niagara.

mand of the Lincs and they responded within two hours with thirty-two vehicles, including two one ton ambulances, all sent to St. Catharines. All the vehicles were four-wheel drive because everything else was considered to be useless. By eleven o'clock that night four vehicles had reached Welland with a total of thirty men and by two o'clock the next morning we had two vehicles and five soldiers in Port Colborne. The response was slow because it took hours for them to make their way down the highways. By daybreak there were a hundred and thirty of all ranks employed in the operation.

We had the liaison officer at the E.M.O. headquarters in St. Catharines and what we called an operation centre in Lake St. Armory which controlled the dispatch of and movement of vehicles and personnel. We then had a practical headquarters in the Regional Police Station in Niagara Falls. I commanded the Welland group and a Captain Wayne Hill commanded Niagara Falls. On the thirtieth, which would be the Sunday, we were ordered to concentrate our main effort into the Wainfleet area and evacuate the school children out of the schools. This is the Welland group I'm talking about and they estimate on that day that we evacuated between thirteen hundred and seventeen hundred children. The same thing happened in the Chippawa area. The main task there was to evacuate children stranded in schools.

Other things that we did very early on the morning of the thirtieth, we evacuated an individual from Port Colborne suffering from a kidney disease to St. Catharines where he was treated. In Fort Erie, we moved a number of people with heart problems to the hospital. We also took medicine out to a diabetes case out in Stevensville and in Fort Erie they picked up two or three pregnant women and moved then to the hospital. No births on the way, it was just a precautionary move. By five o'clock that day the high point of our employment was reached, one hundred and fifty-six all ranks, plus nine regular force soldiers. The military headquarters in Hamilton have a number of regular force soldiers attached to it in a support role to the militia and nine of those were tasked basically in an administrative role in the centre in St. Catharines.

On the first morning that we were there, that would be the thirtieth, I flew by helicopter and we did a survey of the lakeshore. The police had no idea of the conditions of the lakeshore. They knew that they were bad but the Superintendent in Welland was going by descriptions he had had phoned in to him. During that flight I was astounded that the drifts out around Lowbanks were thirty and forty feet high. At Lowbanks church all I could see was the steeple coming out of the snow. The Cove restaurant was identifiable only because I could see the square outline of the roof. I couldn't see anything of the building. A lot of cottages were drifted completely over and almost every road from the highway south to the lakeshore was bogged with high drifts. On that flight we put down and picked up a fellow who had frozen hands and feet and flew him into Port Colborne Hospital. His name was Mulko. One of the first problems that was presented to me when I arrived in Welland was from Superintendent Leigh. He indicated that they had known for about twenty-three hours that this fellow had been out at the Agro place and they had tried unsuccessfully to get him by skidoo. Then the first helicopter came from Niagara Helicopters in Niagara Falls, piloted by an individual named Verdel and co-piloted by Frank Edwards. The weather was quite bad. They were very reluctant to fly but the three of us flew to the lakeshore. I went because I was familiar with the lakeshore and had the ability to map read. We put the helicopter down on the lake because the lake was virtually swept bare of snow. The snow had piled up along the lakeshore as soon as it hit the first windbreak. Edwards and I had taken out with us some shovels, small trenching tools that the military uses. When we reached the Agro house, the snow drifts were up to the eaves all around the house. The only way we recognized the house was from the description Agro give to me on the telephone, regarding one of those metal boat lifts used for lifting boats out of the water in the summertime. When we got there we had to dig down from the eaves to a window. We first attempted to try to get into a door but that was virtually impossible. We found it was easier to dig into a window and we used a shovel to pry it open. He had the crank type windows which opened from the left to right. It was frozen shut so we used a shovel to pry it open and they passed out a step ladder. Edwards and I climbed inside and we bundled up this Mulko. Then we dragged him out through the window and up onto the snow bank. He could walk a bit and we took him to the helicopter. Since the helicopter was only a two-passenger carrier, he and Edwards got on and Verdel flew them back to Port Colborne Hospital. I thought I was stranded because the weather was so bad at the point that I didn't think that he could make a second trip. About thirty minutes later, he came back and picked me up.

When I first went into the house, I couldn't believe my eyes. His hands were like those small footballs that kids play with. It was a very advanced state of frostbite and his feet were very bad. I was amazed that he was able to walk to the helicopter, but that was just one incident on the first morning.

I flew once a day, either by helicopter or in a Cessna from Dan Air out of Welland airport. Usually, just after first light we'd make a survey of the lakefront from Fort Erie to the Lowbanks area.

We were at the disposal of the Niagara Police, those were the orders that came from F.M.C. in St. Hubert. The priorities that we established with the police were to preserve life, clear main arteries into the communities of Port Colborne and Fort Erie, and try to open No. 3 Highway between Port Colborne and Fort Erie. We did not concern ourselves with snow removal at that point. In Buffalo, the army was mostly concerned with snow removal.

Our big problem was to keep No. 140 open between Welland and Port Colborne. It drifted very quickly. If a car stopped within fifteen minutes it would form a drift and block the highway and we had great difficulty convincing civilians not to use the highway. If their car stalled or they ran off the road, the highway would be blocked soon afterwards. Then we had difficulty in getting the vehicles down to open it up again. Our thought was that if the storm persisted, eventually we would have to have a direct link from

St. Catharines into Port Colborne in order to bring in large amounts of food. Therefore, 140 was one of the critical highways to keep open.

In Welland, we organized into what we call vehicle columns, in which there were soldiers and vehicles tasked to go out to do certain jobs such as, the effort into Wainfleet to pick up school children. Then there was another group which were called the standby reserve. This was a small number of vehicles left in Welland for emergency tasks. We were afraid that if there was a large fire we'd have difficulty getting fire-fighters into it. Then there was a reserve that worked in and around Welland which cleared fire hydrants and helped shovel out fire halls and sent people to help shovel out at the hospital and places of that nature.

At one point the Superintendent was seriously considering rationing the gasoline in Welland, because we were consuming an estimated thousand gallons a day, which at any prolonged pace would drain all the stocks in the civilian service stations. At that point we weren't sure how long we would be there but that was just the police and the military consumption. We had no idea what the Ministry of Highways was using and their vehicles suck it up just as fast as ours.

In Welland, the soldiers were put up at Riverside Apartments on River Road the first night. We were graciously treated by the people in the apartments. We were coming and going at all hours and no one complained. The women cooked for us. The second day the numbers arriving in Welland were such that we had to move out of there and we moved into Sunset Haven, the senior citizen residence which quartered us for the duration of the emergency. We were treated very well there too.

At the same time this was going on, the military was very heavily committed in the London area. They had reserves down there called out and they had a full nine hundred man infantry battalion called out. At no time did the Region ask for the air support from Trenton. That's where our military helicopters are based.

In order to get assistance, the Region has an Emergency Measures Organization and they request assistance from E.M.O. at the provincial level. We then have a direct line to what we call the regional centre, at Downsview, which is a military centre. Basically, that assistance is as fast as the telephone because the region would identify the requirements and pass them to Toronto to the E.M.O. in the provincial government. A few more phone calls and either the regular army or the reserves are called out, possibly both. We being reserves, have what we call a lag time in response because we have to call people to report to the army and then they task them from there.

Our contingency plans never envisaged having key people stranded and not being able to respond. We have never made contingiency plans for a snowstorm. We had plans for lost children, fires, floods and wars but never a snowstorm. We didn't anticipate one hitting here. Our biggest problem was that key people were stranded whom we had assumed would respond and be at the Lake St. Armory almost immediately. Our transport officer never got to Lake and one of the key functions of the operation was that of transport. You have to have an experienced person controlling dispatching and the breakdowns and gas and all that, but our transport officer lives in Fort Erie. He never got into St. Catharines. That job had to be done by a senior N.C.O. who did it fairly effectively but in all our contingiency plans, this fellow from Fort Erie was to respond to the emergency. In my case, I'm the operations officer for the unit and theoretically I should have gone right to St. Catharines but by the time I could respond, they already had a functioning headquarters in St. Catharines so I went only as far as Welland. Where they were short of Company Commanders, their companies were organized by somebody else. It was a learning experience to us. This was the first time we'd been called out since the Second World War to aid the civil authorities. So the first time we were called out, it didn't happen according to the books we have in the safe in St. Catharines. Since the storm, we've written a new S.O.P., a standard operating procedure. The first battalion in the R.C.R. in London is equipped with armored personnel carriers which are fully tracked. They also have a quantity of snowmobiles. In London they were not faced with the problems we had here of being confronted with conditions that would eventually stop a four-wheel-drive vehicle. Their A.P.C.'s would have a very good cross-snow capability and if they reached that limit then they do have a quantity of snowmobiles. We could have used some down here, but they were all committed in London. We asked for some out of the Borden and Barrie areas.

 I talked to a meteorologist at the forces base in Toronto and he gave me a description of why the storm was so severe here. His explanation was that during the winter of '77, Lake Erie froze on a calm night so that the lake surface was very smooth. Normally he said that when Lake Erie freezes you have great ridges, high pressure ridges that have been thrust up so that the lake is very uneven with a very rough configuration. However, this year it was relatively smooth. Then we received over a period of time three or four snowfalls and the weather stayed cold so that the snow didn't melt and pack itself. When the storm came up, the high winds picked up all the snow that was lying on Lake Erie and blew it until it hit the first windbreak. Of course, that was the lakeshore. You could see that very clearly when you flew over because from the lake to No. 3 Highway there was a lot of snow and from No. 3 to about the Forkes Road you could see that there was less snow. North of the Forkes Road the fields were swept bare of snow. There was hardly any snow at all, except where there was a windbreak. This description fits in with what I saw. The job I had during the snowstorm was commanding the task group.

 We established a task group headquarters centre in the Regional Police in Welland. We had extra telephones put in. One was a direct line to St. Catharines to our centre at Lake St. Armory and then the others were just regular Bell Telephones that you could call out on. That was our line of communication to the military in St. Catharines. Everywhere we sent a group of soldiers we sent a policeman with a police hand radio. Onto the police communication network we posed a military network also. When I was flying a helicopter, I could talk to any of my officers on the ground via the police radio. It worked very effectively. One of the difficulties in using civilian snowmobilers is that they have no internal discipline. The police could request a guy to go out and search twenty cottages but if the weather got too bad or he decided that he wanted to see his girl friend, the fellow could just disappear without any compulsion to report to headquarters. The military and the police have that internal discipline. Of course, the civilian snowmobilers did an excellent job. However, there is always that potential for a problem. I don't know whether the E.M.O. is considering organizing the snowmobilers and CB'ers into a working group. That procedure worked well whereby snowmobilers reported to police headquarters in Port Colborne, Welland and Fort Erie and to fire stations in places like Ridgeway and Crystal Beach.

CHOW Radio did a very good job in keeping the public informed. One of the difficulties in this type of thing is people who think they are isolated and have no concept of what's going on. They become very worried, but anyone listening to the radio station had a very good picture of what was going on. Anyone could pick up the phone and talk on open line radio without being screened. I think that in the future that there should be some sort of screening done before a person gets on the air. I don't know how true this is but it was presented to me and I was never able to verify this. Someone called in and said over the radio that there was a possibility of a water shortage in Port Colborne. There was no water shortage until about five minutes after that call. Everybody in Port Colborne must have started filling their bathtubs after that call. In the future I would think that the radio stations should screen the comments to make sure that this type of thing didn't happen. On the whole, I think the radio stations did an excellent job.

There was an incident where somebody called in and said that a person had been found dead in a car on No. 58 Highway. It took Superintendent Liegh quite a long time in order to get that message back out over the air that that was totally inaccurate, that nobody had been found dead at any point in the Niagara Peninsula. This is one of the difficulties where they broadcast live. This is not good for people who know that their relatives are stranded and then they hear something like that on the radio.

There was a very long time lag on the telephone if you tried to call. That was one of the difficulties that the Agro's faced until we arrived. They really did not understand that when they picked up the phone, they had to wait for the dial tone. So they thought they were isolated there and they only responded when people called into them. When we arrived there, I phoned my situation and explained what I had decided to do with this fellow Mulko. It took eight minutes to get a dial tone. The average person wouldn't wait that long.

During the storm we did a telephone survey, randomly picking people's names out of the telephone book from along the lakeshore mainly, on both sides of Port Colborne. We would call them and ask them whether they had power. Every hour, two duty officers were tasked to call so many people. It was what I call a cross - the - front.

The duty officer would call and ask if you had experienced power failures. If you answered yes, he asked when, for how long, that sort of thing. This was plotted so that the power people would have an idea of where the problem would be. We also discussed the food problem with them. It's amazing the number of people who do not have one day's supply of food in the house. We found a lot of people running out of food. We flew rations in by helicopter to the Lowbanks area, to Concessi's store out there. These are military rations, they come three meals in one box, three soldiers meals for one day. We call it, an individual ration pack. You get one of those each day.

We received a warning order from the R.R. headquarters at ten-thirty on the second of February. They thought the emergency would cease within twenty-four hours and by three-thirty the next day we had split down and had had everybody return.

Our biggest problem was that when this thing happened, we held no winter equipment. Normally, in the wintertime, on an exercise, we draw the equipment that we need just for that specific exercise out of the supply group in Hamilton. They hold a number of different items and the various militia in the Hamilton district draw out of that pool of stores and return it when they are finished. That weekend, we were caught without radios or winter equipment because on the Thursday, January 27, almost all the winter equipment was sent to Meaford for winter exercizes that weekend. When the big blow came up on Friday, we had no winter pool stores to draw from in Hamilton. So all our winter equipment that we drew, parkas, mukluks, windpants, mitts and everything else, all had to come out of base Toronto, at Downsview. This made it very difficult because we had to send vehicles there to pick the stuff up and bring it down here. It's sort of ironic that all that winter equipment that we had was stranded for four days in Meaford. They had all the stuff up there and they couldn't go anywhere. They were snowed in up there. You know, throughout the period, we equipped the police with winter equipment because their regular uniforms were inadequate for the job.

All our vehicle problems were maintenance problems. We had no accidents. We had a total of fifty vehicles involved in the operations, including two one ton box ambulances. We went on standby at four o'clock on the twenty-eighth of January. The young officer that first arrived at Lake St. Armories thought it would be a good idea to take all the vehicles inside the Armory and check the oil and the gas. This was a disaster because in cold weather you should never take a vehicle into a warm environment. The problem is that the metal vehicle sweats and when you drive it back outside it freezes. He had them sitting inside for about two hours before somebody more knowledgable arrived. Then the vehicles went back outside. The emergency brakes froze on them and some of the wheels froze. Then when you take the vehicle from the outside in, you get moisture condensation on the inside of the gas tank and in a two and a half ton Gun-tracker you get as much as three gallons of condensation. If you try to run it for any period of time inside the Armory you'll find that the engine is not performing properly. As soon as you take it outside you get gasline freeze-ups. So we were initially plagued with many of those problems. We had to go and get a lot of this de-icer for these forty to fifty gallon tanks on some of the trucks. Any soldier who's been around for a while knows that. So it's not a big discovery. It's just a fact that the young officer who was first on the scene at Lake St. Armory didn't have the experience and he thought he was doing the right thing. We ran into that problem but most of the difficulties we had were maintenance problems. There was no problem if the vehicle was our one-ton Dodge trucks. They are almost exactly the same as the one-ton civilian Dodge

trucks. Parts for them are easy to come by. Our two and a half ton trucks and our three quarter ton trucks are strictly military. When a two and a half ton truck idles for a long period of time, the points on them tend to weld together. Well, you can't buy points for a two and a half ton truck in the average Canadian Tire store. Parts have to come down through the supply system which meant we had to go to Toronto to get them. So we were having difficulties there. In order to insure that the truck would be mobile, instantaneously, we had to leave it running for long periods of time.

We thought the operation was very successful. We had no major vehicle accidents, no injuries and no claims against the Crown when it was finished.

And now for some fun. Notice phone line to the left.
Courtesy, The Tribune

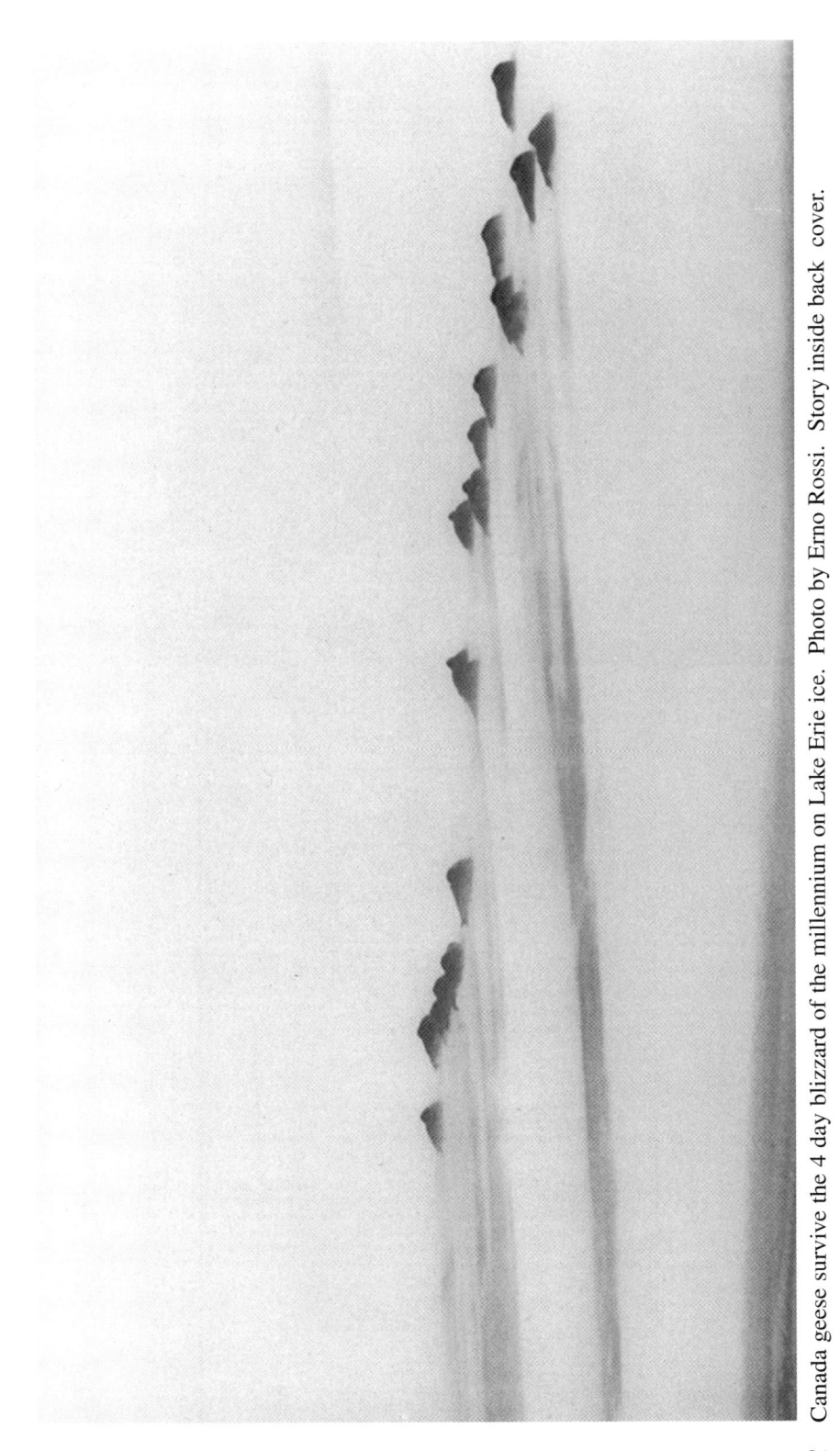

Canada geese survive the 4 day blizzard of the millennium on Lake Erie ice. Photo by Erno Rossi. Story inside back cover.

President Carter signs a major disaster relief declaration for snow stricken Northern and Western New York.

THE WHITE HOUSE
WASHINGTON

February 9, 1977

MESSAGE FROM THE PRESIDENT TO THE PEOPLE OF BUFFALO

This has been a difficult winter for all Americans but especially for the people of Buffalo. You have had your lives and businesses disrupted. Even the simplest daily activities have become impossible for long periods, and the number of dead and injured is still rising.

When Midge Costanza and my son Chip came back to tell me what they'd seen in your city, they told me about police and firemen who were frostbitten rescuing motorists from their stalled cars, and of the fine job Tom Casey has done coordinating federal help. "But one of the great things," Midge said, "is the sense of community, of people helping each other. That is what is holding it all together."

We as a nation have wasted too much too long, and we are having to pay for some of that waste this winter. But we are also learning that we can do better, than we need not use up what we cannot later do without, that we can do with less so that everyone can have enough.

The people of Buffalo have exemplified throughout this emergency the spirit of love and concern for their neighbors that Americans have always shown in times of trouble. You have shown the bravery and the self-discipline and the willingness to work together under difficult circumstances that have made this nation great. I'm proud of you.

Jimmy Carter

PART TWO

THE AMERICAN EXPERIENCE

NORTHERN AND WESTERN NEW YORK COUNTIES

Note: Shaded counties designated as major disaster areas in a declaration signed by President Jimmy Carter on February 5, 1977.

THE WHITE HOUSE

WASHINGTON

August 25, 1980

Dear Mr. Rossi:

President and Mrs. Carter have asked me to thank you for sending an inscribed copy of your book, White Death - Blizzard of '77.

Your interest in sharing your publication is appreciated, and the Carters send you their best wishes.

Sincerely,

Dan Chew

Daniel M. Chew
Director of
Presidential Correspondence

President Carter's son Chip views the damage of the only blizzard declared a major disaster. Buffalo State Courier Express Collection.

Courtesy, U.S. Army Corps of Engineers.

195

Raul Russi - Buffalo Police Officer

"There was no doubt that he was dead."
"It was like the end of the world."

At the beginning of the storm I was finishing a court case. Someone looked out the window and said, "It's snowing. It's really bad outside." So I walked over to headquarters and signed out.

I started my car and got it going. I got about two blocks away—underneath the Skyway—and that was it. It was a whiteout. I parked the car and came back to headquarters and by this time our building was filling up with people. Everybody looked worried.

I work with the streets crime unit and when I came back, there was nothing for me to do. They just told me to "stand by - stand by." So I stood by and I talked to everybody. Once in a while I'd go outside and look at the storm. Finally I went up to Captain Dunford, the Duty Captain and asked him if I could get a car. In some way I wanted to go out on the street and help. "My car's out in front," he said. "If you can get it started and rolling, you can have it."

By this time my Lieutenant, Lieutenant McCann, who also used to be my partner at one time, came in and I said, "Let's try to get this car running." The car was parked in front of the telephone company. We got into the car with two other patrolmen from our unit. They were stranded here also. We jumped in the car and got it started. Then we pushed and tried to get it moving. But we had to come inside the building every couple of minutes and warm ourselves because it was unbelievable. You couldn't stand the wind. At that time it was blowing at 60 miles per hour, along with all the snow and the very low temperature. So we got the car turned around and we got it across Franklin Street and right in the center of that street the car died. Two days later that car was still there.

About nine o'clock that night a Professor from the State University of Buffalo, George Adolf, came in and he has a four wheel drive vehicle. He said, "I'll take two guys and we'll ride around." My lieutenant said that this would go down in history that the streets crime unit would be represented on the street in the worst storm in history. We were car 21 and we started riding around. We answered calls. Our first was for insulin at the Mall. There was a woman who went shopping and had forgotten her insulin. We got within three blocks of her house and we couldn't go any further. So, we ran on foot to her house. We got her insulin to her.

We answered a domestic call where a woman and her husband had a battle. He punched her out, broke her eye open, broke her leg and broke her arm. In the house there was an old black couple and there was only a little space heater and they had about eight kids and they were all sleeping on the floor and the door was wide open and they couldn't close it because the snow had pushed in. They had a blanket across the door and across a broken window and the wind was hollering and the snow was inside the house. It was a pitiful sight. This lady was unconscious on the floor. The Professor was about three blocks away so we had to carry her in our arms to the truck. The doors to the truck were so cold that they would not close so we had ropes tied from one end of the truck to the other. We got her inside the truck and we headed for Columbus Hospital. We got within three blocks of the hospital and that was it. The cars were stalled all across the street. We had to walk to the hospital. We had to carry her. I had to put her on my back and in every position you can imagine. I saw this reporter from one of the news companies, from UPI I think. He had a scarf and I didn't because I wasn't prepared when I came from court for any of this. So, he lent me his scarf and I wrapped it around. Soon the scarf was completely frozen around my neck, so that I could slip it off over my head and put it back on the same way.

Then after we answered about eight calls, a lot of insulin running and things like that, we answered a death call on Niagara Street at apartment 2C. We found the building and apartment 2. I forgot that it was apartment 2C. The doors were completely covered with snow. We knocked at the windows and shouted at this woman to open up. "We're the police and there is supposed to be a death here." She said that the death was around to the side of her and that she couldn't let us in because her sliding doors were frozen. I told her we had to get in there. So we slid down the snow drift to her sliding doors and forced them open with her help. We were in snow up to our waists. When we were inside her apartment we learned several things. We could not shut the sliding door so that the snow was blowing into the room and the body was in 2C not in apartment 2 and we could not get to apartment 2C from this apartment. You had to go outside and approach from the rear. My partner stayed and tried to get her door shut and I went outside and around to the back of the building and found apartment 2C. I knocked on the door and this old lady answered.

"I'm a police officer. Is there a dead person here?"
"Yes, my husband died. He has been sick for some time."
"Gee, I'm sorry but I don't know what to tell you."
"Well come in. Would you like a cup of coffee?"
"Yes please, I could really use one."

While she was making me a coffee she told me I could see him in the bedroom. He was lying in bed with his head on the pillow and the covers pulled up to his neck. He was about 80 years old and very thin. There was no doubt that he was dead.

"You realize we are in the middle of the worst storm in the history of this city," I told her. "There is no way we can get anyone in here."

"Son" she said, "I've lived with this man for over forty years. A couple days more, dead or alive, is all right with me. I loved him then and I love him now. When this storm is over and things calm down then you can tell someone that I'm here with my husband."

I finished my coffee, got to the truck and radioed the situation. Then I helped my partner who was still struggling to get that sliding door shut. I left that place with a deep feeling for that old lady and I'll never forget her as long as I live.

We were on the street from about 5 o'clock in the morning and we just couldn't go any more. The cold had gotten to me and my pants and jacket were soaking wet. There were maybe 8 to 10 cars in the street at that time. No Buffalo police cars. They were civilian vehicles. Precinct 7 was shut down completely with snow. No one could get around in some of the other precincts.

I came back here, went up stairs and I layed down and slept for about three hours on top of this filing cabinet. In the morning I got up, went down stairs and reported to my office. They told me I was still working so I should get my stuff together. I went over to my brother's house and I borrowed a snowmobile suit with the full cover and went back on the street.

Now our duties changed from mainly helping people to stopping some of the looting. Justin Avenue and Williams Street were probably the worst looted areas in the whole city. The trucks coming into the city on the thruway stopped there and got stuck. There and in Precinct 7 on South Park. The looters opened up the trucks and tore everything out.

There was a wig shop in the little market and it was broken into during the day. That evening when we were walking around we entered the shop. We figured there would be looters there. We said, "Why don't we sit in this place. We can't help but come out winners. We'll make 10 arrests." There was Joe Ransford and myself, another officer who has since left the force, and Larry Billings another black officer. We got into the wig shop and we figured that the best way was to blend into the scenery. No sooner did we put on these Afro wigs than we heard them coming. Then we started talking among ourselves, "Take this Jack and let's take that." And they would come right in and join us and say, "Yeah, hey wait a minute. Don't take all that stuff. We'll take some too." They would grab some of the stuff and head for the door. We had two guys hidden by the door and as soon as the looters grabbed the stuff and headed for the door, the two officers would jump up and grab them. So we went this routine for four or five hours and we got about 15 or 20 arrests. We had one of the trucks come over and take them back to the station. We would leave them in the cell block and go back to the wig shop and have a repeat performance. Finally, we had so many arrests we had to go back to the station house and book them.

Then there was a call for any car in the city to go to the Statler Hilton because they had a guy breaking into rooms there. So we left the prisoners and jumped into the truck and went to the Statler. The guy had just run up the street. The only other place he could go was to a small hotel around the corner. We got in there and asked if a guy came in of that description. He was in the washroom. I entered the Jon and went over to this guy. I didn't know whether he was armed so I pulled my revolver and stuck it in his back. He turned around and looked at me and said, "Get that gun out of my sight!" He pushed me. My partner was right behind me. This guy tried to fight us and we ended up in a big battle. He was pretty husky. I couldn't believe that he pushed the gun away. Somebody's holding a gun in his face and he didn't want to know nothing.

I remember another incident about 5 o'clock in the morning. Just before we came in he radioed us and told us that at the foot of Church Street there were people stranded in their cars. The storm had been going on for 14 hours straight. There had to be 150 cars and I can honestly say in 99% of the cars, the only thing you could see was a 5 inch circle of the top of the car roof. We went along and banged the tops of the cars. Then we would listen for sounds in the car. We figured that by this time if anybody heard the bang, they were alive. If they didn't hear it, they were dead. Nobody heard us. They found one or two bodies there later.

I couldn't believe this. Some people treasured their possessions so much that they wanted to stay with their cars. They treasured their car more than their lives. Even if we found someone, it would have been a miracle to get them out of the car. It would have been a miracle if they were still alive. We radioed back that we couldn't find anyone and that we couldn't tell if there was anybody in there.

I've been here for twenty years and I have never in my life seen anything like this storm. I came here from Puerto Rico in 1957.

I know that the day after the storm they released most of the looters from jail because the jails were full and they couldn't handle them. Judge Green released quite a few of them on their own recognizance. He had no choice you know. The jails were full and they couldn't put anymore in there. They took the minor looters and released them. I remember one of my looters was on violation of parole and he was sent away to Attica.

The thing that stands out in my mind is the misery of the storm and yet we still had a ball with it. I love to work. You can check my record. I worked three days straight and when I was done I said, "Now I'm ready to go home." I always said that I wanted to work in Harlem. I think that this was something like it. If there was anything you wanted to do, you did it. If you wanted to do nothing, nobody forced you to go out into the storm.

Such a dramatic thing. People in need, people helping others. People are different in emergencies like that. I loved every minute of it. It gave me the chance to put out like I've never put out before and maybe like I never will again. I went beyond myself. All of a sudden there are thousands of people in need of help. It's there. All you have to do is jump out there and help people. It was a chance for me and my partner to jump into it and sink up to our elbows helping people. We loved it. I don't want it to happen again, but if it does, I'll enjoy it. It's like being in a plane crash. You are the only one in good shape and you can help everybody. There is so much to do that you do not know who to help first.

A situation like that usually comes when you do not expect it. The city felt the need for a lot of equipment, but how do you prepare for something like that? I think that the city and the police department should have vehicles that can move around in an emergency such as four wheeled vehicles and snowmobiles. I think that there should be a plan within the city government to deal with an emergency of that nature—a plan of action they could alter to fit an emergency situation. It should be ready for the police department because I'll tell you truthfully, we were caught with our pants down.

So were families who planned on going shopping on Friday because their husbands just got their pay that day and they had to go a week without much food. Families, the city, the whole state got caught with their pants down.

In a disaster people will come together and they will pull it off. The whole world could come down tomorrow from an atomic war and people will find a way to get out. We came from the cave man to today and we got out of it. We will get out of it tomorrow if it happens again. The city could be completely destroyed and there would be people left to walk on forward to something else. That's the way people are. But I can't see how you can prepare completely for anything like that blizzard. Even when you are ready, God will turn around and give it to you another way.

It was great for me. I helped people and they smiled as I walked away. Then I found myself smiling. "Jesus, I just helped that guy." I felt good about it and nobody had to say, "Hey, good job, you just helped that guy." That's the kind of feeling I had for those two or three days.

I tried to explain that to my wife when I got home. She couldn't understand because she was locked up in the house with the kids for three days. They were driving her nuts—they had no place to go. She had to shovel the driveway. She hated the whole thing.

It was a chance in a lifetime to fulfill my fantasies. I've dreamed about catching people who were falling from buildings and saving people from a fire and they were all right because of me. It was the greatest high in the world. If I left this job today there are some things I would treasure about it and the storm would be one of them.

When I finally got home I crashed for about two days. When I came back to work I got into it again. I wish that everybody lived through something like that and came out of it all right. They would feel different about themselves afterwards.

Many people were jammed into a small bar for a very long time. Some had a ball and loved the people they were with and they never saw them again. They were together and they made love in the phone booth while everybody was there and nobody cared.

It was like the end of the world. For the first time you were loose to do anything you wanted to do because there was no tomorrow. Many people had that feeling.

Policemen were stranded on that skyway and they didn't know if they would be rescued. That has got to be an interesting feeling.

One guy was found frozen to death leaning up against a building in one of the projects. He went around the corner to buy a bottle of wine—he happened to be a wine-o. He never made it. His need for alcohol was stronger than his need for life.

I remember one incident on Jefferson Avenue. I was wearing a snowmobile suit. It has a mask on it and all you can see is a little opening in the mouth. We saw two kids by this store and we thought they were breaking into the store. When they spotted us, they ran. So I ran after the one kid for two or three city blocks and I finally caught him from behind. I turned him around and when he saw me he screamed. I was in a black suit with stripes on the side and a black mask and hood. He didn't know who I was. He just knew that somebody in the darkness had come and grabbed him from behind. He was really shaking.

Then there was this guy who was sitting home with his wife and she is one of those people who claims that nothing bothers her. They were talking about the storm and she said, "Well it's not that bad outside." He said to her, "Look, it's the worst storm we've ever had. People are dying from this storm." Then she says, "It's not that bad, I saw worse in 1939." Finally he got an idea. "Come here" he said, "I'll show you how bad it is." He took her outside with just her housecoat on. Then he ran back inside and locked the door. He left her out there and she screamed, "Let me in. Let me in." He screamed to her, "Tell me how bad it is." She screamed back, "It's really bad. Far worse than 1939." Then he let her in.

Most people under reacted to the storm. They didn't realize how bad it was. The Mayor did the same thing. He under reacted at first and then he over reacted later on. It's because of the blizzard that he is not running for office again. One of the police commissioners had no idea at first. He gave an order that I laughed at. "Good morning. We will issue an order to all the people to get their cars off the street." Who was I to tell him but I did. I told him that a lot of people would not be able to get their cars out for weeks. He didn't believe me at the time but after the next day he got a clearer picture of the situation.

I remember people leaving the building from this one door and others stood there and told them, "Don't leave, don't leave." But they left the building and in 30 seconds they were back inside saying, "O my God! O my God!" In five or ten minutes you would be frozen to death in that wind and cold. It had to be a lot like what happens at the North Pole.

I'll be very honest with you. I didn't pray during the whole thing. I've prayed in other situations but the need was to help and not get down on my knees.

I've never seen a city brought to a halt like that before. And yet some people left their houses and got downtown and broke a window and grabbed a diamond ring.

If I had just sat there for a couple of days and did nothing, I would have hated myself for the rest of my life. I had a ball. I loved every minute of it.

"So everybody struck out."

I'm a very active normal guy and I got stranded in a house for three days with three very ugly women and one male homosexual. No amount of liquor I drank could change the facts of the situation. So everybody struck out.

Harry Usiak - Dispatcher and Morgue Keeper

"In this particular 32 hour period, I received at least 13 calls of people dead in cars."

On January 28, 1977, I reported to work at Erie County Morgue at 6:30 a.m. Everything was quiet. Then the rumors started of a big snow storm approaching. The hospital authorities let all the personnel go home to avoid the storm. I was here alone!

I remained for 32 hours because no one could relieve me. I had to make arrangements with undertakers, hospitals, police and fire departments for the removal of bodies—people who had died outside or in their cars. It was impossible for our morgue wagon or our medical examiners to reach the scenes.

Our usual procedure is to take the call, log it in a book, taking special notice of the time of the call. We then notify our medical examiner and he goes to the scene. He can release the body to an undertaker or leave it in a hospital if it is already there. If there is an autopsy necessary, we return the body to the morgue. In this particular 32 hour period, I received at least 13 calls of people dead in cars.

Because of the storm, we had to improvise. We allowed undertakers to remove some of the bodies. We permitted the fire department and hospital ambulances to take some of the bodies to the hospital.

The storm hit on the 28th. One man died in his car on that day. But the police were so busy that they neglected to call our office until the 29th. The man who died had gone to the bank on the morning of the 28th. When we got him on the 29th, we removed over one thousand dollars from his person. He had intended to use the money to run his grocery store that day.

One man attempted to walk home during the storm on the 28th. He got as far as the packing plant on Howard Street. He entered a parked car in order to get out of the storm and he died there. The employees found him in the car and called me. Of course, we could not get to him. I contacted the plant manager and asked him to have the body brought into their warehouse. It was at least three days before our people could get to the deceased.

There were many elderly people who attempted to shovel snow or use their snow blowers. Some of them dropped dead while they were outside and many of them had been under the care of a doctor. In these cases we tried to contact their doctors, who usually signed them off as coronaries. We then contacted the funeral directors who removed the remains.

I remember the case in Amherst, where a man took refuge from the storm in his car. The police found him dead with his car still running. We did an autopsy here and confirmed that he died of carbon monoxide poisoning.

The biggest problem that I ran into was being alone while our five telephones rang constantly for 32 hours. All the local and national news media wanted me to give a complete run down of

The beginning. Watertown Daily Times.

every case. They wanted names, addresses, circumstances and all that. It was impossible. I didn't eat for 32 hours.

I have some advice for any locality that might get hit with this problem. Stay off the phones unless absolutely necessary. I understand the problem of the media. But they slow down everything when they all call at the same time. They should co-ordinate.

Monoxide Deaths

A young man and his six year old daughter died of carbon monoxide fumes when he started a snow blower in a closed garage. The fumes killed him in the garage and his child in her bedroom.

Silent Killer

Many people die at the hands of a silent and stealthy killer each year. Some are sleeping in their homes, cottages and tents; others meet death in their cars - although there is no traffic accident. They die from carbon monoxide poisoning.

Most combustibles emit some degree of this lethal gas and in a poorly ventilated area, it takes but a few minutes for the CO level to reach the danger zone.

Carbon monoxide has no smell, taste or color, the Ontario Safety League warns. The only way to ensure your safety is to practice prevention. Never barbecue indoors or in tents. Have home and cottage heating systems, along with any propane burning appliances, checked annually by qualified people. Be sure your chimney and flue area are clean and working correctly before lighting the fireplace. Keep the exhaust system in your car in good repair and the engine properly adjusted and timed. Never start a car inside a closed garage. Never sit in a car with the motor idling without the windows open.

If you suspect CO poisoning, get fresh air fast! Exposure to carbon monoxide can be recognized by headache, throbbing at the temples, nausea, vomiting, dim vision and dizziness. The next stages are coma, convulsions, depression of heart and respiratory action and finally, death.

Burials

Although many funeral services were conducted during the week of the storm in spite of the weather and driving bans, very few actual burials took place. Most caskets were stored by funeral directors and cemeteries until conditions allowed actual burials later in February.

Ron Offhaus - President of Tops Friendly Food Markets

"If something has to be done then do it."

We had warnings but I think a lot of people didn't believe the degree to which that storm was going to hit here. When it did hit, we in our offices here had 200 refugees. We went out on the street and got people out of cars and gave them shelter and food. We gave spaghetti dinners to 200 people and we got enough stuff in here to fix breakfast for all those people. We were feeding truck drivers and anybody who was on the road.

We found out there was a bus on Bailey Avenue, near Clinton and there were two young boys between ten and twelve years of age stranded in there. They were on their way by bus to visit their grandmother. Next door we have freezer units, so we got Bob Clifford, one of my executives and two other guys to go next door and put on the clothes that we use in our freezer units. Then they walked down the street and they brought those 2 children back here. The kids were in there with the bus driver and they covered the 2 boys with blankets and brought them back here. Then we called their parents and the kids slept all night here in the office near the heater.

The building itself is not adaptable to sleeping 200 people, so during the night I was on the phone. We had set up phone communications here and we kept the switchboard open. I think everyone made up their minds they weren't going to go anywhere. The people who tried took 3 or 4 hours to go one mile and they came back. They were lucky they made it back. It was a state of emergency.

We have a crew of people here in ecology and landscaping and we have 4 wheel drive vehicles, and we were using them to take people home who lived within a mile. The drivers were bringing in food supplies as well.

It got to be quite interesting because this was the night of Roots and we have television sets here, to give away at store openings. I think we had four televisions set up in the conference room downstairs. There were 100 people down there sitting around and watching television and we had the cafeteria open all the time with hot soups, coffee and tea. Then, everybody sat and watched Roots. We wouldn't allow any alcoholic beverages of course. But there are a lot of stories that you hear about people stranded in the neighborhood bar. When they closed, they closed. 'Everybody out! I don't give a hell how bad it is. You're going home, we're closing! That's it!" We had another girl who was at a hotel and was not allowed to stay because she ran out of money so we put her up here.

The Red Cross was in need of supplies and foods. So I set up an emergency area where they could get food supplies from some of my stores in the area. Remember that a store can be wiped out completely. It cannot take care of the masses of people. It has to take care of the people that live in that community. Our offices and our warehouses during the whole storm never stopped functioning. We got out and supplied all our stores with only one exception for maybe 6 hours. That's the only store in the whole system that had to close. We had store managers who stayed in their stores for 36 hours straight, sleeping there. We had a responsibility to keep the stores open and to feed the people because they had nothing. They panicked. Bread and milk supplies were being wiped out. Come hell or high water, my suppliers were going to get products to me. I wouldn't take "no" for an answer. We donated a trailer loaded with king size bread to the Red Cross. They were working for the community and they were having difficulty acquiring food and I did whatever I could to help them and the Salvation Army.

Mayor Makowski had his no driving ban. I was upset. If we don't drive, how do we open the supermarkets, how do my people work? I called the Mayor's Office, and I talked to Mr. Blair, Commissioner of Police and I explained to him that we must have an exemption, and he gave it to us. So, I got on the phone, and I told the Red Cross and the Mayor's Office that we would act as a spokesman and a communicator for them because they had enough problems. We called all the other people in the industry such as Super-Duper, Bells, Twin-Fair and a few others and we explained to them our problem and what we had to do and how we had to keep our stores open; and the fact that we had all received permission. Don't forget, it was only the City of Buffalo where there was a ban on driving.

The only store where we had severe problems was the Niagara Street store in Buffalo. It was completely closed. I had the Army Corps of Engineers working with us to open it. When our donated truck-load of bread arrived at the Red Cross, it was unloaded by the Army troops.

We had 200 people here for 36 hours. I was here until there was one woman left and I had to get the four wheel drive vehicle to take her home because she had no way to get there. Then, we finally closed up that night.

The people in our stores did a phenomenal job. We had managers who fed and sheltered 250 people in their stores. Various executive and various business leaders' wives and families were stranded there. These stories kept coming back to me. I would meet someone and he would say, "Did you know I was your guest?" We warmed baby bottles, we cooked foods, we had snowmobiles put into action, we had emergency situations and the people responded without panic.

How do you prepare for a blizzard? We are stacking medical supplies, blankets, candles, and sterno. So what's it cost you? A few hundred dollars to be prepared for something that might happen. We were using draperies over the women for blankets. It got cold at night. It was a very costly storm. There were so many things to contend with. We had stores you couldn't get into for ten days. They lost 50% of their business. When we did get it back with food stamps, we didn't get back all of it. It cost us a tremendous amount of money but, how do you put a cost on helping people.

Our company is one of the strongest community minded companies in this part of the country. You name it, there's somebody working at it, myself included. We have doers in our organization and we're pretty proud of them.

My advice to someone in my position in a future emergency is to be very cognizant of the feelings of other people. Don't over react and don't be quick to pass judgement on someone in an emergency. Somebody has to stay cool, calm and collected in order to get the facts, assess the situation and do what's necessary. Don't think about what it will cost you or the repercussions. If something has to be done, then do it. I think a little foresight is always good. I've been through a lot of pressure situations. I have worked a lot of charities with a lot of people. I feel that if you can assess things quickly and make decisions, good, bad, indifferent, you'll be right 90% of the time. In a situation like this, help somebody to control his emotions and make him feel comfortable. Make them forget about what's going on outside.

Dented Roofs

A report from Columbus Hospital on Niagara Street in Buffalo stated, "People have been walking on the tops of cars because the drifts are so high."

Jerry Aqualina - Buffalo Zoo

*"We had a very pregnant camel that we
had to watch on an hourly basis."*

My wife was stranded along with other members of the family in different areas in the city and it was really a strange feeling not knowing where people are or what is occurring. It is difficult to know if you are hearing true things on the radio. You are in a position where you cannot find out what is going on. It was Monday afternoon before I could account for all my family. All of them got home and they survived it very well.

One of the funnier things that happened at the zoo, occurred when phone calls started coming in about the animals being free. One report said our polar bears were out in the snow. One of our security guards and I started out toward the bear pits to take a head count. We must have been fifteen feet away from the bear pits when we both looked at each other and wondered what the hell we were doing out here? What happens if the polar bear is out?

The main problem was food and the distribution to the animals. We were short of manpower too. We ran into animal escapes and animal deaths. The food shortage was a problem because normal delivery of fresh fruit, vegetables, meat and fish come by truck from the areas in downtown Buffalo. The police brought our food for us. They carried the fresh produce and frozen meat and fish in the police cars. They took good care of us. We got hold of a guy on a snowmobile and he helped us truck our hay around.

We had one very pregnant camel that we had to watch on an hourly basis. In order to get to her we had to dig into the barn so that we might check on her. She didn't deliver during the storm but shortly after she did. I stayed here a couple of nights myself just to check on her. She delivered a female which we have in the children's zoo right now. There was no way the baby would have survived in the cold barn so we pulled the mother and child out and kept them warm.

Feeding the larger waterfowl was a great problem because of the amount of snow over the ponds. It's extremely dangerous trying to get across those ponds. All the outside animals were extremely difficult to get to. The hoof stock and the waterfowl animals were especially difficult to reach. The house animals were no problem. Most of the animals in houses could not take advantage of their outside cages because the cages were completely covered with snow. Normally our routine for the small animal house and cathouse is to let the animals out during the morning when we clean up their cages, and they return at night. We couldn't do that because their cages were full of snow. However some of the animals really liked it. We got our snow leopards outside as well as our Siberian tigers and our one black leopard and they all had a ball with this blizzard stuff. It was great fun for them.

The polar bears didn't react one way or another. They would lay out in the snow and they didn't make as much use of their dens. Most of the bears enjoyed it. They don't have any problems with that type of weather.

The animal escapes were a real problem. Those animals that are kept in exhibits that are protected from the public by moats and high fences were in many cases completely free to wander over the drifts that covered the fences. It was this way the reindeer got out on us. They proceded to walk over the top of this beautiful big drift that was covering the barn completely and they were free. These three that did manage to escape were Scandinavian reindeer. A male and two females were in the trio and we were forced to track them to an area down on the edge of the creek across from the Buffalo State College. When we got to them they were clumped together, the three of them, and we did manage to dart the male and when he was darted, the two females bolted and they took off. We packaged up the male and brought him safely back to the zoo and we went on a kind of merry chase throughout the City of Buffalo and the Village of Kenmore trying to get the two females back. The news had picked up word of these animals and they broadcasted it. This brought the community into a co-operative effort with us by helping to pinpoint the location of the females. They could trample off so damn fast, you know they can really move on the snow. We finally caught one on a side-street in Kenmore and we just roped her and tied her down until the vet got there. The other one was caught in the backyard of a house in Buffalo somewhere. This animal was run down by snowmobilers. Some people chased her down with a snowmobile, exhausted her, and then they tangled her up in some ropes and she ended up dying of shock. She was pregnant with a little male fetus at that time.

We also had a couple of sheep that originated in Sicily and Corsica that were able to free themselves by walking over the fence of the children's zoo. One of the sheep has been returned to us but the other has never been found. She's still out there someplace. She may have been killed by dogs. We never heard from her and no one ever gave us a call on her. So we are still missing one animal from that exposure.

We organized shovelling crews to work within the zoo. Everyone that was available went and dug around moats and in many cases this meant digging straight down through 10 feet of snow. We were in no panic. It was a lot of sweat and a lot of cold but we did get most moats dug out. Where we could not dig out the moats we were forced to lock the animals in their barns. This meant that we had to dig our way to the barn first to get the door open and then we locked the animals safely inside. Fortunately, we didn't have any problems with that. The animals all stayed fairly calm and we were able to feed and take care of them from inside their barns until we did get a lot more snow dug out. Terry, the Assistant Director, organized the crews from the National Guard and a couple of other private companies that came in with some heavy equipment to help us dig out the moats. That was a big help. Most of the animals, if they see any kind of drop or trench at all, will not challenge it. This worked pretty well. We just trenched the moats all the way around and we didn't have any more escapes after that.

Shortage of manpower was a real problem. A lot of the zookeepers couldn't get in. Fortunately, I live close enough that I was able to make it and Terry, the Assistant Director was able to make it and a few of the keepers that lived close by got in. We were operating at about one third man power and this involved us doubling and tripling in the areas of our responsibilities. We had to get to every area everyday to check that every animal was present. We were still worried about escapes. It's hard working this way because we usually need the twelve keepers here to work the place efficiently and there were a few times when we had four or five people to do all the work. It seems as though the mornings were clear but in the afternoons it always seemed to snow like hell again and everyone wanted to get home. Nobody wanted to get stuck at the zoo overnight.

We did have permission from the police that allowed us to drive during the driving ban. This was very helpful.

We lost a number of animals from the cold. We lost quite a bit of our waterfowl. Both our black swans died. We lost several of the hoofstock animals. Many that died of the hoofstock animals were older ones that just couldn't take the severe weather. Some, however, were younger animals and we still are uncertain about the cause of death. We lost our antelope through the cold, and we lost a nutria which froze to death for no apparent reason. It's a rodent or rat-like creature that was introduced to the south along the Florida coast. They're working their way up the Mississippi now. They've almost spread throughout the south eastern portion of the states.

We did have to do away with several of the waterfowl and some of the animals after the storm because of the frostbite that they had received. The damaged portions of their bodies were turning gangrenous and though we treated them for a month or so we couldn't get any positive response to the treatment, and we were forced to put them away. We were hit very hard as far as animal deaths are concerned. We lost a markhor. That was a big one of our female population that died for no apparent reasons. It was probably distress, caused by the bad weather that brought it on. The markhor is a type of goat from Russia and from the higher altitudes of Asia. That's a $5000 dollar animal right there and a periated deer died and some antelope died which were worth several thousands of dollars also.

Animals' deaths were really big and no one feels worse than we do. It's just something that gives us a very bad taste. When a keeper goes out and sees one of his animals dead it's a bummer to him. Thanks to our keepers and their efforts to get out to the areas and check these animals on a regular basis, we were able to avoid an even greater catastrophe. We were unable to save quite a few of them. However we did completely empty one of our waterfowl islands. The big island froze over and we just couldn't break up the ice. So in reacting to that situation a few people got out there and we just got a hold of every animal that we could and eventually carted them all to safety or to an island that was still free of ice. We brought a good deal of them right in here. We brought our red-breasted geese and our bar-head geese and some of our swans inside where we made temporary stalls in our children's zoo barn. We kept the birds there until the ponds cleared up enough for them to get out again and get some free running water.

In a zoo such as this, when there is a disaster you need all kinds of help from all kinds of people. The one thing that we didn't need was for the public to come tramping through the zoo at a time like that. It's just too damned dangerous. They don't know where they can and can't go and when you got snow drifts completely over your barrier fences there is simply no way of controlling the people. That was a bit of a problem.

The false rumours were also bad. I'd be sitting home and occasionally I'd hear on the radio that a polar bear had escaped. You had just finished shovelling your life away and you finally sit down for a rest and you hear something that you know very well could never have happened. That's really the only area of the zoo that we didn't have any problems with. Our bear cages or pits, because of their construction did not encourage drifting into the pits. So we knew there was no way in hell that any of our bears could have escaped. You know people like to get a hold of this kind of stuff and play with it; it's certainly not humorous.

There's a tremendous feeling of helplessness when you know damned well the animals are being adversely affected by the weather and all you really can do is feed them and make sure there's no medical problems. Other than that you're helpless. It's really up to the animals to survive. Very few zoos have facilities where they can lock their animals in a heated quarter with water and drains and feeding apparatuses. We just don't have that here. Our barns are old, they are cold, they don't drain well and they are drafty. It's mostly up to the animals to survive and as you look back on our winter losses for the last few winters we haven't really had any problems at all. This storm hit us especially hard and for some reason the animals that died weren't able for one reason or another to make it through. That was the worst thing about it. I came in here very early in the morning around six or six thirty and I made my initial rounds just to see what animals needed help, and when I found a dead one, it would tear me apart.

The animals at the zoo took a very calm view of everything. Naturally, when the reindeer were free that excited them, and we excited our herd of children zoo animals because we had to put up some extra barrier fences around them. They are small brown animals and extremely nervous. They are very flighty creatures and if a truck backfires they will fly off. At the back of their exhibit there was quite an expanse of open space that had drifted over. Since there was no way we could get it dug out, we decided to put some additional snow fencing on top of the regular fencing and we buried it in the snow drifts to keep them contained. One of these little creatures did get out shortly after but she was an animal that we had hand raised and she was fairly easy to coax back. They were calm about the snow and they had no problem walking around. We didn't really have any animals that got super excited about it. The lamas stayed inside their barns which was good for us and them. But a lot of the animals on the inside became nervous when they were unable to get out because this would upset their routine of going out in the morning and doing their stuff. Since their routine was broken this made them a little more nervous than normal. Other than that we really didn't have any weird behavioral problems. When it comes to animals, survival is the big thing and they'll do what they can to survive so they stayed fairly calm about it.

The diminishing fuel supply presented a dangerous situation in most of the buildings especially for the birds and reptiles. The mammals were a little better off in this regard but reptiles are very sensitive to the cold and when the temperature was fluctuating up and down because of our conservation of fuel, it presented an additional hazard to the reptiles. They probably went fifty-five or sixty degrees and that's very cool for a lot of reptiles as well as a lot of these exotic birds. We did lose a few of the reptiles. The deaths of the reptiles were statistically higher during that period than in any of the years before so we can assume that the cold was a contributing factor to the deaths. We did have a few bird problems but we didn't lose many birds down at the bird house. Several of them were treated for colds and congestion problems. We had to treat the birds with antibiotics and water to get rid of the cold. You have to isolate the birds because its a viral infection, and similar to humans, when the bird gets a chill his resistance goes down and if you don't isolate the birds and keep them in warmer spots you'll never have them survive. They usually snap out of it quite easily. By watching their eating habits and feces you can determine if they have a cold. Interestingly enough, his little eyes and nose will also run.

There's no question that we've learned from the storm. We were pretty well stocked here, as far as food goes with our weekly food deliveries. Everything was up, but in the future, I think we will keep an eye on those long range weather forecasts during the winter months. We have already purchased a larger freezer for animal food and we plan on stocking that fairly well for the winter months with fish and meat. Fresh fruits and vegetables we can do without. They can cut way down on them and not affect the animals health because we do have prepared dried foods which are completely nutritious. We do like to add the fresh stuff for diet variety. We plan on keeping the food barn a little fuller than it was last year as far as our hoofstock feed is concerned. We did not run out mind you but we ran low. It would have been more comforting to have a bit more of a cushion than we had this year and we will certainly keep our freezer pretty well filled. Other than that we can't do anything to stop the snow.

In the repairs that are presently being made to the hoofstock barns we are installing different types of doors. The new door will be a more effective wind shield. Physically our animals were in good shape prior to the storm. This is normal procedure because we start feeding them more in late spring and building them up so that they are in extremely good shape by the time the winter season approaches. There's not a heck of a lot more we could do as far as the animals are concerned.

Terry Gladkowski - Buffalo Zoo

" Walking through the zoo, you didn't know if you were in an animal enclosure or a duck pond. It was a very tricky situation. The bison were charging people."

Love at first bite. More snow please. Courtesy, Lee Wroblewski.

Bird Keeper Lee Wroblewski comforts a sedated Scandinavian reindeer during a safe return to the Buffalo Zoo. Courtesy, Buffalo State Courier Collection.

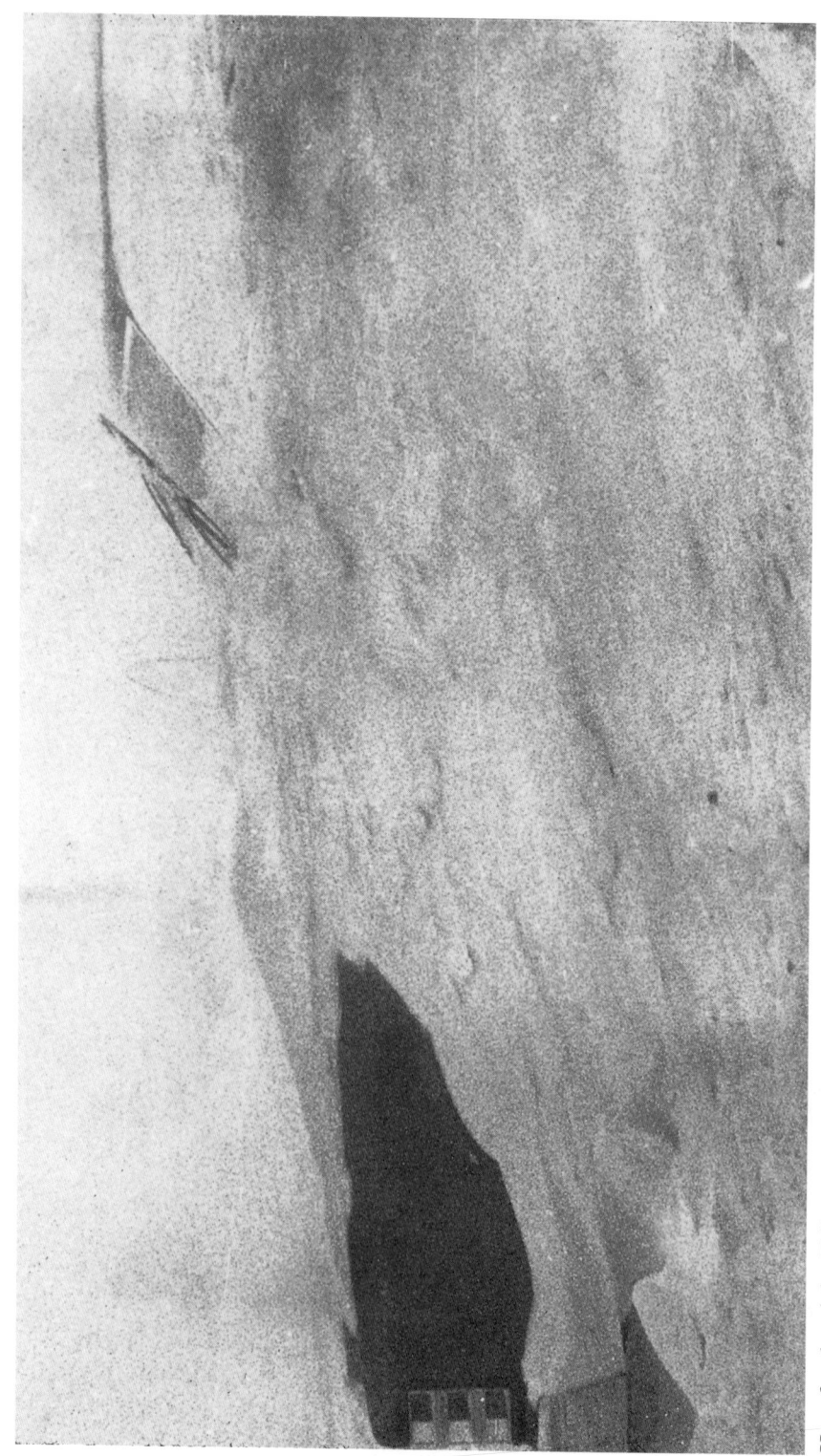

Here for the night. Tribune photo.

Michael O'Brien

"God really hears and answers prayers."

I was on the expressway going north towards Niagara Falls when that thing hit about 11:30 a.m. I was going across Grand Island when I came to the toll booth for the first bridge. Visibility was nearly zero and the bridges were closed. There were many people around so I felt secure in the company of so many other cars.

Because of all the motorists pressuring the people at the tollgate to open, we were allowed to go through. But they had a policman to keep you from getting onto the thruway, so you had to exit onto the island which is a very rural area. I had to make a turn that took me further into the rural areas of the island and from that point on I couldn't see what road I was on. I stopped the car and was stuck in it for the entire night. It's a very rural area and there are miles between homes. The only security I had was the car. I was afraid that if I ever got out and walked five feet away, I would never find the car again.

I was freezing to death. The weekend before I'd been up to Alleghany State Park, doing some cross country skiing with a friend and I'm notorious for leaving the car unpacked for a week or two. I remembered that my equipment was in the trunk of the car, so I went to the trunk to get some of the clothing, such as those insulated snowmobile boots, ski gloves and thermal underwear and an insulated vest and parka. The wind blew up against my hands and my face and it felt like a razor blade tearing at me. It was almost impossible to keep your eyes open. I had to keep my hand on the car and get back there because I couldn't see what I was grabbing. Just in that short time it was numbing. Eventually I changed in the car and I think that was the answer to everybody's prayers.

I knew the signs of monoxide poisoning. I had a new car and the muffler system was probably good. But with the winds blowing the way they were I didn't want to take any chances. I was able to have the window open a crack. I had the loose insulated clothing and it was keeping my body temperature up. I turned the car on once in a while and let it run for a few minutes. There was liquor in the back but I realized that that is one of the worst things to do. I felt the radio stations were being a little bit too sensational. It was scaring me. But if it wasn't for the radio, I would have thought that it was the end of the world.

Luckily, I had a McDonald's cup left in the car from the skiing trip. I could urinate in the cup and toss it our the window. I didn't have to go outside and be frostbitten.

My twenty-one year old brother was in a coma for twenty months before he died as a result of the snowmobile accident. My dad died a couple of years after that from cancer. We had a sixteen thousand dollar fire in our home. My brother and a sister have a rare skin disease. So there has been a lot of trusting and purifying of the faith. It was a very natural inclination for me to pray. I had a Bible in the car and that was comforting because I could sit and read. It was the presence of God with me that really saved me and comforted me.

My survival was really a testimony to the power of prayer and the love of God. I feel a protection in His love and that's the same kind of testimony that this experience was. God really hears and answers prayers.

I turned to God in prayer and felt the assurance of His love, protection and presence. I had a profound trust in his words, "All things work together for the good of those who love God." As I repeated these words I realized that I could not see any good in this terrible storm, quite literally I could not see anything at all! Then I realized a key word — "Together". Perhaps this blizzard, isolated and of itself — seemed of no value. However, God said, "Together things work for the good". The storm could be compared to a piece of a jigsaw puzzle — that by itself was not the entire picture. It needed the other pieces before the whole picture was complete and appreciated and taken for its full value. So with the storm, I could trust in God that together all things would work for the good.

What an important lesson to learn for everyday life! A loving God sends us pieces of a puzzle in our daily situations. Some seem of no value or are difficult. To trust His love and wisdom to work things together is to allow Him to complete a beautiful picture without having the frustration of any missing pieces. This became the source of my peace.

About 11:30 a.m. the following morning, I was rescued by the people in the service station about a mile down the road. By 3:00 p.m. I was able to walk to the home of two friends, Joe and Chris Mombrea in Niagara Falls and they had given me up for dead. They had called the morgue for a description of the eight bodies which had already been brought in. My mom and family had been awake all night praying and were very relieved to hear from me.

When I arrived at my friends' house, I felt so much love in their welcome as they gave me warm clothes, food and rest. Many friends called to let me know that they had prayed and were rejoicing in my safety. My friends made me feel such a part of their family — welcomed for four days in their home, sharing all they had, especially themselves. Everyone seemed to be sacrificing to meet the needs of others, many of whom were strangers. Then the storm became one piece in a beautiful picture that was no longer a puzzle. "All things work together for the good for those who love God."

A friend questioned: "Why do we need a blizzard before we help those in need and express our love and concern? There are always needs and always the need to be loved."

Louis Billittier—Chef's Restaurant

"We had approximately 220 people in here and I was saying to myself, 'Jesus, I hope not too many more come in!'"

I own Chef's Restaurant at Seneca and Chicago in Buffalo, New York. The day of the Blizzard. The great day. I was out in

Kenmore picking up my portable radio when I saw the snowflakes. They were pretty heavy so I thought I'd better head down to the restaurant. At least I got there before the storm started, about 11:30 a.m. We started getting things ready for our regular Friday lunch hour when the winds started. We figured we were going to have a tough lunch.

After a few hours, the Mayor of the City of Buffalo and our county executives said we better let our people go. When our people started to go home, they started getting stranded. Traffic was backed up. They couldn't see and as the day went on, it just got tougher and tougher. People started to abandon their cars and started to walk and take shelter whereever they could. That afternoon we had approximately 220 people in here and I was saying to myself, "Jesus, I hope not too many more come in." You can't turn people away in a situation like that. On the other hand, how many can you handle? So everybody had lunch. Thank God we had plenty on hand.

Around five thirty, no more people came in. Everybody was pretty comfortable at that point. I shut the bar down at eight o'clock after I made a general announcement. Tea, coffee, milk and soft drinks were available. I had one guy who objected to the bar being closed. I told him, we didn't need anymore problems than we had already. I couldn't even see my parking lot across the street.

My friend, Roger Fenlon, from Erie County Emergency Medical Services found his way down here and he couldn't get any further. He was trying to get out to the Medical Dispatch. Luckily we both had our portable radios. He brought in blankets and other medical equipment from his vehicle.

We had a line of people from the telephone booth into our third dining room. I kept one telephone line open so we had incoming calls on it. Everybody was trying to phone home to their families. One husband got mad at his wife because she was stranded here. She said, "He can stay mad, I'm safe and sound."

Everybody got settled down pretty well until around midnight. Then we lost our power and people ran out of cigarettes and they panicked. They couldn't get cigarettes because I didn't have the keys to the cigarette machine. I had to get cigarettes. One of the patrons came over and said he would go down the street to the wax factory and get cigarettes. So he took orders from all the people and walked out into the blizzard. He brought back a big supply. No cigarettes was harder on the people than not having food.

Then Standard Milling called me from down the street and ordered a hundred meatball and sausage sandwiches and a few cases of beer. They had their workers walk over in the blizzard, pick up the food and bring it back to the stranded people and their employees.

I got a call from the wax factory later on and they said, "Look, we'll trade you candles for coffee, sugar and milk, It was a deal. We had light from the candles since the power was still off.

We had one fellow here with a pace maker, with a heart condition and we got a hold of his doctor. He called the emergency hospital. We had a police officer here whose name was Carl Reese and he walked over to Emergency Hospital through the storm. Carl brought back prescription medicine several times and helped a lot of people. Carl died of a heart attack as a result of his storm work. He was a great policeman.

One girl was about to go into a diabetic coma because she needed insulin. We couldn't get her to the hospital. Again Carl Reese walked to the hospital and got her insulin. She was fine after that.

Then we had a police officer who was out there trying to help people and he slipped and fractured his leg. So we splintered his leg and layed him down on a blanket. I said I didn't care if he was breaking rules and regulations, I was going to give him a shot. So we gave him a little liquor and let him rest comfortably and the next day we got him over to the hospital.

Then we had an incident where we had an epileptic boy who needed medication. After many many phone calls, we finally got to the right people. He was a little mentally retarded as well and we got him squared away.

During the night when we couldn't make coffee anymore because we had no power, we had to do it the old fashioned way. The cook boiled the coffee and strained it.

Before the storm, my son came into work with me. Little did he know that we were going to have a storm. He was ready to go out that night for his eighteenth birthday blast with all his friends. We celebrated his birthday here at midnight. We had everybody sing him happy birthday and we had a great party for him.

Luckily the restaurant was hot and with body heat it didn't start to chill down till about eight o'clock the next morning. The power went off from approximately eleven o'clock. We had gas for cooking. But we had no exhaust fan so I asked people if they would refrain from smoking. In a situation like that, they have nothing else to do but smoke. We opened the doors occasionally, but that didn't last but a few seconds because all the snow blew in.

We went through every bit of food we had here, bread, meatballs, spaghetti, chicken cacciatore. We gave it away and we traded with other businesses in the community and it brought a lot of people very very close.

All our patrons left by 8:00 p.m. the following night. Then I closed up the restaurant and I went home and I got a few hours sleep.

I was then able to work my way back to the Medical Dispatch Center. I'm responsible for all the emergency vehicles. I got a call from our operators and their men had been working continuously. They needed socks, gloves, parkas and a change of clothes. I called the Mayor of the City of Buffalo and told him I needed five hundred dollars for clothing. The Mayor committed himself and had to pay the five hundred out of his own pocket. I called a friend of mine who opened his sporting good store on Sunday and we got the clothing. Stanley Makowski is one of the finest mayors that the City of Buffalo has seen. He has a lot of compassion, understanding and concern for the citizens of this community. He has done more for emergency medical services than any mayor I've served under. I'm sorry that he's leaving his office.

The Salvation Army is one great group of people. They assisted me in getting some socks and gloves for our ambulance personnel.

"a blizzard should be named after a man"

Because of the storm some women suggested that a blizzard should be named after a man because you never know how many inches of snow are involved or how long it's going to last.

Births—Nine Months After The Blizzard

Since people were confined for many days during the blizzard, I was curious as to how this would affect the birth rate, nine months after the storm, when compared to the previous year. My suspicions were confirmed in Regional Niagara in Canada where I discovered that the birth rate had jumped almost 18 percent.

I was surprised to discover that for Erie County and Buffalo on the American side of the border that the increase was only about 3 percent. I double checked my figures and their source and then set out to discover why there was such a great difference between the Canadian and American statistics. Much of the explanation lies in the next interview.

Erno Rossi

Marilynn Buckham: Erie Medical Center (Abortion Clinic)

"For March and early April we noted a 45 percent increase in the number of abortions."

The center is called Erie Medical Center. It's an outpatient abortion clinic. We do terminations up to 12 weeks of pregnancy. We found that during the blizzard of '77, transportation was severely restricted for our patients. In this period we found a higher proportion of our abortion patients were from Erie County than usual. Normally, about half of the patients are from outside of Erie County. During that period only 39% of our patients came from the non-Erie County areas. And among those from the non-Erie County areas, very few were from the far away towns usually representing our abortion patients. It appears that the weather of '77 affected the abilitiy of women to get to our center for services.

Because of the storm, we were shut down for a little over a week. Women who were scheduled for appointments at this time were very anxious as to what would happen if they were past the 12 week limit. Many of the women, when we finally did open, came in and took the risk of driving inside the city limits with the driving ban in effect. They were very anxious since they feared another blizzard. They were anxious to the point of being hysterical, knowing that they were still pregnant unless we could get to see them within a very short time. After 12 weeks they would have to wait and have a more complicated procedure done, such as a saline and have to go into a hospital, which concerned them and the people here at the center.

We abort here at this center up to 12 weeks with minimum risk. The women on staff who work and live in the city walked into the office during the driving ban to help the people who were on our answering service. They took calls, assuring the pregnant women that they would all be seen and not to panic. This was a great help during this stressful period. Even though we weren't open for patients, we did answer the phone and reschedule many women 4 to 5 times hoping that the weather would clear up.

The clinic was organized in January of 1972. I've been here since we opened. I found it the most difficult time for staff and for women to come in from a distance or locally because of the blizzard. They were under a great deal of pressure. During this week and a half when they couldn't come in for the normal appointments, they were still pregnant.

The technique used here at the center is a suction curettage, a vacuum aspiration, a very simple technique, which takes approximately 5-7 minutes using a suction machine and curette.

The cost is $160.00 dollars. We are usually booked a week ahead of time and we do them between 6-12 weeks of pregnancy. They have to have a positive pregnancy test before they can have the abortion to make sure that they are pregnant. So these women that were calling at that time were pretty sure. Yet some of them hadn't had pregnancy tests. So we were going to have to wait until they came in because there was no place where they could get a pregnancy test done. They would have to have it done on that day. We were making as many exceptions as we possibly could.

The staff at the center responded very well. We had a meeting upon returning to work when we could all make it in. I told them that during the next few weeks, we were going to be under a great deal of pressure, and that I was going to be asking them to work long hours and possibly even Sundays. We never did work Sunday. But we did work long hours with many more patients than were normally done on a normal working day to accommodate the women who had been waiting and who were often hysterical. Many of the women just finally said that they were going to have the child when they called. They said they just couldn't keep hanging on.

The total amount of Canadian women that come to our services here, I would approximate at about seven to eight percent. Some of the Canadian women prefer to come here because they do not have a board to find out if they are physically and mentally competent to have this abortion.

During January, the number of patients dropped 25 percent due to the blizzard. In February 1977, after the blizzard, the number of patients rose about 25 percent because we were behind schedule. Many women who were scheduled during the blizzard, never did come in to us. We are also busier in a cold month like February than we are in a warm summer month.

For March and early April we noted a 45 percent increase in the number of abortions compared to the same period of March - April 1976 and 1975. The remainder of April 1977 showed a 25 percent increase in abortions, because of the blizzard.

The racial composition of our clients having abortions is disproportionately white. Eighty-eight percent were white, nine percent were black and fewer than two percent were from other categories. One percent would not identify themselves. These figures are from the first quarter of 1977 and this has held true over the years of abortions at this clinic.

YES YES YES

Sample answers given to inquiries concerning the driving ban: "Yes, you can drive your wife to have her baby. Yes, you can go to a funeral, but not to a wake. Yes, the wedding can go on with the guests arriving by car."

Dr. Gerstenzang--Assistant Professor of Psychiatry, University of Buffalo Medical School, Director of the Emergency Clinic, Meyer Memorial Hospital

"In these types of withdrawals, the victim experiences grand mal seizures after 48 to 72 hours and then death."

I'd like to consider the two most important psychological effects of the blizzard. The first type of reaction has to do with people that we can call psychiatric patients. There are about 20 to 40 thousand people in Buffalo who are marginally adjusted to life, people who have had a history of one or more previous psychiatric admissions to the hospital. They will often have a history of difficult adjustments to many things in life such as marriage, jobs, stressful situations in the family, problems with children or deaths of loved ones. Many are borderline individuals, others are stabilized chronic schizophrenics. Others may just have severe neurosis. These people are sittting on a time bomb because they are very vulnerable to the straw that breaks the camel's back. We saw this in the emergency clinic throughout the storm and for a week to ten days afterwards. There was an increase of patients who were marginally compensated from an emotional point of view who were tipped into the compensation, not because of the blizzard per se, but because it happened to be a stressful event that none of us could get away from. Had that stressful event been something else like being fired from a job or having their car demolished in a wreck or having a fight or a marital separation, these things would precipitate many people into a situation where they would come to us or be brought in by a family member. Some of the more extreme examples are brought to us by the police.

An example is a middle-aged secretary who had a 20 year history of psychiatric problems. She was fairly well stabilized and was able to function well when the blizzard struck but she was stranded at work for the night. As the night wore on she was thrown into a psychotic reaction by the stress because she was unable to control anything about her environment or herself. She was brought here to the hospital and admitted. There were many people in the same situation.

With many people, I found an actual improvement in their emotional well being because of the blizzard, whether they had a psychiatric history or not. We tended to see a lot of this in the medical professionals such as nurses and orderlies and people in the helping professions generally. This business of having an overwhelming stressful situation served as a vehicle for people to step out of their own personal problems and mobilize their energies to do things that could help others. This is characteristic of people who choose the helping professions. They could get over any personal difficulties helping others. My guess is that there were as many people who received a therapeutic benefit form the blizzard as there were who received a non-therapeutic effect. I'm limiting myself to emotional reactions. I'm not including any of the elderly who were running out of food or the sick who were running out of medicine.

In this country, as we got into World War II, the incidence of serious emotional and mental disorder decreased dramatically. Admissions to psychiatric hospitals dropped rapidly. People with neurotic traits and disorders benefited from a feeling of joining in the common effort. There was a "real" outside threat to everyone's security and lives. In view of this they were able to put aside their neurotic tendencies that we can call "unreal" in comparison to war. Much of this occurred during the blizzard among people such as the operators of four wheel drive vehicles, ambulance personnel, police and firemen. There was a great boost to their emotional state of well being.

Beyond that, there are some individuals with certain personality traits who would not be considered by most professionals as being psychiatrically ill, specifically the obsessive-compulsive personalities. Some of these people had a difficult time with the blizzard. Being obsessive-compulsive is a valuable trait in our society. Such people tend to be the do'ers and organizers as well as being reliable. They are hard workers and they do everything they can to meet others' expectations. Because of the blizzard, these people became very uncomfortable because an obsessive-compulsive cannot tolerate a lack of control over situations. They were confronted with a driving ban they couldn't break, they had a driveway they couldn't get out of and they couldn't get to their offices. An obsessive-compulsive cannot handle free time well and he therefore had a problem. These people tend to be the most productive and successful segments of our society. An example is a neighbor who is a very dynamic man and a top business executive, largely because of his personality traits, but with the anxiety of the storm, his traits got out of hand. He diligently shovelled his own sidewalk for several days and then proceeded to shovel the entire side of his street. He then crossed the street and shovelled the entire sidewalk on the other side. When I was returning from the hospital, I saw him, the only person in sight trying to shovel out the entire roadway by himself. That's when I convinced him to stop doing that. What is interesting here is the form that his anxiety took when he was not able to control the situation. Instead of being able to handle his anxiety in a more reasonable way, he was engaged in a futile attempt to control things by attempting to shovel the road with only one shovel. These individuals had a severe time with the blizzard.

Then there are those individuals who have a reactive depression or a let down following a peak period of stress. They slump emotionally when the challenge has been taken away. The classic psychiatric example that we are seeing more frequently is the so-called promotion depression. You have a typical business executive who works very hard to rise in his organization. Then he receives a very significant promotion and family and friends are very happy for him, but he develops a significant depression which can incapacitate him. He has put so much energy into achieving something and once attaining this goal, this mobilization turns in on itself and depression follows. This occurred with some people following their energetic involvement with the blizzard.

With respect to suicides during the blizzard, my guess would be that they would have dropped significantly. I have no statistics to prove this however.

Remember the lady I told you about earlier. She became delusional and told us that this whole blizzard was engineered by the Mayor of Buffalo. Such a marginally compensated person as this lady who goes into psychosis will have delusions.

On the other hand, other chronic psychotics in the hospital at the time of the blizzard, actually improved their condition-much like other segments of the population. There was something bigger than them that was happening and this distracted them from their own reality and encouraged them to partake of a shared reality that was compelling. In this sense the blizzard was therapeutic.

Sensory deprivation will often induce fantasies and hallucinations very dramatically--fantasies being much like a heightened imagination whereas hallucinations are real to the person when he sees and hears things. People in a dark room with very little stimuli for a long period or mountain climbers isolated by a blizzard with nothing but white around them— have gone absolutely psychotic. All of us are surrounded by external stimuli such as sound, smell, sight, touch and taste. We also have internal stimuli such as memories and thoughts about the future. If the external stimuli are eliminated as happened to some isolated people during the blizzard, their internal stimuli or primary mechanism becomes a louder voice because it does not have to compete anymore.

I'll give you two other clinical examples of sensory deprivation. One would be the elderly person who has surgery for cataracts and when he wakes up he has dressings on both eyes and he becomes psychotic — seeing and hearing things and becoming very agitated. He has relied on his sense of sight to keep him oriented to who he is and where he is. When the vision is cut off like this, the fantasy grows.

Another example is with some people who had certain leukemias, more so of a few years ago than now. They would be put into a germ free environment, they would essentially live in a gold fish bowl and would stay there for a few months. They never got to touch anybody. Even the food that came in would be sterilized before it got to them. We noticed that the fantasy life of such people skyrocketed to the point where it was difficult for them to distinguish between fantasy and the real thing. So the whole issue of sensory deprivation during the blizzard would be very real for someone who is living alone or is trapped in a vehicle and spent a good deal of time staring at the whiteness of the storm.

For the cabin fever syndrome which some people experienced during the blizzard, there is no one cure which can apply to everyone since one person's need is another person's poison. For myself, reading fiction absorbs me completely and the better part of a day could pass without my being aware of it. For another person, he may want to get the guy next door and another from across the street and get involved in a poker game. If teenagers liked it, they might get involved in a good monopoly game or perhaps listen to their favorite albums. These sort of things make sense as antidotes.

In 1967 I was a ship's doctor for a Coast Guard Cutter with 250 men aboard. We were in the Arctic for three months. We had travelled up the coast of Alaska, crossed the Bering Sea and ended up in the East Siberian Sea for three months doing classified work, fourteen miles off the coast of Siberia. Here was real cabin fever. We even lost our water supply. The people who handled this well were those men who became absorbed in various things. In fact, I had a continuous monopoly game going in my area of the ship — the sick bay — and people kept rotating in and out of there. There were pockets of others kinds of activities. There was one enlisted man who loved to sing and play a balalaika and he did this endlessly and many people could concentrate on this either listening or singing. This wouldn't help for others and so we had other activities for them. I remember that doing puzzles was very popular.

This isn't commonly known but it is true that withdrawal from alcohol or from barbituates is more serious and more life threatening than withdrawal from heroin. The individual withdrawing from heroin often experiences a more intense discomfort and a more intense experience. But he does not face the life threatening withdrawal of a severe alcoholic or barbituate addict. In these types of withdrawals, the victim experiences grand mal seizures after 48 to 72 hours and then death. There are many people who consume tremendous quantities of alcohol daily and don't consider themselves alcoholics because they are so accustomed to it. If, during an emer-

An Army C-5 Galaxy airlifted borrowed equipment from New York City to Niagara Falls, New York Airport. Courtesy, Buffalo Evening News.

gency like the blizzard, these people were cut off from their supply, they would be in a life threatening situation.

Bartender—Statler Hilton—Buffalo

"People were running around, drinking, drinking, drinking."

I came in early on Friday, January 28th. By eleven a.m., all the hotel rooms were taken. The hotel was packed. There wasn't a place to sit down in the bar all night long. There was no place to go. No relief showed up for me so I worked all night. I never went home for a week. I washed my own socks, shirt and underwear. I've been bartending for 40 years and I've never seen sales so high. People were running around, drinking, drinking, drinking.

NEW YORK STATE DEPARTMENT OF MENTAL HYGIENE
WESTERN NEW YORK REGIONAL OFFICE

"He was fearful of leaving his apartment and expressed fears that he would either kill himself or go up on the roof and shoot policemen."

The Blizzard of '77 was "a killer", reported the Buffalo Evening News, "the storm to top all storms in the winter that had already topped all winters". Before it was over four days later, many people had died, thousands had been stranded and all roadways were blocked. There was discomfort and fear of loss of essential services and substances. Telephones didn't work, gas supplies used to heat homes and public buildings were dangerously low, electric failure hit many areas, grocery stores ran out of food, and milk for babies became a precious, ebbing commodity. People everywhere were isolated and separated from each other for long periods of time, often without communication. Working men and women, children sequestered indoors with parents and siblings, elderly persons cut off from usual routines all began to show signs of increased irritability and tension. Firemen, road crews and hospital workers, overtaxed by long hours of hard work, began to weaken with strain and fatigue. To make matters worse, the radio proclaimed the possibility of dangerous flooding in the future.

Scattered information started coming in. Increased use of alcohol was noted, fires in homes and businesses became frequent as people turned up furnaces or used temporary heaters for keeping warm. Automobile accidents of the fender bender variety were common and more serious loss of life accidents more frequent. Few people were unaffected. Loss of work for one day, two days and more were common. Pay checks dwindled and budgets stretched. For those in marginal or low income employment situations, making ends meet became impossible. Already a high unemployment area, Erie County became even more depressed and suicidal depression became more frequent and common.

The psychological and emotional state of some people became precarious. The mental health programs of Erie County were severely affected by the ongoing, continuous bad weather. Staff would make heroic efforts to get to their place of employment only to learn that client cancellations were at 90 to 100 percent levels for the day. The clients already in service (the identified vulnerable) were regressing and losing ground in their struggle for equilibrium. Telephone contact (an inadequate technique at best) became a frequent means "for keeping the lid on". Clients on psychotic drugs were not receiving adequate monitoring and prescriptions and medications were running out. Behavior of clients became more bizarre and hostile. Acting out, a euphimism for all manner of inappropriate behavior was common. Staff resources were low, irritability was common, absenteeism increased and closings of mental health sites because of heavy snow became common.

Administrators of mental health programs were faced daily with the dilemma of closing programs because of health and safety reasons for staff and remaining open because of the client need. Those qualities (warmth, acceptance, understanding, genuineness, sensitivity) which enhance the counselling process were diminished. Everybody was affected. The comfort of routines and the ability to plan was reduced to a shambles. Clearly the whole system was in a state of crisis and service quality was diminishing. Clearly, respite was needed.

The massive job of snow removal continued. Thousands of automobiles were towed to central receiving areas. People who were stranded and trapped had no way of moving or getting to their homes and families. A state of emergency and restrictions on travel existed in the city, towns and villages of Erie County. The isolation continued. The casualties of the storm became more widespread. Loss of employment, loss of property, loss of life were common.

As the snows abated and snow removal accomplished, a degree of normalcy returned. People in all walks of life were glad that "it was over". Factories opened, businesses started up, schools began to open and a feeling of relief began to spread throughout the county. Optimistic pronouncements were cautious. The people were wary. What would happen next? Anxiety was at high levels and remained just below the surface.

Research confirms that disasters produce mental health casualties far beyond the time of the actual disaster. Thus one month after the actual disaster, the mental health service system experienced a demand for its service beyond its capacity. It should be remembered that the mental health professional staff, also experienced the disaster. In effect, the helpers are also victims. As victims, their efficiency, their capability, their effectiveness was lowered. At the same time, their numbers had been decimated and fewer people were available for actual service provision.

Inpatient services revealed an increased utilitzation. E. J. Meyer Memorial Hospital, a short term acute psychiatric facility showed a dramatic increase in its daily census. Buffalo Psychiatric Center had also shown a dramatic increase in the number of admissions.

These individuals are frequently difficult to manage in the community, require regular medication, and high (intensive) levels of supportive counselling and assistance and are particularly susceptible to regression. The snow emergency, with its disruptive and disorienting effects, was especially difficult for those individuals whose maintenance in the community was precarious at best, especially for those who derive social supports from extra familiar sources such as day treatment programs, organized social activities and the like. Each mental health program in Erie County has reported inappropriate, regressed, bizarre behavior from this group of clients.

THE AGED
The Erie County Office for the Aging noted:

The extremely harsh weather of this winter has produced above average hardships on older people in our care, jeopardizing both their physical and mental well being. The inability to battle the elements compelled many people to remain at home. Such forced confinement served to intensify and exacerbate the social isolation to which too many elderly are already victim. Fear of venturing outside one's own four walls also tends to create high anxiety in the individual about his or her ability to obtain medical care and meet other very basic human needs. During the storms of January and February, our office received up to 75 calls a day from older persons unable to get food, medicine or help in shoveling out. The anxiety inherent in such inability to cope with elemental realities tends to aggravate existing physical maladies (such as hypertension) and nervous disorders and to further deflate an already low sense of self-esteem.

The most detrimental effect of the extremely cold weather this season has been the high energy costs it produced. Approximately 25% of all persons over 65 in Erie County live at or below the poverty level, making it all but impossible for them to meet the formidable utility bills they have received. Anxiety about how to pay these bills, plus fear of having their gas or heat shut off, has caused many to experience severe stress and agitation. Outreach workers and case supervisors here, as well as workers in our subcontracting agencies, attest to the emotional distress of their clients caused by these uncontrolled costs.

The overwhelming magnitude of all of these weather-related problems, when compounded, can immobilize the coping mechanisms which the elderly individual might normally be able to muster in order to deal with his problems. The individual's loss of confidence in his own ability to cope with forces from the external world has long-range deleterious effects on the emotional health of many an older person.

FAMILIES
Couples who were already experiencing marital tension experienced relationship breakdown after being confined together during the blizzard. Women who had suffered from depression found that the increased family interaction caused by the storm exacerbated their symptoms. Many individuals used alcohol to combat the anxiety inherent in the storm situation with the result that family

turmoil was intensified.

The following case portrays one situation where further service was necessary as a direct consequence of the storm. A young woman in her late twenties was treated for depression reaction to the trauma of relocation. Counselling and medication benefited her to the extent that she was able to move from one community to another and continue to function adequately. Her reaction to being confined to strange surroundings by the storm was such that she felt isolated in the new community and experienced further symptoms of depression following the storm.

South East Corporation V, which serves an urban, suburban, rural population noted a sharp increase in aberrant family behavior. Intake conferences revealed a unusually high incidence of aggressive physical abuse. Where arguments were once settled by "shouting" or "not talking", husbands and wives were battering each other.

Parent-child relationships emerged as serious dysfunctions. School related problems (due to closings) were more intense and complex. Drug and alcohol abuse by adolescents was a common problem. (Substance Abuse Programs in Erie County were scheduled for elimination effective April 1, 1977.)

INDIVIDUALS

Depression was a common symptom. The underlying rage manifested itself in suicidal and homicidal ideations and attempts. In one instance, a former client called in a state of panic. He was fearful of leaving his apartment and expressed fears that he would either kill himself or go up on the roof and shoot policemen. Rehospitalization was achieved within two hours of the initial contact.

Observers at medication clinics note "increased numbers of clients, high levels of anxiety, loud abrasive behavior, misuse of medication and verbal aggressiveness". Families reported poor eating, sleeping and personal hygiene of those clients least able to cope with stress.

STAFF

The staff of all the service agencies are themselves victims of the disaster. Informal discussions have revealed increased absenteeism, diminished ability to render service, increased complaints about clients, conditions and caseloads.

The Executive Director of Corporation IV sums up the issue of staff morale as follows: "Our staff is emotionally drained and noticeably agitated. They were required to not only manage their own affairs during the siege, but those of clients as well. This double load has been exhausting. Who is helping the helpers?"

Captain Phil Morana—Buffalo Fire Department

"I honestly believed for a while that the whole city was going to burn to the ground."

I came on duty at 8 a.m. and was expecting to be relieved at

5 p.m. But nobody could get into the city to relieve us. Later that night a false alarm came in and as bad as that storm was, there were still false alarms. Some people have no respect for us.

We were trying to make a way to an alarm but the streets were blocked with cars. We made U turns and inched our way by alternate routes. Finally, we got bogged into the snow and we were still three blocks from the alarm site. The Chief asked me to take the portable radio and report on what I could see. We still were not sure if there was a fire. Two other men and I struggled through snow that was over our knees and when we got within one block of the alarm, I could smell smoke and I could see a glow in the sky through the blowing snow. I used the Chief's radio and his signature and asked for a second alarm, an unusual thing to do when you are that far away from a fire that I had not yet observed. When I finally got closer to the fire I couldn't believe what I saw — three houses were burning and the glow lit up the fourth and fifth houses on each side of the fire. Engine number 9 found another street open and made it closer to the fire. Many people from the neighborhood were helping to push the pumper until it got close to the fire hydrant. Then, we started dragging lines and tried to cut the fire off.

I remember that there was an older woman dead in the snow. She probably came out of one of the burning houses and fell down and in no time at all she was covered over with blowing snow and died.

I also remember that by the time I got to the corner where I saw the glow in the sky that I had frostbite on three fingers already. I actually used the fire to warm my hands or else I wouldn't have been able to move them.

When we shut off the hose in order to move it to a new position, the hose burst. By the time we replaced the broken line, the nozzle to the hose was frozen stiff from lying in the snow. By banging it, we finally got it opened.

The first alarm to a fire brings in three engines, two hooks and ladders and a chief. A second alarm will bring in three more engines, two more hooks and ladders but no chief on the second alarm. A third alarm will bring in three more pumpers and one hook and ladder. That fire went to three alarms.

The water kept running down the street to the corner where the drains were plugged. This caused the water to rise to the level of the running boards on the pumpers. The pumpers and hoses had to be chopped out with jack hammers which we borrowed from the power company. A lot of the equipment was ruined. Axles disintegrated on the trucks so that they couldn't be moved. Some of the pumpers stalled and when that happened we could not get the water out. This turned to ice and they split. I think we lost three pumpers that way.

We are not in the habit of using antifreeze in our vehicles since they are kept inside or kept running when they are in use at the scene of a fire. When an engine stalled from snow and ice in the motor, the water froze because there was no antifreeze and we lost the vehicle.

From now on, we should keep sets of chains on hand at all

times, even though we have good snow tires. I should have been wearing two pair of gloves that night or at least thermal gloves which I bought the next day. In weather like that, all firemen should wear ski masks.

Seven houses were destroyed that night and I'll never forget those unfortunate people running out of those houses with their television sets and pet birds and whatever was of value to them. They were abandoning houses all along the street, whereever the sparks were flying in those 50 and 60 mile per hour winds with the wind-chill factor at 50 and 60 below zero. The people lost most of their household goods. I honestly believed for a while that the whole city was going to burn to the ground. Considering the circumstances, the firemen did an excellent job.

A couple of years ago, people in that area would throw rocks at the firemen when we came into the area. During the night of January 28th, 1977, they were helping to push the pumpers and opening their houses to us with coffee and food.

Burke Glasser—Caretaker—South Park Conservatory

"Are you going to move it or am I going to push you off the bridge with my snow plow?"

When I got here on Saturday morning, the ventilator in the cactus house had blown open and about thirty thousand dollars worth of cactus plants were frozen. Then the engineer told us that we were very low on heating oil. We called the oil company but they couldn't get through. They said that they didn't have a truck or driver available anywhere. We had no alternative fuel supply so we had to stay with oil.

By eleven thirty that morning they found that there was an oil truck stuck on William Street in front of the new post office. The oil company said that if we needed the oil bad enough, we would have to get through to that truck.

I took the dump truck from here and plowed my way over to get him. I left here about noon and returned with him about eight o'clock that night. To conserve fuel in the meantime, we had dropped the temperature in the greenhouses to about fifty degrees. There were two hours of fuel left when we got back.

When I got through to the oil truck, it was still running. But his brakes had failed because of the snow and ice. So I led this six thousand gallon oil truck back to the Conservatory. Since he did not have any brakes, I had to stay close in front of him.

The police told me that if anybody got into my way, I was to use the snow plow on my truck and push them off the road. Only one guy gave me a real hard time. He wanted to go down Seneca Street into the city but the police wouldn't let him go. So he wouldn't move his car from the middle of the intersection. "I'm not going to move another inch until I can go where I want to," he told me. So I said to him, "Are you going to move it or am I going to push you off the bridge with my snow plow?" He called me a few choice names. Then I jumped into my truck, lowered the snow plow and headed for him. He drove his car into a snow bank and cleared the intersection. The oil truck followed close behind me and we got through to the Conservatory with the oil. The next day, I got my truck so badly stuck in the driveway that it took a bulldozer to get it out.

When we finally got the oil into our oil tanks at the Conservatory we discovered that it was the wrong type of oil. This caused problems with the boiler and we sprung a number of leaks. Oil blew all over the boiler room floor. The engineers who stayed over during the storm soon solved the problem and everything worked well.

If we had run out of fuel, the estimated damage would have been about six million dollars because the weight of the snow would have collapsed the building. I was really happy because if we had lost a place like this, the city could not afford to replace it. It would have been gone for ever.

Mrs. Toy

"It was a boy, we estimated him at 7 lbs., 13 ozs."

I called my doctor at 10:30 a.m. and told him I was having mild contractions. The nurse asked me to come in so he could examine me. This was my second baby, so I didn't feel there was any big hurry.

It was about five to twelve and the storm had already hit here but it wasn't bad so I didn't think anything of it. The nurse had said to go into the hospital. So we took our little girl to the neighbors. I got my suitcase and my husband headed for the expressway. There was no way that we could get through. We were stuck. He tried for 15 or 20 minutes to get us out and then we both realized we weren't going to get out. The snow had just drifted up all over the car!

Finally, I said, "Let's get out and try and find a house so we can get to a phone or to somebody who has a CB radio." So we walked a little way and we saw a big huge truck that was sitting there and the guy rolled down his window and we asked him if he had a CB. He said no. By this time the winds were 60 m.p.h. and we couldn't see 2 inches in front of us. I asked him if we could get in the truck for a few minutes just to get warmed up. He said, "No!" He claimed that he had valuable equipment in the truck and he couldn't let us in. From there we walked across the intersection to a little tiny pick up truck sitting there with two guys in it. We knocked on the door and it opened. They told us to get right in. We sat there.

The one guy that was in the pick up truck was hit by another car but he had a CB radio in his own car. So he called over the citizens band for a rescue squad and he told them of our situation and the Elma rescue squad picked us up on West Blood and took us to the house of a fire chief where we sat until 5:00 p.m. During all this excitement, my contractions had stopped completely. All the time I was at the fire chief's house I didn't have any. About 5:00 p.m., the East Aurora fire department picked us up. We were back in our house in 10 minutes when my contractions started again. From 5:00 p.m. until a quarter to 11 we were in constant contact with my doctor.

We had gone to Lamaze classes. My Lamaze teacher kept in contact. She had planned on coming down with the doctor who was supposed to deliver me. But neither of them could make it. The fire department got a hold of Dr. Mariniello about a quarter to eleven and they brought him down. He was there about five minutes and the baby was born at twelve minutes past eleven. It was a boy. We estimated him at 7 lbs., 13 ozs.

In Lamaze we learned to have a baby naturally, without any kind of anaesthetic. My purpose in going to these classes was to have my husband with me during the delivery. I learned how to breathe with my contractions, making it easier on me. When Dr. Mariniello got here, I asked him if he could give me something to calm me down and he said no. All I was allowed was a local for my episiotomy. Any drugs would have drugged the baby. Since this was going to be home delivery, they didn't have the equipment they had in a hospital. We were lucky the baby was healthy. We made it through with no trouble.

This delivery was easier than my first one. I felt much better after he was born. My doctor stayed there until midnight and we had two of our neighbors come over and stay about an hour. Then I was up right after they left. I got up and washed the baby myself with the help of my husband. Then I came downstairs and sat on the couch with the baby and talked. I felt better. I wasn't drugged.

When you take these Lamaze classes, your husband is your coach. He helps you breathe if you get off track. He has to learn all the breathing techniques. He can tell you how to start up and how you should be breathing for certain stages of labor. When we went to the classes it seemed to me that he wasn't absorbing, but you know, he really did. He kept me right on track and I don't think I could have made it through without him. He was very much involved.

Looking back on it, my husband was really thrilled. He says that he thinks he was in a state of shock. Everything we went through during the day made the birth of the baby seem almost secondary. When you are walking in 60 m.p.h. winds and its snowing so bad you can't see and you don't think you have much longer to live, other things become less important. All I could think of during the whole episode was that I was going to fall and my water was going to break. Then I thought that I would fall and I wouldn't be able to get up.

While the doctor was here my husband was kept busy doing things during the delivery besides being busy with me. He had to do a couple of things for the doctor and he was almost as busy as I was. The doctor said that my husband was so nervous he couldn't

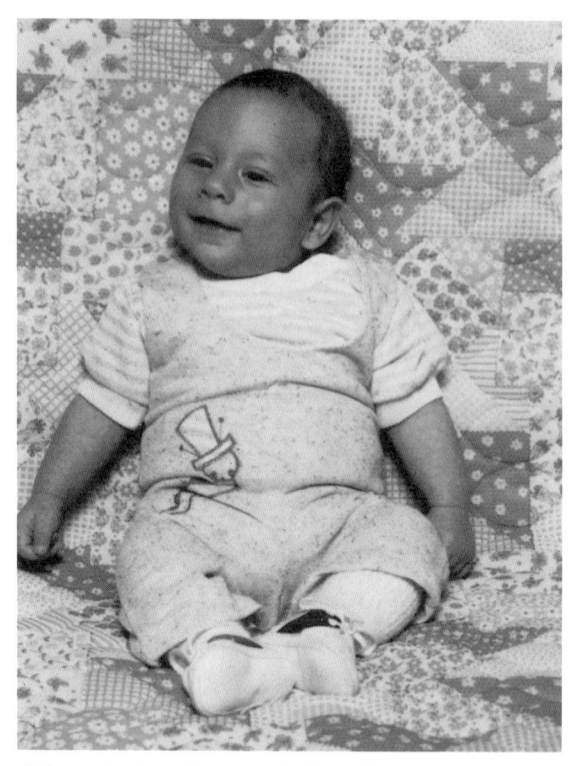

Blizzard baby. Brennan Jeffrey Toy.

boil the water. They don't boil water anymore. In fact, I think my doctor said they never did.

I remember that he asked Don if he had a dryer. He had Don get a couple of the baby's receiving blankets and throw them in the dryer. Then when the baby was born, he was wrapped up warmly.

Delivering this baby wasn't any different than when I was in the hospital except for the absence of equipment. You've got to try to keep yourself calm. I think that everyone should go to Lamaze classes. If I could have all my children at home, I would. There was a more satisfying feeling with my blizzard baby than with the first child.

Everything was quiet so that when the baby was born it was not a shock to him. They don't spank him on the bottom. They just try to keep the atmosphere really quiet because that is what the baby is used to before he's born. It reminded me of that when I saw Brennan. As the doctor gave him to me, the baby looked right at me and he had a smile on his face. Jenny on the other hand just screamed bloody murder when she was born. That's the biggest difference between the two births that I can remember. He didn't cry at all until the doctor suctioned his mouth and his nose and fixed his umbilical cord. I remember lying there saying why isn't he crying? I thought something was wrong with him!

It was funny to see us coming home from Elma with the East Aurora Fire Department. My husband got out of one truck and I came in another. And all the guys in the truck stepped out to say, "No more winter babies please! Make them all in the summer." In the end, the members of the Fire Department were thrilled. They were going around saying we just had a baby boy. They were thrilled to death that everything went well.

The beginning. The Skyway is closed. Downtown Buffalo.
Courtesy, Buffalo State College Courier Express Collection.

ANYONE FOR A BOTTLE

A downtown bar stopped selling individual drinks and began selling by "the bottle only" — $16 a bottle.

Donald Toy

"If I had a gun!"

I had three things on my mind. I was worried about somebody plowing me, I was worried about asphyxiation and I was worried that nobody was going to find us in that storm. That was why I got out and tried to find someone. By this time my clothes were soaked from being in and out of the car. When we got out of the car, we figured there was a house close by. The only thing we could see when we got out of the car was a telephone pole. That's the only thing we had to follow because the drifts on both sides of the roads were banked up about 10 feet by that time. We couldn't see over them. The only markers we had were the telephone poles and the wires. They were whipping around wildly. They were really singing in the 50 mile per hour winds. My wife was really afraid that one was going to snap and hit her. So we started walking. I didn't really know where I was and getting out and walking was just a shot in the dark.

We followed the lines until we got to the intersection. So we walked down to that intersection and spotted a truck. Two guys were in it and they didn't know where the hell they were. We asked them if there were any houses around and they didn't know either. They had a cab and a flat bed rig. He was hauling a bulldozer on the back. He wouldn't let us into the truck because there were two guys in there already and he said he had some equipment on the seat. He wouldn't let us in the truck! If I had a gun!!! But, apart from the time it would take me to pull the trigger, I really didn't have time to argue with him, and he knew my wife was pregnant and about to have a baby!! I didn't have time to argue with the guy or even call him names. I was thinking about what I was going to do next and so we turned around and walked the other way.

Neither of us were dressed to be out in that blizzard. When we left the house, we left to go to the hospital. Both of us were wearing heavy coats. But we didn't have any boots, gloves, scarf, or hat. We dressed only to go from the house to the car, from the car to the hospital, never figuring that we'd get caught out in a blizzard.

We were walking backwards because we couldn't face into the wind. My wife was walking right beside me, practically touching and she was just a shadow. That's how bad the visibility was. You could make out she was there by the dark against the white. So we got a little ways on the other side of the intersection and we come on a pick-up truck, a tree surgeon's truck. He had another guy with him. He let us in. By this time my clothes were as stiff as wood. I couldn't bend my arms and my jeans were frozen solid from the cuffs to my crotch. I couldn't bend my legs. When I got into the truck I had to break them. From getting in and out of the car they were wet and walking into the gale, they froze solid. The wind chill factor was about 60 below.

We could not have walked around much longer. When I got into the truck I was shaking and my teeth were chattering. But it was warm inside the cab.

The other passenger in the truck had a minor accident about 20 feet up the road and he had a CB in his car. When he learned the situation with my wife, he went to his car and put out a call for help. About 45 minutes later, the Elma Volunteer Firemen arrived with a 4 wheel drive for my wife and the back of a snowmobile for me. They took us to the volunteer fire chief's house. They gave us dry clothes, coffee and they really were great. They put my wet clothes in the dryer. They had to peel my coat off because I couldn't do it.

Gloria Kaeselau - East Aurora

"My baby was so alert."

On Friday, the 28th, I had gone shopping just before the storm hit. As a matter of fact, just as the storm hit, I came in the door. I didn't expect to have the baby for another week and I had been to the doctor the day before. I went to bed Friday evening and woke up in the middle of the night to find out we were going to have the baby. We called the police department and asked if we could get out of town. He told me to go back to bed. So that's what I did, very reluctantly, but there wasn't any choice. We called for a doctor to come in and he came in at a quarter to seven in the morning. He delivered a baby boy at 10:15 and he weighed about eight pounds, and his name is Scott Paul. He was a nice little healthy boy. We did not plan to have natural child birth. The doctor very calmly stood there and said, "Now this will be just like having a baby in the hospital except you're not going to have a spinal."

I recommend it highly. It was a great experience. Looking back on it, I was scared to death. Fortunately I have a wonderful neighbor who took my daughter home and took care of their three children plus ours.

I think the most important thing is to try to relax and not be so frightened if you can possibly avoid it. I didn't believe people about natural child birth, but I guess they were right. You are much more alert and my baby was so alert. That anaesthetic puts them under, too.

WKBW Radio

Friday January 28, 1977 - Weather Report

Between six and seven this morning, Indianapolis had a temperature drop of almost twenty-five degrees. A wall of snow moved into the city and they couldn't see anything. And those are the conditions which are moving east. Between seven and eight this morning, Columbus Ohio picked up the same sort of conditions. People were blown down in the street by very strong winds and a wall of snow moved in. All the roads were clogged immediately. If our winds become west south westerly this afternoon, we'll get heavy snow and blizzard conditions and it will be every bit as bad, if not worse than the conditions that we had last week. Prepare for a return of blizzard conditions this afternoon.

James L. McLaughlin - News Director, WKBW Radio

"Yes, we are the only two survivors."

The snow began late in the morning. The winds picked up and the blizzard was in full force. Buffalo schools had already been closed for three days from an earlier storm. Friday dawned clear and cold and everyone was at work. By 3 p.m. it was clear that we had big trouble and WKBW Radio moved into special emergency service programing. At the time, no one could know that it would be twelve days before the emergency would be over, months before the damage would be repaired and generations before the blizzard would be forgotten.

Here are some excerpts from the expanded news at 5:45 in the afternoon of January 28th.

'Erie County is advising no travel. Visibility is zero and there must be 1000 people stranded in vehicles. One hundred accidents in this county are accounted for. Niagara County is also being clobbered at this time. A Sheriff's Department spokesman told K.B news that driving there was very trecherous, almost everything is blocked off and there is a request that no one drive their cars.'

'Jim Wells with the State Department of Transportation, would like to advise that they have suspended snow plowing and sanding operations until conditions improve in Chautauqua, Erie and Niagara Counties. Visibility is so poor that the drivers are unable to operate their vehicles safely.'

'The Town of Cheektowaga is isolated at this time. A police spokesman called K.B. news and reported that the whole town of Cheektowaga has been shut down. If stranded motorists can find shelter, they should leave their cars where they are. There are snowmobilers picking up stranded motorists and taking them to fire houses and police stations and anywhere where they can find warmth.'

'Like the rest of the area, the City of Lackawana is buried under snow. To the south, the situation is bad and getting worse. In the Town of Hamburg, visibility is zero. The community is at the present time - marooned.'

'All motorists are advised to stay out of West Seneca because the highways are all closed.'

'We declared a state of emergency in Amherst because of poor visibility. Visibility is absolutely zero.'

'Deep down in the traditional snowbelt, to the south of the City of Buffalo, sits the town of Evans. The white blindness hit there earlier and a supervisor made this appeal: The towns of Evans, Brant and the Village of Angola are in a state of emergency. We have a total whiteout. We want no travel and only emergency phone calls.'

'Niagara Mohawk Power has about five thousand customers in the Western New York area without service at this time.'

'New York Telephone Company urges those people whose calls are of a social nature to stay off the lines so that calls of a medical nature can get through.'

'With the temperatures plunging below zero and the winds the way they are, you are in constant danger of frostbite if you go outside. In the case of severe frostbite, a large blister appears on the surface of the skin and this blister should not be broken. The tissue destruction will be severe and you should get in touch with a doctor.'

'There are about a thousand people marooned at the Marine Midland Center at Main and Seneca. They are mostly employees and they will spend the night there. Don't worry, they have enough supplies there for three days.'

'The exclusive WKBW Accu Weather forecast - Blizzard conditions tonight, with snow flurries and snow squalls resulting in heavy accumulations mainly south of the city. Extremely strong winds will gust over fifty miles per hour and will cause severe blowing and drifting of snow as temperatures drop to ten below zero by morning. The wind chill factor will read sixty below zero. For tomorrow, continued very windy and extremely cold with snow flurries, snow squalls, blowing and drifting snow. There will be little change on Sunday. Temperatures tomorrow will be mainly below zero. The high on Sunday, five above zero. Buffalo temperature, one degree below zero. The wind chill factor, minus fifty four at two minutes past six p.m.'

Saturday January 29th, 1977

"All social, civic, recreational and organizational activities scheduled in Western New York tonight are cancelled. In fact, everything is cancelled. If anyone has a snowmobile or a four wheel drive vehicle, you are being asked to go to the nearest fire or police station to volunteer your vehicle and your services.

The Erie County Medical Examiner's Office reports at least eight storm related deaths so far. So if you are warm and dry, please stay where you are.

All gas heated schools have been shut down by emergency orders from Governor Hugh Carey. All schools, with very few exceptions, will be shut down for one week beginning on Monday. That's all gas heated schools in New York state. This is estimated at about thirteen hundred gas heated schools."

Buffalo is known as the City of Good Neighbors, and these

good neighbors helped each other make it through this terrible storm. We got some help from others too. Governor Carey sent in the National Guard, President Carter designated Western New York as a disaster area and airlifted troops from Fort Bragg. We made it, pulling together. When it was all under control, hundreds of folks took the time to say thanks to each other and to drop a line to WKBW radio. An example:

" 'You see, I was alone in the house with my three small children Friday evening when your station was giving all the reports. My husband was stranded elsewhere and naturally couldn't get home to us. The kids thought that all the snow was really great as it meant no school. By dinner time, I was really starting to get panicky. Like an answer to my silent prayers for some inner strength, your disc jockey started to talk to the people out in the storm. 'To be afraid is a human emotion' he said. 'And I'm scared myself when I look outside and see what's happening out there. But don't panic. You can control that and if you don't, you could create worse problems for yourself.' I realized that he was speaking to the people stranded in their cars on the expressways but I wanted to personally write him and thank him myself for that small message. It made me feel so much better.' "

From a letter to Dan Neaverth:

Hi!

"I listen to you every morning and I think you are fantastic.

In that disastrous snow storm, your reassuring voice kept me from going completely insane. When I felt the noise of our two little boys was more than I could stand, I turned up K.B. full blast and drowned them out. Of course I'm being fitted for a hearing aid now but I still have my original state of mind. Yes sir, I'm glad to say that I am still the same mentally incompetent person I was before the stom hit.

The suggestions for keeping kiddies occupied were very much appreciated. Why in less than one day we redecorated our entire kitchen in play-doh. The red and green clumps on the wall even match the ones on the floor, the ceiling, the refrigerator and the stove.

I also found a use for the left over alum. Do you have any idea what six cups of alum can do for a child's personality? People used to tell me our boys were dull. Now I can debate that opinion. My rag muffins aren't dull, they are dill.

Well, I have to close now because our Parakeet just decided to go swimming in the gold fish bowl. Keep up the good work and have a sense of humor."

Peg Herman

We are a fifty thousand watt station. We have a ten thousand watt back-up transmitter and if we lose power here at the station we have a generator all gased-up and ready to go for our own power.

We turned the radio station over to the public during the blizzard. We acted as a clearing house for people who needed help for people who were willing to offer it; whether it was food, clothing, transportation or medicine for 24 hours a day and for about twelve days.

We really pride ourselves at this station in being able and willing to pull out stops and break our format. When the snow hits the fan, we adjust everything. We don't sit and wait and figure out how we should respond. We open up the radio station. If it costs us money, that's O.K. If we lose commercials, that's too bad. Many stations are inhibited. They don't want to change and if they do, their machinery makes it a slow process.

We had an intern here from the Buffalo State College of Communications. We have a program where they come in here for a semester. She was here for a week when the blizzard hit. She slept on the ladies' john the first night.

One of the police inspectors paid us the supreme compliment. He said to us, "If WKBW radio had gone off the air, we would have lost the city." He gave us the sense that we held the city together.

During this whole time, I had a toothache from a cracked tooth. I got to the point where I was so tired that I had to think out every word in advance or nothing would happen or another word would come out or it was mumbled. You had to think in advance that 2 + 2 is 4 and then you would say it. Everything had to be slow and precise.

Then we got wacko. One morning I came out on Danny's show and said, "I don't know if I should say this on the air Dan, it's very hush, hush. The city's street department is working on something at the Seneca Street garage. They are putting together a bionic street sanitation man from parts they had over there. It's not yet confirmed, but this bionic street sanitation man is going to go over to Vermont Street and he's going to eat all the cars which are blocking the street." We were really getting punchy.

I walked into the newsroom one morning about 3 o'clock, kind of a quiet time and the lights were out, and I heard someone talking to me and there was nobody in the room. One of the news guys was on the floor cuddled up next to the heater under the news desk grabbing a couple of winks.

I had the tooth removed. But another bit of comic relief was that Danny on the air said, "Our News Director has to have a tooth extracted and I know all the dentists offices are closed and you dentists are just hanging around doing nothing today. Why don't you come down and take his tooth out here, and we will get Channel 7, our sister T.V. station to come over and film it. And I'm saying "God, no!" A guy called up and said, "Look I've got a portable, I can get a nurse and we could come over now and take it out in your newsroom."

"No, No, I don't want any part of it please." So I got a truck and went up to Buffalo General and I'll never forget his name, Dr. Mash, yanked the tooth and stuck in a wad of cotton, and I came back and just kept working.

Accu-Weather is a private forecasting service that we hire. They operate out of Pennsylvania State College. They are all Penn State graduates which has a good weather school. It's a private service and they started years ago, forecasting for ski areas and then they started forecasting for municipalities and industries. We hired them to do our forecasting for us. We think its a little more specific. They'll pinpoint things better than National Weather Service. Actually the national service is a bureaucratic operation. They don't take chances; Accu-Weather will. They can pinpoint for our listening area. They might say, "Well the snow's going to hit here at 11:30." National Service would never use the time. But we use National as a backup. Sometimes we'll compare them. Sometimes we'll even put both of them on the air. National Weather says but Accu-Weather says, in other words, it's up to you. We think it paid off in the blizzard. Right down to the time it would strike.

We went on live with our listeners. You could feel the community coming together. In a sense, it might be one of the best things that ever happened to our city—in terms of finding out who your neighbors were—in terms of people helping one another—in terms of evidence that Western New York is a friendly place. There was a breaking down of those old imaginary walls that some people think exist between neighborhoods and between people. All that came tumbling down.

I couldn't believe Main Street at night. I put on my ski jacket just to get out of here for a second and I walked out into the blizzard at 11:00 p.m. Friday night. It was like being on Mars, not a moving thing, no evidence that the city was inhabited. Then, I saw a single light coming down the middle of the street—a snowmobiler. He could have been out in the country.

Then, the National Guard arrived along with the military and the State Department of Transportation and they started hauling that snow away and they really did a job. They even picked up some curbs and some big concrete litter boxes. If it was in the streets, their heavy machinery picked it up and they really helped a lot.

I went through a post-partem depression after the storm. Things slowly got back to normal. That's when I went through a down period. I didn't want to work anymore. I lost a lot of interest in my routine job and really I should've taken a vacation. Right after that we had to make a business trip to Nashville and we visited a radio station down there.

"You are the Buffalo people?"

"Yes, we are the only two survivors."

I'll tell you one thing that really pissed me off. The blizzard was Friday, Saturday, Sunday. About Monday, I started to get telephone calls from radio stations in Florida. They wanted to know, where they could hire some good radio newsmen cheap. One of the guys said to me, "We figured there would be lots of guys who were really anxious to get out of Buffalo, and we could hire them cheap." I hung up on all those calls.

We got a lot of calls from Southern States - radio stations wanting coverage. I got the feeling that they were calling to portray our plight in such a way that they would make the listeners feel better who were basking in the sun. A guy from Orlando called and I said to him, "I don't want to give you a report because I think that's what you're doing with it." He said, "Take it straight, that's not why we are calling. We are truly concerned about it."

"If you really are and you're listeners are, I'll give you a report." He said, "Let's do a question and answer." So he asked me the usual questions about the status of the blizzard and if people were getting out and all that business, and he asked "Is there anything we can do for you?" I said, "Yes, you can say some prayers for us." He said, "We'll do it." I didn't mind doing that. We got calls from Houston, Albuquerque, Atlanta and a lot from Florida. One young lady called up from Texas and wanted an in-depth report on the theft of a snowblower here. She asked, "Who in the world would steal a machine like that in the middle of an emergency?" I said, "The same kind of guy that would steal a horse in Texas." She understood.

My only regret out of the 12 days of the blizzard coverage is that nobody thought to rack up the tape recorder and record everything that we did. We have these big 12" tapes and we could have put them on low speed and let them run. What a sociological study that would have made! Next time we will think of it.

COUNT YOUR BLESSINGS

A Buffalo resident complained about the jokes Don Rickles and Johnny Carson made about the Buffalo area. He admitted the sun doesn't shine over Buffalo as much as other locations, but he also stated the Buffalo area is not plagued by mud slides, brush fires, earthquakes, smog problems, fresh-water shortages, serious floods, hurricanes, tornadoes or shark attacks.

James Casey Senior - Red Cross

"They came on snow-shoes, cross country skis, snowmobiles."

I'm Disaster Director for the Greater Buffalo Chapter of the American Red Cross and of the New York-Pennsylvania Western Division of the American Red Cross that takes in six chapters and four counties in Western New York and nineteen chapters and nine counties in North Western Pennsylvania.

We have a branch system in our chapter and the branches roughly resemble township lines. We have 23 branches in the Greater Buffalo Chapter of the American Red Cross. These branches are set up similar to the chapter in that they have a branch chairman similar to our chapter chairman; they have a board of directors, service chairmen, and one of the service chairmen is a disaster chairman.

Also in the other chapters in our division I have been preaching to them that help has to come from within during an emergency prior to getting help from us. We might have to get help from outside too.

The calls started to come in for cots and blankets. We have roughly 500 or 600 on hand. We passed those out to the hospitals as they called in. We started preparing food for people but none of us realized how bad it would be.

In our twenty-three branches we try to be prepared to take care of emergencies in advance. Many of our disaster chairmen, especially along the west shore and other areas, put up shelters to take care of people who were stranded or had to leave their homes. Jean Hineburg of the Hamburg area did a fantastic job as usual. He's been a disaster chairman voluntarily for almost twenty years. John Stazinski of West Seneca did a great job.

Over the years, we got together with the volunteer fire companies and when we can't get through, they have taken our courses and are prepared to handle the emergency as Red Cross volunteers. When necessary, we'll pick up their bills.

As it turned out, over the days and weeks, we found that we had been either directly or indirectly responsible for feeding through 92 different stations and outlets, primarily volunteer fire halls, schools and churches. This is because we had set up preparations in advance.

On Saturday morning, we realized that the best way for us to act was to deal directly with stores when people called for assistance. For instance, we had calls from many office buildings including City Hall. They had five thousand people stranded there and they were out of food. Many of the restaurants had run out of food. I told City Hall that we would give them unlimited credit at the nearest supermarket which was on Niagara Street about three blocks away. I suggested that they should get some of the street equipment and clear the cars out of the way at least that far. They went ahead and did this and the bill we received from one store was over $17,000.

Many people did not get their checks. This was legitimate. Welfare people and people on social security were without food. We made a decision that if people were out of food they could go to the nearest store and have the manager call us. If it was a family of two we gave them eight dollars, a family of four received sixteen, five or more received twenty dollars. We took care of thousands of people this way and all the stores co-operated. We pay our bills on time in disaster services and there isn't a store or a supermarket that will not give us credit.

We had many clubs such as the Golden Age and Boys Clubs, which were doing a fantastic job on their own in their own neighborhoods. They would tell us they were feeding families or bringing food to people in the neighborhood. In many of those cases I told them to go to their nearest supermarket and have the managers call me and we were giving them credit for $500 to $1,000 to keep the thing going. This was a bit unusual but it had to be done. We couldn't get out and the people in that community were taking care of themselves. It was a great thing for the City of Buffalo and everybody in it. Many other community centers and community organizations called in and we gave them credit for taking care of their own.

I have to compliment the merchants on their co-operation so that people did not suffer. Ronald Offhaus, President of Tops Friendly Markets donated $1000, and 7000 loaves of bread and gave us a cut rate price on many other commodities.

A good example of the co-operation that was going on occurred about the sixth day after the snow storm started. I had a call from the Erie County Sheriff's Department, and Pete said, "We have a problem out in the town of Colden. Many of the people living out in the hills have not had anything for over a week. They can't get out and we have nothing to bring in. What can you do about it?" I told him to get a hold of the National Guard and stand by. Then I called Ron Offhaus, the President of Tops, and I asked him for the closest store to Colden which still had a pretty good supply of food. He said, "Tops Market on Orchard Park which is right on the way to Colden." So I called Pete back and said, "Okay, you're an old army man. Get a list and put down what you need and then phone the Tops Market in Orchard Park and they'll get what you need." In the meantime, I called ahead to the volunteer firemen in Colden. They were standing by ready to package the food. The county plows were followed by the National Guard trucks and the sheriff's department. They picked up the food and they got through to Colden where the volunteer firemen made them into packages for families. The snowmobiles took them to the hills to dispense to families. Just a few phone calls on our part and they sent us the bill.

On the 30th of January I had to go by snowmobile to get some additional clothing and some medication which I like to have with me. I couldn't believe the 20 and 25 foot high drifts. The snow between my home and the home next door was as high as the house. If you wanted to get to the back door, you'd have to tunnel from the street right through to the back. I've never seen anything like it.

In helping out with cleaning streets of Buffalo, the Army sent in the 20th Engineering Brigade from Fort Bragg. They flew in 200 to 300 men and their equipment into the Niagara Falls Airport. We housed these young men and they did a fantastic job for Buffalo and all of Western New York. I think we probably had the cleanest parking lot in Buffalo with all the equipment in here keeping it clean. These young men were sleeping anywhere they could find a pallet. They worked all their own shifts and they kept their equipment working all the time. Bill Grossman, the executive director of the Jewish Center across the street from us, offered these young men the facilities over there. They could have a shower, steambath or have a swim. Some of them had hardly ever seen snow before in their lives. They were from Arizona and all over the country. Most of them were new in this area.

Many people were concerned about the blood program. They knew that many of our blood visits could not take place because our blood mobiles and blood crews could not get through to sites that were supposed to receive blood visits. This wasn't bad for this reason: Doctors could not get to the hospitals. Therefore, routine surgery

Cleanup on South Park Avenue in south Buffalo slowed by deserted cars. Courtesy, US Army Corps of Engineers.

was cancelled. Major surgery in many cases was cancelled, but emergencies had to be taken care of. So, blood needs were cut drastically. But even so, we still collected about 89% of our blood quota for that week. We kept the blood center open all day long and people walked in. They came on snow-shoes, cross country skis, snowmobiles. They got through somehow to give blood. They couldn't get to work but they tried to get down here to contribute blood. We had calls from all over the country, especially the Detroit, Cleveland, Johnstown, New York and Boston blood centers asking if they could ship blood. We said we had plenty of blood. It was hard for them to believe this in view of the fact that the national television was expressing how difficult the situation was in Buffalo. Thank heavens for the good people of Buffalo. We did manage to hang in there and collect 89% of our blood quota for that week.

Lucy Mysiak—Administrative Assistant in Disaster Services for the Buffalo Red Cross

"Most disasters occur in odd numbered years."

My first disaster was down in the Xenia tornadoes in Ohio in 1974 where I handled inquiries about people in the area and did case work interviewing people in the affected area. My next disaster experience was working with the Vietnamese refugees in 1975 when they were set up in a camp near Harrisburg, Pennsylvania. My job there was Chief of Communications. We organized the section trying to track down families that were sent to different camps and trying to reunite the families and find sponsors for the refugees. My next disaster assignment was after Hurricane Eloise in the Harrisburg, Wilksburg, Pennsylvania area. I did case work dealing with families and setting up emergency service centers in that area. In 1976 I did not go on any diasasters, and that is part of my theory that most disasters occur in odd numbered years such as 1975 and 1977.

The year 1977 has been a very big year for travelling with Red Cross. I started with our blizzard. I was Administrative Assistant to the whole operation. I helped find and co-ordinate volunteers who had to make up sandwiches hour after hour. During one occasion I ordered 300 lbs. of cold cuts and had six volunteers making hundreds of sandwiches until they were going crazy.

There is no way you can compare the blizzard to any other disaster experiences, it was a unique situation. It basically was similar to the ice storm we experienced in 1976 where the people were isolated, had no power and had no way to get out for food. There is really no way to compare a flood or tornado to a blizzard. One of the important things in the blizzard was trying to get people to co-ordinate answering the phones. The phones were ringing one right after another and there was no way to track down how many thousands of phone calls we received. Basically, people called in saying that they were in need of food. But they also wanted somebody to complain to and yell and scream about the snow. The phones rang around the clock. It was an amazing thing to get phone calls at 3 or 4 in the morning. We thought everybody would be back to sleep or back to normal.

One of the best ideas I have about what to do about a blizzard came in a phone call I received. We generally get storm warnings or flood warnings from the National Weather Bureau. On the morning of the storm, one of the gentlemen called up to report that there was a strong storm heading this way and suggested that I quickly hop on a plane to Florida. I do wish I had taken his advice.

I worked on a flood in Albany in March co-ordinating statistical and accounting information. I spent two weeks down in West Virginia working on a flood out in the mining territory, travelling from one assistance center to another, doing case work and accounting. I have just returned from working down in Johnstown, Pennsylvania where they had their 3rd major flood in the past 100 years, in a town that supposedly was flood free after all this time. I spent 14 hours a day working in Johnstown trying to track down people in the affected area and trying to locate families and reunite them.

I find that disasters tend to bring out the best in most people. You remember people who went out of their way to help. People try and help their neighbors. In the blizzard here, we had a gentleman who was one of the leading surgeons in the Buffalo area and he devoted days helping drive a snowmobile and a four-wheel-drive truck around the area. We also had thousands of people who wanted to volunteer. They offered to help but they had no means to come and help. Those that helped, worked around the clock. Once the disaster is over you never see them again. They are always too tied up in many other things to help out. In the Johnstown flood, we had one lady who came in to volunteer. She worked 10 hours a day for about four or five days and after talking to her, I finally found out she and her husband had owned a chain of department stores in the Johnstown area and they had suffered millions of dollars of losses. They lost an entire warehouse and an entire store. She was too busy, tied up with Red Cross, to help her husband. She thought she was getting more benefit from helping the Red Cross and trying to help the neighbors in her area.

I'm not a women's libber but I do notice that I get a different reaction from men than from women on any operation. Going into a place where you are representing Red Cross, you announce yourself as a Red Cross person to do some assistance. You generally will get a reply saying something like "Are you a nurse?" You really have to explain to the men of the world that you are not a nurse. You are qualified in other terms, you are qualified to do emergency service and supervise. They do react badly that you are a young female coming in and they do not realize that you do have a great deal of knowledge and experience and you are able to supervise and co-ordinate an entire disaster section.

Unfortunately, on my travels I hesitate to mention that I am from Buffalo. I tend to say that I am from New York State because I get tired of people saying, "Oh you live in Buffalo? How was the blizzard? Tell us all about it."

Maurice Gavin—State Trooper

The most interesting thing that happened around here was that the Brink's truck got stuck in the snow with one quarter of a million dollars in it. They finally got the money moved by hand into the Buffalo Evening News Building for safe keeping.

Ed Brady—Assistant Director of Disaster Service
American Red Cross at Buffalo

"I've been in all sorts of disasters, but this was the first time in my 68 years that I've seen a city completely paralyzed."

During the blizzard of 1977, my special assignment was supply. At first our greatest problem was to get cots and blankets to locations, downtown locations where people were stuck for the night. The biggest problem was the inability of normal vehicles to move. Four-wheel-drive vehicles could make it through the snow. We issued everything we had in our supply and requested more from National supply which came when the embargo was lifted. We immediately saw the need of food supplies to those various shelters that had been opened like the City Hall, County Building and Ellicott Square Building, Buffalo Evening News, and the Donavan State Office Building. Here were people who were caught and could not go home for the nights of the 28th and the 29th.

Our first source of supply for them were supermarkets. We purchased milk and bread in this store and from wholesale dairies and bakeries. We sent food out in four-wheel-drive vehicles to various feeding centers. The longest route I recall was to Grand Island with milk and bread for the Nursing Home. All this time we were making sandwiches and donuts and coffee for the men working in the clearing operations. They were fed from our van and also from two New York City Vans and one from Glens Falls New York.

The greatest bulk of food requests came from individual families who were hit because of the mail breakdown at the end of the month. They were without funds, without their normal **welfare**, Social Security, **pension** and other checks coming in. At that time we made a bold decision to authorize purchases over the phone. Families would call in here, we would take the number, make an alotment, tell them to go to their nearest supermarket and have the manager call in. We had to identify numbers or use their Social Security number as identification. When the manager of the store phoned us back we guaranteed the purchase. We felt that it was the only thing to do because there was no possible way to make a one to one contact with the people nor could the people come in here to see us nor could we get out to them. It worked very well and later one store brought in delayed slips that had not been paid, I had the opportunity to check over $3,000 worth and found only two people in that group had gone back a second time. Our cheating loss was low. Lower than we expected.

We did have a gift of 7,000 loaves of bread from Tops. We gave 2,000 to the Salvation Army for their distribution. The rest we sent to mass-care centers throughout the city along with 12,000 lbs. of U.S. Department of Agriculture stock which included ground beef, canned corn, peas, green beans, pears, peanut butter, orange juice, margarine, butter, dry milk, and turkey roll. These were in bulk cans for mass-care feeding. We did purchase some family size cans which were given out by groups for individual home feedings. This amounted to nearly $2,000 of purchasing and the total we spent was over $38,000 in food. That included 1,700 quarts of milk, bread and donuts. Our mass purchases for centers was over $29,000 and our telephone authorization was over $6,000 for individuals.

One of the most spectacular and toughest assignments was to get coffee and donuts to the fire crew at the multiple alarm fire at Virginia and Tampa on the night of the 28th. This was done with four men with two snomobiles and is still talked about by the fire department.

I think what I've learned most from this experience is the need for pre-planning. Sources of bulk food, supply sources and available vehicles should be known in advance. We learned that there are Four-Wheel-Drive Clubs. We used the snowmobilers as well. You find your resources and determine how to use them for your needs.

We had no trouble with finances. People were very willing to open up their doors for the Red Cross.

In my 68 years, this was the first time I've seen a storm like this. I've been in all sorts of disasters, but this was the first time in my 68 years that I've seen a city completely paralyzed.

Pam Zini—Office Manager in Safety Programs, Buffalo Red Cross

"I couldn't believe how nice Buffalo people were and I've lived here all my life."

I was working and I kept saying to myself, "We can go home early today." It was a snow day. However I never made it out of here. I ran around like an idiot at first not knowing what I was doing. Then we got things under control and I was working on the switchboard till about 3:00 o'clock in the morning. It was an absolutely long and miserable day. The calls were frantic. You couldn't get in or out on the board. That was the night we all slept here. There were five people sleeping with me and I was the only woman. The man next to me was a minister. At first I didn't want to close my eyes. I slept on a cot for about 3 days with space heaters. This building is so cold that I thought I was sleeping outside.

I got home Sunday and it was storming like mad and I thought if it keeps up I'll have a good 4 days off. Sunday night the phone rang and they came and got me and I brought a little overnight bag with a pair of jeans and a T-shirt. I slept here for 4 more nights, and we made food and we set up a lot of shelters. We had a lot of volunteers who lived in this area. They answered all of the phones. We had blackboards with all of our shelters and numbers on it and where they were located and what kind of food they could get.

Have you ever seen 8,000 loaves of bread? I can't look at Wonderbread anymore. We made peanut butter, jelly and ham and cheese sandwiches. I burn Corn Flakes, I'm terrible in the kitchen and I was slopping these sandwiches together and they went like mad to all of our shelters. People were very nice and very warm. No one really panicked here until I panicked Tuesday night when I found out that one of my co-workers had a hotel room. I really got upset. I ran right over to my boss and told him I wanted a hotel room too. When I got into the hotel room I went into a complete delirium when I saw shampoo and a shower. I was yelling that I could shampoo my hair. I had such a ball.

Then Fort Bragg pulled in and I knew I was an enlisted woman when I put on boots and a rubber coat.

I couldn't believe how nice Buffalo people were and I've lived here all of my life. Everyone usually walks around and minds his own business. I didn't think there were that many friendly people in the city. People would come in from the streets and people would call up and say they had a lot of free time. Towards the end we even had to reject help. But we had a lot of donations. "Tops" donated 7,000 loaves of bread for example and we had donations from a lot of people.

I slept for about three days when it was over.

People will know how to react if it should ever happen again. I think in the winter time people will be more aware if they see a snow storm setting in. I think they will prepare themselves more at home with basic foods and medicine.

Ellen Casey—Buffalo State College Student

"Someone's parrot flew outside through an open window."

I had to go to the Red Cross that Friday morning because it was going to be my last day of training on the switchboard before my job would start on Saturday by myself as a switchboard operator. I worked like crazy that day because I would get five phone calls at once and I had to answer them one at a time while plugging in the jacks. I'd say, "The American Red Cross," and they'd say, "I need help!" and I'd say, "One moment please." Immediately the people would start telling you their troubles and it seems rude but I had to interrupt them to say, "One moment please," and then switch them over to another person at the Disaster Office. At one point I had 13 jacks going and you'd see another red light and you'd have to unplug a jack. Sometimes you miscalculated and cut someone off. I felt bad when that happened. On Saturday, I worked 12 hours on the switchboard and on Sunday I was at it for about 14 or 15 hours.

Callers were really upset. The biggest demand was for medication for elderly people. Many needed food.

This woman called in and she was so upset because her dog was gone and she wanted someone from the Red Cross to find her dog. She wanted a snowmobile to come around. Well the woman called back 5 minutes later saying the dog was in the house — never mind.

Someone went looking for their children and called the Red Cross but apparently the children were over at a neighbor's house. People with lost children were directed to the police station. People on medication were really upset because they thought they would be in a lot of trouble if they didn't get their medication. I got one woman who was hysterical, crying and sobbing. Over all, I didn't have that many rude people. I get more rude people on a calm Saturday than I did during the storm. Over all everyone was pretty good.

Someone's parrot flew outside through an open window. I guess it died. I couldn't understand what a window was doing open during the blizzard.

My advice to switchboard operators during an emergency would be to get a lot of rest because your temper would become shorter and shorter. People start off saying, "Wait a minute, listen to me, listen to me, you got to listen to my problem", and I'd say, "One moment please," and they'd say, "Wait a minute, you got to listen to my problem, don't switch me off!" I had 3 or 4 people like that who were really upset because I wanted to give them to someone else. They wanted me to listen to their problem. They thought I was the person they were supposed to talk to.

We estimated that we had about 17,000 calls. I took about 6,000 at least and I disconnected four calls. What was strange was that I disconnected the same person three out of those four times. He was Mr. Fields our volunteer chairman for disaster.

The switchboard area in an emergency should be a restricted area. Otherwise, people on a break come in to talk and decide they want to learn how to use the switch board. No one else should be allowed in that area in an emergency.

How Much?

A Hamburg snowmobile dealer tells the story of a man coming into his store during the height of the blizzard on Friday and asking, "How much does this cost?" pointing to a snowmobile. "What else would I need to drive it? Any special clothing? Special equipment?" After he was completely outfitted he reached into his pocket, peeled off $2,000, and roared off into the night on his new snowmobile.

Bob Stone - Assistant Manager, Buffalo International Airport

"He handed her a thirty eight revolver that had been concealed in his robe pocket. I was scared shitless."

I think it was the Thursday, the day before the big blizzard. My boss let me go early because of the predicted storm warnings. I got to the thruway and bam!! - it was zero zero visibility. I pulled my car over as close as possible to the guardrail and turned out my lights because I was afraid that someone would follow me and smash into my parked car. I crawled out the car window on the guardrail side and tried to establish my location. I got a glimpse of a house and decided to head for it because I was worried about a multi-car pile-up on the thruway. I waded through snow about three or four feet deep with only my shoes on my feet. I never had any gloves or hat either. I climbed a twelve foot fence and dropped into the back yard of this house.

A nineteen year old woman came to the door and invited me in. I accepted her offer of a coffee and I phoned my boss and wife to explain my situation. Then the woman and I settled down over coffee and we got to know each other a little better.

Then this fellow walked out of the bedroom with his robe tied up in front. He was about six foot four inches tall and he did not acknowledge my presence. He sat down on the couch. I tried to explain my predicament to him. What I got in response was a cold stare. Then he began to cross examine me for about twenty minutes. After that, he said to his wife, "I guess you can take this back to the bedroom." He handed her a thirty eight revolver that had been concealed in his robe pocket. I was scared shitless. Visions of news stories flashed across my mind: "All American Bob Stone shot to death by a jealous husband in the presence of a nineteen year old female."

I wanted another coffee and I was out of cigarettes. What was more important was to get the hell out of there. I made my dash for freedom but I slipped going down the outside stairs and twisted my ankle. I was in a lot of pain but there was absolutely no way in which I was going back to that house. I made it to my car and was lucky enough to have a tow truck stop and pull me out. But he towed me ten miles out of my way because I didn't have any money on me. He had to tow me to his boss. There I had to wait until a friend drove down and paid the bill before my car was released. It was hours before I got home. I think the moral of this story is, "Don't go if your boss lets you off early."

The next day, Friday January 28th, my real troubles began. The snow kept coming down and would not let up. We knew later in the afternoon that we were in trouble. The winds got worse. They were as high as fifty miles an hour. The temperature dropped. Visibility was very poor. We couldn't even see out the window.

I was here from the Friday evening until the following Thursday. My boss was home. The year before, he had suffered a heart attack and when these cold winds hit he was forced to recuperate. I was in contact with him the whole time along with our chairman, Mr Hart and our executive director. He was stranded in New York City. We were in touch with the city officials of Buffalo and the airline managers themselves.

I had with me a little kit that was given to me by the manager of United Airlines a couple of years ago. I had to stay over in the hotel because of bad weather conditions and the next morning went for breakfast. I was being kidded a little because I needed a shave. And questions like, "Where were you last night?" "You had a rough time last night, eh Stone?" Vince Atamitis, quite a personable fellow, was really giving it to me. He said, "Stone, you need a little help," and gave me this little kit that the airlines use. It has a toothbrush, comb and shaving lotion. Little did I realize that I would really need it during the Blizzard of '77.

I didn't have any change of clothes for about eight days. Same thing for my socks. I did wash them out a little, but the underwear I didn't touch. I was afraid they wouldn't dry in time. I was thinking of not wearing them one of these days, but it didn't work out. One of our engineers Jack Stregel, felt sorry for me and he brought me a change of underwear one day. He said he thought I might need it. By the time he got them into me the storm was all over and I was ready to go home. So I had the same clothes on for approximately seven days.

At the airport at first it was fun time! The bar was open. There was plenty of food and drinks and everyone was using the phones for checking on things at home. As time went on however, I saw the tension build. The people wanted to get out after a couple of days.

This is what happened to my wife. She was going bananas. She was inside with an eight year old boy all day. If you want to stay in yourself, that seems to be OK, but when you're forced to do something and you don't want to do it, you become uptight about it.

We couldn't get anybody new in here to work. We kept the people that were here. We put our own employees up in a hotel. As the days went on, the people thinned out.

There was this little old lady who called up here and asked for a pilot to come and pick her up because she couldn't get to the airport. The pilot asked her the length of her driveway.

Help arrives by air. Note buried car lower left. Courtesy, Buffalo State College Courier Collection.

The bar was packed every night while we were at the Airways Hotel. Everybody was in a good mood. We didn't have any really bad scenes. There was more stress and more concern until the storm actually broke late Tuesday or Wednesday.

We had the federal service building people who were stranded without food on the other side of the airport. I was in contact with them every hour. I told them I could radio them loud and clear but I couldn't get them any food. It was hectic. We got the food to them the next day.

We didn't have any access to the roads to truck things here so we had to work on the supplies we had in the airport. I think that was the big thing. We had supplies right here that we were able to handle. Fortunately, we also had the CFR people that could administer first aid. These Crash, Fire and Rescue People are located here at the airport and they were right here on the premises.

We cautioned everybody not to do something really stupid out on the field. They were to go in pairs and let us know what they were doing and where they were at all times. If something ever happened out on the field where somebody got stranded, we would really have had problems. One of our employees had a truck that stalled on the ramp area and he thought that he knew where the building was, about fifty feet away. He got disoriented and found himself at the approach to runway five. As luck would have it, we had a couple of our trucks that were diesel powered and when the storm came there was no way that we could get them back in. So we left them on idle speed and still running. This way they would not stall. Now this fellow happened to jump in the cab of one of these idling trucks. He found it by sheer accident, and he called the tower for help and we went out and got him. Luckily we did, because he was frostbitten.

We got all the aircraft back to the gate positions. We had some that were trying to take off during the storm and we had an aircraft incident. A couple of aircraft that were going to take off during the day of the storm on Friday were lined up. The nose wheel froze and prevented the first one from turning around. And that held up everything. We had some aircraft stranded out on the taxiways. It took up about three hours to get everyone back from the taxi positions.

I heard on the news that everybody was told to get their cars off the street and since my wife was pregnant I was concerned that this could not be done by her. The Mayor lived around the corner and I told Ruthie to call the Mayor and tell him that I was stranded in the airport. Ruthie called the police and the Mayor but we got a ticket anyway. I paid the ticket.

I received a call from my wife at one point early on in the storm. She told me a friend of hers was stranded at the Executive Hotel across from the airport. She had run out of money and didn't know what to do. Her mother was very concerned. Her father had just passed away and my wife told me to make sure that she was taken care of. I called over to Mr. Clark at the Executive and gave him my name and let her charge anything under my name. I did call and set everything up and spoke to her. Her name was Nancy and I told her to stay in touch with me to let me know how she was making out. She wanted to know if any planes were coming in and I said I'd call her every once in a while and I'd try to stop over and see her and maybe have a drink with her. So we were in contact with each other about two or three times a day especially over the weekend. She was there three or four days and I never did get to see her. Finally when the planes started landing in the early part of the week she flew to New York and went about her business.

I saw her about two weeks later for the first time. I was walking my boy around the neighborhood and her mother spotted me and invited me over. She really appreciated what I had done for her daughter and while we were talking, her daughter entered the house. It was like Raquel Welch coming in. She was beautiful. Do you see that mark on the wall? I've been banging my head there ever since!

THE LAST BASTION

The Buffalo downtown YMCA opened its rooms and showers to women for the first time ever during the storm.

Grandma Audrey shows how they shoveled snow in the old days.
Photo by Erno Rossi.

More Army help arrives. Courtesy, U.S. Army Corp of Engineers.

I'm dreaming of a winter thaw in Watertown, N.Y.

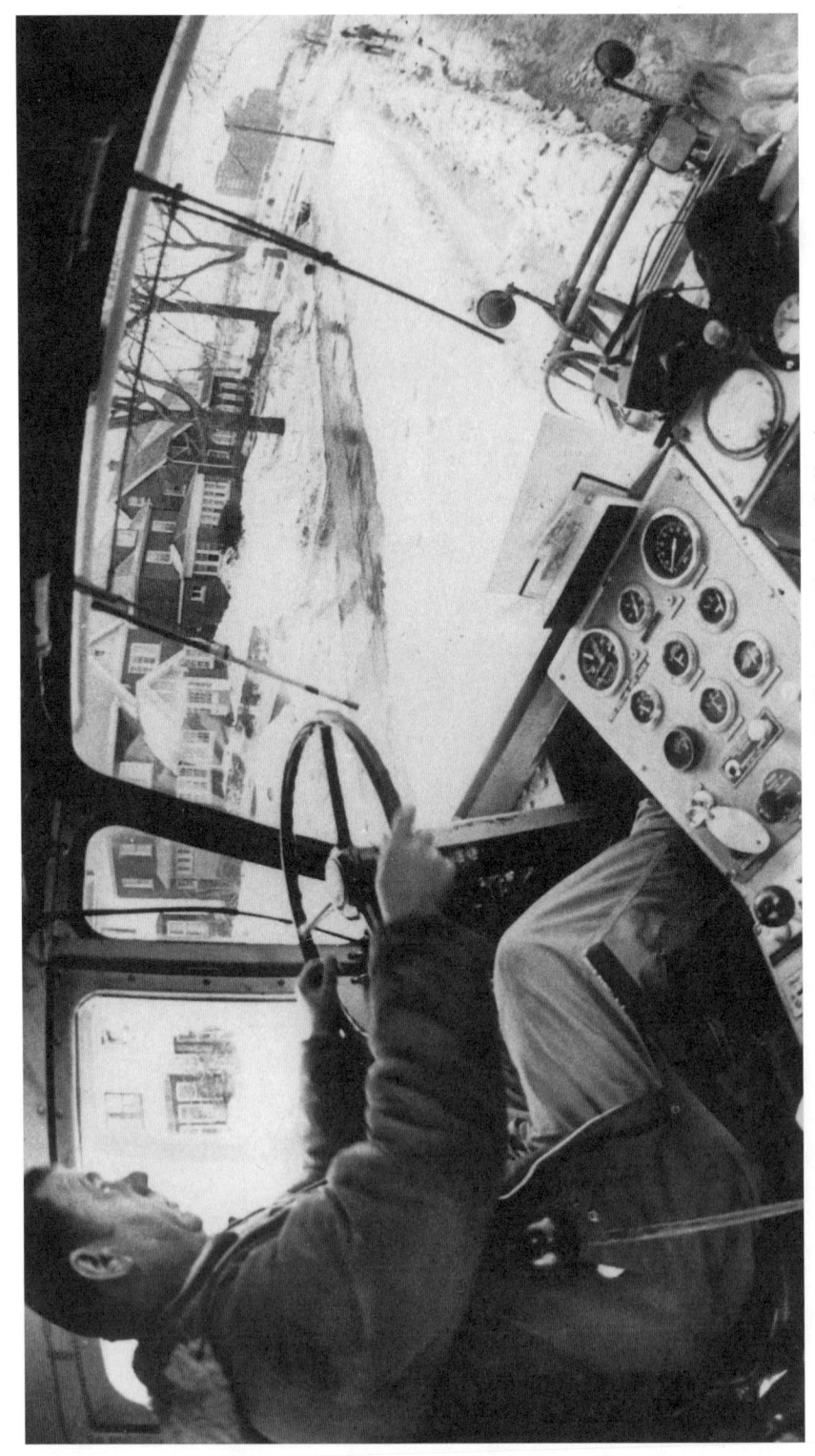

Snow melters on loan from Toronto help with the Buffalo clean up. Buffalo State Courier Collection.

U.S. Army Corps of Engineers co-ordinate their snow attack. Courtesy, The Corps.

261

Mr. Ransom - President, William Hengerer Co.

"Between all three stores we calculate that we fed 7000 people, free of charge."

I'm from the William Hengerer Co. which is a department store organization, located in Buffalo and suburban areas. And we've been in existence here for about 142 years. On Friday, January 28, 1977 we had a very unusual experience here. About 11:30 a.m. it suddenly became obvious that we were going to have an unusual storm, the likes of which we had not seen before in our lifetime. The first thing we attempted to do was to make arrangements to get our downtown and suburban stores closed and to get our people home as quickly as we could. Within the next two hours it became obvious that our efforts to get our people to their homes was not going to be effective although some were successful.

By about 2 o'clock that afternoon, we had a great number of our people stranded in our downtown store. At that point we didn't realize the numbers of other people from surrounding buildings and other businesses who would be left without shelter as the late afternoon and evening came on. By 3:00 p.m., we realized that we were going to have an awful lot of people for dinner here that night and we made preparations. We have a large restaurant operation here in the store and on Friday evening we had approximately 1,000 people for dinner. We served in three shifts and we also supplied food which was taken out for all the people who were stranded in the Niagara-Mohawk complex downtown, as well as the National Fuel Gas offices which are located next door in the Rand building. In addition to those people we had quite a number of individuals off the street and from other small office facilities located in nearby buildings who were stranded. As we were making preparations for dinner that night it became apparent that we were going to have a lot of overnight visitors because bus service or any type of transportation by 4:00 or 5:00 p.m. was really out of the question. So we started making plans for distributing bedding, blankets, pillows, towels, etc. to first of all, the people who would be stranded in our building, which turned out to be about 350. In addition to those people we supplied similar types of bedding to all the National Fuel

Emergency snow clearing on the south side of Buffalo, along Lake Erie. NOTE BURIED VEHICLE. Courtesy, U.S. Army Corps of Engineers.

Gas people and assorted people in the Rand building and other nearby buildings as well as the Niagara Mohawk Power employees.

While all of this was going on downtown similar things were happening at our Eastern Hills Store and our Seneca Mall Store. One of the interesting events that happened at the Seneca Mall Store, which is located off the New York State Thruway, was that among the people who were stranded, there was a bus load of deaf children from St. Mary's School for the deaf here in Buffalo. Their bus broke down on the Thruway and was pulled into the parking lot. The bus load of children were fed, cared for, sheltered and I think very well taken care of by our Seneca Mall Management through that night and the following night. It was not until Sunday, January 30th, in the afternoon, when that bus was repaired that those children were on their way to the Dunkirk area.

Meanwhile, we actually bedded down 350 people in the downtown store. We created a dormitory arrangement; 7th floor was for ladies, 6th floor was for men, 5th floor was for ladies, etc. We supplied them with toothbrushes, toothpaste and towels for freshening up in the morning. I think the most remarkable thing about the experience for me was how co-operative everybody was in following our directions in terms of when to go to bed, when to get up and so forth. When we finished the evening meal, we then had to start worrying about getting ready for breakfast.

The next day, we had roughly another 1,000 people for breakfast. We fed them in shifts and we didn't finish breakfast until 11:00 a.m. By that time a certain number of people stranded in the downtown area were able to get transportation and they left the building.

The next problem was Saturday lunch. At Saturday lunch we had roughly 600 people downtown. It then became obvious that we were there for another night. There would be quite a large number of people stranded again in the downtown store and that number turned out to be 250. They were fed Saturday evening, Sunday morning breakfast and Sunday lunch. At about 6:00 p.m. on Sunday, the last of the people who were stranded in our store downtown were finally either picked up or delivered in some way to their homes. The downtown store, with the exception of security people was finally evacuated. A similar experience was true at both Eastern Hills Mall and Seneca Mall.

I think it was one of the most difficult experiences I've ever been through in terms of trying to manage a disaster situation. We felt very fortunate that we had first of all, this large restaurant operation and adequate food for all these people. Between all three stores we calculate that we fed about 7,000 meals free of charge and we felt very fortunate that we were able to not run out of food during that period when we needed it so badly. I think one of the most impressive things was the tremendous respect which all of these people extended to us and to our management for our efforts in trying to help them. It was a very great human experience, one that I wouldn't look forward to again, but in many respects it was very gratifying. I think one other interesting thing after all this bedding had been dispensed was how diligent these people were in returning all these things to us. And of course because of health laws in N. Y.

State and in Erie County none of these things could be resold even though they were used for one or two nights. So we had a major effort in the 10 days following the storm to collect all this material and approximately $20,000 worth of first quality bedding towels, blankets, etc. were taken and then delivered to the Salvation Army here in Buffalo as a donation. They certainly needed these things because the Salvation Army was perhaps the single, most effective agency in dealing with human beings with problems during the storm period. It was a great experience but I hope it doesn't happen for another 100 years.

Early on Friday afternoon, my wife and daughter were stranded in their car on route 219, just off the Thruway toward Orchard Park. They finally managed to get off 219 and get back on to Orchard Park Rd., going south toward our home, when they became involved in a 25 car pile-up and could go no further and were stranded in their car for about 2 hours. They finally managed to make it into a home, near where the car was stranded and this home took in 12 or 14 people including my wife and daughter and these were wonderful people named D'Amice. My daughter Melissa and my wife Betty were sheltered for 8 or 9 hours. Meanwhile I was busy trying to make all the arrangements for meals and bedding and sleeping arrangements and so forth. But in the middle of this I was able to reach a very good friend of mine who operates the Taylor Texaco Service Station in Orchard Park. This gentleman's name is Charlie Taylor and I reached him by phone at his home knowing that he had a 4 wheel drive vehicle. I was able to tell him where my wife and daughter were stranded. He knew approximately where the house was and at 9:00 p.m. on that Friday night he left the comfort of his own home and went to the address by various routes where my wife and daughter were stranded. He picked them up, got them in his truck and got them home that night. He of course will be a hero in my eyes for as long as I am around.

Another thing that I might add was the tremendous feeling of gratitude and respect that I had for the people in our organization as well as our Mayor and senior executives in particular, who worked so diligently to serve so many people so well. We distributed to over 700 people in the downtown store that Friday night in less than 1 hour. It was a tremendously well organized effort and I will not forget the efforts of my own people for the effort.

The cost to our business was one million dollars. We were closed in all of our 5 locations for 9 days following the storm. At the Seneca Mall Store on the Monday following the storm we had a serious break of water mains with subsequent damage which was very extensive both to the building and to the merchandise in it.

On the subject of advertising on the Sunday following the storm, it's our practice always on Friday noon to review what's running on Sunday. This advertising is very costly. When I saw the extreme proportions that this storm was taking, I decided rather quickly that we should cancel all advertising which was scheduled on Sunday in order to save that money and run that advertising at a later date, when it would hopefully be more effective.

Ten cows died when a barn collapsed in Wyoming County.
Courtesy Buffalo State College Courier, Collection.

DUMPED MILK

One example of the amount of milk being dumped by the farmers in Western New York came from a co-operative report which said three tankers of milk arrived instead of the normal 40 tanker truckloads.

Dr. John Cudmore

"the child was brought in alive"

I live in Buffalo N.Y. I am an Associate Professor of Surgery at the State University of N.Y. at Buffalo, and I'm in private practice, primarily at the Buffalo General Hospital. I am also a Lieutenant Colonel in the Medical Corps, N.Y. Army National Guard. My experiences with the blizzard were primarily limited to the National Guard. We first became involved on the Thursday prior to the actual blizzard because of the increasing amount of snow that was piling up in the City of Buffalo and the apparent inability of anyone to remove it. They wanted to borrow bulldozers and front lifts and dump trucks, just to assist the city officials. We had a staff meeting on that Thursday night in the armory and were staffing a limited mobilization to run this equipment. This was quite fortunate because we already had the wheels and gears, when the real blizzard hit.

Friday I was scheduled to be down town in the morning doing consultations with the New York Telephone Company. I was back in my office at noon for my usual Friday afternoon office hours when my wife called. She is my secretary and handles my books from home and she said that almost all of the patients had cancelled. That night a fellow surgeon who lives a block away from me got itchy and decided to try and get home. I told him he would do very well as a pigeon from the ark. He called about 45 minutes later and said by going through side streets he was able to get home. My house is just south of Delaware Park and approximately a 5 to 10 minute drive from the hospital. I took off for home, arrived in about 45 minutes to the end of my street, spent the next 45 minutes trying to get the 100 yards from the end of my street to my house and only with the help of a bunch of other people who practically picked up the car and put it in the driveway was I able to make it in. I discovered that we had some house guests. We lived next door to a school and one of the women who had children there was the wife of one of my fellow physicians. She was a cute blond and had a daughter who was about 13 who was kind of cute also. The priest at the school wasn't too interested in having them as house guests on a permanent basis so he shipped them over to us and we sat down and had a very pleasant dinner and evening.

    I called down to the armory and found that we were the house guests of about 200 to 250 people and more were coming in all the time. I talked to the people who were there full time. They were unable to get home. Fortunately there were about 20 to 25 other soldiers in the armory who had been there on a special recruiting drive for the week. They lived in New York City, Albany, Schenectady, etc., and they stayed right in the armory. I made arrangements for them to pick me up the next morning with a tactical four-wheel drive vehicle. I got down to the armory and discovered that now we were hosts to 350 people. We had to set up a food serving system. We had food in the armory for our regularly scheduled weekend and we received contributions from the neighborhood.

    We then got word that there was a Puerto Rican Center down the street that was in serious difficulty with several people with frostbite. There arrived a fellow who said that he was an Airforce Medical Technician home on leave and stranded here. We sent him by snowmobile to the Puerto Rican Center. We ran an out patient department there for several days. By Saturday night everyone was halfway settled down. Because we did have a medical facility, the police were bringing in people who had been found wandering in the storm. We treated some 40 to 45 cases of frostbite and hospitalized several of them. We had one case of unusual exposure. This fellow had the lowest temperature that I've recorded. It was only 94 degrees. He was about 72 years of age and he was quite confused. We got him warmed up and we were able to get him with a tacticle vehicle over to the General Hospital and have him admitted. Unfortunately, we were not able to locate his friend whom he described as a balding man with a white beard. We sent out teams to look for him in the same area where he was found. A fellow of that description was found frozen to death several days later when they finally got the streets cleared.

    Thereafter we were the only organization in the area which had the communication and transportation ability and the training to act in a coherent manner to keep such things as emergency medical deliveries and snow plowing in operation during this disaster. Many of our sections were engaged in assisting the fire department and plowing around area hospitals.

We set up an operating headquarters and the three senior officers took turns being in charge of it. I would answer all medical or medical supply problems plus other problems when it was my shift. Generally the shifts were in for 24 hours for the first couple of days. There was a fellow who wandered in off the street and said that he was the local service rep. I told him to put every phone in the armory into this one room for our tactical headquarters. He worked 18 hours rewiring the whole place. We set up a system of answering calls for help according to the nature of the call. If the person said that he was sick we would send out a 4 wheel drive quarter ton with one medic and one driver.

Some medics were Vietnam trained and some were school trained. We discovered that elderly people had a great number of physical ailments and they were cold and without food in the house. So we started taking blankets and lots of tins of soup along with us. That solved most of those problems. The classic call was received from a young man who wondered when we were coming over to shovel his driveway because they wouldn't deliver his welfare cheque if his driveway wasn't clear. We politely suggested he might apply back to shovel and remove his own snow.

We had something like 623 troops activated with selected individuals from other guard units such as tow truck operators and heavy equipment operators. We then started taking direction as to snow plowing and area damage control from the State Department of Transportation. Our principle job initially was hospital and hospital access. Most of our crews were on exposed vehicles. Since we are combat engineers, we didn't have much in the way of closed cab equipment and we were quite pleased that we got through the entire effort including the first several nights without one case of frostbite. We initially started at Columbus Hospital, then Children's Hospital, then Emergency Hospital and finally my own hospital, the General. We cleaned access routes, parking areas and emergency ramps. We moved all of the snow from Children's Hospital to the site which used to be my church, the old cathedral, which was torn down. This made an excellent dumping zone. The only problem was that the pastor there was a little unhappy as to what was going to happen when the snow melted. He presumed it would all wind up in the basement of his rectory. It did not. As the snow melted, we noticed one large cement block with "Do Not Litter" on the side. It had fit very nicely into the scoop of the front loader and then went nicely into a 5 ton dump. Very quietly one day we went back with a truck and returned it to Children's Hospital from whence it came.

We also co-ordinated the medical evacuation of people who were in severe difficulties or had regularly scheduled treatments that had to be taken. We flew people into the dialysis center at the General Hospital using the top of the parking ramp at Children's Hospital as a landing point and then taking the patients by ground over to the General. We had many emergency calls. One was from as far away as Bradford where we had a five month old child who was not able to breathe without the use of mechanical equipment which they didn't have. They were not sure of his diagnosis and he quite badly needed to be transported to Children's Hospital. We put together a helicopter, a flight crew, and a pulmonary technician from Children's Hospital. As soon as we got off the ground, we ran into a blizzard again and wound up following a pipeline from Buffalo to Bradford. We landed, picked up the kid, and flew back in what was charitably called minimal flying conditions. The flight crew was given the Air State Medal For Valor for this effort. It was satisfying because the child was brought in alive, did make a satisfactory recovery, and regretably was found to have a congenital illness which will not allow it to have a full life. But it will survive. When I last checked the child, it was doing quite nicely and was starting to grow again.

Throughout the campaigns, I wore a heavy Irish wool sweater. I received some teasing because of my Canadian background. They thought I was trying to imitate Lord Lovat and his commandos.

I'd like to say in conclusion that it was a remarkable experience. I think it proved the necessity of an organized militia and the function of the citizen soldier in time of stress. Stress is not necessarily exchanging bullets with an enemy. Stress can be defending your community from disasters, either from nature or by accident. I think our experience in this area is growing by leaps and bounds. We are quite able to take care of anything of this magnitude. Anything of a military nature is coming under increased scrutiny as far as money is concerned. Some people believe that the military is against the system of a free society. We need only point to the effective use of welfaring troops with appropriate equipment in natural disasters such as this blizzard.

Frostbite is a condition which could be compared to a burn. It is a thermal injury. Instead of heat, it is cold applied in excess. It causes destruction of cells, both on the skin and beneath it. It can result in loss of an extremity, loss of a finger and certainly loss of the skin. It's initial findings are a pale, firm skin sometimes not particularly painful, until it begins to freeze more deeply. Then you experience deep pain and blisters. This requires acute treatment. Frostbite should be watched for over exposed portions of the body such as nose, ears, eyebrows, cheeks, lips and fingers. If you see your friend with areas that turn white, the time has come to get them out of the cold and into a warm environment.

This is the third time that I have been activated for a natural or man made disaster, the Elmira floods, the Attica uprising and the blizzard of '77. I have decided that I'm no longer going to be in solo practice. I'm forming a corporation with two of my associates in order to guarantee cross coverage of patients at a moment's notice. It's alright to drop your plow and grab your musket and become a militiaman, but when your plow happens to be the private practice of surgery, someone has to look after your sick patients.

Don't panic in a disaster. A survivor is someone who analyses his capabilities, knows his equipment on hand and uses both to best advantage. Secondly, minimal training and equipment is important. You should be able to light your house with some means other than power that comes into it. You should be able to heat it with some means other than the power or gas that comes into it for at least a short period of time; even if it is a cast iron stove or a fire place or something of this sort. Finally, the outlook is essential. If you sit there in your day to day luxurious environment and expect to remain forever in this condition, you may not be among the survivors.

NATIONAL GUARD

National Guard troops reported, "The people on Grand Island were so glad to see our men, they were chasing them down the road with thermoses of coffee and food. It got to be a safety hazard. We had to ask them to keep away from the machines."

Captain Harlan Schlesinger—Precinct 7

"Then the looters would return, cut the locks and continue to loot."

Precinct 7 is adjacent to Lake Erie and the prevailing winds coming off the lake blow everything right through our precinct. We have the smallest population compared to other precincts—only 9,500 people, but we have seven square miles of industrial property—waterfront, trucking, light and heavy industry, grain elevators and bare land. Our precinct includes a small Coast Guard base, a small boat harbor and the Niagara Frontier Port Authority Terminal.

The precinct is about 60% white, 30% black and about 10% Puerto Rican. Most of these people are in the lower income bracket and many are unemployed. There are no middle class people living in the area.

On Friday, January 28, 1977, at 11:30 a.m., that Canadian storm hit us first because it swept over us from Lake Erie and within half an hour we had zero visibility and stalled cars on the thruway exits and intersections. The roads were impassable. The wind was 60 or 70 miles per hour and the wind chill factor was about 50 below zero. You could survive for only 5 or 10 minutes without shelter.

We had to evacuate people from their cars so we formed human chains and had people holding on to each other and we led them to our station house and shelter. By 2:00 p.m. we had 120 stranded people in the station house. Some remained here for two and three days. We were isolated and no vehicles could move in the area. Police cars could not move for at least three days.

We tried to keep a record of the people stranded along the waterfront and in business places. We immediately contacted the American Red Cross for food and medication and the volunteer snowmobilers saved us.

We had no blankets, pillows or sleeping facilities but people were lying on the floor and on tables. Fortunately, we did not have small children here.

Buffalo Blizzard Booty. Courtesy, Buffalo State College Courier Collection.

William Cooley—Buffalo Police Officer—Precinct Seven

"The looters were robbing pop and milk machines, beer trucks and anything they could get their hands on."

I was stranded on Swan Street with about 200 people in a warehouse. There were about 100 people in the firehouse and about 150 at the Puerto Rican Center. I got hold of a snowmobile and answered medical and food calls for precincts 7, 9, and 15. On the second day of the storm, I worked from six in the morning until eleven that night.

The third day of the storm, I was working with my son Vincent who had volunteered. We had an accident and Vincent was in the hospital for a week with a leg injury and operation.

The fourth day of the storm, I answered calls from early in the morning until late at night. That's when I got hurt and I was off work for 30 days and I am still taking medication for my back and seeing a therapist. It was the worst storm I've ever seen in my 24 years on the police force.

The looters were robbing pop and milk machines, beer trucks and anything they could get their hands on. They were hungry.

About three months after the storm we answered a call where people were complaining about this bad smell. We investigated and found three to four hundred pounds of spoiled meat that had been looted during the blizzard and allowed to rot.

Police departments should have snowmobiles for use when things are really bad. They should also have four wheel drives for when conditions improve.

CB's weren't very popular at the time of the storm. They were afterwards.

SHOTGUN JUSTICE

After struggling to keep his driveway cleared, a northern New York resident kept an approaching snowplow from winging the banks back into the drive. He stood in his driveway with a shotgun, motioning the operator around his driveway. The driver complied, lifted the wing, and went around.

Patrolman Patrick O'Brian—Buffalo Police Dept.
Precinct Seven

"Looters unloaded $60,000 worth of coffee using toboggans."

Answered a call at 10 a.m. A woman was being assaulted by her husband. Leaving that scene, the police car got stuck in the snow and was finally pulled out at 12 noon by a tow truck. I tried to get chains at the police garage but they were out of them. We proceeded toward South Park Avenue and did not get there until 8 p.m. We abandoned the car and tried to walk back to the precinct office. There were many buses and cars which were running out of gas and they were filled with people. So, we took a lot of people and led them to St. Valentine's Church where the priests had set up a kitchen and let the refugees use the phone to call home.

We then left the church and proceeded on foot to the bakery on Southpark Avenue where I bought about 5 dozen rolls. We brought them back to the precinct because there were about 200 people stranded there.

We got warm and then went out on foot patrol because cars were now useless. We took people out of cars and into shelter on a number of streets. I worked from 7:45 Friday morning until midnight Sunday night. Then I got six hours sleep and came back to work on a snowmobile.

About midnight Sunday night, nine snowmobiles arrived from Hamburg, New York and they helped us answer calls. We had a call about a gang that was breaking in and assaulting people on Louisianna which is about three blocks from the precinct. I rode as a passenger on the machine and I fell off and hurt my back. I didn't go off sick until February 7th. By then, I couldn't walk anymore and my legs were numb. I went to the hospital for 10 days and was in traction. That didn't help so I went home for a month.

They discovered that I had a ruptured disc. On June 13th they removed a disc and two vertebrae. Today, the 22nd of July, I'm still off work and I saw the doctor this morning and he said that I'll have to lie off for another month or two.

During the storm, the people of this neighborhood were very well organized. They had toboggans and sleds and since they knew that the police had difficulty getting to emergencies, the people broke into factories and homes, taking what they wanted. They were gone by the time the police got there. I remember the semi-truck that was half covered with snow. Looters unloaded it of $60,000 worth of coffee using toboggans. They were well organized.

One day we used a four wheel drive to pick up some food for some old people over on Perry St. When we delivered, we thought we were going to get mobbed by the people in the building because nobody had any food. So, we spent the next four hours shopping for the elderly in the high rise building.

Police Departments all over the country should have four wheel drive vehicles, especially in snow areas. They are safer than snowmobiles and they can transport a lot of people out of isolated areas.

PAPERWORK

A law enforcement officer's nightmare was filling out an accident report involving 50 cars and 113 people. This occurred on Route 31 near Albion, N. Y.

LOOTERS

A Buffalo City Judge visited the Erie County Holding Center and at one point, released without bail some 30 defendants accused of looting during the storm. This was necessary because most of the courts in the area were closed for a week and the jails were swelling.

LOOTERS

The rash of looting in the east side of Buffalo had spread downtown, prompting a local gun shop operator to hang out signs reading, "Trespassers will be shot, survivors will be prosecuted."

Thieves took advantage of the immobilized city and stripped abandoned vehicles, broke into homes and used smash-and-grab tactics on shops, police said. Gangs of youths took furniture, beer, radios, cigarettes and other items. At least 100 persons were arrested. It was estimated $200,000 worth of goods were stolen.

CIVIL DEFENCE

Police reported that some truck drivers in the south end of Buffalo were toting shotguns around to protect their stalled tractor-trailers.

REFRIGERATORS

A truck driver had to abandon his rig during the blizzard. When the storm was over he returned and found that his trailer had been relieved of a load of new refrigerators.

Robert C. Penn—Commissioner
Department of Human Resources
City of Buffalo

"We hired some 1300 people with an emergency grant from the U.S. Department of Labor."

My involvement in the blizzard started around 11 o'clock on Friday, when I noticed a very dramatic change in the weather outside. I started to advise division directors and unit supervisors to let people go at their own discretion but mandated that the division directors must remain on duty no matter what. It was sometime later in the afternoon around 3 o'clock that I realized that the matter was very serious. I had my wife, who is also a city employee taken home so she'd be safe. I tried to get an assesssment of how many people we had within the department in the event that we had to be called into service. When it became clear that 600 people were stranded here in City Hall we started to set up some contingency planning to deal with the people in the hall so they wouldn't panic. We did coordinate with the Red Cross to get blankets and cots and to check the food supply so that we could feed the people.

About 11:30 or 12:00 that night, I went to the Mayor after I had done some brainstorming with some of my staff. Everybody was paying attention to getting the streets clear and no one had thought about the actual consequences on human lives. Since our department is primarily set up to deal with the people, that became a concern of ours. The Mayor listened as he listened to a bunch of other people, but I got the feeling that the people were a very low priority at that particular point in time, not because the Mayor was insensitive and didn't care, I think his experience with hardware was more important.

We started to put together a human service contingency task force and that consisted of liasoning with the Red Cross, the Catholic Charities, the Salvation Army, our own division of aging, a division for youth, a division for manpower, in such a way that we could start to meet the emergency needs. I also offered the services of the Buffalo Information Center which is an information and referral program, of non-emergency telephone calls so that people would feel like they were communicated with. That number eventually got published in the paper and on the radio. We started to give out all kinds of information such as what bus routes would be open, what streets you could travel, what to do in case of food shortages, what to do in case they needed assistance with hospitals. We eventually opened up many neighborhood recreational centers and a lot of our local offices because our offices are all decentralized in every community.

We then started to use 4-wheel drive snowmobiles with emphasis on the elderly because we found that the elderly couldn't get out. We had to get to them with food. The elderly were the hardest to get to move from their residences. They were immovable.

We had a list of the handicapped and the disabled elderly so that it was fairly simple for us to reach those people to make sure that they were safe and secure.

We were co-ordinated with the Erie County Department of Social Services for the out-station people who receive food stamps. We also hired some 1300 people with an emergency grant from the U.S. Department of Labor, to perform several tasks. Those tasks included shovelling of sidewalks and streets, starting first with the elderly and people who were handicapped. We had individuals working for the Railroad to clear the railroad tracks so that the food could get into Buffalo. We found out that after we entered the blizzard it had become very difficult for food to get in. We maintained one liaison with the Red Cross. We arranged for the banks to open up one of their offices so the individuals could qualify for food stamps and get their welfare checks. We also arranged with the Post Office for individuals to come to the Post Office to show their I.D. to be able to pick up their checks because the regular mail had stopped. This was the central command post to deal with people problems. We also directed street crews to where there was an emergency situation.

Afterwards we sat with some individuals and tried to work out a draft plan for an emergency contingency plan in the event that a blizzard, icestorm, flooding or even a riot situation occurred. This was a formal contingency plan that would tell people where they could go to predetermined places for transportation and communication.

Clean quiet streets of Buffalo to enjoy. Buffalo State College Courier Collection.

California Dreamin'.
Courtesy, Buffalo State College Courier Express Collection.

ARMORED ATTACK

A Lewis County man had just parked his car when it was run over by an Army armored personnel carrier. No one was hurt, but the car was a total loss.

Sheldon M. Berlow

"I discovered that this building was one big party from top to bottom."

On Friday morning when the weather started getting pretty bad, it was obvious that it wasn't just a routine winter storm. It was whiter and more furious looking. I began to think of the employees in my office and the rest of the building, whether they were going to be detained later in the day or not. So my first call was to the Weather Bureau. They told me that the worst of it was coming upon us in about a half hour to an hour and it would last about two hours, perhaps a little bit more and then it would pass by. Our decision therefore was to wait it out until the end of the day when it would have cleared. It didn't of course. We gave our employees the option as to whether they wanted to leave immediately or wait until the end of the day. Some put their coats on right away, particularily those who had family responsibilities and children waiting for them at home. The rest said no, we'll wait around and see what happens.

About three-thirty, four o'clock in the afternoon, it became obvious that it wasn't passing over. It was just getting worse and worse and worse. Worse means looking out the window of this building from the fourteenth floor and not being able to see across the street at all for a long period of time. At that time I started going through the building to see what the other people were doing. The Rand Building connects with Hengerer's on our eighth floor. Hengerer's Restaurant is essentially our building restaurant but they are not open for dinner on Friday evening. Around six thirty I came into Hengerer's Restaurant to let them know that there were people stranded. When I walked into the restaurant they had the most exquisite buffet set-up already. There were hot dishes, cold dishes, and appetizers, salads, and tid-bits. They were set-up to feed their own employees, the Rand Building employees, people from the Tishman Building and National Fuel Gas people. People started pouring into the restaurant. Incredibly enough, they didn't charge anybody for any of the food. To me it was just astounding. I think they did charge for beer and wine. They poured food out as fast as the few hundred people that were in here could possibly consume it, and they did it with a happy spirit. Most of the people did not realize that they were not going to be charged for the meal. They didn't realize it until they had these full plates and searched for a table. Then they realized that nobody asked them for a cent. Then there was a party spirit where everybody was one nice big family, all eating together, and it was a very cheerful kind of atmosphere. In fact, the only problem in the dining room was to get people to get up and give their seats to somebody else standing in line. Everybody was sitting around having a wonderful time with the food and drink that was coming.

It then became apparent from all reports that we were here for the night at least. Then Hengerer's opened their second floor, the housewares department and allowed us to take any amount of sheets, pillow cases and blankets necessary for the number of people that we as owners here designated for our employees. We signed a voucher and were billed at the wholesale costs. It was really rather incredible.

Now what was happening in the rest of the Rand Building? I discovered that the building was one big party from top to bottom. There were many well stocked liquor cabinets all of which were opened to employees without regard to social or economic position and to anyone else who might have stumbled into the building. I began to suspect that it would run out eventually until I went down in the lobby. I still was unable to see the other side of the Lafayette Square. Through our main revolving door there appeared this white lump, over-burdened with shopping bags. The lump went straight for one of the elevators and up. I asked the guard, "What's that?" He said that it was the delivery boy from the liquor store across the street. It stayed open and this kid amazingly enough, had been able to get himself across from that store about twenty times in the past few hours. He was delighted about the whole thing because he had never made more tips in his life, nor did he expect that he ever would again. This was fine as far as I was concerned except I had the basic apprehension that any of it could have gotten out of hand. What I did along with several employees was to float through the building from floor to floor and check the tone of the parties. We did have guards in the building in case there was any particular, immediate problem and then we had our employees who were geared to watching for this. Other than that, I took the stance that as long as they were happy, it was probably the best thing that could happen because this was now one o'clock in the morning. The parties petered out and eventually everybody went to sleep.

The next morning Hengerer's were open, cheerfully serving Danish pastry and coffee to everyone at no charge.

My chief engineer, Ted Slifer, did not go home for five days. Each afternoon, I begged him to go across the street to the Hotel and take a room with all expenses paid. He refused saying that he would rather be here in case the boiler went out. He propped himself up in the boiler room with a cushion and a pad. He is an old time navy engineer. I went home on Saturday and didn't come back until Monday morning. Everybody who couldn't get to their homes stayed in the building. No one complained about it.

My wife and two young children in North Buffalo survived comfortably. They regarded the storm as fun. There was no school, there was a lot of snow, and there were lots of kids to play with. It was sort of like a big snow weekend. Instead of driving we walked the three or four blocks and bought a minimum of things so that there would be some left for other people. We easily shifted from one usual type of food to another. The children were extremely resourceful and inventive. They talked to each other, they read magazines that had never before interested them. They played with children in the neighborhood who did not interest them when they were more mobile. I heard tell of depression, but I didn't see it. It became a very leisurely way of going about the day. It was an interesting shift of personal values.

There was a driving ban but I was exempted from it because I am the co-owner of this Rand Building. It was built in 1929. Only banks could construct buildings in 1929. It is a 29 story structure including towers, located on Lafayette Square which is the center of Buffalo's commercial-financial life. It's a building that enjoys a mixture of banks, Western Union, radio stations, law and accounting firms and non-profit organizations.

MARINES

Near Camp Drum, a 52-ton Marine personnel carrier flattened a State Police car buried under 5½ feet of snow. A sub-compact car was marooned alongside it. One report said, "They're both kind of squashed."

Lieutenant McLean—Buffalo Police Academy

"Now we are going to show a great film called Naked City."

The weather began to get bad early on Friday afternoon of Friday, January 28. By 2:30 p.m. the office buildings downtown had begun to send people home. Buses were stuck in the snow. We had 55 mile per hour winds that were blowing off Lake Erie. The windchill factor was something like 67 degrees below zero. Many people who had left the office buildings were stranded in the streets. They were blown around, knocked down and could not get their footing. Our traffic policemen, working in pairs, would pull these people back against the buildings and help them get inside for shelter. Downtown Buffalo, and especially Main Street, was like a wind tunnel that funnelled the wind off Lake Erie.

By 3:30 in the afternoon, we turned this training Academy into a refuge for people who were stranded downtown. Many of the refugees were concerned about their families so we made arrangements for them to use the telephones. There was a pervasive air of anxiety with many people frostbitten. In an attempt to calm people down, we brought out the movie projectors which we use for showing training films. We sat the people down in the auditorium and I said, "Now we are going to show a great film called Naked City." Everyone was immediately interested because they thought we were about to show a porno movie from the police lockers. Some people will remember that Naked City was an old television program about police work in New York City. We saw that one and a number of other training films and they helped people to settle down.

We have police dispatching speakers here and many people sat up all night listening to the constant police calls.

We had two sisters stranded here who live nearby in an apartment complex. One was 76 years old and the other was 78. One is the mother of a Buffalo policeman. Everyday they come to St. Joseph's Cathedral next door and hear Mass at noon hour. It's really important to them. Since they were the oldest people we had here, we made arrangements late at night for them to sleep in the women's cell block where there are cots. They politely refused on the grounds that they did not want to miss anything in all the excitement. The one woman's son is a policeman assigned to the city court detail, about a block away from here. He was stranded downtown and couldn't move. He called his mother's house all night, trying to contact her. About 3 a.m., he learned from another police officer that his mother and aunt were safe in the police academy where they had been since 3:30 in the afternoon. He really gave her heck for not letting him know where she was. She very calmly asked, "How the devil was I supposed to know where you were?"

I remember another couple who were stuck here. The woman had just been released from a hospital and her husband took good care of her.

We had a fellow who was with his wife and they had been downtown. They took shelter here and the fellow had frostbite on his chin, cheeks and forehead. We don't have any medical people in the building. We phoned a police surgeon and explained that the frostbite was starting to erupt. We proceeded with first aid on the doctor's advice. The frostbite victim couldn't get out of the building until 4 o'clock the following afternoon. He didn't speak English so he couldn't help us in trying to locate a member of his family to come and get him. Not that it would have helped because nobody could move. We couldn't move a police car to get him home either.

We had a woman whose daughter was sick at home and the mother used the telephone to keep in touch with the babysitter. The last phone call she made was about 6 o'clock in the morning and she was informed on the phone that her daughter had been rushed to the hospital. That capped the anxiety for the night. She began to cry and then she started to scream. We didn't have anything that we could use to get her to the hospital until eleven o'clock in the morning when an uncle got through in a four-wheel-drive vehicle.

At the height of the storm, the police commissioner asked several T.V. Stations to announce on the television screen that any citizen who wished to volunteer his four wheel vehicle should call this number. When the volunteers started to call in, we asked them their location and asked if they would drive to the nearest precinct. Then we put a police officer in the vehicle with the owner along with a portable radio. These vehicles were hauling policemen to handle all kinds of service problems.

I'm 51 years old and I've lived here all my life except for my

Buffalo Evening News Photo. By Dennis C. Enser.

time in the Navy and World War II and I've never seen anything as frightening as that blizzard.

HAPPY KIDS

For thousands of Western New York students, the blizzard of Friday, January 28, meant as much as two weeks of unplanned vacation. Most schools were already closed as a result of a winter storm which had swept Western New York the previous Wednesday night. It wasn't until February 7 that most schools and colleges reopened, while most Buffalo public schools reopened on February 14.

Mrs. Regan

"It was much like having a baby in that you prove to yourself that you can do it."

My husband is County Executive, much like the mayor of a county. When he heard of our disaster, he was desperate to get back to his command post. He was in New York. The calls for him flooded us during that Friday afternoon. Our name is in the phone book so that we are easily contacted when people need help. We had a public involvement in the blizzard.

Our children were safe here and so was my mother in Orchard Park. She called that evening and told me that there was a call for four wheel drive vehicles. She felt I should donate our vehicle. It's a new four wheel drive Jeep Wagoneer. Coming from her that suggestion was strange because she is the biggest chicken about driving in bad weather, but she gave me the number to call and I followed her advice.

I was told to drive the vehicle to the nearest precinct. It was truly wild outside-whiteouts, snowdrifts, traffic lights swinging wildly and terrible ice conditions. They were flabbergasted at the Main and Utica Precinct when I arrived with my son because this was soon after the call for vehicles and they seemed surprised that someone had made it.

I was beginning to feel like Florence Nightingale so I volunteered to drive while a policeman with a walkie-talkie accompanied us. We cruised mostly around Delaware Park, helping stranded people, taking people home and giving stalled cars a push. I wanted to save a life but nothing so dramatic occurred. The policeman finally took us home and they used the jeep for four more days.

My seventeen year old daughter turned very prissy and was furious with me. I received the hint that one is not supposed to be

Florence Nightingale when one has three children.

My husband was then in Syracuse. He finally got a helicopter to fly him here and he spent much of his time downtown thereafter.

It was one of the most exhilarating periods in my life, much like having a baby in that you prove to yourself that you can do it. I understand why people take high risk jobs and help others.

I noticed that in conversations about the blizzard, Roots was often mentioned. Here was a real media event for the United States through television. It was interesting that so many people who were trapped in their homes and offices were forced to watch this classic program. People who would never have seen Roots because they rarely watched T.V. were forced to do so because of the blizzard.

We felt very puritanical about obeying the traffic ban. We still remember our friends who cheated. They sneaked away to the tennis club or skiing. Here we were, skiing enthusiasts with the most snow we have ever seen and only six miles from the city line and we still obeyed the ban. We felt very prissy about those who did not.

Samon Manka—Buffalo Policeman

"about seventy percent girls and thirty percent guys"

The night before the storm, we left Buffalo for a ski trip to Mount Snow, Vermont. We just beat the storm out of Buffalo. On the way to Vermont and all through the time we were in Vermont, we kept getting reports of the storm. Everyone was quite concerned. We kept trying to call Buffalo, but most times we couldn't get through. During the time it was snowing in Buffalo, the ski conditions in Vermont were the best in five years. We consisted of two bus loads of people, mainly girls from Bryant and Stratton Business Institute. About seventy percent girls and thirty percent guys.

So we spent the weekend in Vermont. On Sunday night we started heading home. We were stuck in Rochester, New York for three days. We were put up in a hotel in two large rooms. We partied a lot. Then we were declared a disaster group by the Red Cross and they started to pay for the hotel rooms. So we got more co-operation from the hotel manager and a couple more rooms and people started sleeping more comfortably. Several of us tried to rent rooms but it was just impossible because there were so many truckers stranded in Rochester and all kinds of people trying to get through. There was no way out of Rochester into Buffalo. At first the manager gave us two big rooms and everybody was just sleeping all over everything. Some lucky ones got the beds and it was pretty tough sleeping. They had to scrounge up blankets and we looked all over the place. Finally the Red Cross came over with some blankets for us. Some of the older people who were with us managed to get rooms, but most of the people all slept in the community rooms. It was tough because there was only one shower and bathroom in each room and everybody was running in and out.

I came into Buffalo with a State Trooper because I was concerned about my family and what was going on in Buffalo. They wouldn't let commercial traffic through, but the trooper had set up a run. Being a policeman, he ran me into Buffalo.

Upon returning to Buffalo it was unbelievable. There was snow everywhere. Many of the roads were closed.

I went back to work in Precinct Seven right away, delivering food on snowmobiles to the needy families. There were paths where there used to be roads, cars abandoned everywhere, only the major arteries were open and even they were touchy.

Lou Barkowski—Senior Toxicologist—Meyer Memorial Hospital

"They were three freaky looking dudes."

The thing that surprised me was that we have this twenty-four hour call service at Meyer and we respond to emergency patients. We serve eight counties in Western New York and so we get a lot of response from different areas. I was on call that week-end and I was home Sunday night. It was two in the morning and I got a call on the radio from Sister's Hospital. They said they had a comatose patient who needed this analysis done. I said that there was absolutely no way I can get there. And they said, "Oh ya?" and they hung up. So about a half hour later I got a call from the hospital here and they said we got three guys here and a four wheel drive vehicle. These three guys had brought the sample of a comatose patient and then they came to my apartment to pick me up. They arrived in nothing flat. They were three freaky looking dudes. The one guy had an aviator's hat with the flaps turned up. They were more out of it than anybody. I got in the back and these guys just loved to drive over anything and everything. I couldn't believe it. They flew over some of the highest dunes that I had ever seen. Shot right over them and they got me here in a matter of ten to fifteen minutes. It was quite a trip and I'll never forget it. I think they were more laid out than the donors of the blood samples.

Once we get the sample, it's about twenty minutes to analysis. It's a simple analysis that covers about fifteen drugs. They don't know how to treat a patient until they find out what they had. There can be a toss up between a head injury and a pass out on alcohol. They want to be certain before they operate on someone like that.

Ben Kolker—National Weather Service
Buffalo International Airport

"There were twenty-nine people who died in some way and most of them died from being trapped in their cars."

You have to go back through the earlier part of the winter in the Western New York area to understand what happened. If we look particularly at the month of January and almost as early as Christmas, we'll get a good idea. We began to get snow at that point and quite a bit of snow fell almost every day. It was piling up and we never really had a thaw during this entire period. We ended up with at least 30 to 35 inches of snow on the ground. Then a cold front came through and a low pressure system passed to the north of us and there wasn't too much wind. It was fairly good weather just before the cold front entered. The winds picked up very sharply behind this front and there was a rapid drop in temperature to down near zero Fahrenheit and the combination of high winds and low temperatures gave a very bad wind chill effect. We had all that loose snow on the ground. Then this high wind condition entered the picture. There wasn't much snow that fell with the blizzard itself—only about seven inches, but the snow on the ground was swept around and driven into drifts. The wind was so strong that it packed the snow. It broke the snow crystals up so they really packed in solidly, almost like a form of cement. Then, add to that the frozen lake and you complicate the problem. Lake Erie had been frozen at the end of December and the snow had been piling up on the lake in the same fashion. There was probably as much as thirty inches of snow out on Lake Erie itself (a surface area of about 10,000 square miles.) All the way down to Toledo and Detroit we had snow on the lake and the winds picked that snow up and blew it over the city of Buffalo.

The city itself, the buildings and the geographic layout, acted like a giant snow fence and when the wind blew the snow off the lake it created the tremendous drifts which were extremely bad. They were packed like granite. If you cut across a snow drift, it looked like a piece of granite rock.

Much of Western New York got hit the same way because of the high winds and because of the snow, but Buffalo got the worst because they got that additional snow that came off Lake Erie. The combination of very cold temperatures and high winds gave you a real blizzard. Gusts of over thirty miles an hour combined with temperatures dropping down near zero continued for a long period of time. The conditions of high winds and blowing snow and very cold temperatures persisted throughout the weekend and isolated people. They just couldn't move.

Buffalo in particular, needed more help than anyone else because they had not been moving the snow as much as necessary prior to the blizzard. They had all this snow accumulated. Record amounts of snow sitting on the ground prior to the blizzard did not help the condition. The city did not do enough hauling of the snow prior to the storm hitting and then the problem was compounded by all this additional new snow and very bad drifts. The equipment they had was insufficient to handle the situation. As a result, they had to call for emergency help from the Guard and the military. They sought help from other cities. It wasn't an ordinary plow that was needed. They needed high lift shovels. They needed a lot of power equipment to actually crack the stuff and chop it.

About three or four days into the following week, I made a trip down through parts of Buffalo. The only way they could move the snow was to dig it out with motorized vehicles. There was no way you could plow it. Houses were actually buried up to their roofs in certain areas where they were exposed and the drifts were up to thirty feet in places where the snow had a good chance to pile up. It was the worst blizzard in local history.

There have been bad snow storms at other times and we received a lot of snow. Several periods back in 1944 and 1945 we got snow from four feet up to six feet falling over a period of a week, but there never had been this type of drifting. Added to that was the extreme cold. The fact that there has been a radical change in suburban living was an additional factor that they didn't have to contend with in forty-four and forty-five. The number of people living outside the city has increased. This has changed the traffic pattern. It really tied the city up and created an emergency situation. It's probably the first snow situation declared a disaster. This meant that the federal government could act to come in with assistance, both financially and otherwise, to help the people in the area to get out of that problem. Usually when disaster areas are declared they are in connection with floods, tornadoes, or hurricanes. This is the first incident where they ever did anything like this in connection with a snow situation.

Buffalo seems to have got socked really well and it was certainly the worst hit. The storm however extended into the county areas. The areas most exposed to Lake Erie, which would have been the Eastern half of Erie County and parts of Cheektowaga County, Niagara County, Genessee County and parts of Wyoming and Monroe County were pretty hard it. Some of the areas back away from the lake where they had several ridges were provided with a bit of shelter and they didn't get as hard hit as we did up here.

A very interesting thing developed during the blizzard. We had here on that weekend a lake effect storm at the East end of Lake Ontario which dropped up to six feet or more of snow. They were not however getting much of the wind effect because of the presence of the lake effect storm so they just got a gradual quiet pile-up of snow. They did not get the drifting and hard packed snow that we had in Buffalo. We had some men in the weather service who made a trip out there to observe the difference between that end of the lake and this end. The snow there, at the east end of Lake Ontario, was in big mounds, not particularly packed, relatively easy to move by using plows, but the snow in this region was packed like a rock hill. With the sun shining, you got those crystaline effects that you get with granite when its cut a certain way. It was like rock.

I have seen drifts before but not that high. We had a couple of blizzard conditions in the past, rather localized, but it was nothing like this. Back in sixty-three we had a condition in the whole of Western New York and the worst areas hit were Syracuse and Oswego. They had some hard packed drifts too. Across the field from our observatory the roads were blocked and I was able to take a picture of it in 1963, but this time in 1977, when I went over the same area it was much worse. To clear the approach road to our observatory, they finally had to come in with the high lift equipment. You really had to go to work with those high lifts. It was like using a steam shovel. You use the high lifts and dig away at it and break it up like big hunks of rock. Big chunks of packed snow were treated like cement blocks and cast away.

There were twenty-nine people who died in some way and most of them died from being trapped in their cars. It was either monoxide poisoning or exposure that killed them. If you stayed out very long in those conditions you were dealing with wind chill factors down to forty and fifty degrees below zero and if you were exposed to that cold for very long, you were finished. There were a couple of people who were actually out and it was obvious they died from exposure. They found their bodies just lying out in the open where they tried to cross quite a distance. An older person who might have had a heart condition at the same time would be in really rough shape trying to move about in a condition like that.

Over the years we have never referred to a storm like this as a blizzard around this region because blizzards were supposed to be associated with a certain kind of weather condition which is normally found in the central plains in Canada and the United States where it occurs often enough to be a notable weather phenomena of that area. The combination of high winds blowing the snow with very cold temperatures creates a blizzard condition. We have now changed the definition a little bit so that we call that particular situation in the East here a blizzard and in the future you'll probably hear the weather services using more blizzard warnings. Usually we used the expression near blizzard conditions, but now we will be using blizzard warnings. Usually we used the expression near blizzard conditions, but now we will be using blizzard conditions in describing similar situations. The storm of the twenty-eighth of January, 1977 was actually what we call a severe blizzard. The winds were over forty miles per hour and the temperature was way down.

We were looking for trouble on this one. We had a blizzard warning out before it actually hit. The situation was followed carefully by other offices because this particular front and its effects were felt through the Great Lakes' region. The only difference was that in most areas, it was rough for a few hours during and after the passing of the front and then conditions quieted down. Here however, we had twelve hours of practically zero ceiling and zero visibility. You just couldn't see anything at all and the worst of it was caused because of that lake situation. Cleveland, Detroit, Chicago and Toledo did not have as much snow. During those brief periods of visibility they sent people home early in many cities. They tried to do that here but a lot of the people delayed too long and they were trapped in Buffalo. Some of them never got out of the city for three days, I couldn't get out of the airport very well. I was here from Friday morning until Sunday morning. We were in need of man power here so we stayed in and kept going to keep the office operating.

The term whiteout may be used to describe this type of condition. A whiteout is what you find in the Arctic, but this storm was the exact equivalent of a whiteout. When that thing hit at the airport, it was just as though there was a white wall out the window and for most of the day you couldn't see much beyond the window.

It was practically zero visibility. It picked up at times so you could see a few hundred feet but most of the time you just couldn't see beyond the window pane.

A whiteout is generally considered to be with fine snow. It isn't necessary to have that much snow coming down. There are very cold temperatures with it and the snow floats from the sky. It isn't necessary to have the wind for a whiteout. It's the white crystals present so everything has a white milky effect. You cannot really distinguish anything for any distance. Objects fade out against the white. In the Arctic, a lot of things are white anyway and that makes it difficult to see them.

There is another reason why this area got the full impact of that blizzard. Lake Erie froze over much earlier than normally in 1977. That meant that we got the full effect of most cold fronts and that kept the temperatures down.

GOODBYE NATIONAL WEATHER SERVICE

The weather was so bad at Buffalo that their Chief Meteorologist, James Smith, said he was retiring from the National Weather Service in February.

Paul Wieland—Public Relations—Buffalo Sabres

"Gary McAdam had five separate accidents with his new Thunderbird on the way home."

I drove from Toronto to Buffalo on the morning of the twenty-seventh of January. The Sabres played Atlanta that night. The reason I mention that is because the team was having problems because of the players who were in the all-star game. Jimmy Schoenfeld, Richard Martin and Gil Perreault had all left Vancouver after being delayed by a fog problem. They arrived in the early morning of the twenty-seventh about one a.m. They had to drive through the beginning of the mini blizzard that we had that day. Officials were recommending no unnecessary travel, but the players got back. They played Atlanta that Thursday night and tied the game one to one.

We have a sell out for every home game. Because of the weather that Thursday night only twelve thousand people were able to make it. We can seat sixteen thousand four hundred and thirty-three and every seat was sold out and paid for, but the balance of the spectators couldn't get here. In fact there was some talk about cancelling the game that night, but we felt a larger majority of people could make it and they did. Rather than get sixteen thousand people angry, we got four thousand people angry. No matter what you do in a situation like that, you are subject to criticism, but it wasn't too vigorous a criticism, especially considering what happened the next

View looking north toward Buffalo, New York. Approximately 100 cars and trucks were still stuck in the snow on Fuhrmann Boulevard along the shore of Lake Erie about four days after the blizzard hit.
Courtesy, U. S. Army Corps of Engineers.

morning.

The morning the blizzard hit I recall I was tired from being in Vancouver and the trip home. I arrived at the office at about ten o'clock. At about twenty minutes to ten, I called down to the auditorium and it was starting to snow pretty heavily, but you know, that's Buffalo. That's our area and you don't think too much about it. A friend of mine, a rewrite man on the Buffalo Evening News had called our office and told everybody to get the hell out of there. A terrible blizzard was coming and if we didn't get out now we never would. That's what my office told me. So I didn't even bother to try and get to the auditorium.

In the auditorium we have a set up called the Aud Club. It's a private club and seats eight hundred for dinner and it's right in the building. Now the Aud itself is in down town Buffalo in the middle of a business area. What happened when the storm hit was that people couldn't move and they started to come in to the auditorium. A lot of these people were freezing in their cars. We started taking them in. We had three hundred people in the Aud Club until late Sunday. We had women and children, diabetics and we had a psychotic guy here. The police were running insulin on snowmobiles for people who were stranded here. It was necessary to form human chains of people. You know that we are right on the waters of Lake Erie. The storm was at its worst right at the Aud. The people from the Aud were actually forming human chains out the side doors and over to the roads to get these people in these cars. It was so bad that you had to be holding on to each other so that you didn't get lost.

Meanwhile, in North Tonawanda, the hockey team was practicing. They don't practice in the Aud all the time. They often use the Tonawanda sports center. The Sabres normally get out there about nine o'clock for physical training. They were there before the storm hit and the practice was over about noon. They shut the doors about 12:15 and walked out into the face of the blizzard. The Sabres were supposed to leave that Friday afternoon for Montreal in order to play the Canadiens on Saturday night at the Forum. Gary McAdam earned a new nick name that day trying to get home from his practice. They now call him "Crash." He had five separate accidents with his new Thunderbird on the way home. Lee Fogolian and Brian Spencer took four hours to drive what normally took five minutes. They got stranded in their apartment and never got out again.

Saturday afternoon they finally got a charter plane in Buffalo. It was a small prop jet. I was sitting there and our coach got there behind a snowplow as well as our director of scouting. They used the phones to see how many players they could get. By three o'clock that Saturday afternoon, they only had ten players. How these players managed to get to the airport is a story in itself. Finally one guy got through in a four wheeler and that brought our minimum up to thirteen players with two goalies. Otherwise we would not have met the starting line-up requirements. We would have had to forfeit the two points to Montreal.

Well we finally got the group rounded up and they took off and the take off itself was pretty hairy. They finally got to Montreal and the weather wasn't that bad. They were bussed into the Forum, they played five men short of the normal roster, and they tied the Canadiens three - three. The Sabres out-played them heavily. That night the game was supposed to be telecast and broadcasted on the radio. Our broadcaster, Ted Darling, was able to pull off a major scoop. He will probably tell you his story himself. It is really fascinating. The players got back on the plane and flew into Buffalo the next morning.

Saturday I was sitting in my home out in the suburbs and the owner of the team Seymor H. Knox called me and said: "I don't think we can play tomorrow night against the Los Angeles Kings." This was to be a Sunday night game at the Auditorium scheduled for the thirtieth. I was directed to make the necessary arrangements to cancel the game. I couldn't help thinking that here is a P. R. man cancelling a National League Hockey game. I wondered if Clarence Campbell would appreciate this.

I finally got through by phone to the Kings who were playing in Long Island that night against the New York Islanders. I got Bob Nevin, who was their assistant general manager at the time, and explained what was happening. It took me two hours to get him because the game was going on and of course he was working. It was imperative that he be informed that the Kings could not fly into Buffalo if they were to leave New York after the game that night. There were no planes landing. So I called him and told him this was Paul Wieland, Public Relations Director and I told him that the game was cancelled. He was very sceptical because you know it could have been some prankster. It took me quite a while to convince him that it was me and that the game was cancelled. The game itself was later played on the make-up date on March 3rd. We were forced to reschedule a game against the Toronto Maple Leafs that was to be played on February 7th. That's a week later. We moved it back to February 14th and did manage to play it on that date.

The most horrifying part was trying to get out of here and play in Montreal. If we hadn't made the game we would have lost the two points. By league rules we are allowed to cancel a game in our rink because of weather, but we couldn't have Montreal sitting there and waiting for someone to play. So we would have been penalized if we hadn't made it. I still can't understand how twelve thousand people made it to see that game on that Thursday night. I understand that many of our fans were involved in the thruway blockage after the game. Many of them were forced to abandon their cars for over a week.

Don Luce— Buffalo Sabres

"Everybody went "Whoops" because it felt like we were going to tip over in the airplane, right there on the ground."

We were supposed to fly out that Friday night to Montreal. But the storm was so bad that they told us we would fly out on Saturday morning. When I woke up the next morning, there was a pile of snow.

Fortunately, my car wasn't drifted in. The office said we were still to go to the airport. I started the car, backed it out and it stalled. I came back inside the house and the phone was ringing. It was the office. I was to stay put until they cleared a plane to fly us out. That took a couple of hours. But I got the car running and clearance to head for the airport.

Terry Martin had already walked over to my house. We left to pick up Craig Ramsey. We tried to get to his house but his street was a wall of snow. So we drove back to my place and phoned Craig. I told him to walk out past the snow drifts so that we could pick him up. When we got Craig, we headed for Billy Hajt's house. The same thing happened there. I drove home, phoned him and told him to meet us beyond the snow drifts. When we got Billy, we headed for the airport and passed all kinds of cars completely covered with snow. Fortunately, we didn't get stuck. Believe it or not, I was driving a Ford Grenada with no snow tires. But there were four of us to push if we got stuck.

The wind was really blowing wildly at the airport. We waited for one and a half hours before we knew if we had a team. Finally, enough players showed up and we got on the plane. The pilot said that above 2000 feet, there was no storm. But the problem was to get the plane off the ground.

We taxied to the runway and made the turn to enter the runway. We were broadside to the wind when it hit us. The one wing tilted upwards and the plane moved sideways a couple of feet. Everybody shouted "Whoops" because it felt like we were going to tip over in the plane, right there on the ground. The stewardess headed for the cockpit and some of the guys heard her ask the pilot not to take off. Someone said she was crying.

I thought we would turn around and go back, but a big jet pulled up behind us so we couldn't turn around. So we took off. It was rough for the first 2000 feet. But after that, it was great.

We left Buffalo at 4:30, got into Montreal at about 6:15. We went straight to the Forum, got into our equipment and played. We didn't have a pre-game meal or anything and we played really well as a team, even though we were short handed. I even got a goal. This wasn't what you call a routine trip.

My advice to anyone in a similar storm in the future is, stay where you are, if you are safe. Don't move. It's not worth it. We made it and we were lucky. If it happens to me again, I won't move. It was a very risky trip. We found out how really bad it was when we got home. Even my neighbor got involved in a pile-up on the thruway. He was cut badly, almost froze to death and was in severe shock. We didn't realize until later how really lucky we were.

Interesting though how the team reacted. We had our backs against the wall and we were playing the number one team. You'd expect us to lose by a big score. We tied Montreal, three-three. This proves that when things get tough, people can face their problems and rise above them. Hard times can make you a better person. It proves too that you can overcome just about anything you really want to. Especially if you have faith in yourself and those around you.

Find your car, dig it out, get it started and try to get it home. Courtesy, Buffalo Evening News. By Ronald J. Colleran, February 1, 1977

Can we go home? Courtesy, Buffalo State College Courier Express Collection.

Ted Darling—The Voice of the Sabres

I have never missed a broadcast for the Buffalo Sabres since I joined the club in 1970.

I have seen a lot of snow in my home region around Kingston, Ontario, in Watertown, New York, and in the City of Ottawa, Canada but I have never experienced anything like that storm in January.

I live in Lockport, New York, a small town about sixteen miles north of the City of Buffalo. On Friday, January 28, I was supposed to go to the International Airport at Buffalo in order to catch a plane to Montreal. The plane was to leave Friday afternoon. I started to drive around noon and was able to get about three blocks from my home. That was it! Visibility was about twelve inches and my windshield was blocked. I turned around and made my way home. I tried again on Saturday and failed. No luck. Somehow, the team assembled the minimum number of players and miraculously their plane took off for Montreal.

I was to do the television coverage with Rick Azar of Channel 7 who was already in Montreal. Rick Generet was to do the radio coverage of the Sabre-Canadien game. But he was stranded on the Canadian side of the Niagara River in Fort Erie and was not able to make the plane. I called Montreal to talk to Rick Azar. They were able to set up somebody else to do the game on television. This, however, left the radio broadcast still in doubt.

I called a radio man directly in Montreal. Most of the guys in Montreal, all the play-by-play men, were either working or they were out of town. I managed to get hold of one chap but he was unable to do it because his boss wouldn't let him. He worked for the CBC and this broadcast would have gone into the Toronto area. So, he was out of the picture. It was at this point that I made a decision. I would call the game over the radio by watching it on television. Rick Azar and Tom McKarthy would do the television coverage on Channel 7 and I would call the game on the radio.

In the old days they used to call the baseball games from the ticker tape as it came across the wire service. No one had ever called a game over radio while watching television. But you can imagine how the old reporters would have handled this little band of paper about a half inch wide, coming across typewritten and the reporters saying such things as, "Joe Blow is up at bat and hits a double with two men on base. He advances to third and moves about," and the reporter would make up the fictitious story to go along with the actual fact. It would be pretty hard to do a hockey game like that because it is a faster sport.

I remember another time when the Carling World Open was being played. I was working for the CBC and calling the golf tournament there on the radio. I had to get on to an extra hole. There were so many people around the green and the water hazard that I couldn't get on location where my transmitter would transmit back. I ended up about a hundred yards from the green. All I could see was Billy and Al's head, but I called the play from that distance because I knew that the two guys would be on the green and since I could see their heads I could assume they were doing certain things. For example, I called Casper fifty feet from the pin and all I could see was him standing over his putt. I could see his head and when he made the putt you could hear everybody "ooing" and "ahing" and I exclaimed that he just missed by inches. Dan Kelly happened to be listening to the golf cast on radio and watching it on TV. One of these putts missed by two or three feet and I had said it missed by a couple of inches. Since Kelly was watching it on TV and listening to me, he thought I was nuts. That was the only time when I did anything that approached what I was going to attempt to do during the blizzard.

It suddenly hit me that I could be talking to the radio station right from my living room and describe what I saw of the action. I called the radio station and explained to them what I was prepared to do. The person at the radio station just about flipped out when I explained the plan. When the night shift man came on at the radio station I explained to him that I had been talking to the engineer in Montreal. When we were on the road to do radio, we have an engineer in each city. He will set up phone lines and have all the equipment there. The microphones, the hook-ups, are all set. So I asked our man at WGR to get in touch with the Montreal Forum and tell the engineer to stay on duty and to proceed as if I was doing the broadcast right from the Forum. The engineer in Montreal was instructed to raise the levels and crowd noise in order to get as much realism as possible. They were to explain to the engineer that I would be sitting in my living room and calling the game on radio.

Now it was time for me to set up at home. I set up a table in the living room and placed my television on it. I placed the phone beside the table. My fourteen year old son Joey sat with his headphones plugged into the television. We had the lines all open. I couldn't hear what was being said over the television. I knew they were there and they were riding the levels and the engineers just mixed my voice from my house with the levels coming from the Forum. This went out on the air to the radio listeners. I had called about 7:15 p.m. and instructed them to stay right on the air because we had a good line. I stayed right through. At 7:30, I called the press room at the Forum and received the line up. When I told them I had to announce the game from my home in Lockport, New York, they thought I was crazy. When the TV reception began at eight o'clock, I was ready. I was given the cue over the phone from WGR radio when I saw the players coming on the ice. I followed the game on TV.

It was a little difficult because I couldn't see the clock at all times, but my son Joey kept me up to date. Through his earpiece that was plugged into the side of the TV, he could get all of the important times to me. He wrote them on a piece of paper for me. I was able to read his notes and incorporate the time factor into my description of the play on the ice. If the television had failed, a confession to my listeners would have been necessary. They didn't know I was calling the game from my living room.

It was a very strange experience for me because for the first time in my announcing career, I was able to raid my fridge and get my own coffee between periods. WGR had news fillers between periods. I really enjoyed that part.

It was the easiest road game I ever handled because when the game was finished, I hung up the phone, turned off the TV set and went to bed. Surely that was better than listening to crazy George in Colorado, banging his drum in my ear.

Jim Schoenfeld—Buffalo Sabres

"they are the world champions."

A lot of our players were snow bound back in Buffalo and yet we tied Montreal that night 3 - 3. I got the third goal. It was passed from the point and I shot and scored. Everything considered, we played very well since they are the world champions.

Stanley Dylong

"One car hit my leg and my leg got pinned against my snowmobile and my leg got broken."

I saw a bulletin flash across the television that they were in need of snowmobile drivers and four-wheel-drive vehicles to help people stranded in different plants in the area. So, I called the local police department in my neighborhood and asked them what I could do to assist. They said that they would be in contact with me. About forty-five minutes later Captain Schlesinger called me and asked if I would be willing to try to make it down to Precinct Seven. Normal driving time is about seven minutes. In the storm, it took me three and a half hours by snowmobile. Visibility was nil. The snow drifts were already over the tops of some cars and trucks. When I got to the precinct, there were about three snowmobiles there already and everybody was exhausted just getting there. I had a cup of coffee and warmed up a bit and then we started delivering insulin shots to people who were stranded in different industries in the South Park and Main St. area. In order to pick up the insulin, we had to travel downtown. Some people down along the lake front were stuck for two or three days without insulin because nobody could get to them. The snow drifts across Ohio Street and Fuhrman Boulevard were as high as the viaducts which is about twenty or twenty-five feet. A few people did try to make it and couldn't. They had to turn around and come back. The next day Al Tatu and I drove the snowmobiles together. We found an underpass with some railroad tracks going underneath it and that's the only way that we got to these people who were abandoned in these different warehouses along the lakefront. On the way back we found a fellow who was in the snow and was all frostbit. We brought him back to the police department and wrapped him up in clothing and took him to the Emergency Hospital where he was treated for frostbite. His face was swelled about three times its normal size. His hands and his fingers were swelled with white blisters. I was wearing a snowmobile mask, but I still got frostbite. It was pretty painful. At first, it starts to burn, and then it starts to itch. Before long you have big blisters and you walk around as if you are a fish with scales for two or three weeks. In some places your skin can turn black and it stays that way when it kills all the tissue.

The people from Niagara Mohawk Power called the Captain here and asked if there was someone here to transport one of the power company's people to repair a power break. I travelled about five miles and picked up the guy and he got all bundled up and we were down there for about four hours in the one power station. We repaired it. They sent me a very nice letter on it, thanking me for helping them. They should have gave me about six months free power or a steady job.

Then there was this bus a short distance from a restaurant and the people were trapped in this bus for six to seven hours because you couldn't even see across the street to get to any shelter.

That way to Florida! Courtesy, Buffalo State College Courier Collection.

VOLKSWAGENS

When a rotary plow driver working an area with drifts 12 feet high was asked if he was concerned about hitting buried objects, he said he wasn't worried about hitting a car, especially small cars. With a straight face, he said, "Volkswagens are okay, they go through the rotary blades."

Frances E. Voermans—General Manager
Hotel Lafayette, Buffalo, New York

"With all those men in the hotel, we soon had six ladies who rented rooms and tried to take advantage of the situation."

When I got the weather reports that Friday morning of January

28th, I told my secretary and administrative staff to go home early. At this time the hotel was half occupied. No one knew that this was to be the worst blizzard in our history.

Then the front desk was jammed with requests for accommodation. We filled all the rooms and asked people to help each other if they could. Five and six guests were sharing rooms with just two beds. Ten waitresses and two bus boys shared one room. Everyone slept in shifts.

For the month of February we had a large contingent of people working to keep the railways clear. They worked for 18 hours a day and slept the rest of the time. Along with them we had a lot of workers from Canada who were especially called by the city on contract to help clear the streets. They brought with them the big trucks and snowplows. So February was an exceptional month for the hotel with all kinds of people coming and going. We didn't know for certain who was here. The workers would pass the key from one person to another rather than working through the front desk. Rooms appeared vacant because many workers showed up with only a toothbrush and toothpaste. The front desk would assume that certain rooms were vacant and then rent the room. While the new guests were asleep, the railway guys would walk into the room and wanted to know why someone was sleeping in their beds. They got really grouchy.

With all those men in the hotel we soon had six ladies who rented rooms and tried to take advantage of the situation. We threw them out as soon as we discovered that they were in business.

I've been in the hotel business for twenty-five years and I've never seen anything that affected us like the blizzard of '77.

Ambulance Attendant—Buffalo

"The baby was safe at her home."

About ten o'clock in the morning we got a call for a woman who had just had a baby and she was bleeding heavily. We finally got to her house about noon hour, with all the snow. On the way to the hospital we got stranded on William Street behind a semi truck. We talked to the driver and he was freezing. He had no heaters, no defrosters and he looked like he was frostbitten. Then we tried to get fire trucks and police vehicles into this woman but no one could get in to us. Then everything died on the ambulance when we ran out of gas - battery, the radio - everything.

We were in the middle of the black neighborhood and a couple of kids came up to us and asked if we wanted to stay at their aunts, until the storm blew over. So we packed the lady up and carried her on a stretcher for half a block to this kid's aunt. It was about six o'clock at night by then. The people were really nice and they treated us very well. Two fire trucks and an ambulance got stuck trying to get to us.

About three o'clock in the morning there were about five or six four wheel drive vehicles that finally made it through to the end of the street. We packed the lady again and carried her through the blizzard to the vehicles. They got her to the hospital after 3 a.m. and I heard she was going to be all right. The baby was safe at her home.

U. S. Coast Guard

"For exercise, we dug snow caves into the twenty-five foot drifts."

There were about 28 people here including three women and we were snowed in for about 12 days. We ran short of food about the ninth day and one of the National Guard helicopters flew in food for us. There was an almost complete whiteout for six days. It was especially bad because we are situated on the shore of Lake Erie.

On the third day one of the heaters blew up. We rewired the system and had to use emergency generators which run on oil for the rest of the time.

Morale got pretty bad for a time, mainly because there were several people with a morale problem, even before we were confined for so long. The Corporal almost got murdered. I remember one fellow would put on his sneakers and go jogging everyday across the snow drifts for about three miles. He was a professional jogger and he would bring back a newspaper. Most people played cards. I stood radio watch for twelve hours on and twelve hours off. For exercise we dug snow caves into the twenty-five foot snow drifts. Some of those caves had four rooms inside them and they lasted until sometime in May.

Every morning, I'd go with our one and only cook and we'd think of things to break the monotony. Our favorite pastime was pancake flipping contests. Then we had an Ed Sullivan look-alike contest and that got people laughing.

In the next office, the wind blew directly against the big double pane thermo-windows so that frost would concentrate on the glass, between the windows and the curtains. Every couple of days we shovelled about six pails of frost off the windows and floor.

Stanley Makowski—Mayor of Buffalo

"She shouted that this driving ban should be a once a month occurrence in which nobody could use automobiles."

I was having a public hearing on the occupancy tax, which was extremely controversial in our community. The hearing was being

Lt. Gen. J. W. Morris, Brig. Gen. R. L. Moore and staff members met with Buffalo's Mayor Sanley Makowski to discuss cleanup operations. (02/05/77)

held in my outer office and this was just about 11 a.m. I felt a cold wind hitting my back from the window. In a matter of minutes the snow began swirling around from this very cold wind and it started to blur the buildings across the street. I became quite concerned. I discussed with some of the people around me as to what the forecast might be for the afternoon. If it was to continue for the afternoon perhaps we should start releasing our employees early because we run into these traffic tie ups when we get this volume of snow. It was around noon hour I think that I decided to let the various department heads exercise their own judgment as to who should remain. If possible they were to release some of the employees so there wouldn't be any jam up as far as vehicles were concerned. Later, I looked outside and I could not see anything. I was concerned and called up some department heads and asked what they had done with their employees and they mentioned that some of their employees were now coming back since they were not successful in getting home. There were many cars stalled and they decided to return to our building and wait. Little did we realize that this was going to be the most unusual storm in our history and from that point onward there was no discussion of getting home because we had more people constantly coming in.

Then the questions began to start about getting our equipment into the streets to plow and we began to start concentrating on what we should do. I called our corporation council Mr. Faschio who was my Deputy Mayor, and asked him to take over by co-ordinating the activities that we would need. He set up a headquarters to organize the cleaning of the streets. Then we realized that the storm was increasing instead of letting up and we knew we were going to have our hands full. We not only had our city employees coming into City Hall but we had others in the downtown area who ended up stranded here. We had people calling from the Red Cross and other service agencies that could provide food. We then requested that the cafeteria stay open if it was possible. From all indications, it looked like an all-night stand and we tried to get our administration to co-ordinate the need for food, clothing and blankets. We had to see about cots for sleeping and medical facilities. This was put in the hands of Mr. Faschio and his staff which included by that time the police commissioner, the fire commissioner, the transportation and public works commissioner, and so on. There was a meeting late into the night as to what action we should take. Since there was no let up in the storm, it was a matter of trying to keep people calm and giving out news reports. The streets commissioner gave us his appraisal. He saw things that we didn't see because he was out in his districts and he said that everything was completely immobilized. There was no way that we could get our equipment into areas to move the snow. The volume of snow made that impossible.

We had a couple of storms prior to January 28 and January had been one of the most severe months in terms of the number of days that temperatures were below freezing. Then, to have this arctic blow come in on us made it much more difficult to cope.

So we got into the second day of the storm and remember it was raging all night long and very little could be done. We have some excellent equipment with some new pieces but they could not function properly because of the blowing snow and the extremely poor visibility. We also had cars that were illegally parked or stalled throughout the city making it virtually impossible for snow removal equipment to operate. Our people were very patient. Many of the employees stayed right within their own departments in their offices and they made themselves as comfortable as possible. Somehow the Red Cross got their four-wheel drive vehicles to bring in sandwiches towards the latter part of the morning. Our kitchen ran out. As soon as the news went out and people in other areas became aware of the disaster in this city there was an immediate response. For instance the Mayor of New York City offered to send in snow fighting equipment such as snow blowers which were badly needed. We did not have any of our own. The City of Toronto and the town of Kenmore volunteered help. Oil companies offered to send some equipment from other states to assist us. Such things as gasoline cans and gloves and other equipment were offered and needed.

Saturday morning we contacted the Governor's office and they had already heard about it. The governor had dispensed his people here to assist us. The Department of Transportation of New York State immediately sent over equipment from surrounding communities. I don't know all of the sections from which they sent this equipment but it did arrive. Sunday the Governor himself flew into the airport. We had the main streets open by then but the sidestreets were all jammed. People in some areas were not even able to get out and we had many of our employees, especially the Human Resources Department, delivering food and medicines. The Red Cross, the Salvation Army and all of the service agencies such as the Catholic charities were involved in distributing medicine and food and blankets. The side streets leading to some of the main arteries were clogged by high snow drifts. This was an extremely slow process trying to clean up.

The owners of automobiles were encouraged over the air to attempt to move their vehicles so that the snow removing equipment could operate. The tow truck drivers were instructed to keep a record as to where the vehicles were being towed so that the owners could locate them. We started this removal process on the main arteries. It was very slow and tedious work because we were aware of possible legal action against the city if any damage was done to private property.

I declared an emergency and asked for all people to stay indoors as long as they could with the exception of going for food. But they were not to use their vehicles. We put a travelling ban on for the use of private vehicles with some exclusions. I don't remember all of the exclusions but we had to make some exceptions. Again this was shifted over to Mr. Faschio's department and they came up with the modifications of what we could or could not do. The ban on travelling lasted 2 or 3 days until we began to make some head way in clearing snow, not only from the main arteries but from some of the side streets. Then, there was pressure to lift the ban because some of the industries were behind in their contracts and individuals were waiting for products to be delivered. No one actually pleaded with me to remove the ban but I was getting the feeling that each day was presenting more and more of a problem for people to meet their obligations and their contracts. So bearing these things in mind I decided to take a chance. My staff met with me and we decided to lift the ban as an experiment, with a plea to our citizens not to abuse it. We lifted the ban and encouraged people to go only to work or for food. Unfortunately, too many wanted to see what was happening. They had been restricted to their homes for a few days and now they were eager to come out. It wasn't long before the main arteries were clogged again with vehicles.

We were declared an emergency area by the President of the United States which meant now the federal government was involved. Surrounding communities from as far away as New York City were sending equipment here to help. The National Guard and the reserves and the Army Corps of Engineers played a tremendous role in shipping this equipment over from New York City. We had troops coming in from North Carolina with their equipment such as tanks and plows. This was a gigantic effort to assist us in our emergency. There were many people that I wish to thank and did thank after the storm but could never repay.

It was near the beginning that we received authority from the federal government to be able to get in private contractors. They could come in with equipment to clear our streets. And this is when we really started to move a lot of snow. They would be able to pick up the snow and put it on trucks and deposit it wherever they could properly do so. Many of the private contractors were authorized to deposit the snow away from the streets. This allowed people an opportunity to move their vehicles. This was a massive clean up and it was successful. We came out of the storm with a relatively low number of deaths in the city, and we thank God for that.

There have been no lasting ill effects of the storm in my judgement. If anything, I believe that people at least learned that they are strong and sturdy. They responded magnificently in opening their homes, their restaurants, hotels and motels. Stranded citizens were given an opportunity to rest anywhere that was available. It showed that the community can stand these kinds of difficult experiences. The electronic media carried our image throughout the world and we were wondering whether or not our community image was hurt as a result of the international publicity but I don't think we were damaged by the exposure. I suppose the immediate response to a storm like that would be that I wouldn't want to live in the City of Buffalo because look at the storm they had. On the other hand, I think it gave us an opportunity to show the openness and the kind of people from this part of the country. We are proud of the Great Lakes and the Niagara River and our wonderful neighbors next door to us in Canada. We are extremely grateful to the Canadians, in particular the City of Toronto which responded to our immediate needs by sending tow trucks, food and snow melters. I was a little embarrassed that we had to have a debate about whether or not the snow removal equipment that Toronto offered could be classed as a proper expenditure for our community here. As Mayor, I wish all of you in Canada to know that we are extremely grateful for what you've done because it helped boost the morale of our community tremendously. The Canadian help saved lives in our area and for this we are extremely grateful. We owe our Canadian friends a great debt of gratitude for what they have done.

We noticed one of the good points that emerged was that people who never had spoken to each other for years began saying hello. Individuals were so accustomed to getting into their cars and going down to the shopping plaza and then coming back home. Now they had to ride the buses and walk and they were able to say things like, "My gosh, I haven't seen you in 10 or 15 years. It's so nice to see you." I had one woman actually call out to me as I was walking to church. She shouted that this driving ban should be a once a month occurrence in which nobody could use automobiles. She said that she felt fine by walking and using the bus and probably it would be better for all of us if we did it more often. This was a really positive effect from the experience we had.

I have some advice to Mayors of other cities if they should run into a situation like this in the future. I think that communication is extremely important. You must keep the people informed as to what is happening and give them honest reports as to what's being done in terms of the city. I've already requested sufficient funds to get some new equipment. I want an inventory of the kind of contractors that could step into this kind of situation. I want to know what equipment they have available and what we can expect in terms of picking up that volume of snow and depositing it in trucks and taking the snow to deposit areas so it would not interfere with the regular flow of traffic. Communication with the private sector must be available for this kind of work. Co-ordinating the man power and getting everyone involved is another major problem. We found difficulty in getting heavy trucks to deliver oxygen to hospitals in some remote areas. This meant that we had to go into neighborhoods that were clogged and we had to unclog them. What we would like to be able to do is to have a predetermined route and then immediately clean that route upon indication of a heavy snow.

The police and the firemen without exception stood up magnificently throughout this ordeal. I have the highest praise for every single man in those departments. The street sanitation crews that had to work around the clock will in the future be able to eat and sleep right in the area where we store the vehicles so that they will not be caught away from their work. Any other mayor will be well advised to start setting up task forces and looking at inventory. Find out what you have as far as equipment and man power is concerned. What is the best way to utilize your resources? How would you establish traffic patterns so that there is the least amount of interference with the snow fighting equipment? Where do you set up your communication brain center? How will the police department handle looting? We were able to apprehend better than 39% of the criminals that were in action in an area. These task forces are in the process of meeting and coming up with the recommendations for whoever takes over from me.

I think the good Lord sent us a message in the storm. I imagine he tried to tell us that we have a pretty good place on earth if we could get to understand one another. Then our petty differences will seem very small indeed. Here we are. We have a magnificent world to live in. All we need to do is co-operate one with another. Remember the poor, remember the unfortunate and the disenfranchised and bring them into the main stream of life and thereby have a greater force to combat whatever might be coming our way. It's one world and we are here for a brief time. Nature won't destroy us, we'll destroy ourselves. I think there is both a spiritual message and one of common sense that came out of this. There's so much more that we could do if we looked at our brother without prejudice, without bias. I think I've learned it. I hope my family has and most of our citizens here.

I think if you are too busy to pray then you are just too busy. Too many of us use that excuse. I can't do this. I can't be with my family. I can't go to church. I can't even kneel down in the morning to say my prayers because I'm too busy. If you're using that excuse you better review your schedule. Because you're just too darn busy to be a living and contributing member of this society.

BE PREPARED

Because of the severe winter, 33 of Buffalo's 79 pieces of snow removal equipment were out of service the day before the blizzard hit.

Chief Sullivan—The Fire Alarm Office—Buffalo

"So cars have to be kept out of the city until the stalled vehicles have been towed away and the streets have been plowed."

In an alarm office there are no windows so we do not know if it is raining, snowing, day or night. I spent twenty-seven solid hours here during the blizzard and finally got home with my son who has a four wheel drive vehicle. When I woke up, I said to my wife that I was going to watch a certain TV program. "You can't," she said, "because that was last night."

"Isn't this Friday?"

"No, this is Saturday."

I was working all Thursday night and all through Friday and Saturday until noon.

We were getting calls of car accidents and abandoned cars as well as our regular fire calls. We tried to check the abandoned cars and often we received a report that someone was dead in the car. We ordered our people to lock the car, take the keys to the fire house, give us the location of the car and license number. Then we would report this to the police. So we handled deaths, accidents, births, fires and everything in between.

Firemen who had snowmobiles would come to the alarm office and we issued them portable radios. We sent one of our snowmobiles down to a person who had to be taken to the hospital, and they put that person in a sitting position on the back of the machine, and two firemen walked alongside of the snowmobile and held him in a sitting position for about two blocks where they could put him into the ambulance. Firemen were using snowmobiles to get trapped people free and to get nurses and doctors to the hospitals. All of this was co-ordinated through the alarm office. The wires held up and the system worked well. We were very fortunate.

A major problem was with people driving into the city to work when some of the streets had been cleared. There was no place to park so the city streets became parking lots which completely closed off traffic. Then the plows were not able to operate. So, cars have to be kept out of the city until the stalled vehicles have been towed away and the streets have been plowed.

Another problem we had was with our pumpers. On them there is an interchange valve so that in the event of overheating you can open the valve and water from the intake side will circulate through the radiator and out the overflow. If you put antifreeze in it, the antifreeze would be washed out continually. Since the apparatus is normally kept in the fire house and then kept running at the scene of a fire, they would not freeze up. But this type of blizzard was something never seen before and pumpers were stalled in deep snow and out of fuel. The bottom hose at the radiator should have been cut to let the water out. Since this wasn't done, some pumpers froze. Fortunately, we had minipumpers flown in from all over the State and we assigned them to fire houses in strategic locations.

Overall, I found people rose to the occasion and helped one another. It showed what a great city it is and how really co-operative people can be.

Duty Deputy DiMaria—Buffalo Fire Department

"She demanded to know what the hell was going on for five days

I was Duty Deputy that day. Around noon the weather really got bad. Of course when you're up here on the twenty-fourth floor you can really tell. You couldn't see anything.

We got stuck here with the majority of our employees and we had 650 people stranded here in city hall. Now that created a problem. Our primary objective is fire fighting. We got stranded with people. We had to find a way to feed them and take care of three pregnant women as well. Two were in the nine month stage and we had to put one pregnant woman in the inhalator down stairs in the Superintendent's office. We didn't have any deliveries but we were ready for them. We tried to get some bedding. We were in touch with

Volunteer firemen use a trenching machine to reach a home in the Village of Depew, east of Buffalo. Courtesy, Buffalo Evening News.

the Red Cross and the Salvation Army. We were trying to find places to feed people. We soon got some food which was stored in the basement in the weights and measures room. I found out about the food and I ended up dispensing it to emergency units and to our fire houses so that we could feed our people.

I remember that there was a bus load of about 50 people who walked in. They got on the bus about 2:00 in the afternoon and at ten o'clock at night they got off the bus. They had travelled a distance of 2½ miles in eight hours. They wandered in and of course they were hungry. With our skidoo people and with our four wheel drives we were able to get food to them. Engine 32 at Seneca and Swann had over a hundred people stranded in it. We tried to feed them and if we had bologna sandwiches that's what they got. We were given cold cuts at first and then later on as things improved we were given ground beef and with the ground beef we were making cheeseburgers for anybody who wanted them. We didn't pay for any of this food. It was given to us and we dispensed it. Not only did we dispense it we took some ourselves because we sure needed it. We worked around the clock. We were here five days.

I am a veteran of World War II and at that time there was a song about the lights going on again all over the world. I knew what it meant pertaining to the war but I also knew what it meant pertaining to the snow blitz because about the fifth or sixth day when I looked out from the 24th floor here at city hall you could begin to see the lights of the city coming through again. It was a beautiful sight and it had two meanings. As we looked out the window you could see the Corps of Engineers, the Military, the National Guard out there working night and day getting things cleared away. You could see a mobile canteen bringing hot coffee, hot soup or sandwiches to the workers out there. You could see cars being towed away. There was activity, but the kind of activities you would only see on an emergency basis.

We made a lot of good friends. There were people who worked right here in this building and we didn't know each other by name, but shortly, we got to know each other by Joe, Tom, Pete, Harry and Mary. We rode the same elevators for years but now we became very close and this was the positive thing of it. We had driving bans and the people got to walk to get their milk and bread and again it brought about a closeness of people. I wish this would stay on a day to day basis, not just during an emergency. I wish it would happen all the time because it was warm.

We would get calls from sick people needing medicine and we would dispatch our people from our service station, which is right behind the city hall here. We would either dispatch them with a skidoo or a four-wheel drive. We would call the hospital and tell them who was coming in. The hospital would give them a free one day supply and we would take it to the patient free of charge. I know that this cost the hospital a lot of money. We ran twenty-four hours a day.

Then we had to find bunks for people to sleep on. A lot of people ended up sleeping on the floor. All of a sudden we got bunks from the National Guard, from different military units, from the Red

Cross and the Salvation Army and we started to manoeuver a little better.

On the second day we used some of our four-wheel drives to get some of our people home. We would dispatch them to different parts of the city, military style, with people in the back of the vehicle huddled together to keep warm. People got within walking distance of their homes in this way because it was almost impossible to get into the side streets. We even had trouble keeping the main streets open because of the winds and the blowing snow.

We transported sick people on skidoos from their homes to a waiting ambulance and then to the hospitals. We had a lot of trouble with some of the industries where the drifts were very high. But we got the people out eventually. We had calls of people dead in cars and we would dispatch our squads. We were back logged for a while, especially the first couple of days. If a person was dead in a car we would lock the vehicle and take the keys over to the police so that they could get that person and his car out of that location. But for a while we were so back logged that we would take the keys, lock the car, and give top priority to removal of the body from the vehicle. If we couldn't get the vehicle, definitely him. I remember at least six cases like this.

Some of our squads would get snowbound and abandon their vehicles. Then when we were able to get back to our equipment, it was pilfered. Our radios, personal equipment like jackets, boots, or fire equipment, were all stolen.

There was a place at 1070 Broadway where the sisters out there were taking in a lot of stranded people and there wasn't enough food. My brother, who drives a semi truck here in the city, works for one of the major supermarkets and they had him out delivering loads of bread. Eventually he needed a police escort because they were robbing him. They wanted the bread.

About the third day, they asked me downstairs if there was anything I wanted. I told them that I wanted an ice cream cone. One of our fellows made it home and he brought back a half a gallon of ice cream and some ice cream cones. The people who were supplying the food downstairs in the basement of the city hall had fresh bananas. So we had banana splits. It was ideal. We didn't have any chocolate syrup but we had bananas with ice cream and believe me it tasted like a full course dinner.

We couldn't hear the phones. The only way that we could tell they were ringing was to watch for the light to flash. The city hall guard tapped me on the shoulder one day and he said "I hate to disturb you but there's a flood down below in city hall." I said, "Oh my God, that's all we need." Sure enough, it was on the mayor's floor, the second floor, the air conditioner broke and there was water all over. So we went down and we found the leak and we got it turned off and we got some people working with hand squeeges because the mayor had a big conference coming in here, with people coming from all over. We watched out the windows and the helicopters were landing outside. It reminded me of a war, like we were going to be invaded.

It was good. It brought people close together and I know it

lasted for a while and I wish it would last forever. I think the biggest story you can learn in any emergency is that people will stick together and they will help but it should be longer. It should be forever. It shouldn't be only in an emergency that we are close together. If we could normally have that closeness that we had during an emergency, I think we could avoid other kinds of human relations disasters, such as murder and rape. That's the most important thing that I learned from this emergency. I think before something happens you should set up a program and be ready for it. I think we always wait until the horse runs out of the barn. We are an emergency unit. The fire department can cope with any emergency and I'm happy that we were here. If this would have happened on a Saturday or Sunday we wouldn't have been here. We would have probably been in our homes. We were able to function here because everybody had a place to call. I think what you should try to do if something is going to happen in any community is be prepared for it. Have some kind of a system. For instance, I think the whole thing is setting up a plan in advance. I think that's the whole substance. You might be ready for a plane crash but a plane crash doesn't happen, but something must be ready. We have gone to several meetings after this thing was all over and discussed how to improve what we did. We gave our experiences ....

Some of the girls were up here helping and it was coming time for one of these girls to have her period. So Eddy called his wife and she asked if any of the women up here needed anything. Sure enough this one girl needed pads. Nine months from the 28th, there will be a lot of pregnant women giving birth. Nobody could go anywhere. Sure enough, Eddy's wife sent up all the necessities for the women here. After this was all done, I drove this one girl home. When she got out of the car she said, "When you see Eddy will you give him back this bag and thank his wife for the stuff she sent us." I hadn't been home and I had lots of stuff to carry into the house. I carried this bag in and gave my wife everything. She opened up the little bag and there's the tooth brush and everything else and one Kotex pad. She said, "What the hell are you doing with this?" I don't know if she ever believed me but I tried to tell her the story. She demanded to know what the hell was going on for five days in city hall. My wife has never let me forget it.

Joanne Cavalieri

"So the "doctor" took the lady's pulse, looked in her eyes and prescribed a cold glass of water."

My mother makes egg salad sandwiches on Friday and she asked me to take some over to Deputy Fire Commissioner DiMaria in city hall at noon hour. I made it with the sandwiches and remained for five days answering the phone.

I remember the Captain of the fire boat kept calling because he was having trouble with the boat. Ice had put some holes in it and the Captain was worried. The boat had to be taken away and repaired because of all the damage caused by the blizzard.

The superintendent of the water treatment plant called and told us he was running out of oil. We had to take emergency measures to supply him because his pipes and boilers would have frozen.

One woman was hysterical down stairs and was screaming for a doctor. Two firemen went down and one told the other to call him "doctor" when they saw the lady. So the "doctor" took the lady's pulse, looked in her eyes and prescribed a cold glass of water. This settled the woman down and she was fine after that.

I slept on the floor and covered my whole body because I was afraid of bugs crawling over me. The janitor from city hall accidently stepped on me one night and then he told me about the flood in the mayor's office.

The firemen's wives were really nice because here I was with their husbands for all this time and yet they called and asked if they could send me changes of clothes, deodorant, tooth paste and such. I really appreciated that.

CHANGE IN LIFESTYLE

A Buffalo businessman was asked how the blizzard affected his lifestyle. He said, "In the fall my wife and kids will move to Florida and remain there until the kids have finished their school year. I'll fly down every Thursday and return to work in Buffalo on Monday."

Neil Hodgson—Erie County Medical Examiners Office

"We have purchased a heavy duty generator that will run both of our houses on its own private power circuit."

During the 5 days of that blizzard I jump started 72 vehicles. We tried 73. The one we couldn't get started was a brand new Chevy with heavy pollution control. It just wouldn't start. Throughout the course of the blizzard, I was driving a 1970 Chevy Impala with positraction and wrap around tire chains in the back. I was towing and starting cars with this unit throughout the course of the blizzard and I never got stuck. I used 80 gallons of gasoline taking personnel to and from the hospital for those 5 days. I now own a 4-wheel drive Blazer with a 4-ton winch in the front end and a heavy duty trailor hitch in the rear.

During those days, the neighborhood spirit emerged as people were shovelling out each others driveways and the street itself. As I was driving people to and from the hospital during the day, my next door neighbor made sure that my driveway was clear so that I could get the vehicle in and out in the morning. When I came home at night, I did my driveway and his driveway just before I went to bed.

During the blizzard, everybody banded together and came out of their shells and talked to and helped other people. Then, when the blizzard ended, everybody seemed to crawl back into their cocoon and they didn't want to say hello to anybody anymore. So, I formed a neighbourhood block party for August. I'm trying to get these same people to say hello and unlock their doors and talk to their neighbors again.

My hope for years to come is that this storm will teach us a lesson and try to get us to say hello to our neighbors and strangers on the street and try to get a little bit closer, much like the days when people used to leave their doors open and talked to their neighbors and stopped in for a piece of pie or a cup of coffee.

During the midpoint of the storm I had my citizen band radio and Erie County Medical Examiner's portable unit in the car. I was leaving the back gate of the hospital in order to take some people home. I picked up this call from a liquid fuel truck that was trying to get here in order to supply the hospital with its oil. The oil supply in the hospital at that time was at a critically low point. The truck was stuck on one of the sidestreets. If they couldn't unload that fuel oil it would begin to thicken and once it reached a very thick point it couldn't be taken out of the truck. So, it was important that we get that truck into the safety of the hospital grounds, unload it, and build up that oil supply that was running low. Using the CB to communicate with the driver and then the Medical Examiners portable unit to correspond with the medical examiners office located in the hospital, we were able to get a plow and a fork lift over to move the cars out of his way so that he could get the fuel into the hospital. Without that fuel the supply in the hospital would have been finished before the blizzard.

We got our minds together on what happened and what would be done to try to change the situation. We formed, among the employees, our own web of 4-wheel drive and heavy duty vehicles. We could make it through another disaster now a little more easily. Now we have a list of each driver. We know the critical people in and around the area of the hospital now. So, if need arises we could pick these personnel up and get them to and from work and hopefully this would end one of the great problems we found in this last storm.

For my own personal safety and I guess personal comfort for any other storms of the future, my neighbor and I are better prepared. We have purchased a heavy duty generator that will run both of our houses on its own private power circuit. The main reason for this is that the gentleman next door is a quadraplegic and has to have electricity to keep his pumps and a lot of heating apparatus together.

Colonel Daniel D. Ludwig
District Engineer, Buffalo,
U. S. Army Corps of Engineers.

"Those 12 days of snow removal cost about 6 million dollars."

On the twenty-eighth of January, a Friday morning, I was conducting a weekly staff meeting. One of my members advised me to watch the weather forecast in view of a potential storm which may require early release of the employees in order to get them home in a safe manner. That was approximately ten o'clock. I was under the impression that the storm would arrive later in the day since it had reached Cleveland approximately at ten thirty in the morning. We proceeded with our work and at about twelve o'clock I received further information that the storm was in the vicinity. At twelve-thirty I notified the employees that they were released from their duties and they were to proceed home because of the storm. Between twelve-thirty and one o'clock the storm became so severe that those who had not departed were unable to leave and many who had departed had returned to the office and decided to weather the storm. With the continuing storm there were about seventy people who remained in our office and who remained over night.

The following morning many of us returned to our homes. I was able to return to my home in Amherst on the Saturday afternoon. I helped shovel my family out. I was informed about seven p.m. that night by the emergency operations staff officer that he had been contacted by the Federal Disaster Assistance Administration in New York. The Corp of Engineers might be called upon to assist in the recovery of the area in the form of snow removal operations. My staff officer indicated that we would receive further word shortly.

In my travels to my home which took approximately two hours, I found that the depth of snow and the severity of drifts were comparable. From up at the river front I found that the drifts were very deep. Many roads were blocked heavily in the suburbs. The normal drive to my quarters would be about twenty-five minutes and I made it to my house by way of a route that had been phoned back to me by other employees who had found their way home. Only a few of the streets had been cleared by that time.

On the Sunday morning I received a call that the Federal Disaster Coordinator would be in the County Office at one o'clock to give me instructions concerning the emergency recovery. I reported to my office at approximately eleven o'clock on Sunday morning and found many of the people still in the office. They were unable to return to their homes and many of these people had to remain over in the office the second night. I went to the Raft Building and met with officials of Erie County and with officials from the Federal Disaster Assistance Administration who had been able to fly into Buffalo during a clear period about midday. We were in the Raft Building for several hours until approximately six p.m. The storm had returned during the middle of the afternoon. I received instructions to provide the contracting assistance to the Disaster Administration for snow removal of the major roads in five counties in Western New York. I began to call my staff together. Some of them had to come in from remote locations by snowmobile and by seven p.m. we had returned to the Buffalo District office in the midst of the storm and we were putting together our plans for the recovery operation. After a brief staff meeting we began to solicit contractors for heavy earth moving and hauling equipment in order to begin to clear the roads that had been assigned to us. We were instructed to work with the State Department of Transportation. It would be the Governor's representative and provide us with the priority for road clearance.

The decision to use earth moving equipment was mine. I realized that the snow was very densely packed and that snow plows would be virtually useless on most of the roads and that snow blowing equipment is not commonly available except at major airports in many metropolitan areas. Fortunately, I had some previous experience with snow removal. I had been assigned at an army post in Kansas and during all the storms it was my responsibility to coordinate snow removal from the post roads. Equipment available to us in those situations was strictly engineering equipment, road graders, bucket loaders, and dump trucks. Consequently, we made immediate appeals to construction agencies that had such equipment, putting the notices on TV screens, and in radio announcements, and by phone calls to contractors within the Western New York area. Response was immediate and with national attention that the storm had brought upon the Buffalo area we also received calls from parts of the east coast and Alaska offering snow moving equipment.

On Sunday evening I had accumulated a total of about ten people in the office and advised the other members to come in as they were capable. The federal disaster coordinator had requested that we get at least one contractor working Monday to give the visibility of federal government assistance. We were able to hire contractors on a per hour rental basis of their equipment with Corps of Engineers supervisors overseeing the work. We were able to put approximately twenty-four of these contractors to work during the first twenty-four hours after we made appeals for their equipment. It was a situation that was very obscure as far as knowing the magnitude of the work required. We were responding to written requests formulated by the State Department of Transportation in communication with the County Highway Department as to what roads needed federal help. Since the storm reconvened in the middle of Sunday afternoon, and continued persistently for approximately two more days, there was no chance to make any personal recognisance either by vehicle or by helicopter.

In the metropolitan area of Buffalo we endeavored to move as much of the snow into the Niagara River as possible. We received permission from the Department of Environmental Conservation to do this. In other areas we used parks and vacant lots within the city to store the snow. On Tuesday, we were informed that the President had added two more counties to the Buffalo District responsibility in eastern New York. I co-ordinated with my sister District in New York to provide the assistance in handling operations in those areas.

My division office in Chicago assisted me by flying in people as soon as the airports were open on Tuesday and Wednesday. Another one hundred people arrived from our districts in Rock Island, Chicago, and St. Paul. These people were primarily used as inspectors of construction equipment and were located throughout the disaster areas of Western New York. Most of the attention was given to the Buffalo Metropolitan area, where we had approximately two hundred contractors working for us. Approximately forty were working in the Buffalo city limits alone. The problem here was there was so much snow and it had to be hauled away. Clearance was slow. In addition, many of the streets had cars parked on both sides of the streets and we had to provide the contractors with wrecker capability to move the cars after they had done their clearing and this made the process move very slowly. In some cases, automobiles were completely buried. Only rarely did we actually damage buried vehicles.

The areas that intrigued me most were in the vicinity of Fuhrmann Boulevard, Ohio Street and the Skyway. Here the snow had piled in heavy drifts isolating many of the facilities along the lake front in the vicinity of the Buffalo Port Authority. Our contractors were instructed to work around the clock, stopping only for refueling their machinery. Supervisors worked on a two shift basis, twelve hours each.

In the Fuhrmann Boulevard area, we had to plow through twelve to fourteen foot drifts using tracked bulldozers that would provide a one way lane access to the Skyway. It took us approximately two days to clear the entrance and get access to the skyway where over one hundred cars were trapped. The project came to an end on the eleventh of February.

We had worked very closely with Mayor Makowski to get the streets of the City of Buffalo open, primarily the bus routes, so that people could return downtown to work again. We were assisted in Buffalo area by a contingency of Engineer troops from Fort Bragg, North Carolina, who had road graders, front loaders and dump trucks. By the eleventh, I informed the Mayor that we had cleared all the major bus routes and all the major streets that had been assigned to us and that the emergency situation no longer justified the retention of federal assistance. At that time he reopened the city to traffic and I assisted the Mayor in contracting with a consortium of three contractors to clear the side streets in the city of Buffalo. That work was done in response to the Disaster Declaration by the President which enabled additional funds to come into the city to help in the recovery.

The response of the people who work for me was gratifying. From the time they were first called in, many of them stayed in the vicinity of the office, only returning home briefly. Many worked around the clock, the first few days, in order to get the operation going and to keep it going.

The Army Corps of Engineers was called into this operation primarily because we have a capability to provide contracting assistance designated under the Public Law Ninety-Nine in emergency situations. Frequently the Corps is called in to help in natural disasters caused by flooding. To my knowledge, the Army Corps of Engineers had never been called to provide emergency assistance as a result of heavy snowfall or storms.

My own family during this storm got by with little incident. We did have a couple of problems at home. My wife's clothes dryer became inoperative and she could not dry clothes. On two occasions the hot water pipes froze causing part of the house to be extremely cold. However the pipes did not burst. My children were unable to attend school and they spent most of their time shovelling the snow away from the house to get access to the streets. The snow in many areas around my house, was ten feet deep. I think that it was a unique experience for people in Western New York and those of us who were involved with the recovery of the emergency. Being right in the middle of the storm, having my headquarters right there and available, enabled us to respond almost immediately.

The other item which I had mentioned was the information on the disaster. We, for several days, were unable to know the complete extent of the damage and were relying strictly upon the reports from local highway patrols and road authorities in the county. We did respond in many cases to emergency requests from hospitals that needed to get fuel or from farmers who needed to deliver dairy products to the market or face the possibility of dumping their milk. In many cases we dispatched equipment to many sites based upon the recommendation of local people and found that the equipment was either inadequate or the wrong kind and we had to make adjustments.

The Corps of Engineers involvement during the eleven or twelve days of the emergency period involved over two hundred separate contractors which in those twelve days required about six million dollars to remove the snow. The contractors were paid an hourly rate based upon the type of equipment that they had. Thus, we were able to get them to work very rapidly without having to negotiate a fixed price for a certain amount of work. Since we were paying on an hourly basis, we could then stop him at any time.

In piling the snow from dump trucks and bucket loaders in many of the local parks and vacant lots, we figured that there would be no significant problem for any future flooding. This proved to be a correct assumption. After the middle of February, the weather became milder on the weekends. The snow that was heavily packed in the parks did melt at a much slower rate than did the snow that was on the streets or on the lowlands. There were concerns that this snow would be around for many months and would provide unsanitary conditions as it melted. We were very fortunate in that we had a number of successive thawing spells over a four week period. Most of the snow melted by early April. By about the tenth of May, the last of the snow that was piled in the parks had melted. We were very fortunate in getting a very unique thaw that enabled the snow to melt at a rate which did not result in flooding of the area.

A little housekeeping in Wyoming County. Courtesy, Buffalo State College Courier Collection.

319

Sharon Gorenflo

"I was directing contractors just like the male inspectors."

I work in Public Affairs for the Army Corps of Engineers in Buffalo, New York. I operated the switchboard for them for 36 hours straight. They were trying to call in personnel, trying to get contractors, etc. We were getting people in from other districts. I was ordering supplies for these people such as equipment, helmets, books, coats, whatever. Finally they were able to get their regular switchboard operator in and I went upstairs to what we call the War Room and I started working in there. We had charts and diagrams and street locations and we were starting to tell contractors where they would be doing their work and we sent out inspectors to check on the contractors. This lasted 24 hours in the War Room and then we got an 8 hour break. We slept at the Corps.

By Wednesday, I was getting a little tired of the War Room and they kept needing inspectors and I kept saying, "I'll go out, I'll be glad to go out and inspect." They kept saying "No, we need you here, we need you here". Well finally they got the rest of their clerical help in by Thursday morning. About 2 a.m. they needed an inspector desperately. They didn't have anybody around. So finally I said, "I'll go if you want me to." So I went out and stayed out in the field for 4 days. I was directing contractors just like the male inspectors. I was telling them where to plow, how wide to make the streets and how narrow to dig the curbs back. We got all kinds of comments because they weren't used to seeing a woman out there. Everyone was really marvelous about it. No problems at all. I worked with about 5 different construction companies around the city.

DISASTER INFLATION

Examples of price gouging - bread $1.00 a loaf, eggs $2.50 a dozen, cookies $1.50 a package.

Carl Geffken
Chesebrough—Pond's Inc.,
Watertown, New York.

"One friendly dog slept in the cafeteria, one not so friendly dog slept in the warehouse."

HOW IT ALL BEGAN

This has been an unusually blustery winter in the North Country and the past week was no exception. Each day seems to bring either crystal clear skies and bitter cold winds or hazy gray air which precipitates its perpetual mist of snow. So, when early Friday afternoon the daily accumulation had reached ankle depth on the freshly plowed pavement, few people were able to foretell what was in store.

To most of us, January 28, 1977 was just another work day at Chesebrough—Pond's, but a greater challenge lay ahead. By about three, road reports started to filter in from second shift workers who wisely judged that travel was too hazardous. At the same time, another major concern was brewing and at 3:15 p.m., Ray Davis, plant manager, called a meeting to announce that we would be curtailing all manufacturing operations for an undetermined period due to the limited natural gas supply. While the employees were assembled, they were also advised about the storm warnings and road conditions in the area. Any employee unable to travel home would be provided with food and bedding at the plant but there were few people who accepted.

There was a flurry of activity as nearly three hundred employees divided into two pursuits. One group lined up at every available telephone in order to make special arrangements for travel while the other group stoically trudged to their snow covered cars and inched along the already drifted access road toward home. By about 4:30, it was clear that about half the employees were going to require food and lodging until they could get out and emergency preparations were already underway. Outside help was being mustered after hearing the news cast about CPI curtailing the second shift and preparing to care for its stranded workers. The first to appear was Frank Macy, the Disaster Chairman for the American Red Cross who arranged to provide blankets for all and cots for about 40. At the same time, Donna and a group of volunteers were busily calculating the amount of food we would need for supper and Saturday breakfast. Mike, with his four wheel drive agreed to make the trek to purchase the groceries since by now, the only vehicle moving was his Jeep.

By six o'clock, 150 grateful employees had been served a spaghetti dinner (a la Ragu from the company store) and the bustle of preparation and regrouping for the morning cooking chores helped to ease the tensions for many. Clusters of employees passed the time with word games, by making their own playing cards from scraps of paper, or just chatting with friends about their mutual predicament. Some watched a television that had been brought in while many assisted in the general task of organizing to help others and prepare for bedding down.

Six employees from second shift continued to work, while sporadically, family and friends of some workers managed to arrive by truck or snowmobile. Some managed to get home, even by car, while others were able to get only as far as a friend's residence. Several people who got to the plant found themselves stranded for the night.

All employees who required special medication or care were questioned about their long range needs and arrangements were made to pick up supplies at the hospital. Because our own nurse, Pat, was stranded away from the plant, two Red Cross nurses were brought in, in order to administer to any special needs. Mrs. Jane Yendell stayed with us for the duration of our ordeal and provided a very stable and constant source of professional help.

There were some very tense moments late in the evening. Waiting for telephone calls from employees who decided to brave the elements and make the trip home kept us on edge. One call was overdue by an estimated hour and a half and would have indicated safety for six employees traveling south on Interstate 81 at midnight. The winds had picked up again and the snow was drifting heavily. One of the passengers was a senior employee who was due for her medication at 6 a.m. At 1:30, the sheriff's office was called to assist in locating the two cars but the weather was too severe for their vehicles. So we waited anxiously until 3 a.m. when the call came in that two were safe at home and four were at another shelter.

The atmosphere seemed more relaxed now, knowing that everyone was at least safe for the night. Some of the employees were too restless to sleep, a few were making the most of the situation and played cards until late, and the others slept soundly on make-shift beds at "the Chesebrough—Hilton."

SATURDAY—A BREAK AND THEN

As people wandered into the company cafeteria for "slim-pickins" of coffee, fruit, toast and left-over spaghetti, it became clearer that we were faced with more than an ordinary storm. Another foot of snow had been added to the half covered ten foot high cafeteria windows and the forecast was for more of the same. With the assistance of Mike and his Jeep, volunteers from the plant staff, who lived within the city were able to band together for a ride home or at least to family or friends nearby. Those who lived in the more remote or distant areas were still stranded.

The continuing snow and chill winds predicted the inevitability of our spending at least another night and the blizzard was now forecasted to last through Tuesday.

Chesebrough—Pond's had been among the first to organize help and the Red Cross was already on the scene to give aid in the disaster. We now considered opening the plant as an emergency shelter and headquarters for the Red Cross and Unicorn REACT (an emergency CB communication team.) Our facilities were well suited to the needs since there was a large cafeteria, adequate rest rooms, a large office area and a sophisticated telephone system. Soon after Ray Davis announced our willingness to help, the activity shifted into high gear. Amid the flurry of helping those who fell victims of the snow, the REACT team moved in and began stringing antennas and before long there were sounds of CB broadcasts emanating from the Personnel Office. The advantages of the CB system were immediately obvious since all radio calls could be received by those who organized and faithfully manned their stations for the duration of the crisis. When an emergency call came in, there was an immediate means of transmitting a call for mobile help. Calls requiring special assistance, medical attention, etc. could be channeled to the right people within seconds.

Dr. Fred Stone and his wife Nella, an R.N., arrived on Saturday as volunteers for the Red Cross and quickly helped to provide a complete medical team at Chesebrough. Both worked long and hard to care for the needs of those who were rescued and needed emergency care and when telephone calls for medical assistance were received, they were again ready to respond.

Many people were helped during the day and by nightfall, over one hundred people were again sheltered at the plant. Twenty students and two professors from nearby Jefferson Community College had been stranded for 24 hours in a cold building with very little food and were among those who were brought in. Other persons had been stranded on Interstate 81 and adjacent roads which were by now heavily drifted with the wind whipped snow. Some had walked to find help and had to be treated for frostbite. There were elderly persons and two who were unable to walk. For those who spoke only French we found someone to act as official interpreter. For those who had special needs, everyone pitched in to help. One friendly dog slept in the cafeteria, one not-so-friendly dog slept in the warehouse.

Late on Saturday night, a very sketchy and abbreviated telephone call was received. The caller said that a woman was in labor and a car in which they were stranded was on a road in a remote part of town. Before giving any details, the caller hung up which almost suggested that this was a hoax. Rather than take a chance, the sheriff's office was called to verify the location and ask for a town plow to be dispatched to the area. Dr. and Mrs. Stone gathered blankets and medical supplies and left with a crew of volunteers in a four wheel vehicle. After two hours of searching in vain, they returned to report their experience and now, we all hoped that the call had been a prank.

Hours seemed to pass like minutes during the bustle of activity. When the armored personnel carriers from Fort Drum arrived at 3:45 a.m. to deliver a new supply of blankets and sleeping bags, Saturday's major chores had been completed and we could now face Sunday. As the willing contingent of Army and Marine volunteers rumbled back out of the parking lot and over the mounds of snow we could not help but think about their southern accents and what experiences they would relate to their families.

SUNDAY—WITH NO SUN

The telephones started ringing at a more frequent rate again at about 6:30 a.m. With another foot of drifting snow, a wind chill factor of 30 below zero and the bustle of getting help to people, there was little to indicate that it was Sunday. There were people to transport to hospitals, essential prescriptions to be delivered, food and fuel to be provided, and hundreds of questions to be answered. The calls were continual. Some by telephone, the rest by CB. Nearly all were emergency calls but there were some who were looking for comfort and reassurance. We all felt that a few calming words to the caller who was aged and living alone was an important part of our work. Sometimes a caller would have to be tactfully told that we couldn't shovel the snow from her awning or clear the front walk because there were other more critical emergencies. But reassurance was always given so that the caller could phone at any time, day or night, if a real emergency became apparent. Many of these callers were telephoned later in the evenings by the Red Cross nurses in order to give them some additional support.

Recognizing that spirits were at an ebb, especially for those who normally spent their Sundays in a more worshipful way, it was decided that a church service would be appropriate. Father John from Brownville had volunteered to conduct Mass in the plant and his presence was clearly appreciated, especially by the JCC students who were able to go home with him.

During a mid day lull in the wind and heavy snow there were some employees, volunteers and travelers, who were able to get to destinations within the city and north into Canada. A few of our Canadian guests, even the ones bound for Florida were obliged to stay. A young woman who had frostbite was taken in by a family in Black River. An elderly woman with multiple sclerosis was moved to Howard Johnsons where she would be more comfortable and one person was reunited with his family at the Ramada Inn. As each person was checked out, his destination was noted and the travelers were all asked to phone our emergency number when they were safely out of the area affected by the blizzard. As each call came in, a note was made on the roster to indicate their safety.

The slight and very temporary easing of travel conditions also brought with it a new group of stranded persons who needed food and shelter. The people who were now safe within our plant would remain for another three days. The snow was again falling heavily, visibility - just a few yards at times, the temperature - about zero, and with gusty winds of 30 - 40 mph, the chill factor easily fell intermittantly to -50 degrees. It would seem that no intelligent being would dare risk such an environment even between the squalls. When the going was roughest, for safety reasons no assignments were given, but the lulls in the storm were never predictable. This risk was the challenge that a group of very dedicated young men and a few not so young men, accepted. In order to provide emergency transportation and bring assistance to those who were stranded without food, fuel or medication, a team of approximately thirty volunteers were registered at our location as snowmobilers and drivers of four wheel drive vehicles. Some were employees, but the majority called to volunteer after hearing appeals through REACT or radio/television broadcasts. Each man was checked in, allowed to volunteer for assignments and checked out in order to keep track of where he was. There were many times when a snowmobiler would come back to the plant after accomplishing his task and after brushing the snow from his clothing and removing the encrusted ice from his face, he would volunteer for another job. The average snowmobiler logged 150 miles in a day to help others who were endangered by the blizzard. Four wheel drive vehicles and snowmobiles all took a heavy toll of wear and tear with such continual and hard use.

Some repairs to machines were made by volunteers who worked in the plant machine shop and warehouse. In time, arrangements were made for a local distributor to provide parts in order to keep the machines in top condition. There were times that when neither law enforcement vehicles nor road plows could move, the snowmobiles and four wheel drivers were pressed into action. Even when the travel ban was enforced by the police, registered volunteers on assignment carried an emergency pass and were encouraged to continue their missions.

MONDAY—KEEPING COOL (AND ORGANIZED)

Another gray and gusty morning with its new accumlation of snow, the telephones ringing as before and the CB chatter nearly constant . . . . . . The powdery drifts had covered all but a couple of feet of window space and there was no let up in sight. As we took stock of what we had already been through and now tried to separate the continuing saga into actual calendar days, it was at first difficult to account for the three nights that had passed. A subtle fear had crept in reminding us that we were all human. Endurance, teamwork, and the vital urgency to help where we could, had carried us through and we had become organized quickly enough to meet the challenge head-on. Co-operation and the willingness to pitch-in and pull together was a fact of life rather than a forgotten dream.

In order to continue at the same pace and remain both efficient and effective, a few refinements helped to keep the system going. Emergency calls were taking a turn from the original "rescue plea" and as the days of isolation mounted, victims of the storm became more concerned about food, fuel, and how to get them.

When a call was received, the basic information was logged and the original message form was handed to the appropriate person responsible for a specific type of aid. The call was immediately transferred to the same worker who would either provide advice or arrange assistance. The basic areas of assistance were identified as 1) Medical, 2) Food. 3) Fuel, 4) Shelter and 5) Rescue, Transportation and Emergency Communications.

All medical and health related calls were handled by Red Cross nurses and Dr. Stone. There were many persons in need of pharmaceutical prescriptions and some acutely ill persons required transportation to the hospitals.

Requests for food were frequent and these calls were also handled by the Red Cross for the first four days. Mrs. Pat Quick was a very dedicated worker. She served the community both at Chesebrough and is now faithfully solving the lingering problems of emergency care during the aftermath. Pat and others provided initial help for the individual families as well as for large rescue centers throughout the county.

Fuel supplies for some persons required immediate attention and calls relating to emergency assistance were handled by Dick and Jim. They were continually in touch with the County Civil Defense Office concerning the larger resources of fuel oil for the area while they arranged for quantities of kerosene, gasoline, etc. to be carried by snowmobile or four wheel drive to people who were without cooking facilities or heat.

Transportation and emergency communications via CB were very professionally handled by the REACT volunteers. Larry, Tom and now Dick Trombley worked long shifts around the clock. When food, fuel or medicine were required, this team would dispatch vehicles and keep in touch with the volunteers along the way.

Many people were given assistance during the first four days and nights and because the state and county agencies required time to organize and respond, emergency centers such as ours had been the focus of activity. Since we had a written commentary on radio and TV bulletins, our storm information was relatively complete and accurate. Listings of pharmacies, food stores, gas stations and fuel dealers who were open were photocopied and given to those workers handling specific needs. Current weather conditions and forecasts were available to the snowmobilers and drivers. Road information and special points of interest (including the temperature in Miama, Florida) were announced over the intercom as received.

Names and telephone numbers for other emergency centers were also on file and because our communications system was well established, we were in a position to offer some early data to the Civil Defense Office. This basic data was compiled during the very early morning hours as we called twenty-three centers and explained that these statistics would be used for the initial request for federal assistance. During the first four days, emergency food and shelter were provided to over 3900 persons in four major centers, four motels, fourteen fire halls, and one shopping mall. Four hundred and thirty-eight key volunteers had been involved with these centers and approximately 155 snowmobiles and four-wheel-drive vehicles were used for transportation. Each snowmobile traveled an average of about 150 miles per day. Unicorn REACT relayed about 25,000 messages and the major emergency centers like ours handled approximately 6000 calls during this time (one per minute around the clock). The statistics are conservative since they do not include many smaller emergency centers, private homes, halls and restaurants. Many thousands of emergency services were also provided outside of the centers and we can account for a large portion of these from our records.

TUESDAY

Dawn was observed through the one foot window pane above the twelve foot drifts and the routine was well known by all. Everyone pitched in for the cooking and whatever else had to be done to house upwards of sixty residents and itinerant Eskimos.

The news media provided a great public service in the community and some stations had been broadcasting around the clock since Friday. They were often called to make announcements, requests for volunteers and in general, keep the public informed. Tuesday night brought camera crews to the plant from ABC and WNEW in New York. On a previous day, WWNY - TV in Watertown aired a visit to the Chesebrough-Pond's center. Numerous radio interviews had also been given to WATN, WOTT, WWNY, MNPE, and CBS in New York.

There were some lighter moments during the crisis and when the weather temporarily broke on Tuesday, it seemed appropriate to recall some of them. The simple pleasure of life to many of us had not included such things as showers, soft towels, clean socks and underwear, receiving a bag full of tooth brushes and tooth paste, a real bed, orange juice in the morning, and the list goes on.

February first, was also Terry Horning's birthday. Terry, a 30 year employee at the plant, was surprised with a birthday cake and ice cream after dinner had been served in the cafeteria. The cake was purchased at a local bakery on a return trip from the hospital. Along with Terry's surprise came a more favorable weather forecast for Wednesday and when word arrived that the major emergency arteries would probably be clear by 7 a.m. there was a long awaited ray of hope that Wednesday would bring freedom.

WEDNESDAY—NEW HORIZONS

All our "guests" arose early and had eaten breakfast and were waiting to check out by 7:15 a.m. Road reports from our emergency vehicles were cautiously optimistic that those who were stranded could retrieve their cars and make it safely out of the snow belt. By mid-morning, calls were coming back from thirty, very appreciative people who were well on their way toward home. There was one exception. A family of nine was on their way to Florida and we received a postcard (in French) to say "merci" and that the sun was a welcome change from their ordeal.

By mid-day Chesebrough—Pond's Emergency Center, Watertown, New York, was being phased down and all the city, state and county agencies were in the process of reorganizing for the massive clean-up.

As some of us were travelling by Jeep to our place called home, we had our first opportunity in six days to witness the five to eight foot snow-fall and drifts which easily towered to 15 and twenty feet. The bright sun seemed to make the whole episode take on a different perspective. As for the people who helped people, we all share a new and brighter perspective.

WATERTOWN SNOW

Approximately 66 inches of snow fell on Watertown between 28 Jan. '77 and 1 Feb. The total snowfall for Jan. totalled 90.8" breaking the old record of 79.4" set in 1940. The total accumulated snowfall at the end of January amounted to 181", and well over 200" at the end of April. The wind chill factor during the blizzard ranged from -35°F to -47°F.

Roads Disappear in Cheektowaga, N.Y. Buffalo State Courier Collection.

GOODBYE REFUGEES

On 2 February, at 7:00 a.m., the travel by auto ban was lifted for five hours in the Watertown area. This was done so that many of the 1,900 stranded travelers could leave the city, so as to lessen the demand on scarce food and fuel resources.

Food Stamps

"It was almost a second disaster."

If you lost one hour of work as a result of the storm, you were eligible for food stamps. There were thousands of people in lines as a result. I suppose about 80% of the people in Buffalo, were eligible for a one month supply of food stamps and that amounted to three to four hundred dollars worth of stamps. People who didn't need them were eligible and went and got stamps. But people who had been laid off before the storm were not eligible because they hadn't lost an hour's work. So they had people who needed help and couldn't get it. You had people who didn't need help and they were eligible.

The second thing was that the program was administered through the government agencies who were used to dealing with people on a one to one basis. The private agencies who are used to dealing with disasters, were not used. It was bad news here for a week. It was almost a second disaster. For instance we had the Armory a few blocks away, one of the largest in the country, where they could have got the people inside out of the cold. It wasn't used. Instead they picked locations that couldn't have held 200 people. We had thousands. It was badly set up. It was done quickly and done earnestly, with the idea of helping people who needed help, but it was not done well.

PRESS INTERRUPTION

On 29 January, the Buffalo Courier Express reported that it was the first time since 1834 that weather interrupted its publication.

Clint Buehlman—WBEN Radio—Buffalo

"Civilization is so thin you can see through it."

I had no difficulty getting to work on January 28, 1977,

because I have a jeep with a snow plow on it. So when the weather gets bad I plow my way to work. That morning there were five cars parked across Elmwood Avenue so I lowered the plow and plowed through the Twinfair parking lot and into the lot of the radio station.

It was the worst storm in my forty-six years of radio work. In the 1930's we did not have the equipment that we have today and the roads were not plowed then and nobody thought anything of it. People accepted that fact that they would be snowed in for a while. People had not yet developed the habit of ignoring nature. The average person today knows nothing about nature. If he needs heat or light he turns a thermostat or pushes a button, and when the heat and light stop-it's panicsville.

That was the longest period of time that I have ever seen the schools closed. We had six people answering the phones constantly and it was a very serious thing with absolutely no humor or even light hearted treatment like some of the other stations. I make no fun of a situation where someone is inconvenienced whether an adult or child.

We developed a system a long time ago for school closings. We have always had direct phone connections with four outside lines - two for schools and two for plants. We give them unpublished and unlisted numbers and threaten them with death if they ever reveal these numbers and we talk directly to school principals, personnel supervisors and plant managers. We use the personal approach but it is expensive and time consuming.

I consider the ice storm in March of 1976 to be worse than the blizzard of '77 because of all the public utilities that were cut off. We had no power at my house for five days during that ice storm.

People are primarily interested in themselves. If you take a lot of time talking about South Buffalo or East Buffalo and they live in the North Side or over on Grand Island - then they couldn't care less. "We are not getting snow here. What's the matter with you?" It takes a couple of days of doing without before people actually became neighborly. They did this during the storm. Someone is without food for a day or so and suddenly the neighbors care. Prior to that they did not care.

The blizzard was expensive for our station because we lost thousands of dollars because we did not have commercials for a long time. After two days the station manager said, "Look, couldn't you manage to squeeze in a commercial or two? The other stations are getting all their commercials in." At eighty dollars a minute it soon adds up quickly.

We run into so many nice people and once in a while we encounter that stinker who phones up and says that he has been listening for fifteen minutes and we haven't mentioned his plant at all. It would take a lot of us to go through the list. Some people are only interested in that one thing and they don't want to wait. They have become accustomed to instant everything and if you don't serve them right away they think they are being ignored.

Civilization is so thin you can see through it. When you run into a civilization you find out what rotters some people are. Such people are the exception of course but you can do a good job for 364 days a year and on that one day you don't pay attention to your job, people will never forget it.

EMERGENCY

The phone rang at 3:30 a.m. in the sales office of L. L. Bean, Freeport, Maine. The caller was from Buffalo. "Can I order three pairs of long johns?" he asked a salesman.

A common post blizzard clean up scene in Western New York. Courtesy, Buffalo News.

Staying in shape Buffalo style. Courtesy, Buffalo State Courier Collection.

Bob Emerling, Boston, New York

"But in the city there is more of a whirling action to the snow and wind and it blows up under your face mask and freezes your eyelids."

The blizzard hit here late Friday morning and we were ready because our Boston Rescue Squad has been having mock rescues for ten years. We work as a snowmobile unit with that squad which, by the way, has its own ambulance. We notify the Red Cross, the Sheriff's Department and the State Police of our service and we have been called upon every year for the last ten years. So, when the blizzard hit on Friday, January 28, we were ready to go.

We are first aid trained, we have sleds to carry patients behind our snowmobiles and we drive four wheeled trucks that enable us to carry our snowmobile as close as possible to an emergency area. Then we unload and drive the snowmobiles from there. We have orange safety patrol vests and carry the big orange flashlights that many firemen use.

Our first call was on Friday morning from a woman stranded in a hunting cabin. We got her out. Actually, I put on my snowmobile suit about 9 o'clock that morning and never took it off until after midnight of the following day.

Our first call from the Buffalo Red Cross occurred around 2 o'clock Friday afternoon. There was a shortage of blood in the hospitals. So we drove our trucks to the South Gate Plaza and snowmobiled from there. We arrived at the Red Cross about 6 p.m. Friday evening and delivered the blood to the hospitals. Then we delivered diabetic medicines, then we got the truckers out of their rigs on the highways, some of whom had been there for thirty hours. We got a number of people out of cars as well. Then we were running errands for those firemen at that bad fire, getting new nozzles because the old ones had frozen. We are prepared to get to the scene of an emergency real fast, do the work that must be done and then pull out as the community becomes organized enought to handle it. We pulled out of Buffalo about midnight on Saturday, because other snowmobiles were arriving and were able to do the work. We had lots to do back around Boston.

For example, we had to deliver a lot of oil to people who were running out. We put the 50 gallon drum in the snowmobile sled and block the drum so that it doesn't roll. Then, you have a man on a lead machine who breaks trail and we deliver the oil. We never allow a man to go alone on a mission and we prefer three, in case of trouble. We also delivered a pile of food to hungry sheep in that manner. When we delivered bread and eggs to people, we always insulated the eggs with the bread.

We found that we don't like towing a snowmobile on a trailer to the scene of an emergency because the trailers get bogged down and are hard to manoevre in the snow. They pull harder too. I've got a custom back on my truck and I can load four snowmobiles right in the heavy duty, three quarter ton pick up with four wheel drive and posi-traction. The posi-traction is important to have.

We fed a herd of wild deer after the blizzard. We fed them bales of hay that we had to break-up and scatter over the snow. Then they paw the hay out of the snow. If you just leave the bale unbroken, the deer don't want to eat it. Some Game Wardens in Pennsylvania where we hunt, were having this problem with starving deer and we told them how we solved it by breaked up the bales. Then it worked for them, but that winter was hard on deer.

We have wild turkeys around here too and they were hurt by the severe winter. A lot of them were found dead.

I remember when we were checking the stalled cars on the skyway in Buffalo, the wind was 60 miles per hour and the wind-chill factor was 50 or 60 degrees below zero Fahrenheit. That wind would push the snowmobile and sled sideways across the pavement. We have the clothes to protect us including a face mask and a shield on the snowmobile helmet. In the city there is more of a whirling action to the wind and snow and it blows up under your face mask and freezes your eyelids. What we appreciated was to be able to jump into an abandoned car for a couple of minutes and take off a glove and pick the ice off our eyelids. Then you are ready to go again. People who left their car doors unlocked sure did us a favor and those that abandoned their cars and left them running did us an even bigger favor — that heat felt good on the eyes.

Other clubs have called us and asked how we can travel in a blizzard when you can only see a few feet in front of the machine. We tell them that you travel that couple feet and then can see a couple of feet more and eventually you get there. That's why it took about four hours to get into Buffalo when normally it is a 40 minute drive.

As far as gloves are concerned, you can't beat a wool lining. The fleece absorbs the moisture from your hand and after you have picked the ice from your eyes, there is a lot of moisture on your hand. You can buy very expensive snowmobile gloves and they won't do the job under extreme conditions unless they are fleece lined.

William Bellis, 42nd Aviation Company, Niagara Falls

"The guys up there have to keep their heads out of their bottoms."

I'm an instructor pilot for the National Guard and I was at home on the night that the blizzard hit. About 5:30 on Saturday morning, Colonel Sullivan called and asked if I could get to work. I tried to shovel out through thirty foot drifts at the end of the street but that was impossible. So I called work and they said that they would send a helicopter with a hoist. Sure enough, they came over and lowered the hoist down into my apartment complex and hauled me off to work. What made it interesting was the 50 knot winds that were blowing at the time.

My job consisted of co-ordinating and setting up all the flights.

Snowmobilers check a car. Courtesy, American Red Cross.

I would receive the missions from headquarters and then I'd assign a flight crew to fly the mission and then give a mission briefing. I would fly as well, depending upon the number of aircraft which were needed. I got about 25 or 30 hours of flight time during that period. These were the worst weather conditions in which I have ever flown because of the ice, snow and wind. Visibility was extremely poor — no more that 1/8 of a mile at altitudes of several hundred feet.

The one flight was to Bradford, about 100 miles distance, for a 5 month old baby who had breathing difficulties. We were to fly him back to Buffalo so that he could make use of this machine at Children's Hospital. With out the machine, the child wasn't expected to live through the night.

We stayed up that night, receiving weather reports from Cleveland and New York Center. We even had an airliner, on its way from New York to Chicago, fly through the storm and let us know the weather conditions. That plane reported that turbulence was so bad that even an airline couldn't last for long in it.

The helicopter that we flew in the morning had a 48 foot rotor system, was 52 feet in overall length and generated 1250 horsepower in its turbo jet engine. It can carry 13 people normally and weighs between 3 and 4 thousand pounds. When we took off to get the child, there was severe icing conditions and severe turbulence with a 100 foot ceiling and visibility of about 1/4 mile. We followed a gas pipe line for 100 miles from Buffalo to Bradford and landed in the parking lot of the Bradford hospital on a helipad that they had built there in the past. We picked up the baby and followed the pipe line back to the parking lot at Children's Hospital in Buffalo. We flew at altitudes of 50 feet for the most part. I'm happy to say that the child survived.

To fly in those conditions the crew must exercise extreme caution as well as co-ordinate with other agencies. A super knowledge of the area is also essential. We were certain that in each aircraft on a mission there was one person who was from the Sheriff's Department or who had flown a traffic helicopter in that area. We also had detailed maps for the territory in which we flew. Someone had to know where the antennas and wires were located.

The guys up there have to keep their heads out of their bottoms if they are going to survive. If the weather gets too bad, don't take a chance. For example, when crews encountered whiteout conditions they landed in a field and waited for the snow to blow through.

For that return flight to Bradford we received the New York State Medal of Valor. We were honored because there have been only about 50 such awards since the State was founded.

OVER 26 FEET

Records kept at Mannsville, N.Y., in Jefferson County indicated 318.7 inches of snow had fallen from 7 November 1976 to 11

ConRail rotary plough clears 15' drifts, 1 1/2 miles long near downtown Buffalo. Courtesy, Buffalo News.

February 1977. The Blizzard of '77 dumped 74.5 inches on Mannsville. The most snow in a 24-hour period was 56 inches on 29-30 December 1976.

Major Donald Nathan—Salvation Army

"But in the midst of all that, the offices of the Salvation Army in this building were looted."

I'm disaster co-ordinator for the Salvation Army. I was a member of the co-ordinating council for the federal disaster administrative assistance program working with Tom Casey, who was the federal head of that program. As such we sat in daily with the co-ordinating meetings. Salvation Army was given the job of human services. Mr. Casey's words to us were that they would clear the roads if we would take care of the people. That's basically what we did. Tom Casey was the head of the FDAP and directed the whole program. I think he was outstanding in his work. There were about 10 or 12 on the co-ordinating council that went on a daily basis.

During the emergency, the Salvation Army fed a total of 176 thousand people in one way or the other. The program evolved from an original emergency station during the first night of the storm. People came into our building because we were there and we were open. We were fortunate at this building, 960 Main because we have a large kitchen, and we have a trained staff here who knew how to handle crowds and we knew how to feed people. There were numers of people who stayed at the Niagara Falls building and at the Lockport building as well. Those were the 3 major centers.

We then went into extensive work with direct deliveries to homes. We made about 59 thousand deliveries to people's homes-medical emergencies, this kind of thing. That was done mostly by snowmobilers. We had over 1000 volunteers with over 400 snowmobiles who did that kind of work for us. We would receive phone calls here and deliver the food to homes. As the roads began to open, we established feeding stations in each police precinct. Snowmobilers then operated out of the police station and we would run 4 wheel drives to the police stations. Then we went into emergency canteen work where we fed another 30 - 40 thousand people. That's basically the kind of thing the army got involved in.

I've been in about 20 major disasters. Some of them were unique. The first one was back in 1947 or 48 when a hurricane hit the Jersey coast, and I've been in 2 or 3 hurricanes. I was stationed in New Jersey when 4 barges of ammunition blew up and flattened about 2 cities with about 62 thousand people each. That was an interesting disaster. Martial law was declared and the Salvation Army was very active. Actually we operated more canteens there than we did in this one. We had 22 canteens operating then.

I was in Xenia, Ohio 4 or 5 years ago when the tornadoes went through there. I've been in 3 major city riots when the cities erupted and burned. It's hard to say what kind was the worst. This blizzard was a very unique disaster. It was the worst in some respects. In every other major disaster, the outside could get in to help. For instance, when a tornado goes through, there is destruction for a mile long at the most and usually it is a few hundred feet wide. By the morning of the next day, you have the mass of aid coming in from the people who are on either side of it. They can shelter and feed most people. What made this disaster unique was it covered 9 counties and nobody could get in. The railroad yards were closed, the airport was closed, highways were closed. At least for the first critical hours you had to help yourself while working from the inside out. That made it different from any other disaster we were involved in. What caused the disaster was not the snow itself but the abandoned cars that were stuck in the snow. We had ten thousand abandoned cars stuck in Erie County. So you had a complete stoppage of all transportation. There was no mobility. We couldn't move. It was a block by block thing. As you got one block open then you could move in that block and the people could go. That's one of the things that made it unique.

When that kind of disaster occurs, normal places such as supermarkets very quickly run out of food, because you can't get delivery vans in. You can't fly food in because there's no place for the airplanes to land. You couldn't bring it in by truck, because the trucks couldn't use the road. So then you had to set up a priority system as to what has to come first and that's where a lot of the problems came from. During the last disaster those priorities were set up on the basis of who needed help and what the critical emergency was, but not necessarily what street would be opened first. It was important that they open the main highways first, but that was only after human needs were met.

What the Salvation Army operated on was over a thousand volunteers. Without them we couldn't have done very much. There was a lot of vandalism, a lot of looting the night of the storm. It was strange because the temperature was about 60 degrees below zero and there were all kinds of warnings on the radio about exposing your flesh for a few seconds. In the midst of all that, the offices of the Salvation Army in this building were looted. In my offices they stole two sets of things, calculators and typewriters. They also stole the amateur radio equipment and this was the equipment we used for the canteens. We had a radio set-up on the first floor. We think that when the youth center closed earlier in the day, someone stayed behind and then let others in. The burglar alarm system was off because we were housing people here. They got about ten thousand dollars worth of equipment. As a result of that we were without communications. Our telephone lines were tied up something terrible and we clocked 1500 calls in a 45 minute period. When somebody wanted to call the Salvation Army, it was almost impossible. The phone didn't ring. If you put the phone down and picked it up, somebody else would be on it. All of our phones were operating that way. So here we were trying to call other Salvation Army centers in Niagara Falls, Lockport, and Tonawanda and we couldn't get them.

Finally, the amateur radio people came in with their own equipment and set up a radio station in the golden age center and they operated on a 24 hour basis. They slept on the floor. They were just fantastic. They made arrangements for someone to be at every other salvation center. That gave us communication, and for the first time we could function with a co-ordinated effort. It was particularly important when we started running canteens because we ran them out of all salvation centers and they would have been passing each other on the road.

The first night we put out over the radio and television that we needed snowmobilers. As I said, about 400 snowmobilers responded and one of the groups came quite a distance. I really don't know how they got here. There is a snowmobile club in Olean N. Y. which is down on the Pennsylvania line and they came up to Buffalo and there was 20 or 30 of them. They did one of the most heroic things that I've seen done. We were taking phone calls, answering medical emergencies. We had a woman who was in Lackawana who called in about 10:00 in the morning and said she was out of food. This was the second day. Snowmobilers could only carry two orders at the most which made it very difficult. So we would put them in groupings and we would have them respond to an area. What happened was that nobody else from that particular area called in, so they couldn't respond to it and it didn't seem like that much of an emergency. About 3:00 in the afternoon she called back and one of her children was sick and she needed some drugs. Again it didn't seem too urgent but we said we'd get it there as soon as we could. About 9:00 that night she called back and it was a real full blown emergency. At that point these people from Olean were here. It was about a 14 mile trip to the woman by snowmobile which is an awful long distance for a snowmobile in weather which varied from 40 to 60 wind chill factor below zero. Four of them volunteered to take it out to her. They figured at least one of them would make it out to her. They left here about 10:00 at night. They stopped in buildings as they went. All four of them did make it. They got back here about 3 or 4 in the morning and when they walked in, they had ski masks on. There were icicles hanging from their ski masks. It was that cold. They were really in pain. And all they said to me when they walked in was, "Hey, would you mind if we rest a few minutes before we go back out?" You couldn't pay people to do that kind of thing.

We had about 200 medical emergencies, most of them for insulin-people going into a diabetic shock-this kind of thing where they needed some drugs. We had them call the doctor who called the drug store. Usually by the time that was done we would pick up the medicine and take it to their homes. I remember one man who called and his wife was going into diabetic shock and she needed insulin. She was really quite far into it but we were able to get to her in time and I think that probably saved her life. Medical emergencies were given top priority.

One of the things Tom Casey did was to go around the table and each one of us would tell what the problems were that we had that day. The first priority I mentioned was milk. By the morning of the second day we were getting phone calls from mothers of new born babies who were running out of milk. They had to have milk or else the babies would suffer. About 91% of the milk was being dumped because they couldn't get to the dairies. We diverted enough snow equipment to get the major farms open to get the milk to the dairies. Then we opened a milk center depot and we delivered milk to these people. That to me was a major emergency.

The FDA did a number of other things. For instance, we were running out of gas for snowmobilers. The gas station across the street was out of gas. They diverted a truck which went out onto the thruway and got a gas truck and brought him all the way in so we could have gas to deliver food. Priorities were set on the basis of human need first and then getting the roads open.

We had an officer on the west side of Buffalo, Lieutenant Patrick, who is now in Oswego, N.Y. He happened to be in the west side of Buffalo, and it was the hardest area hit. The roads were impassable. One of the cars that got buried was his stationwagon. He would call in here and we would tell him who needed food. He would pull food by sled to people who needed it. He walked miles and miles through that first day and it was cold out there.

One of the things that we would get a lot of phone calls on, were people who were concerned because they were trying to call friends in this city and couldn't get an answer and they were frightened. Most of the calls concerned elderly people, and one of the phone calls we got was directed to Lieutenant Patrick. It was about an elderly man on the west side and one of his relatives had tried to call him from out west and couldn't get an answer. Patrick found out that this person had a son and the father and son hadn't talked to each other in years. Patrick found the father who was ill and then he went to see the son. As a result, he got the father and son back together again. So that is one of those things that worked out very well.

We had one of those unusual stories about shipping the snow south. That was a strange one. One of the problems we had was there was a train sitting over at Erie filled with feed for cattle. And cattle would begin to die here because they couldn't get any food. So they had to get the railway open to get that train in. The main problem was here in the control yards in Buffalo itself. There was so much snow that they could not move it. We had our canteen down there when they began to clear out that yard in order to move the train in. There was a long load of empty hopper cars that were going south as soon as the rails were opened. Somebody had the bright idea of filling these empty cars with the snow and we saw it happen. The idea was, that the snow would melt by the time it got to Florida. That's exactly what happened. The train with the feed arrived in time.

The major problem of course, was supplies. The local food stores run out quickly since delivery trucks couldn't get into the center of Buffalo. There was very little hoarding and there was no panic and there could have been quite easily. We were almost in a panic ourselves at times because we had two sources of food when it began. We do have emergency kitchens and we have emergency canteens which we keep stocked. They ran out pretty quickly. The second thing that really had helped us was that we had at Christmas time a surplus of donated canned goods. We had them in the basement of this building and we used that. By the second or third day that was gone. Incidentally there was a naval reserve unit in Buffalo that spent week-ends here and did cooking for all the people we were handling. They did that instead of their regular training. That happened to be their regular training period time and they came over here and worked for the army center.

We had all kinds of volunteers. The FDAA had put in a special phone for us with a number we only gave to salvation centers, to the FDAA itself and to other emergency agencies so they could call and get us without going through the regular lines. We found out through a phone call that came through our regular line that the Toronto Salvation Army was trying to get us. So we called back on our own line and Commissioner Brown in Canada wanted to know whether we needed any help. Within a day, there were two large trailer trucks of food sent from Toronto. The only thing I was requested to do was to see if I could help get it through Customs, because that is usually a very slow process. I called Customs and they assured me that they would have to do the usual thing unless I could get somebody to authorize that it was not to go through all the normal procedures. On the strength of the First Army we assured them that everything would be all right. When the federal government speaks, Customs listen because I was downstairs about 9 o'clock that night and I heard sirens from a police escort. They had met these trucks at the Customs and they were cleared immediately. I think it was the fastest anything ever went through Customs.

We were getting all kinds of people stopping in because we were handling human services and there were a lot of human interest stories going on in here. People from newspapers, radio, and television were here. There was a TV station in here from Boston, we got a call from one of the newspapers in San Francisco, etc. U.P.I. was here, A.P. was here and somebody was here from a French newspaper from Montreal. He came in and when he heard about this food from Canada he asked if we could identify any. "Well," I said, "I think it's in some of these bags," and I reached in and pulled out a can and here the label was in French. He took a picture of me holding this can with a French label. National Geographic was here and so were most of the major magazines.

The obvious advice in a situation like this is do not panic. Stay where you are until you receive direction. When you receive direction, follow it. I don't know how much you could prepare for disaster, because the very nature of it says that each one is going to be different. You don't know what facilities are going to be knocked out. I was there after those tornadoes in Kentucky when every building in the community was completely flattened. The police station, the library, the city hall were all gone. They had to buy tents and that sort of thing. So, whenever you have a disaster, the first thing you've got to do is find out what you've got available for use. Then you go with that.

Courtesy, U.S. Army Corps of Engineers.

We got calls from all over the world. We got money sent to us from an American colony on some small island in the Pacific that I had never heard of. They took up a collection and sent the check here to help people in the storm.

Most of the time in a disaster, you've got to start helping yourself internally. What made this unusual was that internal help had to last longer than normally, before that massive help could get here.

The roof caved in at a department store in one of the shopping malls, 15 minutes after the mall closed. That happened from the weight of the snow on the roof. If that had happened earlier, hundreds of people might have been killed. It's amazing there weren't more deaths.

We had canteens up here from New York City with volunteer crews. Some of those guys were interesting. One of them was John Oppenheimer, big heavy guy who was a stunt driver for the Kojak movies on TV, he's the guy that drives the cars off the cliffs and hits other cars. Another volunteer from New York City, was a fireman who took his vacation and came up here as a volunteer. That's the kind of help we were getting. Almost all of our staff volunteered to work nearly 24 hours a day. Our major problem with our own people was that they didn't go home to sleep. They just didn't want to quit.

We had one local guy named Jack. Young guy, one of those drop outs from high school. He works cleaning bars and this kind of a thing. He had volunteered the night of the storm for an agency, and they didn't have much for him to do. He was passing our building and he saw everybody coming in so he came in and saw how busy we were. So he decided to volunteer. He turned out to be our number one volunteer. He knows the City of Buffalo like a book, and he worked over a week without sleep. He would sit on the back of a snowmobile and direct these guys, particularly the ones from Olean, as to where to go and how to find streets. When that began to taper off, he chauffered people around, he drove canteen, he helped with the cooking, he helped with the clean up, he helped handle people until he was exhausted and with a partial frostbite he ended up in the hospital. We couldn't get the guy to stop. He slept for 72 hours, came back and started working all over again. Just a fantastic young man, who we are going to try to help. This guy has a lot of potential. He gave and gave of himself. He was one of the first volunteers we had, and he was the last volunteer to leave. He took the last canteen out. We couldn't pay him. I didn't know his name for the first three or four days. I'd say, "Hey, what's your name?" He'd say, "Hey, I'll tell you later". and he'd run and I finally got his first name out of him. He never asked a thing for himself. You know a lot of people would look at a kid like that and say he's no good.

We estimated the total cost to the Salvation Army at about 150 thousand dollars.

Auto Death

A young man was killed in Wyoming County while attempting to free his car from a snow bank. A truck hit his auto and then his car ran over him.

Two Lowville, N.Y. boys were buried alive when a large overhanging snowdrift fell on them. They were dug out by a neighbor and parents and treated at the hospital. Photo courtesy of Inco, by Dino Iannandrea.

Colonel Mike Sullivan—National Guard

"By Monday evening, we had approximately 614 people activated."

These comments pertain to the involvement of the New York Army National Guard, more particularly, Task Force Western, in the Blizzard of 1977 in Buffalo and the surrounding area. On Thursday evening, January 27, I was notified through our alert system that there was a distinct possibility that elements of the 221st Engineer Group would be activated to assist the City of Buffalo in snow removal operations. Upon receiving notification, I left my civilian occupation and my office in the Hotel Statler where I follow the profession of the law and proceeded to the Connecticut Street Armory, the home of the 221st Engineers. I had already requested that my executive officers summon technicians who are employed here daily on a full time basis to a meeting at approximately 7:30 that evening. The meeting was held here at the armory and we discussed the role that the 221st Engineers would play in assisting the City of Buffalo in snow removal operations. Our alert indicated that we would commence snow removal operations on Monday evening, January 31st. Our instructions consisted of organizing a plan whereby the engineer group and the 152 Engineer Battalion which is located in its entirety in the Connecticut Street Armory would accept missions from the city concerning snow removal and that we would work on city streets from 8:00 p.m. every night until 8:00 a.m. every morning until such time as the city felt our services were no longer required. The 152 Engineer Battalion has bulldozers, front loaders, dump trucks and other equipment for the removal of snow. At the meeting on Thursday evening I met with many of the technicians who are mechanics and I met with the battalion commander of the 152 Engineer Battalion and my own staff and we organized the plan to assist the city commencing on the following Monday.

I then left the armory at approximately 11:00 p.m. and proceeded to my home in Snider. I spent the night there and the next morning I decided to stop at the armory about 9:00 a.m. and make sure that our plan had been implemented. I was in my office, which is on the corner of Connecticut and Niagara Street, when I heard the wind blowing. I looked outside the window at 10:00 a.m. and was unable to see the street corner, seventy feet from my office window, because of heavy blowing snow. By eleven thirty a.m. that morning of January 28th, civilians had already begun to come into the armory seeking shelter. There were people from the federal building, some people from the neighborhood, people from plants that are out in the Black Rock section of Buffalo and people from the Chevrolet plant. By approximately 4:00 p.m. that day we had well over a hundred civilians in the armory seeking shelter. During the day, the forty-five technicians who were at the armory, went about setting up an aid station for people who might suffer frostbite and rounding up some food in the form of hot soup, coffee and some sandwiches to feed to the civilians who were coming into the armory.

I had been requested by my headquarters in Albany, the state capital, to stand by and prepare to activate as many people as I thought would be needed to assist the city in the event the storm continued in its severity.

In the early evening hours of Friday, January 28th, I spoke to the civilians who were in the armory and informed them that we would be able to provide them with a place to sleep and some food and that we had an aid station if any of them felt ill. By this time we were able to summon one of the doctors who serves in the National Guard and he was on his way to the armory. In the meantime we had two civilians who were medics or aid men in the army and navy while on active duty and they assisted some of our people in administering to those people who were ill. Fortunately, we did not have anyone who was seriously ill. We did have to assist in the removal of one person from a bus which had stalled outside the armory. She did not want to remove herself from the bus and probably would have been frozen if she had not been carried from the bus into the armory.

The people stranded here were allowed to use the phones in the armory in order to call their families. Blankets were issued to people. We tried to keep them generally in one or two larger rooms so that they would not be wandering throughout the armory.

By late that evening we had begun to alert national guardsmen to report to the armory the next morning so that we could form a task force to assist in the snow removal since the snow was quite heavy and drifting by that time. On Friday night as well, we started an emergency operation center here at the armory, operating out of the headquarters of the 221st Engineers and at that time we had limited telephone lines into the armory. So we made arrangements to add to those lines and were able to do so the next day. The emergency operating center began handling requests for emergency delivery of food and medical supplies. Our equipment was unable to move through the streets because they were blocked with stalled vehicles.

By Saturday evening approximately two hundred and twenty people had reported to the armory for duty. We had mustered four or five snowmobiles from civilians who had volunteered to help us out in the emergency delivery of medical supplies. On Saturday night, Albany headquarters asked me to move my activation date up to Sunday and start snow removal on Sunday evening rather than Monday evening. We began the snow removal operation at 8:00 p.m. on Sunday evening and our operation was set up in such a manner that the New York State Department of Transportation would assign snow removal tasks to the city employees and to the National Guard so that there was a central co-ordination point for snow removal tasks. We received our first tasks late Sunday afternoon and they consisted of snow removal operations in and around the Emergency Hospital, the Columbus Hospital, Children's Hospital, Buffalo General, the Deaconess Hospital, and Meyer Hospital. They commenced work at about 8:00 Sunday night.

By that time the chill factor was about forty degrees below zero and our equipment such as bulldozers and front loaders did not have windshields. Consequently the men would work approximately ten minutes in the bitter cold and then we would change operators so that none of our men would suffer from frostbite. The hospitals were most co-operative in that they provided sandwiches, coffee and a room for the men to warm themselves while they were off of the equipment. The men worked all night and until eight o'clock in the morning. We made considerable progress although there was a vast amount of work to be done.

The emergency operation center was operating on a twenty-four hour basis since late Friday night and continued to operate on a twenty-four hour basis. Although our men were not involved in snow removal operations during the day, except in the extreme emergency cases, they were involved in the delivery of food and the movement of people from one location to another. They picked up laundry linen in Batavia for use in five local hospitals. The hospitals had run out of clean linen. With the assistance of the New York State plows and our heavy trucks, our people were able to get to Batavia, pick up the linen and deliver it. It took a considerable effort and a long time but the job was done.

We also had five helicopters standing by at the Niagara Falls Airforce Base, under control of Task Force Western and they were used for emergency medical runs. In one instance on Monday or Tuesday of the first week, a run was made to Bradford, Pennsylvania to pick up a small child who was in considerable difficulty and the child was flown to the Children's Hospital here in the City of Buffalo where it was able to receive medical treatment. The flight was made by an Army National Guard helicopter, two pilots, Dr. John Cudmore and a medical technician from the Children's Hospital. We had many emergency medical requests. As they came into the armory through the emergency operation center, Doctor Cudmore would assign priority to the missions so that the more serious ones were handled first. This went on for three or four days.

On Sunday, I alerted more people because of the great demands being made upon us for extremely strenuous physical work and very long hours. By Monday evening we had approximately six hundred and fourteen people activated and performing various tasks. Every night the people would go out on the street and conduct snow removal operations.

The helicopters were used to pick up food at wholesale food distributors and fly it to various locations. There was a flight to a Gowanda hospital and to a hospital in Springville. Road transportation was virtually impossible. Also we delivered food over the city streets by means of heavy army trucks to hospitals and to those facilities which were in desperate need of food.

In the meantime, the city had requested through its Ambulance Board, that the task force provide army type ambulances to the city to assist in the movement of emergency patients. I think by the first Saturday, which would have been on the 29th of January, there was about one civilian ambulance operating in the whole city. We were able to give a total of nine or ten ambulances with operators and assistant operators and these ambulances were all attached to the various hospitals. Ambulances were dispatched wherever they were needed and this worked quite successfully.

In addition to this, the Sheriff had requested seventy people to assist in snow removal operations in many of the towns surrounding the Buffalo area. Off hand I can remember Evans, Lancaster, Alden, Hamburg and Cheektowaga, and those seventy people acted as road guides in helping to stop traffic from moving over roads. The plows could then undertake their operations without being impeded by traffic. These men worked long hours under extreme weather conditions.

In the meantime we were running a mess hall in the armory on a twenty-four hour basis so that the troops were able to eat during their off duty hours.

We were assisted greatly by the Salvation Army which sent food trucks to the various work sites. They did a very commendable job.

We also provided blankets to neighborhood centers such as the Puerto Rican Center, so that the people who were stranded there had something to keep them warm.

We were in almost hourly contact with our headquarters in Albany. As a matter of fact we have a teletype system whereby we could transmit messages in a couple of minutes and there was a constant flow of information from the operation here to Albany and from Albany to Buffalo. We also co-ordinated with the regular army people who came to Buffalo on Tuesday, February 1st to assist in snow removal operations. They were from an engineer brigade in Fort Bragg, North Carolina and we had a liaison man affect co-ordination with them. We knew what they were doing and they knew what we were doing. This man was in the person of Colonel Robert Lowery who was sent here by Albany to help us in the co-ordination so that our own people would not be diverted from their major effort of assisting the city and the surrounding communities in their time of extreme need.

Most of the people involved in this operation remained on duty for many long hours. After three or four days, many of them had to be ordered to go home for a little rest. I remained here from Friday through the following Wednesday before I was able to get home for a night to see my family and during the approximate twelve days that I was here I got home twice. Many of the officers did the same thing as did many of the enlisted people and the non-commissioned officers. They all felt that they were serving a purpose.

After we were on active duty approximately six days and some of the pressure had been diminished, I had an evening meeting with all the men, some six hundred and fourteen of them and asked if anyone wanted to be relieved because of financial problems or family problems. Out of that number of men, there was I believe six who asked to be relieved. The rest of the men felt that they had started the job and they wanted to finish it. Their efforts were highly commendable.

During the operations we ran daily flights for the Sheriff in our helicopters so that he was able to move throughout the county and observe the conditions that required his assistance. We also assisted in a visit in which Senator Javitz, United States Senator, State of New York visited our community. I believe this was on Thursday of the first week. That would have been about February the third as I recall. We had numerous other visitors including the Governor who came within a matter of a couple of days after the storm started, to view the situation personally. I myself went up in a helicopter almost every day to look over the situation and it was truly amazing to see the extent of the snow, throughout the whole area.

After we finished working in the hospital areas we began to work on some of the streets in and around the armory and also we were assigned a task to clean and to remove the snow from some of the major truck terminals in the city so that heavy trucks loaded with food could move easily in and out of the city. Our men were received with the greatest enthusiasm by the local population who came from their homes with hot soup, coffee and some other things which I won't mention at the moment and were most receptive to seeing the National Guardsmen working. This had a distinct effect on the morale of our own people. I know of one instance out in Orchard Park where the men worked for four days trying to get to a place where fifteen people were stranded. They finally got there and got the people removed.

This is generally a thumb nail sketch of what went on. The emergency operations center ran on a twenty-four hour basis. Our job was expanded one hundred fold from the original mission of snow removal assistance for the city. I can't help but comment on the co-operative attitude of the New York State Department of Transportation. We worked very closely with them and their people were extremely hard working and sincere in their efforts. We were on state active duty, having been activated by the order of Governor Carey. The Mayor of the City of Buffalo came to the armory twice and personally thanked the men for the work they were doing. On February the tenth, our last day of active duty, he presented me, as a representative of Task Force Western with a very nice plaque and bison statuette as a gift from the city. Also the mayor signed a proclamation praising the efforts of the National Guard in the snow removal operation. As the effort began to wind down, approximately around February the sixth, we began reducing the number of people on the active duty on a gradual basis, keeping enough to perform whatever tasks we had. Finally, on Monday I proposed a release plan to my superiors in Albany and requested that we be allowed to work on Tuesday, February the eighth and then have a day off on Wednesday the ninth and come back in on February the tenth and do maintenance on the equipment. The men were to be released on February tenth. I can't fail to mention the effort of the mechanics involved in this operation. Our heavy equipment we had on the street was maintained at about a ninety-two to ninety-three percent operational status throughout the emergency and this was exceptionally high. I might say it exceeded the operational status of the regular army equipment which had been flown here from Fort Bragg.

The hard working efforts of the maintenance people had much to do with the success of the operation because the maximum pieces of equipment were able to be kept on the street. During the course of the active duty period we had a couple of visits paid us by the sheriff of Erie County, Sheriff Braun who expressed his appreciation of the National Guardsmen. On February tenth all of the men were released except for a rear contingent of approximately twenty-five people who were kept on active duty for the following week to clear up the mounds of paper work that had accumulated. Records were kept straight.

During the course of the two week period, our operation here at the Connecticut Street Armory was visited by Major General Vito Castellano who was Chief of Staff to the Governor, Brigadier General Francis Higgins, and Lieutenant General Jeffery Smith, who was First Army Commander and in charge of the whole First Army area which is comprised of the greater part of the eastern United States.

The helicopters flew many missions. I recall one where they picked up a plow engine down in one of the rural areas and flew it to Buffalo so that it could be put into a city plow. We were able to satisfy approximately ninety-five percent of the requests made of us. There were some minor type requests which we turned down because they were of a nature that the people involved could render some assistance on their own part and solve their own problems.

There is one other thing that I would like to mention. During the course of this operation, my superiors in Albany sent some National Guard finance people down here to arrange partial payment for the men so that after we had been here about a week they were able to be paid for whatever number of days they had served. Then at the end of the period, they were able to be paid the balance of what was owed to them and this had a considerable effect on the morale of the people.

My advice to anyone who might reasonably expect that such a disaster could occur in their part of the country would be to have some type of plan that can be implemented. In fairness to the military, we were the only people who had a natural disaster relief plan where there was a lot of preplanning. There plans were implemented after the floods of 1972. The basic idea of the plan can apply to any natural disaster. This is why we were able to get into operation on a rather short notice.

The thing that stands out the most is the willingness of the men involved on behalf of the National Guard to work long arduous hours in an effort to bring the community back to the point where it was able to operate. Then there was the co-operation of the great majority of civilians in local governments and the people on the street who assisted us in many ways.

There is another thing that I would like to mention. On May 18th, 1977 the Honorable Hugh Carey, Governor of the State of New York, came to Buffalo to the Connecticut Street Armory to talk to the people who had been activated during the blizzard of '77 and to present to them a military award for their work. Some people got more than one award depending on the nature of their activity. It was the first time I can recall when the Governor took the time to come to this armory and personally express his thanks to the people. My name is Colonel Michael T. Sullivan Junior and I am the commanding officer of the 221st engineer group of the New York Army National Guard and I was the commanding officer of Task Force Western, the official designation of the National Guard organization which was involved in the blizzard of 1977. Task Force Western headquarters was at the Connecticut Street Armory, 184

Connecticut Street, Buffalo, New York.

WBFO—Buffalo

One thing that you should be aware of is that there had been T-shirts sold through J. C. Penney called the Blizzard of '77. There was a series of four blizzard post cards that were sold in various small places in the city. You might want to know that papers in Chicago were printed articles by Buffalonians about the blizzard.

One thing that happened was the City of Toronto called here and offered the City of Buffalo 3 snow melting machines that were very efficient and Buffalo rejected them. Somebody called Channel 2 and told them about this rejection that he read in the newspaper in Fort Erie. Well, my husband got on the phone to Toronto first and confirmed it. Then he called our City Hall and they said, "Maybe we ought to look into that a little further and we will get back to you." It worked out just fine. The machines were very helpful and there was a great debate about their expenses not being paid and it's still going on in terms of who's paying what, the federal, state or city government. There were contractors allegedly ripping off the city by charging outrageous fees.

During the blizzard appeals were placed on TV saying this is the number to call if you can provide your snowplow or your four-wheel-drive truck. The next day they had to run things saying, "Volunteer your four-wheel-drive truck," because people were charging for their services.

BLIZZARD AMNESTY

On February the fourth, Buffalo officials announced that a general amnesty was going into effect, cancelling all fees and fines for persons whose automobiles were tagged or towed away between noon Friday and midnight Wednesday. They forgave a $12 ticket placed on 2,632 abandoned cars and waived a $25 towing fee for an estimated 500 vehicles.

REFUGE

Unofficial estimates place the number of abandoned vehicles in Erie County at 3,500, while approximately 13,000 persons were sheltered in public buildings, hotels and taverns during the storm.

Jim Casey, Jr.

I watched television news reports about the blizzard when I was in Australia. Then in Aukland, New Zealand, the front page of the newspaper had a picture of the boxcars that were carrying snow away from Buffalo.

Anyone for snow? Courtesy, Buffalo Evening News, by Richard W. Roeller.

Local Bars

Many people who had to take refuge in local bars reported that it was like New Year's Eve.

WHERE'S MY CAR?

A Buffalo newspaper reported that the city had lost track of literally thousands of cars that were towed away during the snow emergency. "They weren't necessarily stolen, just misplaced," said the article. Approximately 4,400 autos had been towed.

WEATHER FACTS

Between 20 Dec. '76 and 10 Feb. '77, Buffalo had 53 consecutive days of below freezing temperatures.

Lowest Average Jan. temperature in 107 years at 13.8° F. Previous record was 14.1° F.

Greatest one month snowfall Jan. '77, 68.3", old record Dec. '76, 60.7".

Greatest snowfall for one season, 1976-77 = 199.4", old record 1909-10 = 126.4".

Most snow on ground, 4-7 Feb. '77 = 42".

NIAGARA FALLS

Two fires in Niagara Falls, N.Y., on Friday evening, January 28th, and Saturday morning, January 29th, resulted in 20 fire fighters being taken to the hospital with injuries suffered while battling two multi-alarm fires. All were treated for frostbite, exposure or smoke inhalation.

Refugee Sparrow of '77 Blizzard Takes Final Flight

Stormy, the refugee sparrow of the Blizzard of '77, took his final flight inside the Erie County Hall Annex, in downtown Buffalo, N.Y., 9 years after the storm of the century and millennium. Stormy was laid to rest in a flower garden at the corner of Delaware and Church Street in downtown Buffalo. He became a pet and friend of employees. His song kept spirits high for 9 years. May Stormy rest in peace. Amen. Oct.9/86.

Niagara Falls. Note the American falls frozen over to the left, the ice bridge across the Niagra River and the Canadian falls to the right.

Epilogue

Mrs. Furry expressed the feeling of many people when she said, "It's up to yourself in a disaster like this." With such a crisis and social paralysis, some people have asked why the death toll was not higher.

Part of the answer is that people helped each other spontaneously, in life threatening situations, not waiting for orders from someone in a position of authority. This type of help confirms my basic faith in human nature and leaves me with a feeling expressed by Buffalo policeman Russi when he said, "We will get out of it tomorrow if it happens again."

As important as immediate help may be in an emergency of this kind, we should remember that we received a blessing in disguise in the form of the worst ice storm in our history in March of 1976. At that time in the Niagara Peninsula and western New York, freezing rain caused the massive destruction of trees, power and telephone lines. If it was weak, it was destroyed in the ice storm. What was restored was a healthy power and communication system that withstood the 60 and 70 mile per hour winds of the Blizzard of '77. If that ice storm had not occurred, power and communication failures would have been massive and prolonged during the blizzard. I shudder to think of the number of storm related deaths from both a blizzard and blackout. If such a blizzard should strike Toronto, New York, Chicago, Detroit or Montreal at rush hour, with or without a previous ice storm, the death toll would be horrific.

Two suggestions come to mind for an early warning system with respect to blizzards. We are more accustomed to winter winds than we are to snow powder. Both wind and snow powder can prove disastrous. Canadian and American weather people should tell us the depth of snow powder once it begins to accumulate, much like we hear on ski reports. If you have snow powder on the ground and the forecast is for moderate to high winds, then be careful.

The second suggestion is for Canadian and American weather services to report the ice conditions on large bodies of water that have the potential for surface freezing. When the surface of a lake is partially or completely frozen, we no longer have a lake but a vast ice desert, much flatter than most deserts in the world. Add to the surface of the ice an accumulation of snow powder, in combination with a strong wind and you may find yourself buried in your car, your house or your city.

Beware of snowflakes!

43Y347

JAMP-CLINDAMYCIN 300mg
CLINDAMYCIN-HCL

####
L5407